HIGHFELL GRIMOIRES

Langley Hyde

BLIND EYE BOOKS

blindeyebooks.com

Highfell Grimoires
Langley Hyde

Published by:
Blind Eye Books
1141 Grant Street
Bellingham WA 98225
blindeyebooks.com

Edited by Nicole Kimberling
Art by Dawn Kimberling

This book is a work of fiction and as such all characters and situations are ficticious. Any resemblances to actual people, places, events, or magical grimoires are coincidental.

First edition May 2014
Copyright© 2014 Langley Hyde
ISBN:978-1-35560-28-9

Printed in the United States

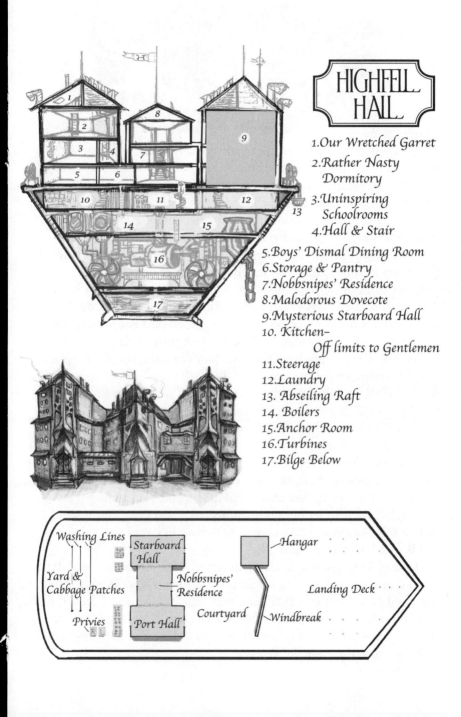

HIGHFELL HALL

1. Our Wretched Garret
2. Rather Nasty Dormitory
3. Uninspiring Schoolrooms
4. Hall & Stair
5. Boys' Dismal Dining Room
6. Storage & Pantry
7. Nobbsnipes' Residence
8. Malodorous Dovecote
9. Mysterious Starboard Hall
10. Kitchen— Off limits to Gentlemen
11. Steerage
12. Laundry
13. Abseiling Raft
14. Boilers
15. Anchor Room
16. Turbines
17. Bilge Below

Washing Lines
Yard & Cabbage Patches
Privies
Starboard Hall
Port Hall
Nobbsnipes' Residence
Courtyard
Hangar
Landing Deck
Windbreak

1

When it came time for me to say goodbye, I clasped my sister's gloved hands in mine. I wanted to say too much. I wanted to speak a spell that would give Nora the strength she would need to make the best of this bad situation. But choked by emotion, I said nothing. No such spell existed. I could only wish for her safety and hope for her happiness. And neither wishes nor hopes were magic.

We stood together at the edge of the airfield. The summery golden grass crackled under our feet, smelling sweetly of hay.

Nora wore mourning silks and a narrow bonnet that protected her face from the afternoon sunshine. Although she was more delicate than I was, we both shared our mother's golden skin and small build.

Yet where I had my wastrel father's russet curls, she'd inherited the darker hair of my stepfather. When her hair was straightened, it passed for aristocratic. Today, her skin was sallow with grief and her doe-dark eyes were marked with the mauve crescents of sleeplessness.

"When will you be back?" Nora asked.

"I'll see you soon." I hoped I wasn't lying.

"You're an ass, Neil. You'd best write, or I'll have to hijack a glider and hunt you down." She embraced me fiercely. Her orange water perfume didn't hide the faint singed scent of her ironed-straight hair. She smelled so like our mother that I couldn't breathe for grief.

I didn't want to let her go. I wanted to protect her, but instead I told myself Nora could take care of herself and I gave her a respectful nod before I turned to our uncle.

Gerard Franklin was a tall man, gaunt with stress, but still dignified even in his mourning black. During my childhood, on the few visits he'd ever made to our family home out in Midshire, I'd disliked him for no reason I'd ever been able to articulate. Now he made an unlikely savior. Without his intervention, I would have been transported halfway across the globe to Newland.

"I'm grateful for the opportunity to teach in your school. I know you can't pay me much, but this is a right and honorable living you've given me," I told him warmly as I shook his hand.

Uncle Gerard smiled modestly, an expression that sat thinly on his aquiline features. "Remember what I've told you about your pupils. Your duty is to better them. Although our methods may seem somewhat harsh, the stubborn ox listens only to the whip. If you can tame them and teach them the rewards of work, then you will have done well."

"I understand, Uncle." I smiled at him. I doubted the students would be so unfortunate as that. I knew that life treated some harshly. But I was sure, between myself and the other teachers at the institution, we would manage to create a curriculum that would get the boys excited about their letters. Whatever their backgrounds, I hoped to show them the joy that could be found in learning.

Goodbyes over, Uncle Gerard and Nora walked me across the airfield in silence. My sister kept her posture rigid yet graceful, while my uncle's gestures quickened, rough with impatience. We reached the glider as the airman finished snapping the launching lead to the craft's nose. My uncle's coachman finished loading my trunks behind the leather seats in the open cockpit.

The time for me to leave had arrived too soon.

I gazed at the distant city. Small brick buildings cobbled the horizon, dwarfed by the scores of anchored aetheric vessels that floated in the air above Southside and the River Wyrd. At this distance, the stately towers built upon their ship-like hulls looked small, high as they were above the city smog.

I had attended boarding school on an aetherium, and now I would return as a teacher. I'd never expected this.

I climbed aboard the glider and swung into the second seat. The sun-heated leather, the beeswaxed silk wings, these familiar smells filled me with a schoolboy's anticipation of the oncoming adventure. That overrode my regret at leaving the familiar behind. I snapped myself in and fitted the leather straps before the airman came to double-check me.

He gave a low whistle of appreciation.

"You've been a boarding boy, I can tell." The airman vaulted into the front and revved the engine. "Got your own parachute and all!"

"Yes, I attended Evermore and after that Elmstead." I buckled my top hat beneath my chin, removed the goggles from the brim, and fitted them onto my face. The tailored ostrich leather hugged me like a mask, even as the smoked glass in the goggles darkened the sky's blue from robin's egg to cobalt.

"Elmstead? Highest of the high! And now you're going to Highfell Hall... Suppose none of earn our fates." He signaled to the winch man with a wave of his hand.

The winch man cranked at the mechanized winch until its motor purred into life. The winch wound up the lead attached the glider's nose. The line hissed through the grass, grew taut, and reeled us forward. Then the wind caught beneath our wings and we swung up into the sky like a kite.

The lift-off pressed me into the padded seat and squeezed the air from my lungs. As wind roared past me, I wondered what he'd meant by that. But it was too late to ask. We were aloft.

I felt but the barest tug on the craft's nose as the lead grew taut. The pilot released the winching lead. It snapped loose, falling to earth. We shot free.

The city of Herrow stretched out beneath us. To the north of the murky river sprawled the city's Central Mile and the richer neighborhoods. I glimpsed Knave's Court District, where Nora would reside with our uncle in his townhouse. There the streets broadened, with the buildings made of brick or stone.

As we gained altitude, I could see how the streets sprung out spoke-like from old town centers. Villages had grown outwards and entangled themselves to create the labyrinth of the modern city.

The pilot angled our glider away from the Central Mile.

On the Southside, the aetheria shadowed the neighborhoods. The wood-and-tar tenements, locked in nearly perpetual twilight, formed a dense warren. Beyond the Southside, smokestacks belched out coal dust.

The airman piloted us upward, above Southside and toward the gravity-defying vessels called aetheria. Hanging in midair, the aetheria still filled me with awe. Powered by the invisible current of aether, the great floating ships' upper decks supported educational institutions, laboratories, and also the wealthiest peers' mansions.

Although I had no iolite lens with which to see it, I knew that the natural aether gusted and rolled around us, scentless and intangible. The aetheric current running above the River Wyrd was among the most powerful in Higher Eidoland.

Like navy vessels on fleet review, the great ships pivoted in unison so that their prows faced into the airstream. The massive chains that anchored them to earth glittered with frost.

Gliders, their silky wings glimmering in the sunshine, scudded around the aetheria like skiffs. Insectile trackers, their metallic bodies the size of teakettles, buzzed through the air, delivering messages and small packages.

Higher aetheria, outfitted with belowdecks boilers and adorned with promenade-level gardens, held marble universities and academies. Our craft plunged past their stained glass windows, gilded domes, and fluttering pennants.

As we descended, palatial residence halls and half-domed astronomical observatories gave way to varnished wooden hulls studded with massive intake fans. These drew in aether along with atmosphere through wind tunnels lined by copper wires inscribed with aetheric trapping spells.

Steamy exhaust from the turbines gusted around us. It smelled hotly of metal, edged with an iron tang reminiscent of blood.

Positioned between the mooring chains of higher aetheria and caught sometimes in their shadows, the lesser institutions hovered. These were dingier, their gardens less extensive. Although I had often viewed them from above, never in my life had I thought I would step foot on one in any capacity. As we dropped into their midst, I felt determination as well as curiosity.

Finally, wind whipping and roaring around us, the pilot circled one aetherium in particular. Absurdly small, like a river trawler, the institution below us had a small brick house flanked by two adjoined halls. From above the buildings formed a letter "H". Whether it stood for Highfell or was merely an architectural accident, I could not say. I saw no garden and no one awaited us on deck.

The airman descended toward the aetherium's prow and landed the craft expertly, catching the arresting wire on the first go round and rattling to a stop across the landing deck.

Unsnapping myself only a second slower than the airman, I disembarked. The ice had mostly melted in the midsummer afternoon warmth. The footing wasn't treacherous. Since no servants had come to meet us, I helped the airman heave my trunk out from behind the leather passenger seat.

We carried the trunk across the landing deck and deposited it behind the windbreak. I tipped the airman a shilling. As I tucked my goggles and straps up onto my hat's brim, I saw my welcoming committee approach.

A rotund man, followed by his thin wife and two adult children came forward. The Nobbsnipes, I supposed. Apart from them, only two maidservants and one uniformed manservant stood at attention.

I had expected there to be more of a turnout. At the very least, I had hoped to be introduced to the other teachers. What a shame. In my school days, usually the teachers would assemble their pupils to greet any new arrival. Seeing a new face had always been reason enough for festivity.

This dismal entourage looked like they might be about to attend the funeral of someone who had not been well liked. I hoped they hadn't dressed up on my account.

Barnabas Nobbsnipe, the schoolmaster at the head of the subdued family, wore a fine suit done in gray wool. He stepped forward with his hands perched on his round belly and a self-satisfied smile on his face. Nobbsnipe favored me with a too-brief bow.

"Lord Franklin," he said, "welcome to Highfell Hall."

"My letter of introduction." I handed over the envelope with an inclination of my head. Although he had to be aware of its contents, Nobbsnipe feigned perusal.

I looked away politely. The courtyard around us was a barren cobbled space—remarkably plain. In other aetheria, high-altitude gardens occupied this area. The building looming above me bore greater resemblance to a prison than a school. Yet the stern middle-class house squatting between the two halls would have looked at home on a Herrow street.

"All seems to be in order, Lord Franklin." He tucked the letter into his coat. "It's an honor to meet you."

"The pleasure is mine, Mr. Nobbsnipe." I smiled and bowed. With his round torso and ruddy face, Nobbsnipe resembled a drunkard more than a do-gooder. But then, I had not suspected my uncle of being a man who would pay out good money for a charity school either.

"If I may introduce you to my wife, Mrs. Eudora Nobbsnipe, and my daughter, Miss Louisa Nobbsnipe." Nobbsnipe indicated the ladies with a grandiose wave.

His wife, Mrs. Nobbsnipe, was a narrow woman draped a black velvet dress embroidered with red poppies. She wore a dreamy yet discontented look on her face.

Her daughter, Miss Louisa, too thin and yet too broad shouldered, tried to pull off a gray and unfortunately lacy dress. A size too small, the dress compressed her bosom enough to create the illusion of cleavage.

The ladies of his family gifted me with demure curtsies. I bowed in return. Nobbsnipe then introduced his son, Roger.

With his curly chestnut hair and golden skin, Roger looked enough like me to be a relative. Yet he stood fully a hand taller than me and was significantly broader. But what I noticed most about his appearance was his garish waistcoat.

Embroidered with a scene of Demos ravishing a mortal woman, the waistcoat defied good taste. I wondered if it had once been part of a Darkest Night Masquerade ensemble. Roger, returning my appraisal, twirled an ivory-headed cane with brass bands around its mahogany length.

After that, Nobbsnipe gestured to the manservant, who was uniformed in a modest variation of a military kit. His jacket sported small epaulets adorned with double Hs. "This is the head of our watchmen, Mr. Arnold Jerome."

At this point, Mrs. Nobbsnipe assumed her duty as hostess, saying, "Please, my lord, would you be so kind as to join us for afternoon tea?"

I left my luggage in the courtyard so Jerome could bring it to my suite and followed them inside. The maid-of-all-work took my woolen greatcoat and parachute. Then she showed me into a drawing room furnished with stately dark walnut pieces and conservative taupe satin draperies.

Contemplating what it must have been like for Roger and Louisa to grow up in this dull environment, I could not fault them for desiring excitement in their wardrobe. Clearly the freedom their parents had permitted them in choosing had gone to their heads.

Compassion welled in me as I realized what level of isolation these two young people must have suffered, to see such outrageous choices as acceptable. I hoped, suddenly, that I would get the chance to introduce to them society's more cheerful pastimes.

Nobbsnipe inquired about my qualifications.

"As I'd intended to acquire my doctorate at Elmstead, I've completed my basic studies in the trivium and quadrivium and refined my focus in my preferred field, linguistics. I am passing fluent in five modern languages and seven ancient tongues, and I am broadly familiar with another sixteen dead tongues. I know it's not customary for schools such as yours to take on a teacher without a full master's or doctorate. So I must thank you for giving me the chance to work at your esteemed institution."

"Well," Nobbsnipe said slowly, "your uncle's a right lucky man, having such a fellow of such promising intellect fall right into his grasp."

Ignoring his uncomplimentary tone, I bowed my head graciously. After all, a true gentleman never lost his composure.

Before I formulated a reply, the young tweeny maid, who ran various errands and performed odd jobs, returned with tea on a silver tray. The daashtar tea was tepid and the refreshments were those that could be seen at any modest affair—scones, clotted cream, lemon curd, as well as excellent cucumber and cress sandwiches.

"Why did you study all those languages?" Miss Louisa asked.

Before I could answer, Roger spoke up. "Most grimoires are written in ancient languages. Lord Franklin can use them to cast spells."

"You cast spells?" Miss Louisa gasped.

"Well, I can. Anyone can," I explained uncomfortably. "You don't even need to read them aloud to cast them, as long as you're tracing your finger across the letters in the right order. The touch of a finger across the metallic inks and the metal wires embedded in the spell page will activate a spell."

Miss Louisa listened attentively, but Roger rolled his eyes.

I shrugged and finished, "But knowing what the spell is about before you cast it is, well, advisable. But no. I use the languages to study spells, mostly."

"But you could cast spells," she asked, "if you really needed to?"

"Certainly." I gave her a gracious, inclusive nod. "As could you, Miss Louisa. Having a spell in the first place, and the aether to power it, is really the trick."

Miss Louisa looked disappointed that I had not confessed to great supernatural power while Roger looked vexed by his sister's questions. Nobbsnipe tolerated his progeny's conversation with complacence. Mrs. Nobbsnipe merely gazed sleepily down at the table as if she hadn't been listening at all.

Shifting the discussion away into gentler small talk, I apprised the Nobbsnipes of the gossip that hadn't made it to the newssheets— not that I brimmed with much knowledge myself. Queen Isolde was rumored, according to the court diviners, to be pregnant with her fifth girl.

The queen's laboratories had discovered that the outbreak of Herrow's mysterious ague had been caused by a misused spell, but had been unable to determine from which grimoire the spell had originated. As we spoke, Mrs. Nobbsnipe silently sipped her daashtar tea. Roger ate his way relentlessly through the plate of scones.

In turn, Nobbsnipe described to me recent raiding incidents suffered by the lower aetheria. Air raiders, quicker and more organized than smash-and-grab gangs in Herrow, often preyed on the smaller and more vulnerable aetheria. After several bad break-ins during spring thaw, Nobbsnipe had recruited additional watchmen.

"We are building a strong room in the starboard hall for the safekeeping of valuables," Nobbsnipe announced.

Roger finished the scones. Brushing crumbs from his fingers, he asked, "Speaking of the strong room, Father, may I be excused? I need to attend to Leo. He's still in punishment."

"Ah yes…" Nobbsnipe waved a hand in what he clearly believed was an upper-class manner. "I suppose you should release him, or we'll get no work out of him tomorrow."

"Oh, Papa, I do hope you'll let me sit in on Lord Franklin's lectures. I would be ever so grateful!" Miss Louisa gushed as her brother bowed and left the room. "I would love to see how he intends to better that lot."

"We'll talk about it later, my poppet." Nobbsnipe gave her an indulgent smile.

After tea, Nobbsnipe led me downstairs to the dining room, where I would join the family for meals.

He indicated a door, concealed in the wood-paneled dining room wall, that led to the adjoining port-side hall. Nobbsnipe showed me through a cold storage room filled with massive metal crates secured by dangling padlocks.

Nobbsnipe indicated a spiral stairwell tucked into the corner leading down to the kitchen and then he brought me to the boys' dining room.

The unheated room was a far cry from the boarding school dining halls I'd known. The tables, rude trestles, wouldn't have been fit for the poorest establishment in Herrow. Anyone unwise enough to run a hand across their grayed boards would lift away a dozen splinters at least.

I had expected a school like the one I'd attended and loved. I had envisioned this dining room to be filled with long polished cherry wood tables, with fireplaces against the walls, candelabras with dripping stalactites of beeswax, and a dais with the professors' table overlooking the students like the top bar on the numeral pi.

I'd imagined dozens of servants rushing between the dumbwaiter and the tables, carrying with them flagons of claret and platters heavy with steaming cuts of roast beef.

How could Highfell Hall be so inferior? Then again, Evermore not only had significant endowments whose value had only grown over time, but also accepted student fees.

Whereas Uncle Gerard supported this institution alone. He most likely had to focus his limited funds on the necessities, such as keeping the aetherium's boilers in good repair, rather than spending on luxuries. My uncle did his best. I felt suddenly grateful I'd be taking my meals with the Nobbsnipes.

"My uncle is very charitable," I remarked, more to affirm the thought to myself than to express this to Nobbsnipe.

"Yes, he's a man of many graces, your uncle," Nobbsnipe replied. "Now, let's go upstairs and introduce you to your charges. Some of them are very promising boys."

"I'm sure." At the prospect of meeting my students, my despair at the dining hall abated. Now I was curious.

I followed Nobbsnipe up the stairs.

I had never considered the profession of teaching, because as a peer I had expected to have a legislative or ministerial position. Even if it had only been as a minor administrator in the queen's labs.

But now that I had, by circumstance, been charged with this good work, I itched to begin. I wanted to introduce these boys to the joy that I found in academia. I aimed to share the bliss of losing oneself in a folio, the fascination of discovering the distant past, and the serene concentration required to form perfect copperplate script.

So many people superstitiously feared writing out letters because of their association with grimoires. But I wanted to show these deprived children that spells and letters also offered knowledge they could never otherwise access.

Nobbsnipe led me past several schoolrooms. Through the glass windows in the doors, I saw school furniture shrouded in white dustsheets. Then he stopped in front of one scuffed door. About three dozen or so boys loitered within. They lounged on the desks, jabbering. One younger boy, perhaps twelve or so, drew lewd pictures on the dirty chalkboard using his finger and spit.

I spied no evidence of a teacher's presence. Nor could I spot another occupied schoolroom. I had a horrid inkling of the real faculty situation at Highfell. I couldn't possibly be the only teacher, could I? No, certainly not.

Nobbsnipe opened the door and beckoned me in after him. I adopted an air of authority, though I felt off-kilter, and entered. Nobbsnipe smiled a little too broadly and said, "Boys, this is Lord Cornelius Franklin, the nephew of our illustrious founder. He'll be your teacher. Say 'pleased to meet you' to Lord Franklin."

"Pleased to meet you, Lord Franklin," they repeated in unison.

I felt my smile freeze. I found myself petrified by the idea of lecturing for these urchins. The boys now returned my gaze curiously. I had no idea how he meant me to do this—they ranged in age from mere toddlers to surly teens, and their clothes were more fit for the rag-and-bone man than the chilly temperatures at this altitude.

Finally, after my pause had become painfully long, habit prompted me to say, "It's a pleasure to meet you all and I look forward to getting to know you."

"Don't worry, Lord Franklin," Nobbsnipe said with a kindness that rung false. "I won't expect you to lesson them until tomorrow. The boys have been excused from their vocational training just now to meet you. Boys, you're to head back."

"Yes. Yes, of course." As I watched the boys file out, I wondered what trades they trained for, but felt too overwhelmed to ask. Nobbsnipe had said "your teacher" in the singular.

"Would you like me to show you to your room?" Nobbsnipe said.

"Please," I said politely.

Nobbsnipe led me back into the hall and up a spiral staircase to the boys' dormitory. Afternoon light poured through large frost-limned windows to one side. The beds were lined up in double rows, about two dozen of them, and a petite iron stove squatted in the room's center, stovepipe sagging up into one wall. Stacked in a pyramid beside the stove, like so much meager treasure, were three lumps of coal.

The beds looked like boxes with straw tucked in them, more suitable for animals than growing lads, and the rucked bedclothes seemed but thin sheets.

Then Nobbsnipe gestured to a ladder at the far end of the room. "That there leads to the garret, where you'll be staying. Right upstairs from the boys, so you'll be able to make sure they get up to no mischief in the night. Now, if you'll excuse me, I must see to the boys' other education."

"Certainly, certainly…thank you for your time." Even as I said it, I wished I weren't so polite. I felt very much inclined to give Nobbsnipe some choice language, except I wouldn't know where to begin.

Nobbsnipe left me standing alone in that shabby open room.

As I looked closer, I noticed that the beds all had the touches of boys trying to make a home of such an inhospitable place. Drawings made from charcoal adorned the boards of one boxbed. Little collections of knickknacks and feathers lay near another. All at once I really did want to get to know the boys, who tried so hard to make this place just a bit better.

My position at Highfell wasn't what I thought it would be, true. It seemed I would have to be as much a nursemaid as a teacher, but I could still impart much to these boys. I could still show them why I valued reading and learning, and hopefully, I would also be able to bring a spark of joy to this poor place. Mentally, I thanked my uncle for presenting me with such a challenge.

So thinking, I climbed the wooden ladder to view my new lodgings. The small cot, pushed up next to a wall that radiated heat, had been neatly made up. The diminutive writing desk, made crudely from three boards, looked out a triangular window. A half candle melted onto a pottery shard sat on the sill. In the corner lurked a small pile of clutter that would've looked more at home in a barn. My luggage wasn't present.

My face burning with embarrassment though I was alone, I realized that I had left my luggage in the courtyard—and it must have remained there. Highfell Hall had no manservant to take my trunks for me. I would have to heft my luggage up two spiral staircases and a ladder.

What a contrast from what I had expected. I'd anticipated that a teacher's suite would have more than one room. Evermore, the boarding school I'd attended as a boy, had possessed all of the amenities. Massive and beautiful, Evermore's five floating aetheria had been connected with retractable, covered bridges.

The high-altitude gardens surrounding the skating rinks had contained ice-evolution sculptures so fine that masters of the art had come to view them on a daily basis. Poets, artists, and musicians had resided there to tutor us. There had been weekly recitals in the hothouse gardens—those sweltering tropical paradises filled with exotic flowers and birds.

I remembered gazing down from the heights at lesser aetheria. At the time I'd wondered who could possibly live there.

Now I knew. Beggared peers who'd come but a breath away from debtors' prison, dishonored lords who'd given up the family grimoire as collateral for debt, those sorts of wretches subsisted here. In short, I lived here.

I sighed and reminded myself I must not dwell on my changed circumstances. Then I headed to the deck in order to collect my luggage. Because I could only carry a few of the parcels up the ladder alone, I had to unpack my trunk in the open and ferry my possessions up in stages.

After the first trip the tweeny took pity on me and lent me her laundry basket, for which I tipped her a shilling. At last only the empty trunk remained on deck. Too unwieldy to wrangle solo, it would have to wait.

By the time I made my final trip, the afternoon shadows had lengthened into evening. As I approached the dormitory, I realized the boys now occupied the room. Nobbsnipe must have released them from their duties. I entered the room, laundry basket in hand.

Evening light filled the room with a golden glow that somewhat mitigated its squalor. The boys silenced the instant they saw me striding through the room. One twelve-year-old boy, bronze-haired and freckled, perched on the shoulders of a slightly older boy with dark hair. The younger one seemed to be attempting to spit on the ceiling, Wyrd knows why.

Only the lanky teen, absorbed in drawing on the side of his boxbed with the burnt end of a stick, didn't seem to realize that I'd entered. A very small boy sobbed inconsolably as a slightly older child comforted him.

Setting aside the basket, I paused beside the youngest child. I removed my handkerchief from my pocket and dabbed at the three-year-old's face. For a moment, this seemed to startle him into quiet. But then, presumably because he did not know me, he began to wail. Stymied, I handed the handkerchief to his older companion and turned to address the boys.

I said, "I'm to be your new teacher. Starting on the morrow, I hope you will be on your best behavior. I intend to help you learn all you need to know to prepare you for meaningful employment. You may call me..." I paused.

I retained my title, as only Crown and Parliament could strip it from me, but I had none of the trappings which befit a lord, no monies and no estate. Having these children call me a lord would be beyond pompous.

So instead I said, "You may call me Mr. Franklin."

I hefted my basket and marched to the ladder. I tried to look like a leader, decisive rather than unnerved, and gave them what I hoped was a confident smile as I wished them goodnight.

The boys watched me, apparently perplexed.

As I ascended the ladder, I heard one of them murmur, "Should we tell Leofa?"

Ah, Leofa—could that possibly be the "Leo" whom Roger had gone to release from his punishment? Perhaps he was a leader among the boys.

Once upstairs, I dropped the hatch. I removed my writing box, my paper, the miniatures of my parents from my luggage, and set them on the desk. I gazed out the window.

Visible below, Herrow's Southside slums looked a labyrinth of tarred roofs and timbers blackened from old fires and soot. They were shaded by the exalted aetheria floating above. If my uncle had not gifted me with this position, teaching in his charity school, then I wouldn't have even warranted a life in the slums below.

Still, over the course of the afternoon, one fact had become obvious: I had to escape this school as quickly as possible. Gratitude to my uncle notwithstanding, Highfell Hall was no place for any person with aspirations, intellectual or otherwise. How I would escape I did not yet know, but I vowed that I would find a way to repair my situation before the new year.

Quickly I drafted a note to my former advisor, Professor Ambrose Pike. I stated I would continue with my studies if he would grant me the honor of advising me, even though I had lost my student status.

That decided, I set about preparing for dinner. A spigot jutted from the wall, a bucket beneath it. It gave forth freezing water that smelled faintly of both metal and algae but seemed clean enough. I completed my ablutions as best I could. I brushed off my dinner jacket and waited.

And waited.

The sun fought against the pull of the horizon, then at last succumbed to night, as if she could no longer resist fainting from wearied hunger. A knock at the hatch elated me. I lifted the wooden door to discover the tweeny standing halfway up the ladder, asking for her basket back.

"Do you, by any chance, know at what time supper will be served?" I inquired.

"Supper's long over," she replied. "Bell rang at half six. Didn't you hear?"

Many replies ran through my mind—none of them appropriate for a man addressing a young servant girl.

I said no, thanked her, and restored her property. As I watched her go, I heard the watchman calling for lights out.

I shut the hatch and went to bed. The cot was a sheet of canvas stretched between two poles, oddly stained and worn nappy. After preparing for bed, I eased myself onto it, surprised when the frame held my weight without even a groan. The bed smelled faintly masculine, but I wouldn't barge in on my hosts at this hour demanding cleaner bed linens. The blankets seemed too pathetically thin to repel the nighttime chill.

Yet, since the cot backed up against a scalding hot wall, I convinced myself it wasn't entirely unpleasant. If I turned often enough, I could warm my front almost before my backside froze. When facing the window, I gazed at the stars. The visible Mortal Constellation, the Righteous King, twinkled.

I missed my—my everything, my parents, my old life. But eventually I began to doze.

Sometime in the night, my blankets were whipped aside. I blinked, startled and dazed. Then a man sat on me.

I jackknifed up, out of pure reflex, and somehow managed to clobber my nose against warm flesh.

The man cursed colorfully, using words the like of which I'd never heard, and sprang up. His footsteps thudded across the wooden floor. Then came the snick of a striking match. The flare of light steadied as the room's single tallow candle burned.

The man towered over me, tall and broad-shouldered as if from sport. He had aquiline features, haughty cheekbones, full lips, and a strong chin. Straight hair the color of black coffee fell across his dark eyes.

His garments could only be described as bizarre. He wore no shirt. Ropes acting as bracers held up his rough grayish trousers. He looked like a man who, on the run from the law, had avoided all civilization for years. I'd seen better-dressed beggars.

"What the fuck are you doing in my bed?" His low voice resonated through the air.

"What right have you to demand answers of me?" I stood up and stepped toward him. "I am Lord Cornelius Franklin, and my kind host, the schoolmaster Mr. Barnabas Nobbsnipe, has given this room to me as mine. I am to be the instructor at this school. Who are you?"

He turned away from me, flushing slightly, as if embarrassed by my presence. Only then did I realize I'd been acting like a complete fool, standing before him in nothing but my smallclothes. The humiliation did not make me like him. I yanked my dressing gown from my trunk, clothed myself, and waited for his answer.

"My name is Leofa. But the Nobbsnipes call me Leo," he stated. "I'm the mechanic and gardener."

"The gardener," I said, as if displeased, but inwardly I rejoiced. There was a garden!

"Yes. The gardener. And the mechanic." Then he said suspiciously, "Why did Barnabas give you my room?"

"You should not address your superior by his given name," I corrected, out of habit. Then I shrugged. "Nobbsnipe told me that I'm meant to keep order among the boys below and that this vantage would help in that."

"River Wyrd, if you believe that, you're naïve!" Leofa snorted contemptuously and stalked over to the bed. "Well, you can have the bed, but I'm taking the blankets. I don't know about you, but I have to get up before dawn."

I watched, open-mouthed with shock, as he took the bed linens, wrapped them over his shoulders like a cloak, and then pinched out the candle. Where he settled, I could not see.

I fumbled my way back to the bare cot in the dark, hot with fury. I'd never been spoken to like that my life, nor met anyone so unbearably rude.

"By the way," Leofa said in the dark, "you should probably think about moving your things. You've put them right where the roof leaks."

2

The clang of a school bell announced the arrival of morning. I woke bundled in my dressing gown and coat, not believing that I'd managed to sleep. Leofa had vanished as nightmares did before daylight. But, in what I would call a pointed gesture, he'd left his blankets folded neatly at the foot of the cot.

I dressed in my second-best suit, a dark gray wool with navy pin-stripes that complimented my sapphire cravat. I flattened my curly hair with pomade as best as I could, and headed downstairs. In the mess hall, the tweeny evenly and carefully divided grayish porridge between the boys' wooden bowls. She ducked over to me and told me the Nobbsnipes expected me at their table. I thanked her, passing through the storeroom and thus entering the dining room. Ravenous because I'd missed supper night before, I was pleased to see that the Nobbsnipes enjoyed the usual breakfast foods—bacon, boiled eggs, fish, kidneys, bread, butter, and marmalade.

Nobbsnipe shared the *Herrow Inquirer* with me while the ladies discussed embroidery knots. I flipped to "The Daily Progress," a column featuring various innovations that I sometimes followed. Today featured Professor Elias Hammerton, a vocal and sometimes controversial advocate for servants' rights. He also happened to be one of my old professors at Elmstead.

His column related that a study on a workhouse population had found that, by adding eggs and fish to their diet, productivity increased, along with health and the ability to accomplish abstract, complex tasks. Remembering the gruel I'd just observed the boys ingesting and feeling sympathetic from starving the night before, I related these intriguing facts to my host.

"What nonsense!" Mrs. Nobbsnipe gave me a scandalized look. "Plain food starves out animalistic urges and reduces insanity among the lower classes."

"I never read 'The Daily Progress,'" Nobbsnipe said. "I don't hold with it."

"Such boys have bad blood, my lord," Mrs. Nobbsnipe continued. She seemed oddly wakeful this morning. "If coddled with rich foods, their blood becomes heated and they cause no end of trouble! Besides, the deprivation teaches the ungrateful to appreciate what they do have."

"But it is a most noble sentiment, Mama," Miss Louisa said. "Isn't charity the greatest of all causes?"

At least someone here thinks of the boys, I reflected.

"Kindness is the purview of women. Lord Franklin need not worry." Mrs. Nobbsnipe sniffed and said, "Nothing goes to waste in our household."

I said, "You know, speaking of frugality, I understand that it does cost coal to heat rooms, but must I share in that chilly little garret with your man, Leofa? It seems highly irregular. Certainly there's a room more suitable for my standing?"

"We're aware that you're accustomed to being waited upon," Nobbsnipe explained. "We thought that Leo, rather than watching the boys, could serve you. In addition to his regular duties, he ought to do any work you deem necessary."

"With all due respect, this is a large complex," I said. I could not imagine asking that man to do my ironing. "Can't you find a corner or a closet for your man to sleep in?"

"I'm afraid we simply don't have the rooms to spare," Mrs. Nobbsnipe said. "Considering the construction."

"I apologize if this is less than what you're used to." As Nobbsnipe served himself a kidney, he bestowed upon it a pleased smile. He added, "But once starboard hall is complete you'll have proper lodgings, I promise."

"Really, it is the best we can do now," Mrs. Nobbsnipe insisted.

I tried to accept this with grace, but I felt the butt of a prank. "Very well, then. I'd appreciate it if you found a man to take my trunk upstairs then, in the interim."

"Of course," Nobbsnipe said. "You should have asked."

My attention nearly drifted off as the Nobbsnipes shared several thoughts about how I should conduct my teaching, and most of them seemed to involve introducing the boys to the Old Pantheon. I explained to them that no serious school taught these superstitions any longer, not since Archibald Barton had definitively proven that aether was a natural phenomenon, not of divine origin.

As Miss Louisa slavishly argued how the Old Pantheon symbolically represented internalized morality, I nicked two largish bread rolls and tucked them into my pockets.

I didn't think of it as doing anything wrong, like thieving. Back at boarding school, I'd filched food from the dining hall tables, keeping a midnight snack in reserve. As an adolescent, twelve hours without food had been just too long. Surely, the same principle applied here. And they owed me for last night.

After breakfast, I climbed up the stairs to the schoolroom, where the boys awaited me. I clapped my hands to get their attention and requested that they organize themselves by age. Immediately, they started whining and bickering. I breathed deeply, using a lung capacity I'd developed via playing the flute, and then I belted out, "Quiet!"

The boys stared at me, impressed into silence.

"You're loud," one boy complained, and then the rest of them laughed.

I sighed. "What's your name, boy?"

"Vaughn Hooker."

I recognized his bronze hair and freckled skin. He'd been the one who'd been trying to spit on the ceiling the previous night. His older friend with the dark hair loitered beside him.

"Well, Hooker," I said, "when you're in the schoolroom, schoolroom rules prevail. That means, when you want to speak, you will raise one finger to indicate a question, and you will address me as sir."

The process of taking roll stretched across an hour. At the end, I discovered that only twenty-eight boys attended from the even forty I'd been told I'd be teaching. The older boy I'd seen drawing on the side of his boxbed numbered among those absent. When I asked where the other boys were, my students didn't answer.

"I know you want to cover for them," I said patiently, "but in order to teach you all you need to know, I do need to have you present. It will be their own loss if they aren't here to take my lessons to heart. Now, do any of you care to tell me where they are?"

"Sir—" Hooker blurted out.

His older friend, Ashby, elbowed Hooker so hard in the ribs that he actually started coughing. I watched, bewildered and concerned.

A gawky, swarthy lad named Hugh Quincey, stuck his bony finger in the air and stared at me expectantly.

I nodded in acknowledgment. "Quincey."

He replied, "Pardoning your honor, sir, but they're out at work starboard, where they's got construction. Or sometimes we work down in the boilers too, when they need an extra hand."

"And Roger said he'd whup us good if you went to look for them," Hooker chimed in.

"I see," I said.

I pinched the bridge of my nose, annoyed. How could I teach these boys, when at any time they could be called from their lessons to do manual labor?

"I'm not becoming a clerk," Yorick Upping said. "I'm going to become a watchman after this and then I'll get meat for breakfast, dinner, and supper. Jerome says so, and he picks all the watchmen."

"Don't speak out of turn, Upping," I automatically echoed my own professors. At this, Upping stood, gave me a gesture not suited for polite company, and departed.

When Yorick Upping left, the three-year-old Thaddeus Paxton began to cry. He said he feared Upping would return and push me off the aetherium and Thaddeus didn't believe me when I told him that would never happen. The other boys didn't comfort him.

"Is anyone else going to leave?" I asked.

"Fuck this. Not like that door's locked," Frank Smalley said, and also took himself away.

"Morons," Ashby said. "Yeah, what do they think, that we're all going to be watchmen here? How many watchmen do they need? What do they think is going to happen? Demos! What idiots."

"I'm going to teach you all you need to become clerks," I said. "With my help, you'll be able to find a good place in any house in Herrow. You'll be able to work as a gentleman's personal assistant or secretary. You'll be able to do accounts for households and businesses alike."

Hooker regarded me with such a weird mix of skepticism and hope it discomfited me. He said, all serious, "Do you swear it on your blood?"

"Yes," I lied. I couldn't help these boys. I couldn't even help myself, but we needed to get on with lessons. "Now please be seated."

I felt the boys measuring me. I—and my future as a teacher—hung in the balance of their distrustful regard, and then I removed the bread from my pockets. I placed the rolls on my desk, sat down on my creaky chair, and I waited.

I almost felt guilty. If their evening's fare resembled their morning's, if their shrunken cheeks proved any testament, they dwelled on the brink of starvation. I broke the bread. A faint scent rose into the air.

"Now," I said, "these will go to Quincey, for being kind enough to answer my question. Your reward, Quincey."

Quincey rose, took the bread, and to my shock, began to divide it out between all the boys. At this, Hooker protested that they needed to save some for the boys who were away. Some of the others grumbled, but in the end, everyone agreed. They portioned out bread rolls evenly until each serving was but the size of a finger. Nonetheless the boys acted like the rolls came as manna from the goddess Senna herself.

They either wolfed the food down or savored it, depending on their characters, while I watched, amazed. Perhaps, I thought, more decency dwelt in these wretched boys than I could've guessed.

I inquired about their prior education. After two hours with them, I discovered that their skill levels had little to do with age and much more to do with origin. The boys who had been brought in from poorhouses had been taught some reading, writing, and figuring, but mostly they'd been hired out to do hard work.

They'd labored at every job from chimney sweep to dung collector. Several boys came from the slums and had grown up more accustomed to thievery and begging than service. But a couple of them could calculate odds and interest rates like professional money-lenders. Other boys, raised in lords' households, seemed to be almost classically educated.

After we recessed for dinner, the boys eating in the dining hall and I with the family, we returned to the schoolroom. I intended to discover the boys' linguistic accomplishments.

Shortly after I had started this, another boy came in. I recognized him as the older boy I'd seen drawing on his bunk with the stick of charcoal, lanky and thin, a black-haired teenager who hadn't quite grown into himself yet. He eased himself down at a desk. Ashby and Hooker darted up to greet him, speaking in low voices, and I moved over to see what had gotten them in a tizzy.

The boy's hands were covered with dozens of little purplish blisters. His palms looked as though he'd grasped the most poisonous nettles imaginable. He couldn't bend his fingers to eat his reserved portion of bread, so Hooker stuck it his mouth for him.

"You can't do it, can you?" Ashby asked.

The boy with the stings on his hands looked down as he chewed his bread, as though on the verge of tears, and then I touched his shoulder.

"What can't he do?" I asked.

"Fix the boiler," Ashby finished. "He's all into those mechanical drawings of his, but he can't even fix a boiler."

"Why don't they just hire tradesmen?" I wondered aloud.

"Overall, you'll notice, sir, all due respect, they're skinflints," Ashby said.

"Your opinion is duly noted, Ashby," I said. "Now back to your seats. Both of you."

"But I want to—" Hooker began, but Ashby physically dragged him away. Hooker didn't know when to stop talking and leave well enough alone. I'd known the boy for but a few hours and even I could see that. Still, he returned with Ashby to his place and I directed my attention to the injured boy.

"What's your name?" I asked him.

"David Stanley, sir."

I could feel the other students watching me.

"Like Baron David Stanley, who was the first to circumnavigate the globe in an aeroplane?" I said, trying to be friendly, but he just shrugged.

"Exactly like Baron David Stanley," he agreed. "Only not well off, sir."

"If you can behave yourselves," I said, raising my voice, "I'm going to take Stanley to the garret to care for his hands. Quincey, you're in charge."

Up in the garret, I brought him to the spigot and ran cold water over the youth's hands. He flinched at the chill water but didn't complain, seemingly resigned to the pain.

"I have some salve, I think," I said. I saw that my trunk had finally joined me in my journey. It sat askew in the center of the room as if hurled there from the ladder. I searched through my heap of belongings for the supply of medicines my sister Nora had insisted I bring with me.

After the third time I went through them, shoving aside my flute case, I found myself wishing for my mother's seeking spell. But then

I found the jar wedged beneath my parachute. I applied some balm to the boy's injured hands. The faint gold flecks in the white cream shimmered and a soft scent of lavender wafted up as the balm began to take effect.

Stanley gazed at his hands, curious though not surprised.

"I discussed education with the other boys this morning," I said to him. "I'd appreciate it very much if you could tell me about your background and what you've studied."

"I know basic astronomy," Stanley said, "but not more than the Mortal Constellations, and I've studied advanced geometry and mathematics."

"Anything else?"

Stanley flexed his fingers slowly. "I'm fluent in Siovanese, Rithen, Haedesch, and I've learned a little Accadian and Old Eidlish. When I can hold a pen, I've a good hand. Is this balm from Itoile?"

"Yes, yes, it is." I tried not to show my surprise that he'd recognized it. His excellent classical education seemed worthy of a lord's son. I did not doubt that Stanley had studied these subjects. His diction sounded clean and his accent refined. I said, "If you don't mind my asking, you're…what, sixteen, seventeen, aren't you?"

"Yes, sir," he said. "Seventeen."

"Have you given much thought to what you will do upon gaining your majority?"

It disconcerted me to learn his age. I would have assumed that most of these boys would have been apprenticed out by sixteen or younger, as was common among the lower classes. This young man, more than educated enough to be any man's clerk or assistant, could begin work immediately. Why had Stanley not yet found a place?

"I meant to…" he began, and then started again. "I mean, if I were to have gone to a school like—like Elmstead or Alton, I would have loved to study engineering."

The hatch banged open, flipping back and hitting the floor. Startled, I glanced over. Leofa climbed into the garret, barging in on us.

"So, you're a surgeon too." Leofa appeared to be carrying trapped birds in a net. The birds swung head down, all thrashing wings and panicked twisting. "Well, can't you just do everything, Lord Franklin?"

I ignored what I perceived to be an attempted jibe. I would not give him the pleasure of eliciting a response from me. It would be below me to bicker with a servant. I tightened the cap on my jar.

Leofa dug one of the birds out of the net. I was horrified when I saw the creature's plumage. My old professor of natural philosophy had developed the breed. He only ever sold a handful to fellow academics and dove fanciers. I knew for a fact that they were rare birds.

"Wait!" I cried. "You can't—"

Leofa twisted the bird's neck. The thrashing changed from a live bird's struggles to those of a bird that did not yet know it had died. The dying bird's ruffled feathers looked fine as silver filigree. Leofa looked up at me.

"That's a Silver-Edged Thurgeon!" I cried out. "That's someone's pet! That's a two-hundred-guinea bird."

"Do you think it's any tastier than a hundred-guinea bird?"

I found myself actually speechless. I couldn't believe he intended to eat it. In the corner of my eye, I could see young Stanley slinking away.

Leofa moved over to the desk, opened the window, and flipped open a straight razor. He slit the skin, yanked it off the poor creature as one might remove a stocking, and dropped it, feathers and all, out the window. A horrible stench filled the tiny space. Gore streaked Leofa's fingers.

The netted pigeons shrieked in distress.

Leofa went to the washbasin and gutted the bird right there on the stand. He set the heart and liver aside in his tin cup and chucked the remaining guts out the window.

Riverbirds immediately converged in midair, squabbling over the offal. After that Leofa tied a length of string around the pigeon's feet in order to hang it from a hook in the ceiling. At this point he set the razor aside. That was when I noticed the instrument's distinctive ivory inlay.

"Are you using my razor to do that?" I asked. I felt the blood draining from my face from rage.

"Got a good edge on it," he said.

He had to have gone through all of my things to find it. I couldn't believe he was so blatant. Leofa didn't even seem to care that he'd been caught red-handed—not so metaphorically speaking.

Heart in my throat, I crossed the garret floor. I could not allow him to seize my belongings.

"My razor, please." I held out my hand, hoping that Leofa, crude as he seemed, would have some shred of decency.

Leofa locked his eyes with mine. He did not move. Nor did I. But then his head tilted slightly. His eyes crinkled with a repressed smile. He took a rag from his pocket, wiped the razor clean, and then matter-of-factly laid it in my palm.

"Thank you." I walked over to my trunk and knelt before it, replacing my razor in my shaving kit. I left the shaving kit in plain sight. "In the future, please do not hesitate to ask before you borrow. And, if you do not mind, I must return to the schoolroom. Good day."

After turning to leave, I felt a creeping sensation between my shoulder blades. Doubtless, labor had hardened the man so that he could thrash me if he chose. Before I descended the ladder, I glanced back at Leofa. He'd sat himself quietly on the floor beside his netted pigeons and regarded them thoughtfully. I had not expected to see sadness there.

As I returned to the schoolroom, I wondered whether Leofa had meant to intimidate me. Granted, I had usurped his quarters. But that had not been through my own choice. Was he aware of that? I should have informed him that Nobbsnipe had given me the room without telling me of his occupancy.

Once I reached the schoolroom, I removed all thought of Leofa from my mind and focused on the task at hand. The boys looked tired and cross. I decided to ease up on them. I'd been quizzing them all morning verbally and they were unaccustomed to the rigors of study. The boys had started to fidget, and unless I gave them some reason to like me, they'd all walk out that door.

"At my boarding school," I said, glossing over the truth only slightly, "your year indicates your skill level and what you study. But the students also have houses, which compete against each other for sport, and each house has its name, colors, and house crest. Houses band together, with the higher years helping the lower years, so they perform better both academically and in sports. I would like to implement this system here today."

I gave each skill group a "year" ranging from one, the least advanced, to five, the most advanced. The groups were not numerically even—I counted twenty-seven boys in years one and two, while group five contained only Stanley. I asked everyone to stack the furniture in the corner of the room in order to create more space. Then I reassembled the boys into their new houses.

I said, "Look around you. The young men standing beside you are now your housemates, your brothers."

I watched the boys begin to grin at each other, at the ridiculousness of this, though some boys seemed disappointed because they'd been split up from their friends. Hooker tried to sneak into Ashby's group even as I spoke. I gave him a sharp look and he subsided.

I added, "I want you to spend the rest of the day deciding on your house name, your colors, and your crest. You should pick your house's name from an animal, preferably a fierce one. You're going to have to pick a house ambassador, as well, who will go to the other houses to make sure that you're not picking the same colors."

When the bell had rung, signaling the end of the day, three of the houses had decided on their animal names: Falcons, Wolves, and the Beasels. After asking what a "beasel" was, young Thaddeus Paxton informed me that it was beagle crossed with a weasel and that they were very mean, if somewhat imaginary, animals. The last group remained undecided.

I dismissed the students and let them go galloping out of the schoolroom. They talked about house colors, wondering aloud what kind of sports and contests I would set up. Even as they chattered, I mentally took notes about what excited them. Clearly, they normally had no opportunity for play. Their liveliness gladdened me.

Before making my way back to the garret, I paused to investigate my schoolroom's premises.

The mismatched wooden desks and chairs looked like the deranged remnants of the world's saddest flea market. The chalkboard at the head of the room was filthy, and upon examination I understood why Hooker had drawn on it in spit. I saw no slate pencils or chalks. In fact, I found no slates at all.

Nor could I discover any folios or texts for the boys to learn their letters from. Indeed, my explorations uncovered no paper, ink, inkwells, quills, penknives, pencils, styluses, nibs, or blotting paper. I decided that I'd ask Nobbsnipe if Highfell had a foliarium, though at that point I held out little hope.

Over a modest supper of cold roast beef, bread, pork pie, carrots in aspic, trifle, and cheeses, Nobbsnipe informed me that the only folios present at Highfell were the religious texts that comprised his own personal library. Then he requested that I join them in the drawing room for a game of cards. Roger refused to play and sat sullenly to the side as we played Priest Joan.

Nobbsnipe cleared his hand first and won. Miss Louisa insisted on a game of Beggar Thy Neighbor, which she then lost graciously. She showed me a few of her watercolors. I recognized the view—she'd drawn the bucolic hills and the few freehold farms at the west. She'd selected harmonious sunset colors. At the night's close, I sat down at the piano and played them *Sonata in D* by Helmud Schader.

"It's very popular right now," I explained to Mrs. Nobbsnipe, who hardly looked impressed by the tune. "I think Schader will be remembered as one of the greatest composers of our time, honestly. He does use some unusual time signatures, but I think that adds… a piquancy where instead there could be pomposity."

"How well said!" Miss Louisa said, clapping her hands together. "I found it so very dramatic. Isn't it, Mama? Has Schader produced any comparable pieces?"

"Oh, we have heard enough from this Schader fellow," Mrs. Nobbsnipe said ungraciously. "Can't you play anything more classical? Play something we all know, like *Etherea* or *Damea*."

"Of course, dear lady," I said, even though I found those tunes incomparably dull. How typical to request the least interesting hymns from an older generation's era, back when the debunked gods of the Old Pantheon had to be placated in their temples. But they were repetitive pieces most beginners learned, as easy as running through scales. I tripped them out.

"Do you shoot?" Roger asked. His other contributions to the discourse tonight had mostly been grunts of acknowledgement, the barest minimum that was socially acceptable. So this felt invasive and rude, by virtue of its suddenness.

"On occasion," I replied, cautiously.

"Are you any good?"

"Only fair to middling, I suppose." I didn't like to brag and I believed that any mention I'd been a member of Elmstead's marksmanship society would only serve to goad Roger. I had no interest in getting involved in any sort of spitting contest with the schoolmaster's son.

"Well, I just thought we could shoot a few pigeons tonight while we still have sun," he said. "You get them right, and they just fall like stones." He mimed a dead pigeon plummeting into the city below. "Don't you think that's just a surprise?"

Was there anyone who didn't murder these domesticated birds down here? As for the element of surprise, I could only imagine that the people below had experienced even odder things than dead pigeons raining from the sky.

The sheer number of boarding boys pissing over the aetheria's edges would guarantee the city directly below could experience showers on the sunniest of days. And many schoolboy pranks involved tipping everything from schoolmasters' tea sets to harpsichords overboard. But I smiled and said, "I mostly enjoy match shooting. Targets and the like."

Roger seemed disappointed. But I couldn't find it within myself to agree to spend the remainder of the evening with him. I didn't want to blast away at the local avians either. Greater obligations called me. I excused myself and departed.

On the way back, I passed two watchmen on patrol. The stringy men watched me like wolves contemplating a reindeer—as if they wondered whether trying to take me down made good sport. Apparently not, for I climbed up to the dormitory unscathed.

The delicious scent of roasting meat greeted me, tainted by the smell of unwashed adolescents. The boys gathered in a semicircle around the iron stove, where Leofa crouched, roasting several skewered pigeons.

"—told us to get in groups," Hooker said, "and these are houses, even though we don't have houses and we're brothers now and have house names, and we're called the Skunks!"

"I still think you should just be called the Farts instead," Ashby said, which made the other boys crack up.

I supposed the last group had decided on their name.

As I passed through, the boys quieted down and Leofa looked up at me. He seemed to measure me. I felt myself flushing, grateful for the room's dimness. The coals' red glow in the stove surely hid the heat in my face.

For all Leofa's coarse ways, he had been watching over the boys. He'd probably been doing it for some time. Some of them perhaps knew him better than they'd ever known their fathers or older brothers. Surely, I'd induced a few of the students to like me, tentatively. But they were loyal to him. His approval could mean my success, and his disapproval my failure.

"See you later," he said.

"Good evening," I replied and climbed up to the garret.

Judging from the still-roasting state of the pigeons, I surmised that I would be free of Leofa for an hour more at least. This gave me time to do some work. I lit the candle and fetched the polished wooden box that held the supplies I used for my studies on aether.

In part, I studied the more arcane languages in an attempt to unravel a particular spell in my family's grimoire—the pyxis spell. The pyxis spell could be inscribed onto a gold-and-copper mesh that could hold aether even outside of an aetheric current. The amount of aether it could capture naturally could only power small spells—perhaps a critical healing spell or message spell, but nothing more.

I wanted to change all of that. I wanted to build a spell that would allow me to load aether into the pyxis. Current trapping spells, such as those used to feed aether into the turbines that kept the aetheria aloft, were incompatible with the pyxis spell.

If I could create an interface with one of these trapping spells, well, then I'd have a handy little device. It would be able to capture and hold vast amounts of aetheric energy to be used at the owner's leisure.

Building this interface, which I called a transducer, had comprised the backbone of my studies while at Elmstead. An aetheric power source would change the world as we knew it.

Flying vessels, for example, could journey beyond a direct aetheric stream and still remain aloft, rather than plunging to the ground as they currently did. Trains now powered by coal could run cleanly. Aether-powered mills and other industry could be built up anywhere in Higher Eidoland. Lights could banish the darkness in even the poorest sections of Herrow.

My invention could power the greatest revolution the modern world had ever seen.

If only it worked.

As a boy, I'd watched my parents struggling with this very same problem. I'd hoped I'd be able to repay my stepfather for all his investment into my education. I'd wanted to formulate a device that could transform the pyxis trap from a curiosity into a tool of technological revolution. But without the pyxis spell, which was locked up my family's grimoire and now in my uncle's possession, I could currently only formulate untestable hypotheses.

Grimoires were inherited either through the mother's or father's bloodline. They stood not as only symbols of ancestral power but also granted the peers actual power. Protected by bloodlocks, within the leather-bound covers, the spells were wired into the pages. Proprietary, the spells could heal or harm.

Some ancient spells held the potential to propel forward developing aetheric technologies. Other spells, always sought after for leasing by the queen's military, could decimate armies or bring down plague.

But most, of course, only helped with small tasks, like finding the neighbor's lost hound. And many of the volumes had, over time, become untranslatable, as the last speakers of arcane languages took their knowledge to the grave.

Our own family grimoire was unintelligible. The meaning of only a few spells had been passed down by word-of-mouth. But many of the pages remained an utter mystery.

Now my mother's grimoire was in my uncle's hands, acting as collateral for the loan he'd given me to repay my parents' debt. At my teacher's salary, my mother's grimoire might as well be as far away as the Mortal Constellations.

While my boyhood plan to change the course of history now struck me as fanciful, I thought I might be able to patent plans for the transducer. Maybe I could make some money. I clung harder to the idea of recapturing my fortune more with each passing second I spent here at Highfell.

I laid out several copper wires inscribed with spells. Letters etched into the copper glinted as they collected aether from the atmosphere. The shimmer of the aether ran down their lengths and dissipated pointlessly.

Usually, my studies and dreams of a glorious future had been enough to distract me from any worries, making me focus on what I deemed important. But today, my work filled me with vague despair.

The smell of roast poultry had intensified, drifting upwards to where I sat. I heard laughter. I hoped the boys joked about beasels and flatulence rather than their new teacher.

∽

Leofa did not return to the garret that night. Nor did he return for the next two. In that time, I attempted to convince Nobbsnipe to provide alternative rooming arrangements. Nobbsnipe ignored my entreaties. By the end of the third day, I had become certain that we would have to share the small, drafty, and unevenly heated space above the dormitory.

As sunset deepened, I decided to walk the grounds. I did not exactly search for my unwanted roommate, or so I told myself. I only wished to take in my surroundings.

I left via the door in the boys' dining room, exiting into the front courtyard.

Our aetherium's prow shifted slowly to face the wind, away from the sunset in the west, casting me in Highfell's shadow. Highfell's peaked port and starboard halls, done in gray stone, framed the Nobbsnipes' recessed brick home.

Construction on the starboard hall appeared to be finished. The gray stone hall looked identical, from its plain wooden front door to the weathered window fittings, to the port hall where I taught the boys. The large second-story windows were dark. It had definitely been built, and dare I say, completed at the same time as the port hall. Yet watchmen slumped in the doorway of the starboard hall, the location of the boys' dubious vocational training, around the clock.

I frowned at it suspiciously. What were the boys learning in there? What damaged Stanley's hands so, causing such bizarre blisters? I didn't believe the story about them being burns from a boiler for an instant. Especially not when Ashby and Hooker showed up sporting them the following day.

I shook my head, unable to satisfactorily answer my own questions, and continued on.

As soon as I stepped out of the courtyard and the windbreak's protection, air gusted around me. I paused, annoyed by how the humidity and wind would return my hair to its innately curly state, and regarded

the narrow stretch before me. Only five feet of clearance stood between the building and the railing-less edge. Near the edge clustered
pulley systems and an abseiling raft, which dropped down and around
the hull so that ice could be removed.

I glanced up at the aetheria hanging above. Several construction
platforms floated around an older aetheria, a private vessel in the process of being refitted. A tugship lifted free an ancient turbine, which
from here looked to be nothing but blades twisted into an ellipsoid.
Wyrd, that turbine had to be one of the first mass-produced models,
well over forty years old.

Up above on the Nobbsnipes' house protruded the small shape of
the dovecote. A dingy gray flag fluttered from a flagpole protruding
from the roof, its crest unrecognizable.

In most aetherium, the dovecote was a public space and boys could
access the birds at any time to send letters home. Here Nobbsnipe did
not even permit the school's sole teacher to do so. I'd discovered as
much when I'd tried to write my uncle for supplies. All letters went
through Nobbsnipe's hands before being mailed out.

I hunched my shoulders inside my black woolen coat against the
wind.

Passing around the mysterious starboard hall, I again entered the
yard. The outhouses were across from me, the cabbage boxes arranged
in a grid, and an empty clothesline pole stood beside me. No gardens,
I thought to myself. What did Leofa do around here? And where had
he been sleeping?

Certainly, though, that did not concern me.

Three doors led out into the yard. One was from the starboard
hall, one went to the Nobbsnipes' residence, and the last, which I took,
led into the boys' dining hall.

Dissatisfied, I returned to the garret and sat down at the desk.

I knew I should write to my sister. I took out my flute case instead.
The case's tooled ostrich leather was smooth as butter beneath my fingertips.

The case, and the flute inside it, had been a gift from my mother.
I wished I could guess what she'd tell me now. She'd always had something good to say. I'd never been as close to my stepfather, but yet I
had never doubted that he'd stand up for me, that he'd support me,
that he'd defend me as his own.

Gone. So suddenly. I could not believe it still. I could feel my own incredulity overwhelming my grief. I could remember standing over their corpses. How it had felt, the denial, the certainty that this had to be a cosmic joke, that this was impossible. I could still feel the child within me shaking his little head in stubborn disbelief.

I unsnapped the case and assembled the silver flute with the ease of habit. I played scales, warming up my fingers in the room's evening chill. Outside, it gently misted as the clouds lowered themselves upon the aetherium. I could hear a few droplets pinging around in the pipes and the gurgle in the nearby tanks as the rainwater drained.

No, my parents couldn't have died of ague. No, they would have never been so irresponsible as to leave us in such debt. No, they would have never left us in such penury, never beggared us, not even to pay for our school fees, never impoverished us by gambling on stocks. Never.

I'd read a novel once, one where an adventurer's son confronted his father on his death bed, and he did not see a man larger than life, the image he always failed to live up to. No, the son saw a man, withered and lonely, and he thought, 'The Mortal Constellation brought to ground.' I did not want to think these thoughts now that my parents were gone.

"What song is that?" Leofa asked.

"It's not—I haven't chosen what to play yet." I felt embarrassed. I lowered the flute. I'd been playing snatches of songs. I had to have sounded indecisive and demented. "I'm sorry if—"

"No, I liked it," Leofa said. He sat down on the cot, his legs akimbo, his elbows perched on his knees and his hands hanging down between them. Leofa leaned forward, and he had no right to be so impressive in such rags. "Look, you may look like a—like a Silver Surgeon—"

"A Silver-Edged Thurgeon," I corrected without thinking.

Leofa waved it away. "You know what I mean. What I'm trying to say is, you may look like Roger but you seem all right. We both know they shouldn't have put you in here with someone like me."

I nodded slowly, accepting this.

"But Nobbsnipe likes seeing us both brought low, I guess," Leofa continued. "So we're stuck with each other and there's no helping that. And I can't keep on sleeping out in the hangar."

I frowned as I contemplated his words. He let me think about it, at ease in a way I wasn't with the silence. It made me both envy him and hate him, how he could lecture me so and then wait patiently for me to accept the truth of it.

The difference between our stations, though I was beggared and all but indentured, made what he'd said laughable. I remained still Lord Cornelius Franklin, a son of peers, and my ancestors had hundreds of years of history granting dignity to our name. I did not share a bed with a gardener or a mechanic or whatever true function Leofa performed for this place.

"Shouldn't we at least search for a second cot?" I asked.

"You can look," he said. "I already did. There isn't one. Asked the maids, too."

While that fit with my dire assessment about the school's lack of supplies, the implication that we would have to share did not sit easily with me.

"Unless, of course, you want to try and nick yourself some straw from one of the boys' beds," he said.

I did not.

I asked instead, "Do you truly think that Nobbsnipe wishes to humiliate me?"

Leofa shrugged. "Well, I think he's trying to teach us both our place."

But then I snorted at myself and shook my head.

I was hardly a fop, to shrivel at the slightest hardship. Work remained my only exit from this predicament. I wasn't such a snob that I'd overlook the clearly practical arrangement. Plus, between keeping on this man's good side for the sake of the boys and the fact that I seriously doubted he'd ever take an order from me, my decision became exceptionally clear.

"We'll share the bed," I said. "And you will *ask* me before taking any of my belongings in the future. I'm not in a position to replace any of them, so I'd very much appreciate it."

"I'll keep that in mind." He removed his shirt. "You mind if I sleep naked?"

"Yes." I cleared my throat. I felt my cheeks burning as I averted my face from the candlelight. "I may be broke, but I am certainly not bent."

Leofa laughed, a deep and pleasant noise that filled me with instinctive warmth. I could hear him undressing, the slither of the rough cloth on his skin, and I refused to look, though something in me dearly wanted to.

"Just a joke, Your Majesty. I'll leave my drawers on," he said.

The cot creaked beneath his large frame. When I looked back at him, he'd curled up, facing the hot wall. His back had a few thick pale scars on it. I cleaned my flute, repacked it, and prepared for bed.

When I climbed into bed with him, wearing naught but my smallclothes, I realized how very narrow the cot was. In order to remain on the cot at all, we had to be in full body contact. Apart from instances in the gymnasium, I hadn't ever been so close to any other man before.

His skin radiated heat, like one of the boilers Leofa supposedly repaired, and I felt flushed, awkward, and nervous. After a time, I did begin to relax. At least, I thought drowsily, this arrangement conserved heat.

As I started to drift off, I recalled that I had not yet written my sister. Or Madeline. My former fiancé deserved to hear what had become of me. But, before I could begin mentally drafting my epistle, sleep's soothing weight settled in and consciousness softened into darkness.

3

As the next two weeks passed, slowly we developed a routine. Always Leofa left before I rose. I spent the early mornings planning lessons, breakfasted with the Nobbsnipes, taught, ate again with the Nobbsnipes, and lectured in the afternoons on what subjects that caught my fancy.

Then, after supper with the Nobbsnipes, I begged off as early as I could. By then I'd already endured three hours with the tedious and increasingly parochial family.

In the evenings, I pursued my private research. Leofa inevitably returned after I had fallen asleep, to share the cot with me.

Aside from the intimate overtone it disturbed me to contemplate, our situation reminded me somewhat of the folktale concerning Iskar, the god of death. He could only gaze upon mortals when they slept, lest they die under his dark gaze. But I hardly thought of myself as a beautiful mortal woman, to be kidnapped and kept in an enchanted sleep in the underworld.

Over the course of that fortnight, the lessons progressed well. Although Upping and Smalley did not attend my class, the other boys did seem to be trying hard, even though by now they'd learned that I truly did expect them to memorize their times tables.

Stanley's blistered hands had initially swollen to the point of being unusable, but gradually his symptoms subsided. After his condition had improved, he volunteered to assist me in teaching the youngest children their Eidlish alphabet.

To do this, he used a semaphore card that displayed the letters along with their corresponding flag positions. This was because the supplies I'd requested from my uncle had not yet arrived.

At first, the boys protested strenuously at learning their letters. Apparently they had the superstitious impression that the actual letters held the aetheric power. They thought that writing and reading, therefore, could trigger the accidental release of spells.

But I corrected them. The letters in grimoires were drawn out with metallic inks over wires embedded in the pages; the touch of a finger activated them. Hooker was disappointed that there wasn't a "most magical" alphabet.

I was teaching the boys their times tables by rote when Miss Louisa entered the room. Her severe day dress was a deep blue, and her straight bangs framed her face under her wide-brimmed bonnet. The faintest scent of lilac wafted around her in the room's changing air currents.

The tweeny, that starveling sparrow of a girl, darted in after her. Peggy's eyes widened, her chest heaving, as she looked around the room fearfully.

The boys quieted, watchfully, and I suddenly felt as though I stood on stage, a player in some pivotal scene.

"Miss Louisa, may I help you?" I asked her.

"No, not at all," Miss Louisa said. Her eyes flicked around the room. She held a folio tucked beneath her arm. "I wanted to check in on your progress. You may call me Louisa, if you please."

"Ah…" I had no wish to do so, for we were neither engaged nor related. I said, "Indeed. Miss Louisa, I'm afraid—"

"I brought the Good Writ," she said and stepped forward to the front of the schoolroom. "If it is no inconvenience, I would like to read to the boys and educate them in the ways of morality and good hard work. The Good Writ is the best way to better the morality of man, you know."

"Actually, I am rather in the middle of a math lesson—" I began.

But Miss Louisa glanced at me, with a gracious but silencing smile. She had several pages in the folio marked, and she flipped to the first passage. She had an excellent reading voice, I noticed.

"Before the sea and sky had separated, before the earth knew it differed from the underworld, Demos sculpted man from that ignorant clay. Demos made all the orders of man: from yeoman to monarch, and all the forms of woman.

"And to the greatest, he sacrificed three drops of his blood, and to the least, he gave but one. Then he breathed life into all his creations. And the remnant of Demos' breath that remained after all creatures had been awakened is what we call aether."

Her sudden sermon usurped my planned lesson. But how could I stop her—or even interrupt her—without being astonishingly impolite? I could hardly manhandle her from the room. I crossed my arms and waited.

She read on, "So should we all remember that our formation from the clay of the earth, the lowest of soils, that we may serve our gods' purpose with no thought of self-advancement or worldly gain."

The tweeny slumped against the back wall, teetering on the verge of sleep.

I had never been a believer in the Good Writ and I disliked this passage in particular. Historically, it had been used to justify the subjugation of the servant classes.

But many did not see the Good Writ as such. I had to accept that Miss Louisa might well be referring to more standard interpretations of this passage. These had to do with accepting your role within an unfair cosmos and behaving selflessly despite a lack of resources to call upon.

But to my mind, all this religious text did was perpetuate misinformation about the nature of aether.

When she had finally gone, I said, "Well, after that interlude, I suppose we should return to our studies."

"You don't believe in any of that stuff, do you? I could see it on your face," Quincey said. Although fourteen, he observed the world keenly. "The Good Writ and Demos creating man and all that."

I strove not to smile. I replied, "Science has conclusively proven that aether is a naturally occurring element, not the breath of Demos or any other god."

"Does this mean you don't believe in rebirth or the underworld?" Hooker asked, intrigued.

"That is correct."

"What do you think happens when we die then?" Stanley challenged. Something like terror glinted in his dark eyes.

"I think we die. I think it's the end." I shrugged and I could feel my eyes stinging, as my throat tightened with the unfairness of it. I did not want to discuss this any longer; my parents' loss was too fresh.

The boys stared at me and suddenly I became aware of Leofa standing in the open door, leaning against the doorframe. When I took in his commanding stance, I tried not to think of how I'd slept beside that body every night for the last two weeks.

Leofa watched me, assessing me. I hated that he did this. He had no right. But what I hated even more was how much I wanted to know what he measured me against, exactly, and how I could shatter that unknown standard by surpassing it.

"You're wrong. I'm coming back as a lion," Hooker announced.

Leofa snorted. The boys laughed and chattered about what animals they'd like to come back as and why. Only Quincey couldn't let this go, and now he drew near to question me about being an unbeliever.

I launched into a lecture about how, once, magic and spells were seen as divine manifestations. They were linked to certain regions where the gods' cults had presence and were thought to be fueled by worship. But over time, a series of different thinkers and early scientists had proved that divinity had little to do with making the spells work.

"It's now a well-accepted fact that the spells in grimoires work whether or not you invoke gods or goddesses," I said. "The spells work anywhere there's aether—and if there isn't any aether, whatever deity you invoke, the spell will fail."

Again, I looked up for Leofa, but he had vanished.

⤳

That night I had expected to find Leofa in the garret. But as he wasn't there, I chose to discover more about this reclusive roommate of mine, who seemed content to judge me.

So, not with the noblest of intentions, I searched his belongings. The heap of debris in the corner included several roughly woven nets, an ice hook, and beneath these objects I saw a floorboard with a dented edge. I fingered the rough side and then looked around. I pried up the board and peered underneath.

A pair of iolite goggles, such as you'd see in any lab in Elmstead, nestled in a dingy rag. I drew them forth gingerly and peered through them without strapping them to my head. The bluish polarization lenses still worked, making visible the swirls of silvery aether gusting past. The aether slithered and rolled, like a thick liquid caught in water.

The supper bell rang five o'clock. I had to hurry.

When I returned the goggles, the world seemed poorer for it.

Leofa had stashed fragments of metal here as well. Some were un-worked, but others had been looped onto something like a key ring. Silver, copper, iron, steel, and even wood had been fashioned hook shapes, needles, hairpins, and more. A floral hilt of a silver butter knife was lodged to the side.

A pair of worn cowhide leather gloves had wood sewn onto them, gauntlet fashion. Only when I found the music box and the packet of letters, all addressed to Leofa, did I begin to feel any shame at prying.

I should've stopped there. But still I twisted the key on the music box and listened to the plaintive notes of a long-forgotten melody. The old national anthem for the rebel Hetons. It was so associated with the brigands' liberation movement in the Barrens that to even hum this tune in Herrow would be taking my own life into my hands.

I wondered what it was like for a man who listened to this anthem to be called by the Eidlish version of his name—to be renamed by his employers like a pet.

"Well, I guess I should've expected this." Leofa strode past me and slid his length onto the cot. He held his hands oddly, curled protectively against his chest.

"Your hands…" I stared at them. The music box continued its tune. I moved to shut it.

"No," he said. "Let it play."

The anthem continued, melancholic in its minor key. He closed his eyes as he listened. The music soothed him, I could see, even as it ratcheted up a nervous tension in me. When the song petered to an end, I lowered the box into the hiding place and replaced the board.

"My mother gave it to me when I came here," Leofa said.

"I see."

"Does it bother you that I'm a Heton?"

"Honestly, you look like you'd be more at home in the House of Lords than the Barrens," I said. "But no, it doesn't. I must assume you've been too busy here at the school to go around bashing tax collectors on the head and setting houses on fire."

He snorted but didn't disagree.

I stood up and stomped the floorboard back into place. Then I turned to face him. He'd almost fallen asleep.

"Do you speak Hei?" I asked.

"Yeah. Well, I used to. Haven't used it much since I came here."

"If you'd be interested in teaching me, I'd love to learn. I'm afraid there weren't any Hei grammars available in Elmstead." I did not have to tell him the politics behind that. "So I never got the chance. I'd very much enjoy learning it."

Leofa regarded me sleepily, but also as if he couldn't believe what he'd heard, and then he finally gave up and went to sleep, his hands hanging limply in front of him. This uncomfortable position did not seem unfamiliar to him.

I moved toward Leofa, sinking to the floor beside the cot, and took his hands gingerly in my own to examine them. He flinched, so slightly I could feel more than see it. The multitude of tiny purplish blisters concentrated most strongly around his fingertips. Some speckled the inside of his palm and sprayed along the backs of his fingers and hands. Hundreds of fleck-like scars whitened his otherwise tan skin.

"Stop it," he said, startling me. He hadn't been asleep after all.

"Stanley had blisters like these," I said. "I've never seen anything like them."

"Got a new machine," Leofa said. "Can't get the fucking thing to work."

"At the very least, you should let me rub some balm on them. It helped Stanley quite a bit when he couldn't get the—" I paused for effect— "thing to work."

He sighed. "Not right now."

I contemplated pressing him. He was weak right now, but I decided I didn't want to chance it.

In the end, I retrieved the balm from my trunk. I left it on the desk, already open, in case when he woke his hands were too swollen for him to pry off the stopper.

᠆᠆

Over supper with the Nobbsnipes, Miss Louisa handed me the day's post. I'd received a letter from my sister, a confirmation from Professor Pike that he would be glad to advise me in my continued studies, and another from my uncle. But I hadn't yet gotten a missive from the girl who'd once been my fiancé.

Seeing my sister's handwriting on the outside of the envelope gladdened me so much that I offered my apologies and drew aside to read her note.

Inside, folded very neatly, was a thin silk handkerchief embroidered with green vines. Between the vines she'd rose-knotted red threads. Preceding Nora's current passion for mathematics had been a fascination with cryptography. I recognized the knot formations as the only code she'd kept up with, mostly because she liked embroidering subversive messages on her clothing.

But this handkerchief read only: GOOD LUCK.

Smiling, I tucked it in my pocket before starting to read her letter.

My dearest brother Cornelius,

I am glad to hear that you are well. You know how I ~~worry~~ when you travel by glider, as ~~unexpected storms~~ can sometimes seize the sky. I am grateful to Uncle Gerard for all that he has done for us. His house is very well appointed, and though the fashionable district of Knave's Court has much to offer by way of diversions, I do ~~miss~~ the Collegiate School for Girls. I hope to ~~return~~ soon, but in the meantime I am corresponding with my friends and ~~attempting to keep up~~ on the class work.

Although I hardly interpreted that as negative sentiment, my sister had been careful to strike those words out as politeness to ensure it couldn't be read, superstitiously, as an ill-wishing. Words, at least the ones in grimoires, had power, but most polite individuals took care when writing even a casual epistle.

I ~~miss~~ you so, after all of this ~~turmoil~~. I've successfully petitioned Uncle Gerard on both our behalfs: I asked him that you be permitted to visit me on your next day out in but a few days' time. He has sent his request that you be taken below to the schoolmaster, and so it should have arrived along with this letter.

It is only a thought, but I would so appreciate it if you could escort me to the museum. I have seen the handbills for a new exhibit—a traveling one—that features some of the original papers of Pierre es Tel. It would be such a treat, such an honor, to see these! As ever, I remain

Your loving sister,
Honoria Franklin

I almost laughed aloud when I saw Pierre es Tel's name in her letter. Nora had worshipped Pierre es Tel for his work in mathematical renderings of non-aetheric atmospheric dynamics. Of course she'd be excited about seeing his original scribblings. I was only surprised that she hadn't yet hared off to the museum with maidservants in tow.

Since she'd mentioned my uncle in her letter, I begged the Nobbsnipes' pardon and broke the red seal on his envelope as well.

His note was quite short, saying merely that he'd arranged with the Nobbsnipes to have Roger fly me to meet Nora. School supplies would be held for me at the rental hangar.

I glanced up at the Nobbsnipes, who watched me pensively or, in Miss Louisa's case, attempted conspicuously not to. I smiled at Roger. I said, "Uncle Gerard has informed me that you will be so kind as to fly me down the surface to visit with my sister. I am grateful, sir."

Nobbsnipe nodded, a small satisfied gesture. His daughter smiled tentatively. Mrs. Nobbsnipe looked startled and smiled in a confused manner, like she'd only just become aware of the conversation.

Roger said, "You're welcome." Then Roger exchanged a glance with his father. "I mean, it won't be a problem at all. I'm always happy to go below."

"Oh, Mama! If Roger's going, we can take the large glider," Miss Louisa said, flushing and bouncing slightly with excitement. "I would love to be introduced to Lord Franklin's sister. We're almost of an age!"

I tried to look as though this delighted me.

"And I haven't had an outing below in so long," Miss Louisa continued. "I must see the fashions, and perhaps I can even visit the milliner with his sister! I'm sure she knows all the best fashions of Herrow."

Mrs. Nobbsnipe sniffed. "Very well, my dear. If it isn't too inconvenient for *Lord* Franklin, I suppose it can be arranged."

I found myself vexed by the suggestion. I'd hoped to see Nora privately. But now, rather than catching up with my sister, I would have to spend my day out entertaining the younger Nobbsnipes. Or worse yet, in facilitating their social climbing. Upon mentally reviewing who would be attending, I realized our party would rather resemble the cast of a comedic play—of the type where everyone ends up married at the end.

The thought of being linked in holy matrimony to Louisa Nobbsnipe made my soul wither.

I suggested hurriedly, "If we're going to be shopping with ladies, we'll certainly need a boy to carry our things. What about Stanley? He has nice manners."

Mrs. Nobbsnipe eyed me, as if I'd tried to pull the wool over her eyes, and then she tilted her chin slightly. "I do believe Smalley and

Upping are much more suited to such manual labor. Stanley is not a very vigorous child."

"Well, there's no better way to build his strength," I said. I dreaded having those duller boys with me. I hadn't seen them often, since they did not deign visit the schoolroom, and I couldn't imagine them suddenly obeying me below.

Mrs. Nobbsnipe regarded me for a moment before relenting. She said, "I suppose he can attend you, provided we send Leo as well. But you must make sure to promise me that Stanley won't run. If he does, the fault will rest on you. The truancy office does not take kindly to stray boys."

"I understand. He won't run," I said. I thought it odd that this concerned them. Stanley would only hurt himself by leaving.

"Oh, Mama! I am so happy," Miss Louisa said, and she truly sounded it.

4

With the prospect of my day out to anticipate, all that had verged on being unbearable now transformed into a mere inconvenience. I now found it humorous that the leak in the garret's roof made an icicle every night that melted again over the course of the day. Just like a bizarre timekeeping device.

I settled into teaching. I spent mornings teaching mathematics, reading, and writing as best as I could, given the limited tools in my possession. In the afternoons, after the boys' dinner, Miss Louisa generally read from the Good Writ. Afterwards, I lectured them on the history of science. The boys were spirited and curious, especially about aether.

"Although spells seem magical, the aether in our world is a natural force," I told them. "As the magma in a volcano rushes to the earth's surface and spews forth from the volcano's mouth, so does aether have certain origin points, called founts. As per many naturally occurring materials, there are some lands that have more founts and are more aether-rich than others. Our nation is particularly lucky in that regard."

Hooker raised his hand. "Sir, what's a volcano?"

I blinked at him in astonishment, flummoxed by his ignorance.

"It's kinda like a pimple on the earth," Vernon said. "Only giant. And instead of spewing pus, it erupts fire."

"Yuck." Hooker leaned back, seemingly satisfied and deeply impressed.

Stanley stomped into the schoolroom. His hair had grown—remarkably. Long raven locks rippled down past his shoulders. He scowled at us, daring us to say something, and instinctively I looked at Hooker. Perhaps still caught up in the contemplation of volcanoes, Hooker stared into the distance, unaware of Stanley's grand entrance.

"My hair grows," Stanley announced. "Fast."

Stanley thumped himself down behind one of the desks and glared. Right.

Continuing on as if this interruption had not happened, I said, "At the time that the great grimoires were written, people had not yet invented the methodical reasoning behind modern science. In spite of the superstition they may have attached to aetheric currents, they did observe that the higher up a person was when saying a spell, the better the spell worked.

"So," I continued my lecture, "the great spellmakers of the second middle age started to work from the tops of hills and mountains. Then from towers built on hills and mountains. Can anyone tell me what happened then? Stanley?"

"We went to war with the Hetons who unleashed the Red Ague. That killed almost everyone and knowledge of the grimoires was lost for over two hundred years," Stanley answered without enthusiasm.

"We don't know which side initially spoke the spell that unleashed the ague," I corrected. "But Stanley is correct about the loss of knowledge of how to build devices powered by aether. Then, sixty years ago, Lord Cyrus Fulton managed to translate enough of his family's grimoire to build aetheric turbines to power flying machines. And why do you think that was?"

Stanley held up a finger.

"Anyone but Stanley?" I asked.

Hooker's hand shot into the air. When I acknowledged him, he said, "So he could fly to Newland?"

"Not quite," I said. "As I said, the higher into the atmosphere one goes, the more aether accumulates into drifts and currents. That is why the highest institutions for the study of spells and spellcraft, such as the queen's laboratories, are located where the air is very thin, but the aether is dense."

I told them about how aether, like water, seemed to have impure elements that also affected its dynamics. Aether seemed to act both like water and air with varying densities, often weakening as the aether traveled further from its fount.

Keeping the location of aetheric currents secret from other nations had been a key to Higher Eidoland's successful establishment of overseas power and military might. The boys seemed taken aback by the idea that somewhere, where the aether thinned, the great aetheric warships would fall from the sky.

There, I said, grimoires would be nothing but locked-up *books*.

"So—so why can't we take all the old locked grimoires there?" Quincey said. "The bloodlocks wouldn't be able to work, right, so we could open them."

"A professor named Ambrose Pike tried that once," I said. "But the grimoires are so aether-dense themselves that, when opened, the aether dissipates from their pages into the surrounding atmosphere and the ensorcelled pages crumble. It turns out grimoires need aether to sustain their spell matrixes and to power the preservation spells in the physical book itself."

"I wish I lived there right now," Stanley said, toying with his long hair miserably.

At this point two things occurred to me. All the boys had a higher than average interest in grimoires and Stanley's instantaneous hair-lengthening could only be attributed to magic.

I'd often heard that a black market existed, one that traded in spells and curses spoken from pages and partial pages cut from stolen grimoires. Could Nobbsnipe be a cursemonger? It certainly fit with my experience of his personality.

But cursemongering was a dangerous business. Oftentimes the stolen grimoire pages, their contents marred by time and vandalism, rebounded hideously on the speaker. Deep fear filled me as I realized what possible dangers Stanley and the other boys faced when they were called from my lessons to work in starboard hall.

And it would explain the plethora of watchmen as well.

But how could it be possible that Nobbsnipe could be perpetrating such crimes on my uncle's property without my uncle's knowledge? It stretched credulity.

"Does your family have a grimoire?" Quincey asked, breaking into my thoughts.

"Certainly. Green leather bound with brass." I indicated it could fit in my two hands.

At this, Hooker peppered me with questions: "Have you ever opened it? Have you ever read a spell? What spell was it? What did it feel like to say a spell?"

"No, I've never opened it or read a spell." I had seen my mother read a spell more than once, but didn't bother to share that information with them. "My research has always been theoretical, not practical."

Sadly, the boys seemed to lose interest when I said this.

After a few days, both Stanley's and Leofa's hands had healed. The pink scars denting their hands reminded me of how cloth looked after a monogram had been picked out.

Whenever I dined with the Nobbsnipes, I attempted to stuff what I could into my pockets. It became a game. I even stole a hunk of butter in my handkerchief, got it out of my pocket before it melted, and gave it to Leofa. The gift perplexed him, even after I explained how it could help with roasting of the birds. Afterwards I caught him feeding it to young Thaddeus straight.

In the evenings, I played songs that Mrs. Nobbsnipe disapproved of, but that I knew my sister would've enjoyed. Miss Louisa seemed entranced by what culture her parents permitted me to reveal. Once, we played a quite excellent flute and harp duet. Nobbsnipe, for a schoolmaster, did seem to take a hands-off approach to the boys' education.

Over these past few days I had become increasingly certain that Leofa actively avoided me. He kept on sneaking into bed long after I'd fallen asleep and leaving before long before dawn.

By this point, an ungenerous thought had occurred to me: Could Leofa be masterminding the activities in starboard hall, using Nobbsnipe as his pawn? I shook that thought aside. If Leofa controlled the criminal activities in the starboard hall, he'd dine better.

Or perhaps the Leofa and the boys truly did engage in vocational training. Had Stanley alone somehow gained access to a page from a grimoire? I wished I had more information, but trusted no one enough to ask.

For the first time I realized how isolated one could become on an aetherium. If I did live alongside villains, who would stop them from harming me? I would wait and watch... and keep track of my parachute.

So I observed. I learned that Molly had taken on the box gardens as her pet project. Molly, who was the maid-of-all-work, cared for the cabbages as tenderly as though they were children. Young Thaddeus often liked to join her, playing in the dirt as she worked.

Sometimes in the afternoons, when I lectured, Leofa drifted into the room to listen. He even asked questions, which seemed to encourage the boys' interest, as many seemed to look upon him as a role model. But he left always before the ending bell, before I could say a word to him privately.

One day, beyond frustrated, I gave the class some problems and decided to go search for him.

Leofa wasn't in the garret or the dorms. I did not find him in the schoolrooms, the mess hall, or the bathing room where the boys went for their biweekly bath. I checked the storage room and then went on downstairs. Invading the kitchen was an implicit criticism of Mrs. Nobbsnipe's housekeeping skills. I knew myself as rude for this.

Cookie, a massive woman with sharp eyes whom I rarely saw or spoke to, gave me an evil look. She said, "You aren't getting seconds. I got my orders concerning you, my lord."

"I wasn't—I'm looking for Leofa," I admitted.

"Leo's not here," she said. "Nor should you be."

I glanced around the kitchen at the fireplace large enough to roast a whole ox and the enameled pots. Whole cured hams hung from the hoof with funnels at the bottom to catch the fermenting meat's dripping fat. Grain bags were stashed in dry storage. Once, it would've looked normal to me, but now this bounty looked obscene. So much food, and yet the boys dined on flour soup.

I quit the kitchen and headed downstairs to the boiler room. Inside the dim and windowless confines of the lower decks, the smothering stench of aetheric byproducts wafted strong. I could taste it in my mouth, a thick tang, that reeked like recently spilled blood and had been known to make men gag. The only light came from the hot coals in the boilers and the gold glow of the aetheric trapping spells.

Carlsworth shoveled coal into a boiler, which powered the turbines. The turbines drew the aether into the trapping spells, which in turn powered the spells that kept us aloft.

Around me, shimmering wires ran along the walls, suspended within water-filled pipes made of thick glass. Glass, unlike spell-worked metal, could not transmit aether. It insulated the workers from involuntary exposure, while the water served as coolant, keeping the copper from overheating. The spell-inscribed wires glistened with trapped aether, though some had dimmed, corroded and in need of replacing.

Carlsworth seemed focused on his work and his skin was blackened with soot. He alone tended the two boilers; the third boiler appeared defunct.

I passed him quietly, unnoticed amidst the noise.

The cavernous space felt maze-like with its walls of pipes. I strode through it, looking for Leofa and careful not to touch the hot glass.

Extra spools of inscribed copper wire were kept out of the super-charged atmosphere in glass boxes. Glass pipes were stacked like wine bottles in a cellar. Other spare parts stood on shelves, loose in crates, or on plain wooden trays. The aetheric turbine exhaust, ever-present here, had left a grayish film over everything and the floor felt slimy underfoot.

Davingham and Quincey lounged near the anchor chain in case it had to be wound out or drawn in to maintain its correct tension. Quincey gave me a casual wave but did not otherwise greet me.

My search for Leofa took me even as far as an aetheric intake tunnel. Pulling my jacket around me, I stepped out onto an insulated bridge. Here the turbines loomed as tall as three men. The sound of their massive metal blades deafened me almost as much as the wind roaring past.

The tunnel was lined with the same glass tubes that held copper wires all inscribed with trapping spells. These glowed from the accumulated aether. Condensation from the glass pipes dribbled into the filthy bilge water at the bottom of the tunnel.

I returned to the stifling heat of the boiler room, certain now that Leofa was not here.

I had seen three boys down here, but fifteen had been absent from the schoolroom today. I'd been informed that they tended the boilers when not in lessons. Were the missing twelve boys with Leofa?

Leofa wasn't in the courtyard, landing deck, or hangar. Nor was he in the privy or the yard—but Hooker and Ashby were. Apparently having skived off, they had assembled semaphore flags from their laundry. They currently waved shirts frantically at the nearby girls' school, which had drifted terribly low and close this morning.

The message they so urgently conveyed?

SHOW ME YOUR TITS.

Oh, for Wyrd's sake.

Frowning, I confiscated their laundry and sent them back to Nobbsnipe. But I got the feeling that they would be back as soon as they could. At least they had learned their semaphore alphabet.

So, two more boys accounted for. But ten still at large.

Continuing my search for Leofa, I even ventured through the Nobbsnipes' residence, down the stairs and into steerage. The periscope had been retracted above the wheel and a faint smell of tobacco lingered in the air, as if either Nobbsnipe or Roger enjoyed smoking down here.

The wheel, parallel to the ground and fixed upon a thick brass central column, had been locked into place, as the skies were calm. The barometers, thermometers, and other such meteorological instruments were embedded in the wood-paneled walls. They indicated that this would likely remain the case for the rest of the day.

I paused in front of the stabilizer. The glass globe had copper bands running longitudinally and latitudinally. A copper device floated on the pool of mercury, directly in the center of the globe.

Without this small device, the aetheric turbines could not keep the aetherium level relative to the earth below. I always found it remarkable that such a small thing could govern thing as powerful as a turbine.

As per boarding boys' tradition, I touched it for luck. The glass cooled my palm. The stabilizer was solidly locked into place. Then I left steerage.

Leofa had to be in the starboard hall.

I had nowhere else left to search.

Up in the yard, I ducked under laundry, strode around to the starboard hall's backdoor, and stepped in.

Watchmen, presumably off duty, played cards at a mess table. Several curtained bunk beds hung anchored to the walls, the first time I'd seen that sensible safety precaution taken on this aetherium. The watchmen began to stand as soon as they saw me, a gesture rendered threatening rather than respectful because of their intense, abrupt quiet.

From above, a loud popping noise, a crackle, and a boom reverberated the air. I made for the narrow wooden stairs without even thinking about it. As one, the watchmen moved to intercept me.

"You're not allowed up there, sir," Jerome said firmly. His young swarthy face tensed. "It's dangerous."

I glanced up at the door. Upon it a large bronze bloodlock bristled with spines, much like those one might normally find upon an old Rithen grimoire. The art of making bloodlocks had been lost two centuries ago, and since they were primarily used to safeguard families' grimoires, finding an unpurposed bloodlock was rare. Paying to have it repurposed to safeguard a doorway had to be expensive.

"I wish to retrieve my students," I said, now truly annoyed. "If you do not move away, I will report you to Nobbsnipe."

"As you wish, sir," Jerome said. I could tell from his tone that he dared me to do it. He knew Nobbsnipe would back him up. In Jerome's black eyes I saw a hardness, no prevarication. Head of the watchmen, indeed. He'd stop me whatever it took. Unease shivered over me as I noticed Jerome's gun, a clunky old revolver. A second boom rattled the floor above our heads.

"I demand at least to see Leofa," I said. He had to be upstairs.

Jerome regarded me, his expression bordering on insolence, before he sauntered over to a bellpull beside the stairs. He raised his eyebrows at me and tugged it.

I flushed, feeling humiliated by his insubordination.

Seconds later, Leofa stomped down the stairs.

"Shit—shit—shit—" Leofa stopped when he saw me. "Shit."

I stared at him. He stared at me. And the watchmen stared at both of us.

"Come on," he said. "Let's go outside."

He led me out past the stairs to the front door. I resented his easy command, but I went with him anyway. I had been trying to track him down, after all.

Seeking ice in the summer's shade, we ventured around the stony courtyard to the landing deck's side of the windbreak. Only there, in the shadow of the hangar, did we find some. Leofa cracked some off and pressed it against his burns, sighing.

"Not a good day," he said. "Not a good day at all. Construction's not going well."

I watched him. Weariness and frustration seemed to emanate from him. The wind thrummed around us, whipping his shaggy dark hair around his face, pressing his clothes up against his long muscular frame. Even now, when I was suspicious of Leofa and annoyed with him, I found pleasure in looking at him. I cracked free a chunk of ice.

"Come here." I pressed the ice lightly across the new blisters forming on his forearms. He had a spray of reddish speckles across his forehead, which turned purple even as I watched.

I pushed back his smooth dark hair to apply the ice to his forehead.

"You're not a gardener or a mechanic," I continued, "and the starboard hall isn't under construction."

I gestured up at the starboard hall, which looked perfectly functional, its gray stone neat and its windows tightly shuttered over. I said, "What are you and the boys truly doing in secret up there?"

"Wyrd," Leofa said roughly. "I wish you—I wish you were anyone else but you."

"Why?" I asked. I tried not to feel insulted.

"You just try to be friends with everyone, like everyone should just get along."

"Giving it a try is only civilized."

At this Leofa bristled. "You're Gerard Franklin's nephew before you're anything else. I'm not your friend. So stop trying. Stop following me. And stop asking questions you already know the answers to."

With that, he stalked away, leaving me nonplussed.

It felt like I hadn't understood what half of our exchange had actually been about. It infuriated me. I hated it when I didn't understand something. Worse, I despised myself for feeling as though he'd ripped a hole in me—that he could do that so easily. He was a nobody and meant nothing to me. So why did I even care?

My rational mind understood that our physical proximity when asleep did not constitute adequate basis for trust or friendship. The fact that I'd gone so far as to hunt Leofa through the bowels of the aetherium when he did not return to our shared cot was something I disliked to contemplate. I had to look at my desire to pursue intimacy as an abstraction.

Some men wanted other men. But those men were not and never could be called gentlemen. Even if I knew myself to number among them, I knew it was my duty to force those thoughts aside and subsume those desires beneath more worthy pursuits.

Rarely did circumstances require me to acknowledge that I wanted a man's attention. Not to mention that I enjoyed the feel of his skin against mine. Now, though, I had to accept this irrational longing my part—so that I could dismiss it. I couldn't allow myself to imagine a relationship between us that did not exist.

Never before had I achieved a goal—I had found Leofa, after all—and afterwards felt so defeated.

꩜

That night, when he returned to the garret, Leofa brought a new blanket. He handed it over without a word, and when I took the thin nappy wool in my hands, I knew I had just accepted an apology as well. I did not press him. But why, I wondered, had he thought I'd know what passed on in the starboard hall?

In spite of this truce between us, still Leofa and I were tense around each other. Yet sleeping beside him came as a welcome respite, when boundaries naturally eased, one that I wished I dared to enjoy. But I could not forget the words we'd exchanged outside.

I watched Nobbsnipe closely to see if I'd divulged too much, when I'd asked Leofa what occurred in starboard hall. Leofa had known Nobbsnipe long before I'd shown up. I did not know the extent of their history or where Leofa's loyalties truly lay.

Yet Nobbsnipe encouraged his wife and progeny to use the Eidlish version of Leofa's Hei name. So that indicated a hostile gulf. But was that a ploy? Did Leofa's interests align more closely with Nobbsnipe's than I'd thought?

Leofa played a primary role in whatever went on in the starboard hall. Was he Nobbsnipe's second-in-command within those confines? Surely he'd make a more capable lieutenant than Nobbsnipe's son.

I could not yet determine the hierarchy and balance of power between those two—but I did know that Jerome had reported my visit to Nobbsnipe.

"With all of your manners, Lord Franklin," Nobbsnipe had said to me, "I'd think you'd know better than to go prying in what's clearly a private matter. And I'd hate to think that you're getting the wrong idea."

"The wrong idea?" I had bridled at his condescending tone. "My students come to me with burns on their hands so extensive they can barely write. It is time you explain yourself."

"They're learning to make the glass tubes that buffer the spells in channeling wires," Nobbsnipe had said with disgust. "Heating glass possesses no few dangers for rowdy boys."

With such skills, a boy could obtain gainful employment. I doubted my uncle would have sent me here to train these boys as clerks when they could engage in a skilled trade such as that. But then why, when I had first arrived, had Nobbsnipe even bothered to lie about the starboard hall being under construction?

When I'd dined once with Professor Hammerton, he'd explained that many workhouse wardens could make a mint from inmates' labor. Did the Nobbsnipes turn a profit from this exploitation? Could it be possible that my uncle didn't know of Nobbsnipe's manufacturing center in the starboard hall?

Manufacturing aetherium parts wasn't illegal. But it was dangerous work for children. Perhaps Leofa thought that Nobbsnipe did this at my uncle's bidding and that I had to be in on it. That would certainly explain his comments—and his anger toward me—but it also brought into question his role. How could he countenance this?

Yet I'd never seen anyone deliver or pick up any goods.

But doubts like these flourished as I lay beside Leofa quietly at night, not enjoying our shared warmth as much as I wished I could have.

5

When the day finally came for our outing to Herrow, I dressed in my cleanest and nicest suit. The fine wool, the color of dark chocolate, complimented the bronze silk vest and my cream cravat. I did my best to tame my unruly curls the best I could with pomade. Curly hair—so embarrassingly lower class.

I lent Leofa my extra ostrich leather bracers. He permitted me to adjust them to his larger frame with a sardonic smile, commenting, "What, rope isn't good enough for you, Lord Franklin?"

"Your sporting a clean white shirt is a coincidence then?"

Leofa tilted his head and smirked.

When we met Roger, Miss Louisa, and Stanley behind the windbreak, I saw that they as well wore their best for our little outing. Roger smoked a cigarillo, his bright yellow silk waistcoat and red pin-striped trousers making him look quite the dandy.

Stanley, though shaggy-headed from Leofa's questionable barbering skills, all but looked like a lord. He'd knotted his silk cravat expertly, but had left his tailored woolen waistcoat open to reveal a cream vest embroidered with golden vines.

Miss Louisa wore a rose day dress with fashionable puffed sleeves and flounces. She had a closed parasol with her, which she spun upon her shoulder, and had tied on a large stiff flying hat to preserve her hairstyle.

Roger tossed his cigarillo down, ground it out with his heel, and led us out to the landing deck.

The school's large glider was locked up as though it were Queen Isolde's own crown. The school apparently had only three gliders. I saw one large four-seater and two emergency gliders, where one passenger could fit under each wing, sliding in like bullets in a front-loading revolver. Once the gliders had been painted a cheery gold, but now all had faded to a sickly yellowish green.

Roger unlocked no less than six padlocks. With Leofa's help, he slung back a chain-like net that had been securing the glider to the surface. The two of them shifted the glider into takeoff position.

When Roger gave us the nod, I assisted Miss Louisa into the glider and strapped her in. She flushed and watched me from beneath her lashes, squirming as though the process tickled. I also checked Stanley's buckles, but he'd done an admirable job.

"Used to go flying with my father," he explained. "Summer jaunts, mostly."

I strapped myself in, buckled on my top hat, and pulled the goggles down from the brim, fitting them onto my face. I could see Roger attaching the glider to the belowdecks winch with its tear-away lead while Leofa searched the wooden frame for any warping or water damage.

"Don't worry," Stanley called out to Leofa. "I patched it up last week!"

Leofa nodded in acknowledgment and hopped into the luggage compartment behind me. As the glider was a four-seater, he had no straps to secure himself. He braced his knees against either side of the glider's thin body, and he leaned forward, tucking his arms back between my waist and my seatback, gripping my seat securely. When I looked back at Leofa, our faces but inches from each other's, he grinned like a madman.

Roger fixed his own hat and goggles. He pulled the winch. Then Roger had thirty seconds to run back across the short deck, swing around the windshield into the pilot's seat, and buckle himself in. His hands flew across his buckles as the winch dragged the glider forward across the landing deck. The teeth-clattering experience ended as we tipped off the landing deck and plunged silently toward earth.

The winch's lead snapped away and the glider's nose jerked up. Roger revved the aether-powered engine to life, manipulated the wing-flaps, and suddenly we soared over the landscape. The air roared into the passenger compartment, making conversation impossible. Leofa, stuck in the cubby-like baggage compartment, actually occupied the most sheltered position in the glider.

We circled around. Roger was actually a rather skilled pilot.

Below us, I glimpsed Southside slums overshadowed by the dozens of floating aetheria overhead. Heavy coal smoke drifted around the tarred rooftops, compounded by factory towers belching sulfurous gasses and the sewage miasma of the river. Roger kept us well out of it, swinging us over the brownish river and bringing us north to the cleaner and more fashionable districts in Herrow.

The carefully thatched roofs and courtyard gardens of middle class homes gave way to purplish slate roofs and vaster private pleasure gardens, and here green elms shaded the broad cobbled streets. In the distance, to the far north of the capital, the chains anchoring the Mile Palace to the ground glimmered, just visible.

I'd visited the Shadow Gardens beneath the palace, a veritable riot of shade-loving blooms. Some exotic species even phosphoresced. When it rained, they became quite the destination; the palace acted as a vast umbrella, and the waterfalls pouring down from the palace's edge above created a misty veil around the gardens.

Roger navigated to an airfield to the east of Knave's Court. It wasn't busy. The flight control saw us circle three times and flagged us.

Roger brought us down to land. The glider thudded and skidded across lumps of earth and grasses, a bone-jarring experience that always made me wonder if my eyes could be shaken from the sockets. We lurched to a standstill. After that came the usual pause, as everyone appreciated not having died.

"Landing gears," Stanley muttered in front of me. "Shock absorbers?"

Roger helped his sister down onto the grassy airfield and escorted her to a clapboard building so she could remove her flying hat and fix her hair in the powder room. Stanley clambered out and stood there awkwardly. Leofa assisted the flagger with taking the glider into the hanger.

The packages from Uncle Gerard had been delivered early this morning, and so while we waited for Louisa, Leofa and Stanley loaded the glider up. I checked over the basswood crates.

I could not wait to see what my uncle had given me from my list, and frankly, anything would be an improvement in terms of supplies. As the packages mounted in the back, I wondered where Leofa would sit on our return flight.

With our business here dealt with, our party assembled before the hangar's front door. Along this street several small foundries and steelworks emitted the clatter of industry. At Roger's order, Leofa crossed the cobbled street to the conveniently located coach stand and hired a six-seater hackney coach for us. It felt good to be away from the dismal atmosphere of the charity school and out again on the streets of Herrow.

"Oh, gracious!" Miss Louisa said, fanning herself. "I forgot how hot it gets below in the summertime. It must be nearly twenty-five degrees out."

As we made good distance from the airfields, the foundries quickly gave way to tanners' markets and slaughterhouses. Vendors sold from stands, carts, or even barrels strapped to their chests. Mumpers screeched from mucky alleyways and urchins crowded up against the carriage, shaking tin cups and presenting mischievous grins.

Within minutes, we passed into the broad streets in the city's Central Mile District. Here, shop windows shone with fashionable silks and milliners displayed the latest exotic plumes from Newland.

Young women carried small dogs under their arms. Men strutted with gold-headed canes. Housewives occasionally paused to buy bright little bouquets of carnations from a flower seller. A pair of drunken young lords raced through the streets on high-blooded stallions, scattering hawkers and tinkers.

When the hackney coach drew up to my uncle's respectable townhouse, my sister immediately came out to meet us. She must have been waiting directly in the foyer, I thought with surprise. Nora looked fine in her elegant black mourning silks, but to my surprise, no maidservant followed her.

Leofa left the carriage to assist her in. Then he reseated himself in the front beside the jarvey, clearly with the expectation that Nora's maidservant would take his place in the hackney.

Nora took a seat across from me, clasping her gloved hands over mine. My joy in seeing her surprised even me. I had gone many months in the past without seeing my sister, when we'd both been away at school. But now, relief and happiness caught at me as if I had feared without even knowing it that she would die when I wasn't looking, much as our parents had.

"Oh, Neil, I am so glad to see you!" she said, and I remembered my manners. I introduced my sister as Lady Honoria Franklin to Roger and his sister Miss Louisa. Nora gave me a curious look when I did not introduce David Stanley to her, as his fine clothes indicated a gentlemanly background. But he wasn't here as a social equal, I refrained. Stanley didn't seem taken aback by this.

"Mr. Nobbsnipe," Nora said graciously, placing her small hand on Roger's forearm from where he sat beside her. "I'd like to thank you for piloting the glider that brought my brother to me. Without your assistance, our little outing would have hardly been possible!"

"Of course, dear lady," Roger said in a pleasant tone I'd never heard him use. "Had I known what a lovely girl Lord Franklin's sister was, I would have surely facilitated a visit sooner rather than later."

While Roger's fine phrases did surprise me, his attempt to impress my sister did not. I would have been happy to see him strive were his comments less forward.

Nora's delicate golden skin showed her blush clearly. Her close-brimmed bonnet made it obvious she had not yet been presented to the monarch, so she was no marriage prospect. Complimenting her like this was inappropriate.

"I like your bonnet very much." Miss Louisa stepped into the awkward quiet of the conversation. I liked her very much for taking that social onus from me. She said, "Do you possibly think you could introduce me to your milliner?"

"Certainly, later this afternoon," my sister said. "Perhaps after we visit the museum and have afternoon tea? Uncle Gerard was ever so kind as to set up an account for me at a local teahouse, and I must say, they even serve coffee!"

I loved coffee. I grinned at her and Nora smiled.

"The museum?" Roger sounded disgusted.

"Yes, to the see the original papers of Pierre es Tel," she said.

"Pierre es Tel!" Stanley perked up immediately. He said, "I didn't know we were going to see Pierre es Tel's papers! Do you think they'll have diagrams of his flying machines? I used to love looking at the selection of his work in *Early Flight Mechanica* but it did frustrate me, because I couldn't make out the propeller mechanism in the woodcuts."

"*Early Flight Mechanica* is a good basic reference folio, a good launching point, but the woodcuts are rather poor," Nora said, forgetting in her enthusiasm that we had yet to introduce her to Stanley. "Have you read—"

"Is this really a suitable topic for young ladies?" Roger asked loudly. "If you'd rather do something more interesting, we can always go out on the promenade. It's a lovely day, and it would be my pleasure to treat you to some ice cream."

Nora became quiet, clearly embarrassed. Girls her age weren't supposed to babble and she no doubt took his comment as a tacit criticism of her loquacity.

"The museum first," I said politely, so that my sister didn't have to refuse him.

At the museum, Roger attempted to persuade my sister again to go elsewhere, perhaps riding, or he'd take her to the market and buy her some trinket. Roger seemed to be under the impression that attending the museum exhibit had to have been my idea and that Nora had be here against her will.

When she exclaimed over some mathematical modeling she'd found in one of Pierre es Tel's papers, Roger left Nora out of obvious annoyance. He went outside to slouch on the broad marble steps, smoking.

Stanley, however, went over to see what interested her and ended up finding the diagram of the propeller he'd been looking for. Miss Louisa, apparently bored with these proceedings, asked if Nora wouldn't like to visit the fine arts display. Nora demurred.

As the two women chaperoned each other, I wandered into the section with ancient artifacts, passing slowly through part of a tomb from Ollundi, an ancient city that had fallen into the desert. On the other side, I found the section with the newest Imrian artifacts. A display, donated courtesy of Lord Cyril Slackleigh, was tucked away into an inconspicuous side room.

Burgundy velvet curtains obscured a wall-mounted glass case. The artifacts hidden behind the curtain had to be inappropriate for women and children. Curiosity piqued, I glanced around to make sure that none with delicate sensibilities stood in the immediate vicinity. The curtain's metal rings clattered conspicuously along the brass curtain rod as I drew back the velvet.

The sandstone tablets were all in ancient Imrian glyphs. I knew of the risqué contents of these tablets, so it did not surprise me that no translation had been made available to the public. As I sketched out the symbols in my pocket folio, I caught the drift. What a fun exercise it would make to translate this properly!

"Must be real shocking." Leofa startled me with a heavy hand on my shoulder. How long had he been standing there?

I flushed, feeling caught out.

"What's it say then?" Leofa asked.

"The Imrians had behavioral standards that would be taboo here," I said stiffly.

Leofa glanced around the empty room, meaningfully, and waited for a more complete answer.

I hesitated. "It's about…well, it mentions, rather, inversion."

I expected Leofa to make a disparaging comment or at the very least to move away with deliberate disinterest. Although homosexual acts, along with heresy and other such crimes, had been decriminalized over a generation ago, even speaking about them in public society could result in nasty rumors. Some more outspoken lords quite openly favored reinstituting the old punishments, which at worst had involved burying the offenders alive.

More than anything I did not want to know to what degree of contempt Leofa held homosexuals. I found myself holding my breath. The air seemed heavy with expectation.

But Leofa only regarded the tablets with mild curiosity.

"You sure you read it right?" he asked.

"Well, yes. It's a series of love poems between two gods," I said and moved my hand to hover above the glyphs as I translated. "Anthar, the god of the growing grasses, is trying to seduce Hemnan, the god of the spring rains. Anthar is young and beautiful, green in both senses of the word, and Hemnan is wise, he's traveled the skies, and he's trying to draw Anthar forth—"

When the implication of what I said actually occurred to me, I found myself flushing and I let my hand drop. Leofa laughed and stepped back. I floundered for more words and managed, "It's *religious* literature from *Imria*," as if that could explain away any eccentricity.

"How's it sound aloud?" Leofa asked.

"No one knows." I yanked the curtains closed.

Leofa looked at me as if intrigued. "Huh. And here I thought you didn't have any interest in religion, Lord Franklin."

I returned Leofa's look, startled by his even tone and his lack of disgust. I felt suddenly less at risk. I wanted to say something, anything, that would make him close the distance between us. I desired to feel the weight of his hand on my shoulder again—only this time to let it linger.

"Lord Franklin!" Roger shouted in another room. His voice, obscenely loud, echoed in the museum's halls. "Time to go!"

I moved away from the exhibit hastily, as if I'd been caught in the midst of a crime, and Leofa chuckled. The two of us rejoined the rest of the party.

If the museum was uncomfortable, then tea afterwards was truly awful. Roger seemed both sullen and furious because my sister had spent so much time talking to Stanley about non-aetheric vehicular flight. On the ride over, she'd been describing to Stanley the work on atmospheric dynamics done by a group of natural philosophers in Haedel.

Now, at the teahouse, Nora, aware that Roger was upset but perhaps not entirely sure why, attempted to lighten the mood but her false gaiety fell flat. Miss Louisa scowled at me for my accidental snub and also because we'd spent so much time in the museum that the shops would be closed after we'd had tea.

Leofa and Stanley stayed outside the entire time because the teahouse had no back room for the servants. Stanley's absence clearly baffled Nora—in spite of being so finely dressed and well spoken, he remained outside with the servants.

She made a comment about inviting them in and Roger forbade it on the grounds that it would be inappropriate. I had to back him in this, as it wouldn't do at all for Nora to indulge the young man, who seemed to be already infatuated.

Nora withdrew and refused to speak at all after that.

Slightly after we received our pastries, it began to pour down rain. While the steaming coffee in my hand was truly delectable, I found it hard to enjoy when I could see Leofa and Stanley standing directly outside the window, drenched to the skin. It seemed cruel to eat and drink right beside them like this, but I knew that inviting them in was impossible.

How awful it had to be, for Leofa and Stanley to be left outside, like dogs with nothing better to do than to await a master's homecoming. Certainly, in the past, I visited establishments where my servants had waited for me outside in the rain. How had I never noticed this before?

Honestly, the dismal silence at the table made me long for Stanley and Leofa's company, rain notwithstanding.

Nora seemed especially depressed when we dropped her off at our uncle's house. I left the carriage to help her out, lifting her over the morass of mud, sewage, and debris that rolled stickily down the street's gutter.

"Would it be quite all right if I made an unexpected call on Uncle Gerard?" I asked Nora, for in truth, I wanted to voice my suspicions about Nobbsnipe and see what Uncle Gerard had to say on the subject. I'd feared putting my concerns in writing, considering the close watch Nobbsnipe kept on the post.

"Oh, no, he's not inside," she said. "He's at the Tremont Reform Club, I expect. His carriage has been gone the past few days. I'm fair rattling around in that townhouse of his."

"Has he hired no governess for you? Or a lady's maid, at the very least." Hearing her talk like this perturbed me. Nora liked to be active, to have much to do and much to engage her mind, and having to overcome grief without any diversions would be especially hard for her, I knew.

Little wonder she'd sunk into childish and ill-bred silence at the teahouse.

"I have neither a companion nor maid," she said.

The knowledge alarmed me; providing a chaperone was the least of a guardian's duties.

I reached out to take her hand and suddenly Nora flung herself against my chest. Her hands clutched at my clothes, wrinkling them, and she kept her head down so that I couldn't see her face. Her bonnet collided with my chin.

"I miss Mama and Papa so much," she whispered.

I grew quiet in the cool summer rain. I replied, "I do too."

Nora released me and bolted indoors. The door slammed behind her, the knocker swinging up and landing with an extra thump.

"Your sister's a good-looking girl," Roger said when I returned to the carriage. "But all that math stuff, I mean, how do you expect her to get married when she won't shut up about it?"

I was speechless. I couldn't believe he'd said that to me—as if he'd expected me to agree with his assessment.

"I'm sure her future husband will appreciate her for all that she has to offer," Stanley said in a rush. "Any man would be proud to have a wife like her!"

Roger's expression darkened into a scowl and his grip tightened on his cane. In that instant, I thought he meant to strike Stanley.

Leofa shifted casually, resting his elbows on his knees.

Roger sneered in Leofa's direction but appeared to relent.

"No one cares what you think, Stanley." Roger slammed his cane against the hackney's ceiling and bellowed, "Drive on!"

6

When I woke to the bell in the morning, Leofa had flung his arm across my chest. Though I could still see my breath pluming in front of me, the ragged blankets had trapped some heat between our bodies and I basked in the warmth. Hoarfrost crusted the far wall. The school's prow must have shifted overnight, for morning sunshine poured all shimmery through our ice-glazed window.

I loathed the idea of moving, much less doing so to breakfast with Roger Nobbsnipe. But I resigned myself to my duty. I removed Leofa's arm from myself and stood to dress. I donned my gray wool suit with my sapphire cravat, although I did note that my jacket lining had begun to fray. I had no idea how that had happened and no plan on how to fix it.

Since the spigot to the rainwater tanks had frozen in the night, I couldn't get any water to splash my face. I attempted to flatten my hair with the pomade. I struggled particularly today, truly annoyed because I would not obtain any coffee among the tea-drinking Nobbsnipes.

I turned around. Leofa had been watching me. I started out of surprise. He'd retucked the blankets tightly around him.

"Morning." Leofa yawned, hugely, without bothering to cover his mouth. He poked a finger out into the cold air, indicating the crates stack in the corner. He said, "I bought up your packages last night before Roger could get to them."

"My thanks!" I hadn't even thought that Roger would attempt to pilfer the classroom supplies. But still, I appreciated Leofa hauling the crates up the stairs. It couldn't have been easy. When I told him so, he merely shrugged as if he'd thought it too insignificant to be mentioned.

I tore into them, cutting through the twine around the smaller crates with my penknife. Leofa watched me, curled under the blanket and smiling.

Inside the crates lay bounty: slates, chalk, and paper, which was of poor quality, but better than nothing. Beside those nestled uncut quills and a few penknives. Underneath I found syllabaries and grammars.

Uncle Gerard had even sent some grammars in languages I hadn't requested, including Far Eastern tongues. Curiosity stirred in me. I set them aside for myself.

He'd also included astronomy charts and maps, geometry and history folios, and other essential texts. I wanted to grin—but I schooled my face into a more respectable expression. At last, finally, I'd have something to teach from. I wouldn't have to exhaust myself on improvisation, behind which lurked the fear that what I taught was incomplete.

"You've always wanted to be a teacher, huh," Leofa said.

"Me?" I looked up from the grammar in my hands with a startled laugh. "No! No, certainly not. It's simply not done, for people of my class. I suppose I expected to get into government or continue on in academia. It would have depended on what offers I received."

"What about the Franklin estate?" Leofa said.

"No, I never interested myself in that," I said. I did not wish to explain the circumstances under which my stepfather, Lord Franklin, had adopted me. His natural-born daughter and my half-sister Nora had always been set to inherit all. "I hoped to take a position that would give me the annual income where I could support a wife of a comparable class. Perhaps in the government's grimoire laboratories."

Leofa seemed in deep thought, perhaps even depressed, but I had difficulty reading him. The blanket fell across his shoulders like a cloak. How graceful and commanding he seemed when simply seated, the golden early morning light shining across his bronze skin. For the first time I wished I could breakfast across from him every morning, basking in that quality of his that was too powerful to be serenity.

If I had command of this place, I would have invited him to breakfast. I wished I could. But, instead, he would remain in the cold and I would proceed downstairs to the main house. Once again the walls of class would stand between us, as they had done at the teahouse the previous day.

Downstairs, I discovered the Nobbsnipes were absent and there had been no breakfast laid out yet. I inquired with the maid-of-all-work and Molly informed me that the meal had been postponed until the master finished speaking to the dung collectors in the courtyard. I peeked out my head in time to see an industrial glider, heavy barrels loaded into its fat body, lumbering into the air.

Nobbsnipe marched back inside, his face purple with anger. Roger trailed right behind him. Miss Louisa and her mother seemed annoyed, but not unduly so.

I stepped back to let them pass into the house, slightly perplexed.

As he passed by Roger rounded on me, fast as a snake. He said, "I want the boys lined up in the yard in five minutes."

I looked after him, astonished that he'd dare order me around so peremptorily. Miss Louisa placed an over-familiar hand on my arm. She advised me, not unkindly, that Roger was in a high temper and it would be best to get along with him when he had a mood. I hoped his annoyance had no connection to yesterday's visit with my sister.

I looked to Nobbsnipe for confirmation of this order, but he stomped past me. He headed upstairs toward his study. A slamming door resounded.

I went into the hall where the boys breakfasted. When I informed them that they needed to line up in the yard, they became so quiet that I could hear Peggy scraping the bottom of the gruel pot with the ladle.

Hooker said, "Shit!"

Quincey hushed him.

"Please attempt to refrain from vulgarity," I said.

Hooker muttered something about it being okay when Leofa did it. I ignored him and reiterated my statement that Roger expected them in five minutes. They scrambled out. I followed them through the backdoor in the dining hall out into the yard. Roger waited, leaning on an ivory-headed cane with a cigarette dangling from his lips. Jerome stood behind Roger. Three bulky watchmen flanked them.

The boys, shivering in their shirtsleeves, marched between the cabbage beds. Empty laundry lines, which stretched above the small kitchen garden, snapped and hummed in the wind.

I scanned the yard for Leofa.

As a boarding boy I'd had to line up a time or two when someone had pulled a prank on a teacher or broken curfew. But something about how the boys refused to meet each others' eyes filled me with an unreasonable dread. The punishments at Evermore had been unpleasant, certainly; but even the worst only resulted in a few embarrassing yelps, followed by a three days where it'd been rather hard to sit down.

"Strip," Roger said.

The boys removed their clothes and hunched down against the wind. The morning light starkly revealed their malnutrition. How gaunt they looked without their flopping shirts, how branch-thin their limbs—and how thick their knees and elbows seemed in comparison.

These boys looked but a few meals away from death. I felt irrationally furious to see their thinness. I'd known it, of course, but to see it so raw burned me.

"You boys know the rules," Roger said. "You piss on the left and shit on the right."

I stared at him, incredulous, and then I understood he spoke regarding the privy. I'd had no idea. It hadn't even occurred to me. Now, the dung collectors' presence this morning suddenly meant something else. The Nobbsnipes had been selling the boys' excrement for manure, and their urine to the indigo-dyers. The separation of fluids no doubt brought a better price.

Roger walked the line of boys, thumping them in the back of the thighs with the ivory head of his cane, a punishment commonly done with a switch. He either didn't know that caning wasn't done with an actual gentleman's cane, or he didn't care.

Roger whacked them so hard that an instant red lump rose beneath their goose-pimpled skin. He threatened to hit tiny Thaddeus, lifting his cane, and then, oh-so-gently, tapped the boy on the head. Thaddeus screamed in terror.

Behind me I heard a small sharp cry like that of a seabird. I turned and saw Molly standing there, her hands clutching her skirt in red-knuckled fists, her eyes wide, and I couldn't help it. I stepped forward.

"It was me," I said. "No one told me."

Roger turned to me. His disappointment and annoyance mingled with ugly pleasure. He sauntered up to me.

"I guess the boys have you to thank for this then, don't they?" he asked.

I didn't have anything to say to that. I regarded him coldly.

When he left, the boys clambered madly into their clothes and Molly rushed toward Thaddeus and dressed him quickly.

Jerome and the watchmen chuckled among themselves before heading back to wherever it was they spent the majority of their time.

I did not return to the Nobbsnipes' table. My appetite had abandoned me.

That morning, my fury with myself made it hard for me to concentrate enough to teach the boys. Frankly, they seemed relieved somehow that I attempted to stick to my self-imposed schedule.

Stanley picked up the slack, looking over the answers to the long division when my distraction grew too great. I was grateful to him for that. The boys who found sitting difficult were allowed to do their work while standing.

Miss Louisa came personally to fetch me to midday dinner. There she told me, noble though she found my sentiment, how I shouldn't pity these boys. According to her, the lower orders concerned themselves only with taking advantage of such softer feelings. I didn't bother to challenge her idiotic statement.

Roger smirked at me throughout the meal.

Nobbsnipe wore a slight smile as he ate—as though he thrived on the venomous atmosphere. His wife, on the other hand, seemed barely aware of her surroundings, murmuring an occasional, "That's nice, dear," when addressed.

I did manage to secrete several slices of ham in my pocket, though the honey glaze made a mess of my handkerchief. After dinner, I headed through the storeroom and caught the tweeny licking the plates. Peggy froze when she saw me. I gave her a slight nod and acted as if I tipped an invisible hat.

After depositing the ham in the garret, I climbed downstairs to the schoolroom for the afternoon lecture.

A dull sickening anger remained in me from this morning's ordeal. But the boys seemed somehow nonchalant, joking about their bruises and making mock of Roger.

"He hits like a drunken fishwife," Quincey said, and some of the boys hooted with laughter, miming it to the others' delight.

"Nah, I been walloped by one of them before." Northwall gave what he no doubt thought a knowing leer. He said, "That was nothing but love taps, gentle as a baby's fist."

"He had to go soft. He was afraid he'd hit the stupid right out of Hooker." Ashby tossed his arm around the Hooker's shoulders and tightened it into a friendly headlock. Hooker twisted free.

"No one could do that!" Hooker shouted, puffing up, and Carlsworth broke out into laughter. When Hooker realized what he'd said, he defended himself proudly. "Nobody could hit the stupid out of me! No matter how long it took!"

"It's true," Ashby said in a mock-gloomy voice. "I'm afraid I got to tell you boys, the stupid's here to stay."

"At least I know my left from my right." Hooker grinned at me, and I realized he referred to the ridiculous privy rules. He added, "Not like some people."

I blinked, startled by being brought into this.

The boys tensed, expecting swift reprisal from me. If I'd been a teacher like any of the honorable men who'd taught me, I would have punished such insubordinate comments. But I couldn't bring myself to do so. The boys had each borne a wallop for my ignorance. Acknowledging one complaint would not ruin me.

I said, "I do most humbly apologize for my oversight. I shall strive to improve my sense of direction in the future, Hooker." I executed a genteel bow before him.

Hooker nodded dumbly, stunned. The boys' clear fear of reprisal dissipated. I heard a few relieved sighs. Redirecting their attention, I said, "Let's get back to our letters."

The boys took their seats. Soon every head was bent in study.

⌒

The summer's warmth deepened even as we passed into early autumn. The skies were mostly clear with the morning's crisp breezes softening into sweet coolness over the day's course. The boys made slow but methodical progress in both letters and figures. Leofa and the boys routinely sported strange burns on their hands.

This deepened my suspicions. I could not quite bring myself to believe Nobbsnipe's explanation. But if he lied, then what happened in there that Leofa and the boys felt compelled to hide it from me? Did my uncle know of this, or did Nobbsnipe act alone? Whenever not otherwise occupied, I concocted theories. Were volatile chemicals being developed there? Perhaps unusual narcotics were involved.

Yet so far nothing I theorized quite fit. I kept contemplating hypotheses, waiting for an opportunity to discover more.

After the grammars arrived, Nobbsnipe took to observing my lessons. He even brought a few puzzles for the boys. The puzzles were intricate interlocking mechanisms of wood and iron, requiring both manual dexterity and complex cognitive reasoning to solve.

As per Nobbsnipe's orders, I reported back to him on how well each boy did. Hooker, the destructive mastermind, could dismantle any of them in less than five minutes. Stanley refused to even try—a piece of information which I kept to myself.

A new theory emerged: Nobbsnipe used the boys for safecracking. Cracksmen in Herrow often employed young boys in burglaries. But no boy ever left Highfell and I couldn't imagine any of the Nobbsnipes possessing enough stealth for housebreaking.

Nora wrote to me often. Although she lived in central Herrow, I got the feeling from her letters that she remained isolated and lonely. She maintained a correspondence with several of her friends from school as well as her instructors, so Nora continued her education in spite of the fact that she had not yet been allowed to return to school.

Still, I had received no letters from my former fiancé Madeline Havensea. In my letters to Nora, I had hinted that I would appreciate any information regarding Madeline, but Nora had yet to answer my discreet inquiries. I found this pointed oversight of hers worrying.

I did receive an invitation from my uncle: There would be a dinner in honor of my sister's eighteenth birthday.

The invitation hadn't been issued by Nora's own hand, which took me aback. But I found myself relieved that my uncle hadn't invited the Nobbsnipes as protocol dictated. Still, as a teacher I was subordinate to the schoolmaster, so I had to inform them of my plans to leave the aetherium.

I announced, "I'm invited to a very small dinner being held in honor of my sister's birthday."

"Maybe for a present you should sew her a new dress," Roger said. "Demos knows you can't afford to buy her one."

"Roger!" Miss Louisa spoke up on my behalf. "Please, don't."

"So high-spirited," Mrs. Nobbsnipe said, as if put upon, which was ridiculous given that he'd aimed his comments toward me.

Roger laughed and slapped me on the shoulder, as if we were schoolboys and we'd had some fun at each other's expense. I hadn't had any such friendships at school. I'd never been part of the wrestling-in-the-gymnasium crowd. It always seemed safer, for reasons I disliked to go into even with myself, to stay away.

"Well, Leo can pilot you down on the emergency glider," Nobbsnipe said. "You'll have to unlock the gliders for them, Roger. You say it'll be on the—"

"Her birthday's on the twenty-first," I said. "He's given me two weeks' notice exactly."

"Very good," Nobbsnipe said. He seemed to have the same hands-off approach toward his offspring as he did toward his pupils. He in no way chided Roger for his inappropriate comment.

"Oh, yes! Silly me. I almost forgot, Lord Franklin," Mrs. Nobbsnipe said, and picked up a letter from a small table beside the dining room door. She pressed it into my hand. "If you wouldn't mind handing this over to Leo, I would be much obliged."

"Since you ask, it will be my honor." I smiled at her, and she brightened under my regard, pleased.

Exquisitely ladylike lettering slanted across the high-quality cotton paper.

Leofa Blackwater
Highfell Hall Over River Wyrd

When I turned the letter over, the seal gave no hint as to the letter's contents. The lilac gray wax indicated a woman must've sent the letter. The anchor motif impressed upon it, associated with no crest I recalled, symbolized well-wishing and hope. Was Leofa married? If so, he'd never mentioned it.

I tucked the letter into my breast pocket and we went to the table to be served.

Since I had wearied of the discussing the Old Pantheon and the Good Writ, and rehashing why I didn't believe, I had developed a secret diversion when dining with the Nobbsnipes. I artfully rearranged my leftovers on my plate for the tweeny and filched other tidbits to share with Leofa and the boys.

After supper, Nobbsnipe asked whether I'd like to join him and his son for a smoke. I always declined. Instead, I headed to the drawing room with the ladies. As always, I instructed Miss Louisa on the piano. Her mother watched us, embroidering embellishments on a tablecloth, until finally I took my leave.

Curiosity prompted me to deliver Leofa's letter in person rather than leaving it in the garret for him to find. As did an underlying jealousy I dared not contemplate too deeply. I wanted to be there when he opened it. I sought Leofa and couldn't find him in the schoolrooms, dormitory, or garret, which came as no surprise. I headed belowdecks.

As I descended, I racked my brain for a present I could afford to give Nora, one that would suit both her and her birthday. Passing through a narrow corridor, I heard a muffled cry from the bathing room. Suddenly, I feared that young Thaddeus had strayed from the other boys again. A young child unsupervised in an aetherium could find a world of trouble. I flung open the door and stormed in.

Roger had tied Peter Vernon to one of the bathing room's pipes. He beat the shirtless boy with that ridiculous ivory-headed cane of his. I could see two bored watchmen standing nearby, along with Upping and Smalley.

Traitorous little boot-lickers.

When he caught sight of me, Roger said, "I thought Louisa would keep you busy longer. We're finished here."

Roger turned away, smirking. He waved his cane at the boys and said, "Come on, now. Let Nurse Franklin tend to the boy."

The two watchmen gave an obligatory chuckle that sounded more dutiful than mirthful. Upping and Smalley sniggered at each other and followed Roger out. I rushed to Vernon and began untying him from the pipe. Whoever fixed the ropes had done it so tightly that Vernon's skin was marked with reddening lines from his bonds. His straight black hair hung down, hiding his spotty skin.

I'd never taken notice of Vernon. His mathematics and handwriting stood him in good stead but no more. He kept his head down during class and never misbehaved.

Vernon wept now. He had got his head down at his knees. The welts on his back were swollen. He clenched his puppy-large hands into fists on the floor.

Crying at age thirteen would humiliate any boy, whatever the cause. But at least I knew that Roger couldn't have broken any ribs, otherwise this level of sobbing would've been impossible.

"I want—I want to go home to my mother." He spoke between sobs.

"I thought you were an orphan."

"Who told you that?" Vernon wiped his nose on his knees and stared at me, his skin blotchy red.

Lacking a handkechief, I pulled off my cravat and handed that to him instead. Vernon wiped his nose on it.

"I'm not an orphan," he said. "My mother's still alive. She's a crofter in Pelzwold."

Confusion made me repeat, almost stupidly, "But this is a charity school for—for—"

"Lady Mavin paid for me to come here," Vernon said, "after my father, Lord Mavin, died. Her son was to inherit, but I'm older by a year, and everyone knew it. She told my mother—she told her that this school was where lords' sons went to be educated. They don't let me write her. My mother probably thinks I'm dead by now."

"Your father is the late Lord Mavin?" I repeated, not quite able to imagine Vernon springing from the loins of the peerage.

Then a dim recollection rose to the surface of my consciousness. I remembered how I'd commented on David Stanley's name. Just like Baron David Stanley, I'd said. Yet I knew that the aeroplane-flying baron had no legitimate son. And Stanley had agreed with me so quietly that I hadn't even remarked upon it.

Two bastard sons in one decrepit school couldn't be a coincidence, could it?

"How many of you boys are actually orphans?" I asked.

Vernon said, "Smalley's one. Upping, too. The arse-lickers."

"Language."

"Sorry, sir." Vernon offered the soiled cravat back.

"Keep it," I said. "Besides you and Stanley, how many of you boys are…" I stopped, unsure how to make such a rude inquiry.

"We're all bastards, sir, if that's what you mean," Vernon said miserably. "Except Hooker. His dad's a bastard."

Now I felt the idiot.

When my uncle had come as a savior to our indebted family, when he had offered me a job at this school, I had never once asked: "Why haven't I heard of this marvelous institution? Why haven't I heard of this charity aetherium? Why have you not been lauded in newspapers for your philanthropy?"

Perhaps I had unconsciously assumed he did not speak of this from modesty. I couldn't say.

But now I knew. The secrecy was the point.

Uncle Gerard received payment for housing illegitimates. He left them in this aetherium school, a mockery of the higher schools that the true-born lords visited.

"What do they have you doing in starboard hall?" I asked now.

Vernon shook his head.

"I want to go home," he said, more softly. "I'm really good with pigs, you know. Pigs are smarter than you'd think. Siovanese cooks used to travel to get my mother's swine. The key's the exact right amount of fish, you know."

I knew that if I kept at it Vernon would confess. But what then? Would Roger beat him to death? What, for that matter, had Roger been beating Vernon for? Some crime? The mere pleasure of it?

I considered asking, but knew already I wouldn't. From how the boys evaded telling me what happened in the starboard hall—even Hooker, who otherwise blurted out everything—told me that they were under prohibition. If Vernon confided in me, would he earn another beating? I could not risk it.

I had to contact my uncle. But as the Nobbsnipes did not permit me into the dovecote, they had the opportunity to read my mail before sending it. The chance that my letter would be intercepted seemed high. Perhaps I could get a chance to draw him aside and speak to him at my sister's birthday.

And what of Leofa? He seemed pleasant enough, but was his attractiveness blinding me? Whatever infamy passed in this school, he was deeply involved. How far did his association with the Nobbsnipes extend? No, I could not trust him, knowing what I did.

Although my questions remained unasked and unanswered, I had to let Vernon go. I could not let my curiosity endanger him.

"Well, in that case, it's more essential than ever that you have good penmanship," I said.

"It is?" Vernon asked. He looked taken off guard.

"If you're going to build a culinary empire on your pig business," I explained, "you'll have to keep your own records, at least in the beginning. It's essential. Otherwise, you'll have nothing to show the tax collectors when they come for the queen's due. Also, keeping good records and knowing how to reckon well will keep your employees from embezzling and help you know where it's most profitable for you to invest. You can't make money unless you can keep track of where it's going and why."

"I guess so," he said doubtfully.

After several minutes of my attempting to cheer him up, Hooker, Ashby, and Leofa found us. Hooker galumphed around them, summarizing the events in the *Great Beasel Hunt*, a play of his own making that he'd put on to entertain Thaddeus. His antics actually prompted Vernon to smile, and they helped him up to the dormitory. Leofa and I followed them up, returning to our garret.

Leofa went to the spigot. He turned the water on, leaned over the basin, and splashed some over his face. I hadn't spoken to him since the day on the landing deck and now I'd had my fill of silence. I wanted to demand who had sent this letter.

"I have a letter to you." I removed the envelope from my breast pocket. "It's from a woman."

Leofa took it from my hand. "My mother."

Silence settled over us. I wanted to ask him about her. I wanted to know why he was here at the school and what he actually worked on.

If my uncle profited from stashing away bastards, then he had no reason to actually educate them as long as they remained out of the public eye. So why had he brought me here to teach them? Was my uncle trying to hide me away, among the bastards, because of my own parentage?

"I'd really like a moment to read this," Leofa said. "Alone."

I realized that I'd been staring. I would've asked Leofa these questions—if I hadn't had such suspicions of him. Besides, we had so thoroughly established that I was Lord Cornelius Franklin and he was the nobody whose rooms I had commandeered.

"I'm sorry you must endure my presence," I said.

In reply, he reached up and rested his hand over mine, grasping my fingers lightly. Leofa brushed his thumb over the back of my hand, as if he tested me. I could feel my blush deepen, a heat that discomfited yet pleased me.

"Hmmm," he murmured, "that's interesting."

I snatched my hand back, looking at anything but him. "Yes. Well, I hope—I hope it's good news."

Leofa met my eyes. "Me too."

7

My sister's birthday dawned cool and breezy. The least worn suit I owned was laid out—embarrassingly, the chocolate-brown cuffs looked dingy and the elbows in the coat seemed worn into a pale muddy hue. I went to the bathing room to take a true, but extremely chilly, bath. Then I returned upstairs to shave and dress, drawing on my thickest coat.

Leofa had kitted himself out for the flight, wearing an oiled canvas coat over his usual getup. His undyed linen shirt had been recently washed and his rough grayish trousers had been brushed clean. His worn leather shoes even seemed shinier than usual. With my permission, he'd again borrowed my bracers for this outing.

Downstairs, the boys knew my absence would mean a day working at cleaning the boiler room and already made a ruckus because of it.

As we passed by, they hooted or pretended to hide from me out of a false and unfounded fear that I would grant them extra assignments. Leofa's threats to bring me back early so that I could give extra lessons made them yelp. Hooker scuttled out of our way and tried to offer up Ashby, who'd been trying to take a nap, as a sacrifice to appease an angry god.

Leofa and I left the tussling boys and headed downstairs to meet the Nobbsnipes in the dining room. Nobbsnipe handed me my first term's pay.

Roger took us to the hangar. We passed by the larger glider, which looked like an elongated carriage with broad double-layered wings, going over to the smaller of the two gliders. The two-person glider had a narrow hollow body for transporting cargo. An aetheric-turbine engine occupied the craft's pointed noise. Beneath the stiff tapered wings, the pilot and passenger seats closely resembled slings.

Leofa and I slid ourselves in and buckled up. I fastened my top hat's buckle and withdrew the goggles from the brim. The goggles' smoked glass lenses shaded the sky and the smooth ostrich leather straps felt cool against my temples.

Roger set up the winch and launched us into the air.

As we began to dive, Leofa revved the engine and adjusted the wing flaps so that we arched upward to soar around the aetherium.

The two-person glider was by far my favorite way to fly. Lying prone as if I myself were a bird, the wind roaring over my face, only my goggles, harness, and the glider itself separated me from the sky. As Leofa brought us up higher into the atmosphere, the dark craggy shape of Highfell Hall retreated below us.

Other small swift gliders swooped and dove around us, their shimmery metallic colored silks blinking in the morning light. Buzzing trackers whizzed past us, shaped like dragonflies.

The flying season in Herrow had come almost to an end, but the sun shone today, and many young courting couples would be taking a last whirl in a glider. So commonly did men propose marriage at this time that the *Herrow Inquirer* had featured a cartoon this morning to that effect, i.e., "the last flight and the first plunge."

I couldn't imagine taking my former fiancé Madeline Havensea up in a two-person glider like this. Somehow I couldn't envision sharing this level of trust with her.

But with Leofa this sweet exhilaration felt natural. Perhaps it came from how closely we lay together at night, our breath sometimes mingling, his skin brushing my skin, his hand tightening over my hip, as though we waited to—what a ridiculous notion!

I could not believe I even entertained these thoughts. Firmly, I shifted my mind away from these ludicrous speculations and focused my attention on the geography below.

The smoggy streets below were laid out rather less clearly than a real map. Hedgerows embroidered the distant hills, golden with the oncoming harvest.

When we finally landed at an airfield on the city's outskirts, Leofa summoned us a hansom cab. The seating was tight. We pressed thigh-to-thigh.

I found myself wondering what it could be like if we were simply two young people, courting and carefree. Would I rest my hand on his thigh, slide it gently upward as I leaned in to steal a kiss? What would his lips feel like against my own? What sensations would the rough stubble of his jaw evoke, were I to trace that strong line with kisses? What quiet sound would he make?

My foolish thoughts shamed me. Nothing like that could exist between myself and another man. I would not succumb, simple as that. I had to stop torturing myself lest I develop a complex.

I picked up my sister's present from the jeweler's. Once outside, I turned to Leofa. I was nervous. I'd contemplated asking him this for a while, so it wasn't exactly spur of the moment when I proposed: "It's early yet, and I must admit that I hoped you'd help me pick out a few things for the boys."

Leofa studied me. He said, "Sure. But we should go down to the Ells. Your money'll go farther there than here and the boys have got no need for beaver-fur ladies' hats."

"I don't know," I said. "Beaver fur would suit Ashby."

I'd never had cause to visit a district like the Ells. Distant from the fashionable Covert, Harecocks Gardens, or Knave's Court, everyone knew the Ells for their costermongers and street food. Somewhere between middle class and seedy, it was in that neighborhood that well-to-do men housed their left-handed "wives."

"Let's walk," he said.

The city streets were packed full of people. Young ladies with parasols tipped street sweepers to clear the road so that they could pass without staining their skirts. Old women with dog carts delivered the last of the morning's milk. Newspaper boys shouted out headlines and young men trotted fine horses around beer carts.

When I tipped my hat to a lady or nodded at a lord, my shabbiness encouraged them to ignore me. How odd, I thought, to be overlooked by my fellow peers.

The shops here on High Street were fine. Brightly painted square columns framed broad windows. Milliners displayed ladies' winter hats. Antiquitarians had old sabers competing with new pistols on show. Other merchants flaunted glistening silks from distant nations or painted porcelain dishes.

High Street shops gave way to the Theater District. In the daytime, beneath unlit oil lamps, the large gaily colored double doors looked tawdry and worn. Among the closed-up stages, pale-skinned foreigners sold tobacco and glee-singers sang for change.

A balding singer followed us briefly, belting out out-of-tune limericks meant to embarrass us into paying him to stop. After the third rendition of "A Girl from Haswick," my annoyance prompted me to give him an earful.

As we strode away into a plain cobbled square, Leofa laughed quietly to himself.

"What?" I asked, peeved.

"It's only..." Leofa took a breath to master himself. "You were so polite about it. I don't think he knew what to do."

His amusement dissipated my irritation, leaving me in fine spirits despite our depressing surroundings. We circumvented a group of ragged children, who watered their milk at a pump to make it last longer.

Gloomy, mud-spattered brick boarding houses had playbills pasted in the windows. The smell of lye and ironing in the air hinted at the presence of many seamstresses, tailors, and washerwomen. We walked down a crooked lane so heavily draped with laundry that I could barely see the sky.

Then the laundry abruptly cleared and we entered the Ells.

Here a perpetual market seemed underway. The buildings stretched taller here, pressed together like gherkins in a jar, with flat tops and made of cheap weathered slats. Slop guards, made of thin tin sheets, extended from the roofs as protection from objects discharged from the aetheria above. Laundry was draped from narrow unglazed windows.

On the street, hawkers, costermongers, paper boys, matchstick and flower girls, they all sang out the praises of their products out of sync, like a confused chorus. A barber performed surgery, yanking out teeth and leaving the bloodied victims to, mumbling, beg a brandy-and-water from the nearby pub. Snake-oil men sold morphia, calves' foot jelly, and electrical remedies.

I saw a crooked cursemonger selling what looked like scraps of perfectly normal writing paper with arcane scribbles on them. He also had snippets of aetheric trapping wires, which glimmered with aether and had been stuck into oil lamps like wicks.

The sweet smell of roasting chestnuts and coffee vied with such savories as eel pie and pea-and-turtle soup.

Coffee. I loved coffee and missed coffee, but I needed to spend my earnings on more practical things than such indulgences. I searched, instead, for used cots so that I could have my own bed.

I found a merchant selling a foldable cot, its supports bending flat and its mattress naught but canvas suspended between two poles. The price did astound me, but I supposed that had to be normal, given the essential nature of this furniture. The merchant assured me that no one had died in it. Funnily, I hadn't asked.

As I folded the contraption into a manageable package, Leofa, who had hung back during our exchange, stepped up. He and the merchant regarded each other for a long silent moment. Leofa smiled and said, "Give him his change."

The merchant returned fully half of the price we'd agreed upon.

"Now give him the rest," Leofa added.

The merchant returned to me another third, which Leofa seemed to think fair, and then Leofa turned, catching a boy by his shirt. The boy, who'd been dodging around us, playing tag, squirmed in Leofa's grip as Leofa extracted some change from the boy's hands.

"Your mother would be ashamed of you," Leofa said.

"Aw, sir, we was just playing," the boy said.

I counted my change. I understood what had occurred. I sighed. I'd been pickpocketed by this little delinquent. Everyone in the Ells seemed to see me as an easy dupe.

"Well, take your games elsewhere," Leofa said. "Wyrd, be grateful I didn't call the guard on you. Boys younger than you are strung up on the bridge all the time. Now, apologize to Lord Franklin."

"M'sorry, my lord."

Leofa released the boy into the crowd.

I said, "He couldn't have been more than six."

"Eight, I think. But he's underfed," he said. "You're terrible at haggling."

"I know." I always had been. My friends back at school always teased me for never quibbling over prices. Even though I knew it was a problem, somehow that never stopped me from doing it.

"Do you think I ought to get the boys something?" I asked.

"I thought that was your first paycheck," Leofa said. "Don't you have a debt to pay off?"

I shrugged. "Well, at this rate, it's going to take me a lifetime to pay it."

"You know, you're being cheated," Leofa said. "Your uncle should be paying you triple."

"You misunderstand," I said. "Being on good terms with my uncle is a priority. He's childless, and when he dies, I fully expect my sister to inherit."

Leofa gazed at me thoughtfully. "But that could take forty years. That's a real long time."

"That's better than a lifetime in Newland." I did not say that I had plans to pursue my own work on the side, though I did consider it. Would Leofa like me more, I wondered, if I confessed to him that my true hopes still lay in academia and what I could discover? But why should I confess, when he had not told me the truth about his own work?

"What are you and the boys making in starboard hall?" I asked.

"Do you really not know?" Leofa asked curiously.

"No," I said. "I don't."

"Then you shouldn't." He shrugged and looked away.

"But my uncle—"

"Neil, please." Leofa shook his head. He spoke in a low tone. "If you really care about those boys, you'll stop asking."

I considered insisting, but I could feel his resistance as though it were palpable. My line of inquiry truly did discomfit him.

"So what about getting them some blankets?" Leofa asked.

I recalled we'd been contemplating gifts for the boys. His change of subject further signaled that he'd closed this discussion. This frustrated me, but I let it go. I didn't want to ruin the day.

"We couldn't pack a bundle that large in the glider. We'll buy knit hats instead," I said.

When Leofa did the talking, the seller threw a number of unattractive but functional scarves at a lower price than I would have dreamed possible. Eventually, a fragile sense of camaraderie redeveloped between us.

I learned from him that most of the boys couldn't skate, a chief pastime for anyone growing up on an aetherium, so I bought two pairs of adjustable skates that could be strapped onto shoes. And although the barley sugar sweets lacked the nutrition the boys needed, I knew they'd go down a treat.

"And I still have enough that we'll be able to catch a cab back to the airfield, should the need arise." I tossed the few remaining coins in my hand, proud of my day's work, although I'd mainly watched Leofa do the bargaining after my initial attempt.

"We still have an hour and a half before we should start ambling over to Knave's Court," Leofa said, hefting up the unwieldy but light bundle of hats. "Let me buy you a coffee."

I picked up the skates, now eager. I said, "Do that and you'll be a god among men."

He laughed. "If I'd known you'd think that, I would've bought you some long ago. Come on. I saw a good-looking coffee room back there."

The coffee room was tastefully done up for this side of town, with golden Siovanese wallpaper, gilt-edged mirrors, walnut tables, and a tiny fireplace. But for the fact that it seated only six people, it could've competed with any coffee room in Knave's Court. Leofa bought me a cup made in Rithen style, strong and dark, and then purchased a Dayshon tea for himself.

"I used to live around here," he said.

"I thought you went straight from the Barrens up to Highfell."

"Sure, and then I stayed on," he said. "But I took a year or two out—ran away when I was, oh, don't know, fourteen, sixteen. I did about every job known to man requiring hands."

"Like what?" I was intrigued. I would have never thought of doing such a thing at the same age. At sixteen, I'd still been at Evermore. I'd just started developing my interest in my mother's grimoire and the unusual pyxis spell it contained. I'd still been half-developed as a person, like a chick not yet ready to burst from the shell.

"Docks. Tannery. Butcher's. Smithy. I'd a few apprenticeships. Real positions."

"How did you find them all?" I asked. "Didn't you need to pay the apprenticing fees and have letters of introduction?"

"Forged the letters," Leofa said. "Most people around here can't read, and I have a good hand, so I'd seal it up, hand it over, they'd bring it to the clerk and crack it, and there you go. It's not like they'd be able to recognize a hand and most of them couldn't afford to verify it themselves. As for the fees, I'd promise to work them back. Usually, someone would take me on."

"And then what?" I asked.

"Well…" He looked embarrassed. "Let's just say I wasn't the ideal worker."

He didn't elaborate and I didn't ask. More criminality, I supposed.

Outside, it began to rain. Herrow's black rain was famous. The filthy slurry falling from the heavens actually came from the Southside aetheria. Coal smoke from heating, ash from burned refuse, a stink like blood that was a signature of aetheric turbine exhaust, all suspended in raindrops that left grayish slimy streaks wherever they fell.

"But you went back to Highfell," I said. "Why?"

"Needed the money," he said. "Nobbsnipe offered me a lot."

"Whatever he's offering you, whatever hold he has over you…" I met his eyes. "I could help you. I'm not entirely friendless."

Leofa said, "What, are you talking about that fiancé of yours who doesn't even write to you? Or how about your uncle, who's holding that debt over your head like it's the headman's axe? That uncle of yours keeps you like a slave and your sister like a hostage."

"My sister isn't a hostage!" I said, because his words stung.

He shook his head and added quietly, "Thanks, Neil. But I think I can handle this myself."

Leofa gulped his tea and set the cup firmly on the table. With an oddly precise gesture, he rotated the cup so that the handle faced in the opposite direction. "Look, Neil, working for Nobbsnipe isn't awful. A sure sight better than the stink of a tannery or hauling crates up and down the same cursed dock every day."

"Ah. I see." I didn't see. I couldn't imagine going through all that work to make a life in Herrow below, merely to go back to the grim institution above.

Leofa started telling me a story about a day at the docks. He'd pursued a thief who'd stolen an entire crate of bananas all the way around town—even around the Royal Shadow Gardens, twice. By the time he got to the part with the dog, I laughed so hard I could hardly breathe.

After that, he told me about his aged landlady who'd tried to seduce him. He'd had run-ins with a local smash-and-grab operation who'd had such a hard time trying to rob him that eventually they'd given up and invited Leofa out for a drink. Before I knew it, we had to head over to Knave's Court for my sister's birthday party.

As we walked, the knowledge that our afternoon out had come to an end saddened me. Once we reached my uncle's townhouse, Leofa and I would assume our disparate roles. Separated by our stations, the time we'd passed together today would become irrelevant. I would dine with peers while Leofa ate scraps at the kitchen table.

At the very least, I hoped Leofa would have to chance to steal something from my uncle's larder for the boys. This thought cheered me, but when I suggested it to Leofa, he recoiled.

Leofa said, "And get the cook fired for thieving? What do you take me for?" Then, seeing my mortification, he softened. "Well, I know you didn't mean it like that. You've a good heart. We got the boys gifts enough already."

When I knocked at the door, my sister and my uncle greeted us. To my relief, my sister looked well. She wore a new dress, still done in mourning colors but fashionable nonetheless. I bowed to my uncle and embraced Nora. She smelled of flat-ironed hair and orange blossom water, exactly like our mother always had.

"I'm glad to see you looking well," I said, and I meant it. Nora had regained some of the weight she lost after our parents' deaths. Her skin had a golden tone and her dark brown hair again had a healthy sheen.

A manservant took my hat as well as Nora's present. Leofa bore away the results of our shopping like a dutiful manservant.

After taking a few quiet refreshments with the other guests, who seemed to be mostly my uncle's business associates, we seated ourselves in the dining room. Done out in ebony and green velvet, my uncle's furnishings expressed an expensive, oppressive sensibility and bordered on starkly unfashionable.

Uncle Gerard sat at the head of the table, with me at his right and Nora to his left. Only then did I realize that my sister was the sole female at the table.

Nora was petite, even for a girl of her age. Height did not run on our mother's side of the family and we'd both inherited a much more diminutive frame than either of our fathers had possessed. Now, seated and surrounded by lords, Nora looked truly small.

Uncle Gerard served my sister perfunctorily even as the lords served themselves. Uncle Gerard introduced me to the man seated at my right, Lord Cyril Slackleigh. He was a thin man in his fifties, with dark straight hair. His whiskers framed his mouth. His clothes were superbly expensive—the fine Adurian wool of his jacket dyed an uncommon jet black.

It took me a moment to place his name, but then I remembered he'd donated the Imrian tablets to the museum.

Nora brightened when I reminded her of the afternoon we'd spent at the museum. She asked after Stanley. I almost told her he hadn't been well—his hands had been burned badly yet again and he had been more than a week healing. Then I realized that her showing any concern would be inappropriate in this setting.

"He's well," I lied instead. "But, what I meant to say, was that Lord Slackleigh donated Imrian tablets to the museum. It had religious poetry on it that hasn't been published yet."

"Poetry!" Lord Slackleigh laughed, derisive and disgusted. He said, "Why, I had no idea what it was when I brought it back, I can promise you that! When Professor Vassily told me it was about inverts, I donated it immediately. Got it off my hands—and got a tax reduction for my pains!"

I cleared my throat, trying to interrupt, but Nora had already flushed and turned her eyes down demurely as if her hands in her lap fascinated her. The raucous conversation further down the table died as older gentlemen tried to pretend they hadn't overheard the word "invert" and younger gentlemen tried to display their disgust.

Slackleigh had realized he'd said too much too loudly. He tugged at his cravat as if straightening the knot. Carelessness like this could ruin a gentleman's reputation. Permanently.

"Of course you wouldn't have brought it back if you'd known," I said with a lightness that I did not feel. Sickness and sadness roiled through me. "And how could you have known? To my knowledge, there are but a few who are even vaguely familiar with the language."

Slackleigh laughed as though I'd made some witty remark and Uncle Gerard looked at me meaningfully, which sparked a certain measure of odd guilt.

"I found it when traveling through Zisth," Slackleigh said. "I'm rather a collector of antiquities, you know. I studied archaeology in

Elmstead, and although I'm hardly an academic, it does remain an interest of mine."

"Oh, Zisth!" Nora smiled. "I've always wanted to visit Aduro. It used to the center of all learning in the world, you know, and some of the greatest mathematicians have lived there. I would die to see the Palace of Imrod, where Amurad the Great hired Sekul. We still use his function to calculate how much force is needed for a winch to lift a glider into the air!"

The men watched her as though her loquacious excitement pained them. After that, Lord Slackleigh spent most of dinner talking about the various countries he'd visited, the adventures he'd had, the misconceptions about the cultures as he'd seen them, and so forth.

Nora, who had always wanted to travel and who had never left the shores of Higher Eidoland, acted thoroughly intrigued by what Lord Slackleigh had to say. For almost every place he listed, she knew of some famous discovery that had taken place there, or a mathematician who had called that city home.

She loved the history of discovery almost as she loved the actual equations. Her knowledge and passion discomfited the men around Nora, who shared condescending smiles, as if to say, *women*.

I beckoned a servant closer and spoke quietly. "I'd like a word with my man."

"Yes, sir," the manservant said.

Shortly afterward, Leofa entered the room. He didn't move like a servant. Leofa strolled as he owned everything he deigned to step upon. I found myself instinctively aware of him. He lounged behind me. His voice, richly sardonic, sent shivers through me when he leaned down to whisper in my ear, "My lord?"

"Would you perhaps fetch my gift for my sister?" I asked in a low voice. I wanted to give her the present sooner rather than later, to brighten this poor gathering for Nora.

"Yes, sir," he said.

After dinner, the sexes usually retired to separate rooms. Customarily, the men used this time to smoke tobacco and drink port without offending the ladies' more delicate senses. Usually, ladies refreshed themselves and helped each other in rearranging any garment that had become disarrayed during dining. This provided a relaxing interlude for all.

Yet on this occasion, when the men all retired to the smoking room, my sister was left to sit alone in the drawing room. Some birthday celebration this was for her. When I suggested I go with her to the drawing room, as I did with the Nobbsnipe ladies, my uncle laughed as though I'd made some clever joke.

In the usual muddle after dinner and before the men had withdrawn completely, I accepted the present from Leofa's hands. He drifted a step behind me, obviously not knowing what to do with himself and yet not quite as inconspicuous as a true manservant. I drew my sister aside and gave her the present. The wrapping was poor, naught but a twist of colored cloth, but I hoped that the gift itself would make up for it.

Although no expert in women's fashion, I'd read a recent article in the *Herrow Inquirer* about the ludicrous sums being spent on chatelaines. This medieval symbol of womanhood comprised of a simple flat chain, meant to be looped over the belt, that normally held keys and other baubles.

The one I had made for Nora had miniatures of our parents in locket-style casings—the very miniatures that I'd once adorned the desk in the garret with. Plus a small case for her reading glasses, a small purse, and a portable unbound notetaker.

The notetaker, a plain bronze box-shaped magical device with a few jeweled buttons, had cost nearly as much as the chatelaine itself. It could record approximately an hour of audio material, about the length of an average lecture, although such transient sounds could only be played back once.

"So you'll always have a way to record it, if an idea strikes you," I explained. "Also, I know how you like attending those lectures at the Royal Institute of Mathematics."

"Oh Neil… you shouldn't have. We really can't afford this." Nora lifted the chatelaine admiringly.

"As the lady of our house," I added, "it's only right that you carry the keys."

"You insufferable… I miss you so," she said, embracing me.

By now, we had to part. I paused before I left with my uncle, having a word with Leofa. It seemed strange to me, to have my sister wait alone in the house with all these men around and no female company to chaperone her at all. But I trusted that Leofa would always protect my sister. He would disregard social protocol if necessary. That was what she needed now.

I caught his gaze and said quietly, "Please, would you watch out for her?"

"Yes, sir." Leofa nodded, slowly, and ambled after Nora. His gait made me shake my head. I had to conceal my smile before I followed my uncle, last into the smoking room.

Once there, I accepted a glass of port, declined a cigarillo, and tactfully drew my uncle aside to speak with him. Uncle Gerard seemed in a good mood, rubicund with alcohol, his lanky frame slouching. But he showed no interested in listening. I spoke to him about whether or not Nora could go visit friends or have some friends over, some feminine company, but he wouldn't hear of his house being filled with children. Frustration sharpened my temper.

"At the very least, she needs a maidservant," I snapped. "She needs someone to chaperone her. Demos the Guardian, you could at least get her a governess! I must insist upon this."

"You must insist," he said derisively. "How can you insist on anything, Neil? I own you. I own you both."

I could not believe he spoke to me like this. My hand tightened the stem of my port glass. I said, "You must be drunk, sir."

"You forget yourself. You're not of Franklin blood."

"I never *forget*—" I blazed with anger, but I forced myself to swallow it back. I threw back the port. The cloying wine coated my throat with a syrupy alcoholic warmth. I held out my empty glass and a servant refilled it.

I could not make these circumstances any worse for my sister. I had to make him see, whatever it took, that this situation was insupportable for her. And there was no way for me to address my concerns about Highfell in these surroundings either.

I took a deep breath and said calmly, "I never forget your brother's kindness in adopting me, sir. But what you cannot seem to see is that letting my sister go unattended like this will wreak havoc on her reputation. If you do not change this, she will be unmarriageable. And Nora is of Franklin blood. She's your brother's only child—the only heir."

I gazed at him unflinchingly.

"Fine, fine," he said. "She'll get her maid. You've got more fire in you than it seems, don't you, boy? I didn't expect that out of your type."

"Sir," I said evenly. I would not ask what he meant by that jab. I sipped my port and searched for another topic of conversation. Although Highfell weighed heavily on my mind, I asked, "Have you received notice from the queen as to when she expects my sister to be presented to her?"

"The Darkest Night Ball," my uncle said. "It's quite a social coup."

I nodded. Anyone with the slightest pretentions to society would brave the winter weather for the ball. Sometimes traveling weeks, bogged down in snow and mud, all traveled see the most expensive and astounding spectacle put on by the Crown. It was the largest masked ball.

"I will be escorting her," Uncle Gerard said, smiling at me again. "As her guardian."

I felt my shoulders tighten. I sipped my port, working up a response. I'd thought I would escort her to this event as her older brother and closest surviving relative. But my uncle claiming it…

He acted as though he thought my sister's life a pissing contest. If I fought him on this, it would only get worse for Nora. I knew that with instinctive certainty. I didn't like this at all, and I decided to withdraw. At least I'd won her a maid, I told myself.

"Very well," I conceded.

I spent the next hour mingling with businessmen who were not of my generation. I used whatever conversational skills I had to entertain them, anticipating the next part of the evening, where Nora would join us to play cards.

I awaited my sister at the piano. I took the opportunity to play "My Lady Night" by Percy Ottwark. Even though I'd informed Mrs. Nobbsnipe that "My Lady Night" concerned a metaphor for death, Mrs. Nobbsnipe had disagreed. She had believed, firmly, that it concerned a harlot and thus forbade me from playing it in her house on the grounds of lewdness.

On the last verse, Nora entered the drawing room with Leofa on her heels. Leofa took up a manservant-like position by the door.

Apparently in a fair mood, Nora sang out the last verse, wherein the old man finds his lady-love in the hands of thugs. Her voice, cultivated by years of music lessons, rang clear and bright. Curtsying before the men's applause, she declared that we'd play Whipples because it cheered her.

None of us had ever heard of Whipples. Nora explained the rules. It turned out to be a doubles game, where partners played each other.

"As it's my birthday, I think you'll humor me by allowing me to choose my own partner." Nora had a sparkle to her eyes and a sharpness to her smile that I immediately distrusted. She drifted past Slackleigh and touched Leofa on the shoulder. "And my partner will be this fine young man here, Leofa."

"Nora, I really must protest," my uncle said. "You can't select a servant!"

"Nonsense, Uncle!" Nora smiled at him. "It's my birthday and my privilege!"

"You dishonor my guests," Uncle Gerard said stiffly.

I understood Nora would not be dissuaded from her plan, whatever it was. Yet her choosing Leofa would be social suicide. She had to be truly frustrated to want to attack our uncle so openly. And desperate, if she would risk being called a harlot for associating with servants.

"Come now, Uncle," I said with a smile. "We all know Mr. Blackwater isn't truly a servant."

"Blackwater?" Uncle Gerard started.

"He isn't?" Slackleigh sounded skeptical.

"Mr. Blackwater is a fellow teacher at my uncle's school, Highfell Hall," I went on, improvising and hoping that Leofa had the presence of mind to attest to my claim. "We thought it would be a lark for him to pretend to be my man to get below stairs."

"Why would he want to do that?" Uncle Gerard asked with a dismissive gesture that betrayed rough impatience. Yet I could see that he welcomed my face-saving intercession, although he had to be aware of its fraudulence.

All eyes turned to Leofa. He relaxed against the doorframe, taking on a haughty, lazy air.

"I'm writing a novel," he said.

A brief but significant silence hung in the room as my uncle's guests weighed the veracity of our claim. Finally one of them began laughing. He said, "Don't you boys have something better to do?"

"No women," said another, provoking more laughter.

"At least he's not a journalist snooping around for that workers' rights advocate. What was his name? Hammerson?" said another guest, who guffawed. "You'd be in trouble then, wouldn't you, old fellow?"

Uncle Gerard smiled dourly. But as Leofa's presence had been legitimized, he gave Leofa a permissive wave, allowing him to take up Nora's offer.

As the men began to sort themselves, forming partnerships and then groups of four, I went over to my sister, hoping to discover what she schemed. Slackleigh tagged right at my heels, loudly intending to protest Nora's choice of partner and present himself as more suitable. Nora had already chosen a table by the fireplace and seated herself on opposite Leofa. As a result, I ended up paired with Slackleigh.

In the initial round, I saw immediately that card counting would be especially useful in this game. No wonder Nora had wanted to play it. Nora had a keen eye for numbers. Unsurprisingly, Nora and Leofa won the first hand.

Accepting their condolences good-naturedly, I finished my glass of port, stood, and prepared to give up my seat to the next team. In doubles games like these, the teams rotated through so that everyone would have the chance to play one another.

But Slackleigh refused to move. He still clutched his hand. Suddenly, he slapped his cards down on the table. "I was unfamiliar with the game. I demand a rematch!"

"Oh, come now, Slackleigh!" chided a member of the team waiting to replace us. "Let someone else sit next to the pretty lady."

Slackleigh glowered.

Nora perked up and smiled at the challenging team. She glowed with the pleasure of the compliment and her win. She said, "Sit down so that I may trounce you immediately!"

Leofa grinned as he shuffled the deck.

"No," Slackleigh said. "I'll get my rematch."

As everyone realized Slackleigh would not move of his own volition, our collective embarrassment became oppressive. But as no one intended to haul him from his chair, we had no alternative but to play on.

I offered the challenging team an apologetic shrug and reseated myself. Nora's disappointment was slightly assuaged when the gentlemen promised to call upon her another day, so that they could then have the honor of being her victim.

We lost the next round.

"You play a bad hand," Slackleigh snarled at me.

"I've never been overfond of cards." I drank more port.

Leofa snorted and shuffled the deck. The next team we were supposed to swap with didn't challenge Slackleigh for his seat, instead paying courteous respects to Nora before moving on. We'd been effectively cut out from the rota.

As we played and lost to Nora and Leofa, Slackleigh grew increasingly agitated. Being his partner was rather tiresome, and by this point, I resigned myself to losing. I found cards hideously boring, so I went through the motions of playing and drank by way of entertaining myself.

I'd grown accustomed to the port, which I'd initially thought unpleasantly sweet. Now, even more thirsty, I found the cleaner flavor of claret dreadfully appealing. I requested a glass from a servant.

We played again and lost. Slackleigh's color burned high as his cheeks flushed with anger. While I saw this ominous fact, I couldn't bring myself to care.

"How am I meant to play, with a sot for a partner!" Slackleigh snapped at me. "Will you not stop drinking?"

"No, I won't," I said.

Leofa chuckled. He sounded so very fond of me.

"And you!" Slackleigh leaned on the table and jabbed a finger in Leofa's direction. "You've been dealing me bad hands. You're cheating. I demand that you concede!"

"Aren't you a little too invested in this?" asked my card-counting sister. "It's only a game, after all."

"Stop this," I commanded Slackleigh. "If you continue to cast such ungentlemanly aspersions in front of my sister, I'll have to ask you to leave. You're a poor loser!"

"Now, now," Leofa said mildly.

"You swindler!" Slackleigh threw his wine in Leofa's face.

I stared, shocked and also furious on Leofa's behalf.

Leofa lunged at Slackleigh, upsetting the table, sending cards and drinks flying. A glass shattered against the hearthstones. Wine gushed across the stones and soaked into the hearthrug. Leofa had all but wrenched Slackleigh off his feet. Slackleigh spat curses at his face.

I seized Leofa by the shoulder. "Wait outside. Now!"

Leofa released Slackleigh slowly. His insouciance spoke clearer than words. He let Slackleigh because I requested it—because he shouldn't waste his time on such filth. Shooting me an amused look, Leofa sauntered toward the door.

Slackleigh leaped up to pursue him, but Nora stepped in his path. With a growl of frustration, he attempted to brush past her. But Nora pressed her hand to his chest.

"Let him go," she said.

"You ungrateful, dimwitted fool." Uncle Gerard struck me, taking me utterly by surprise. His hand left my cheek hot and stinging. I gaped at him as he snarled, "I cannot believe you brought such infamy into my house! Get out. Now."

Furious beyond words, I stalked away.

Outside, Leofa fell into step beside me. We had a good two-hour walk before us, traversing the boggy and refuse-laden streets of Herrow.

"Did you and my sister speak while she was in the drawing room?" I asked, trying to cool my head.

"After a while."

"Is she well?"

"Bored. Lonely." Leofa shrugged. "Lord Slackleigh came by. He said he was lost. I told him I couldn't give him directions because I was lost too. Then I taught your sister Whipples."

"Lost, was he?" I shook my head, despising the man. Walking in a unilateral direction challenged me more than it ought to have. I was definitely drunk.

"You're going to have a hangover in the morning." Leofa caught my shoulder to steady me. "After all that port."

"I know!" I snapped.

But then I softened, because Leofa's hand rested so gently on my shoulder. I faced him. Our aloneness in the city made the tight walls of the nighttime street seem surprisingly intimate.

Barely lit by the ambient lights from the aetheria above, I found him so handsome. The impulse to kiss him—I could not bear it! I wanted to commit wonderful, unspeakable acts upon his body. I leaned forward, prepared to cast my fate into his hands.

He pushed back, steadying me. "Whoa there."

"Leofa…" I paused. I wanted share thoughts with him I knew I'd regret confessing. I bit that back. Instead, I said, "Thank you. For the coffee. And for watching out for Nora."

He gazed at me, and smiled. "Anything for you."

"I can't believe he accused you of cheating," I muttered.

"I was cheating," he said.

At this revelation, a surge of betrayal sank through me. I swayed. I'd put myself on the line for him, in my uncle's home. I'd most likely lost my uncle's concessions for my sister's comfort because of Leofa. I'd defended him!

"I just didn't want him to win," he said.

Feeling a fool, I twisted free from his hands and staggered away.

As I was too drunk to fly, we spent the night sleeping separately in the hangar. In the morning we returned, without speaking, to Highfell Hall.

8

On the following morning, autumn fully arrived. The wind coughed up skeletal leaves from the city below, the bird populations migrated, and the rain carried slushy ice within each droplet. Hungover and angry at Leofa, I didn't wait for him when it came to distributing the boys' gifts.

The forty hats led to questions about money, which slid easily into a lesson on currency, as I soon discovered many did not know how many pennies were in a sovereign. This lesson in economics spurred me to contemplate how impossible it truly was to ever repay my debt to my uncle at my current wage. I could remember my uncle's words all too clearly. "I own you. I own you both." He'd said it outright.

Leofa had been right. I was a slave. My sister was a hostage.

"You have to remember to write out the units," I told Vernon absently. "Or how will anyone know that you meant pence and not shillings?"

Outside the schoolroom windows, dim foggy clouds flanked the aetherium. The subdued light made the walls around me feel closer than normal and prompted a surge of jittery claustrophobia. Could I escape? If I snatched up Nora, we could flee to Newland, assume new identities, and start again!

But how possible was that, truly? Perhaps a desperate villain in a penny dreadful would act like that, but reality never presented such an uncomplicated narrative. Could I condemn my sister to an outlaw's life? I certainly couldn't abandon her to my uncle.

What did I expect to do? Leap off the edge with nothing but my parachute? What would that truly change?

No, fleeing would change nothing but my surroundings. I had to find another solution, one that erased my debt and released my sister from my uncle's clutches.

Nobbsnipe entered the schoolroom without warning, interrupting my thoughts. His paunch strained his waistcoat and it seemed to me that his jacket had been left unbuttoned not because of fashion, but out of necessity.

"You told Louisa you would start the boys on languages today," he said.

"Yes, I am." I gestured to the grammars stacked behind me.

"Here you go." He handed me a slip of paper and turned to leave. He'd given me a list—boys' names along with the languages they'd learn. I glanced up at him.

"Nobbsnipe, if I may have a word with you?" I asked.

"I only have a minute," he said, irritated. "I have to get back to supervise work in the starboard hall."

"Indeed." I did not question his obvious lie, but instead I held up the paper and set it on my desk. I tapped out the rhythm of the second measure in Schader's *Pensive Sonata*.

"I'm afraid I don't have a grammar for Ishar," I told Nobbsnipe. "I cannot teach this one, either. I do not know it. And this boy...he isn't prepared to move along yet. Also, teaching the languages in this order...it's not productive."

Nobbsnipe scowled.

"Pythian was the first phonetic written language," I explained, "but the spoken language died out but a few centuries later. So its alphabet was mostly used in conjunction with other spoken languages—"

"Guess it can't be helped that you don't know that one," Nobbsnipe said. "As for the others, you do your best."

He bustled back over to the doorway, where he paused. "Remember, I decide on what the boys learn."

"I *am* aware of that, Nobbsnipe," I said.

I glanced over the list. Why these languages? What did they have in common?

They were all in grimoires, but I had expected that. Although this affirmed the hypothesis that Nobbsnipe engaged in cursemongering, that couldn't be true.

If the boys were casting spells—spells that they couldn't even read enough of to determine their nature—then surely I would see a higher attrition rate among the boys. Not to mention the bizarre effects from spells being spoken daily. No, they could not be casting curses on a regular basis. What then were they doing?

When the answer came to me, I felt as stupid as a man who, in playing blind man's bluff, had fondled a donkey. The boys needed to know these languages to construct spells. Their work in the starboard hall involved building aether-powered magical devices.

As the development of magical objects was exceedingly dangerous, very few labs and institutions were granted licenses by the Crown. I doubted very much that Nobbsnipe had papers signed by the queen. Operating without a license was a felony punishable by hanging.

No wonder Leofa hadn't wished to confide in me.

I distributed the necessary grammars, setting the boys to reading the first chapter. I would have them do written exercises and then I'd verbally quiz them. The youngest boys—the ones too young for study—sat on the floor in the corner, having built a metropolis out of bird bones. Gripping pigeon skulls, they zoomed them over the city like war aetheria on a bombing run.

As my students quietly worked, I considered what spells they could be working on. Most of our extant grimoires came from the second medieval renaissance, so it was no wonder they were written in Old Eidlish or Accadian. Old Modern Zisth as well as Medieval Siovanese also frequently occurred in the grimoires I'd studied.

It occurred to me that Nobbsnipe didn't understand that a spell could be written in any language. As long as the metallic inks crossed the wires embedded in the page at the correct intervals, the spell would work.

Halfway through the lesson, Leofa made an appearance. Not a half hour before I would have questioned his attendance. But now I understood that he, too, needed to learn these languages to pursue his work in the starboard hall. Now his interest in my lessons made a grim kind of sense.

He seated himself beside Hooker and Ashby. I had the two learning Accadian together, because if they didn't sit together, they schemed about it. At least this way their misbehavior could be slightly contained. With Leofa beside them, suddenly the two of them became the most diligent students I had.

In the afternoon, we had a house tournament out in the yard beneath the laundry of the Nobbsnipes. Snow drifted down on us. It had to be one of the most unusual games of stickball ever seen. The bats were old table legs and the balls, scavenged wine corks with ropes wound around them, did not even resemble spheres. The game came to an end after all three balls had been lost over the side. The Beasels won.

At some point during this silliness, my anger at Leofa from last night's escapade wore away. I could understand why he'd wanted to bring that supercilious man, Slackleigh, down a notch. Granted, I didn't appreciate his methods. Berating the sky for its foul weather would have had as much effect as remaining frustrated with Leofa for his actions.

As the wind rose and the clouds whitened with snow, I decided we ought to go in. Blinding blizzards could rise quickly in these heights.

"I'll check the barometer in steerage," I said to Leofa.

He nodded. "I'm going to help secure the landing deck."

I ordered the boys to close the shutters and secure their belongings. The barometers confirmed my instincts, so I sought the Nobbsnipes. I encountered Roger leaning over Peggy in the receiving hall beside the stairwell. He looked annoyed when I first told him the snow worsened, but then he went down to check the barometers in steerage for himself.

Peggy darted belowdecks.

Soon after, Roger charged upstairs, looking determined.

"The pressure's dropping," he announced, as if I didn't know. "Tell Leo to flatten the landing deck's windbreak and close the rain intakes. Louisa's upstairs. You tell her to ring the bell, take down our colors, and make storm ready. She knows how to do that. I need to find Father."

"May I ask who's piloting?" I asked. I'd been taught how to handle an aetherium in a storm; everyone knew emergency protocol at Evermore and Elmstead, because no one could prepare too much for the troubles of a sudden storm.

"Stanley will come when the bell rings. About the only thing he can do around here is fly." He headed for the starboard hall.

I found Louisa upstairs in the drawing room, practicing her scales on the piano. She looked up at me, startled and delighted by my interruption. When I told her of the approaching storm, she sighed in disappointment. Louisa asked me to bar the doors and shutter the windows while she ran upstairs to ring the bell.

Rather than the usual subdued peals to indicate the hour, I could hear a clangor meant to rouse everyone in the aetherium.

I finished fixing the windows on this floor and checked to see if the cushioned display cupboards were locked shut.

"Neil!" Louisa called out, her voice coming faint from upstairs. "Neil, I need your help!"

I ran upstairs, past the bedrooms, and up into the narrow communications tower at the height of the house. The signaling windows had been shut and the cotes closed down. Pigeons flapped and jostled on their perches. The papers from a nearby writing desk fluttered across floor, caught in the wind that whistled down from the ceiling.

The flagpole, protruding through an open porthole in the roof, was still raised. Louisa hung on to the line like a sailor about to be washed out to sea. She wouldn't let go, so I got behind her and helped her heave the colors down.

Louisa turned in the circle of my arms to face me, leaning up on her toes and with her face inches from mine. A cold dread stole over me, and by purest instinct, I turned away.

I slammed my hand on the button that allowed the flagpole to telescope down.

Her chance at illicit romance apparently stymied, Louisa very sensibly tugged on the wire that closed the flag port in the roof. As soon as it snapped shut, the wind cut off and the whirling papers fell to the floor. I dropped to my knees, gathering them up. I stood to replace them on the writing desk. It looked like most of them were invitations, written in an old-fashioned but ladylike hand. Mrs. Nobbsnipe's, no doubt.

The aetherium shuddered as wind hit us from the side. Louisa gave a small cry and I reached out to steady her. She turned to me, placed her hand on my chest, and looked up into my eyes. I backed up and thudded into the writing desk behind me. She laughed as if we shared a joke, but I felt it was much the same joke a shark shared with a drowning sailor. It was funnier to the shark.

"I have to go check on the boys…" I began.

"Leo will take care of them," Louisa said. "He always does."

"But still." I sidled sideways, attempting to evade this face-to-face business going on here. I said, "He has other duties. He has things to do. He can't watch out for them all the time, you know. I really should go there right now."

"Please, it's not as though he needs you to help him," she said.

"What? Miss Louisa, please, will you desist—"

"We're alone now. You can call me Louisa," she said.

I did not know what to say to that. My doom approached all too suddenly. I never thought I'd have to fend off a woman and I had never heard of this topic being covered by etiquette folios. If this situation had been reversed, it would be clear that the harried party should slap the pursuer, storm off, and immediately inform a sturdy older brother. But for me that was hardly a viable option.

I needed a diversion or an excuse. I had to flee. Somehow.

The school lurched and shuddered as a hard wind hit us. I took that opportunity to stutter something about young Thaddeus, and I ran.

In the dormitory, I performed a head count. The younger boys were all present, but for those who had the duty of keeping us aloft. Stanley worked in steerage, I knew, while Carlsworth, Northwall, Quincey, and Hooker labored in the engine rooms. Smalley and Upping no doubt loitered with their watchmen chums, as per usual.

I wanted to go down to the boilers or to steerage to check on the boys there, but Ashby told me they'd done this a dozen times before. I had to bite back my response. Whatever responsibilities they'd taken on in the past, they remained children. I was a member of staff.

The air was chill but lighting a fire in such turbulence was foolhardy, so the boys huddled in their boxbeds with blankets over their shoulders. Young Thaddeus Paxton cried. Already at a loss, I attempted to comfort him. I told him he'd be fine, the storm would pass, but he didn't seem to believe me.

Ashby told the toddler to shut up. He said that if the Nobbsnipes intended to leave Thaddeus outside to die, they would've put him out *before* they locked the doors. Since the doors were locked, now no one would be thrown out. Much to my surprise, this actually consoled the toddler.

"You really think we'll be okay?" Derby asked.

"Yes," I said. But outside the window, I saw bright beams of light catching on the flurrying snow. They looked like searchlights. Alarm shot through me.

Footsteps pounded up the stairs. Leofa burst through the door. "Neil, come on. I need your help!"

I started to ask him where and why, but the raw urgency in his expression told me that now was not the time for conversation. He turned back in the door and I bolted after him. As we pelted downstairs, he called back to me, "A girls' school flagged us. She's coming down fast and right on top of us."

We needed to evacuate the boys and ourselves, I realized. Memories of the countless emergency drills I'd participated in as a boy came to me. Between just the two of us I wasn't sure if we could get all the boys harnessed into their parachutes in time. But the older boys could help. And Thaddeus would need assistance with more than just the buckles of his harness.

I began, "Once we've distributed the parachutes, one of us will have to carry Thaddeus—"

"Parachutes?" Leofa's voice dropped to a hoarse whisper. "What fucking parachutes? Have you ever seen any parachutes here?"

"No, but there have to be…" A terrible clarity struck me. There were no parachutes—no viable means of escape for Leofa, myself or the boys. We were all trapped aboard this decrepit aetherium.

Leofa bounded down, taking two steps at a time, and I hurried behind him. The gusts and howls of the storm outside lulled. The staircase rang with our harried footsteps.

"We've got to get Highfell clear of that girls' school," I said.

"Easier said than done." Leofa hit the landing at the bottom of the stairs and glanced back at me. His strain showed clearly on his face.

"What do you mean? We just have to haul ourselves—"

"The anchor's port has frozen over," Leofa spoke quietly as if to prevent his words from carrying up the stairwell to the boys above. "We can't move the anchor to haul Highfell down, or reel out enough chain to allow us to maneuver clear of the girls' school. Right now, we're dead in the air."

I stared at Leofa, struggling to come to grips with the full extent of our disastrous situation. No parachutes and a frozen anchor chain—the stuff of penny dreadfuls, or nightmares.

"We have to do something," I said. "There must be a way to clear the anchor port of ice."

Leofa nodded and started down the boys' dining hall towards the door.

"It's dangerous," Leofa said when he reached the door.

"More so than crashing into another aetherium and plummeting to the city below?" I inquired.

"Nearly," Leofa replied. "We're going to have to lower the abseiling raft down the outside of the hull and break the ice off the port."

"In this storm?" An abseiling raft was little more than a dingy lashed to the aetherium by two small pulleys. It offered all the protection of a rope swing. In these winds, we'd likely be dashed to pieces against the aetherium's hull before we even reached the anchor port.

Leofa nodded grimly in acknowledgement, no doubt seeing my progression of thoughts revealed on my face. He seemed to share my dread. Leofa gripped the doorknob so hard that his knuckles whitened. Outside the wind wailed and buffeted the walls.

"I can't do it alone." Leofa met my gaze, his expression almost apologetic. "The pulleys require two men—"

"Well, that's why I'm here." I did my best to sound hearty. "Shall we get to it?"

A brief smile curved Leofa's lips. He threw the door open. Together we skidded and slipped across the ice-glazed surface of the deck as the wind hurled cascades of snow down onto us.

Halfway across the deck I stole a glance up into masses of rolling clouds and snow. A strange whine cut through the wind. Alarmed, I realized that the huge gray shadow, sweeping through the walls of white snow overhead, had to be another aetherium. She was nearly on top of us. The storm twisted and muted the shrieks of her alarms to an almost insectile drone.

"Neil!" Leofa called to me and I quickened my pace to keep alongside him.

We reached the abseiling raft quickly, but already my hands felt numb and the tip of my nose might as well as have been a chip of ice.

Shaped like a dinghy, the abseiling raft offered some shelter from the biting wind, and we clambered down into it. Leofa muttered something that sounded like an oath as he worked open the rusty lid of a large metal toolbox stowed in the belly of the raft.

As I leaned over his shoulder I saw that the toolbox brimmed with ice-chipping tools used for routine maintenance. Stuffed between the picks and axes lay several mismatched and battered woolen gloves.

Leofa took two for himself and handed another stained pair over to me. I pulled them on and clenched my hands, trying to work feeling back into my icy fingers.

"Ready?" Leofa shouted over the storm.

I nodded.

Using two of the scraper poles from the toolbox, we pushed off from the deck and skidded across the ice. We heaved the raft over the side and for a sickening instant we fell hard as a stone. My stomach lurched and I felt the blood drain from my face. With a jolt the pulley lines on either end of the raft caught us. Leofa grimaced.

Between us, Leofa and I fed the lengths of spooled ropes out further and descended unevenly. Wind buffeted the raft and twice swept us up from the side of the hull, only to hurl us back against the wood with a resounding crash.

The force shook my entire body. Once I nearly lost my grip on the pulley rope. My arms ached. Despite the biting cold, sweat beaded my shoulders and back, wetting the inside of my coat. At the other end of the raft Leofa worked his rope going hand over hand and snarling something in Hei. He'd never taught me those oaths.

We descended through white walls of ice and snow. At times I could hardly make out the hull of the aetherium directly before me, much less Leofa crouching five feet from me.

Then I glimpsed a great curve of gray metal and ice.

"The anchor port!" I shouted to Leofa, and we both pulled up on our lines taut and then quickly secured the ropes. We scurried to the center of the raft. A massive crust of ice loomed up from the aetherium's hull, entombing both the chain of our anchor and the dark opening of the port that the chain fed out from.

Leofa took up an ice-axe and handed me the other. Side by side we hammered at the ice, breaking away great hunks. With each blow ice chips flew up, stinging my exposed skin.

The raft shook as furious gusts caught it. Leofa and I swayed, but neither of us paused in our assault against the ice. I struck with all my strength and then hurled all my might against the ice again.

Distantly, I thought I could hear a rumble and clang from the interior of the aetherium. Metal groaned and whined. Then suddenly an immense chunk of ice shattered. Ice sprayed out over us as the freed chain clanged up into the hull. The aetherium lurched.

Leofa and I toppled together—caught each other, trying to steady ourselves without encountering an ax blade. For a terrible second we both tottered at the edge of the raft. My heart raced wildly. Leofa's face appeared bloodless with fear.

He clenched his arm around my chest and heaved us both back into the belly of the raft. I landed with the flat of Leofa's ax under my shoulder and my own ax buried in the floor of the raft only a foot from Leofa's head.

"Neil?" Leofa gasped against my ear. His breath felt shockingly warm. "I'm fine."

We lay together, stunned and exhausted. His eyes met mine. He tilted his face toward mine. Our lips were only inches apart. Our frosted breath mingled hotly. The anchor chain continued to grind and clatter up into the aetherium, shaking our raft violently.

"We've got to get back above deck," I said.

Leofa only nodded. Then we both scrambled to our knees. We stowed the axes and then set to the aching labor of hauling ourselves back up the side of the aetherium.

My breath burned and rose in white plumes. The muscles of my arms and back felt like leaden weights as I dragged endless quantities of rope through my hands. Across from me Leofa moved in a steady rhythm. Despite my aching body, I forced myself to keep pace with him. Through clouds and wind we continued to rise.

The roar of the anchor chain dulled, only to be replaced by a new noise. The whine of distant alarms grew louder. Looking over my shoulder, I recognized the fast-growing shadow of the falling aetherium. The girls' school sliced through the churning clouds as it plunged past Highfell. Its gold prow narrowly missed our hull while the bulk of the girls' school kept coming.

"Shit," Leofa said and we both paused at the pulley ropes. We were dangerously close and there was no time to tie the ropes off.

I watched the other aetherium as its sirens grew piercing and the beams of its searchlights struck the surrounding clouds. The aetherium flew at an altitude barely higher than our own. The girls' school, piloted by some brave soul, coasted between other aetheria, barely under control. The white canvas of emergency sails shone in the searchlights like great wings spreading out from the splintered hull.

The girls, their small shapes illuminated by the beams of light, leaped. Dozens of them. White parachutes bloomed in the darkness. Like so many dandelion seeds, they gusted away.

The school's broken anchor chain whipped into sight, lashing behind the school like the tail of an infuriated cat. It swung away and then flicked back towards us.

"No, no, no," Leofa groaned. But we were helpless.

The chain's impact rocked the entirety of Highfell with a wrenching boom. I clung to the pulley ropes as the force jarred through my entire body. Leofa and I bounced with the raft, swinging out from Highfell's hull, only to be slammed back against it.

The second strike knocked the breath from my lungs and my legs slipped under me. I hit the frigid planks of the raft hard, but somehow managed to keep my grip on my pulley rope. The wind roared over me and my ears rang.

"Neil?" Leofa called to me. "Are you…"

"Still here," I assured him as I regained my feet. "Did the chain rupture our hull?"

I could feel my heart pounding as we both craned our heads to take in the damage. A deep gash cut into Highfell's stern. Cobblestones trickled off the deck like grains of salt tumbling from a shaker. Under other circumstances I likely would have been shocked by the sight, but now I felt only immense relief. The damage, though deep, was largely superficial.

Bemused by my own reaction I muttered, "I never thought I'd be so happy to see Highfell look even uglier than ever."

Leofa laughed. I'd never heard a sound so beautiful as that laugh, bright with joy. It made my chest hurt with a pain that made me happy to be alive.

He grinned at me. "What do you say we go back to our palatial rooms upstairs, Your Majesty?"

"Sounds perfect, Lord Blackwater," I replied.

After that, hauling ourselves back on deck seemed like no work at all.

9

After the storm, I confronted Nobbsnipe about the parachutes. Nobbsnipe promised to get them, unctuously, but I knew he'd say anything to make me desist. Shortly afterward Nobbsnipe ordered the boys out to chip the ice from the sides of the aetherium. We lowered the abseiling raft down on chains, which looped around the aetherium's hull. It was horribly like the boys were being keelhauled.

Smalley and Upping seemed exempt from this duty. When I asked after them, Nobbsnipe informed me they'd graduated from the school and had been recruited to work as watchmen for my uncle. I was irritated that no one had told me about this. Why hadn't I been notified? Wasn't I supposed to be in charge of the boys?

Nobbsnipe and Jerome, when I confronted them about this, shrugged and said it wouldn't happen again. But their assurances rang false.

When the boys were winched back up, they offloaded the ice. The Nobbsnipes sold the ice chips to frostmongers, who would in turn sell it to wealthy households for food preservation and ice-a-penny men who would use it to make ice creams. After watching the boys pissing on the ice—it was, quite literally, a pissing contest—I swore I'd never to eat ice cream again. Hooker seemed to find it hilarious that I'd eaten ice cream at all.

Miss Louisa rejoiced in this windfall as it would fund her parents' Herrow-on-Fire party, which celebrated the palace's historic escape from a fire. Louisa seemed oblivious to the near brush with death the storm had brought with it.

At my uncle's discretion, a work gang was flown up to replace the bent girders and to cobble the yard. As the actual mechanisms of the engine had escaped unscathed, we were rather lucky and the principal repairs had to do with maintaining the overall appearance and integrity of the aetherium.

The *Herrow Inquirer* reported that Duchess Sybil's Finishing School had gone down due to a malfunction in their anchor chain.

Luckily, the staff had been able to decrease the aetherium's altitude before it had been blown out of the aetheric current. The aetherium's eventual fall to earth hadn't been from a great height, though twelve teachers and crew had died.

The crash had damaged a factory where aether-powered steamers were built, injuring twenty-seven workers. Several of the girls who'd parachuted had landed in the river and luckily been recovered by the passengers on a commuter river-bus.

After the repairs had finished but a few days later, the Nobbsnipes began preparing for their large party. Roger forced the boys to unload and carry crates filled with ripe oranges, sweet almonds, hams, and many other delights down to the kitchen. It seemed a cruel torture, and I lent my hand to the proceedings to get it over with as soon as possible.

Once up in the garret, we could still hear the boys. The boys, who had cleaned the promenade decks after the work gang had left, were exhausted yet rowdy. So we pretended we could ignore the shouts and thuds as they tormented each other.

Leofa, partially undressed, stretched out on his cot, one arm folded under his head, and gazed up at the ceiling. Illuminated by the candle and half swallowed by the darkness, he looked like he modeled as a young god for a chiaroscuro painting.

I swallowed nervously, tried to think of something to say, and remembered the newspaper I had tucked inside my coat. I removed it, the rough paper warm from my body heat.

"I nabbed you a copy today." I'd been trying to get him the paper whenever I could filch it inconspicuously, because he loved reading it. Also, we'd been papering over the cracks in our room's walls with it.

"Thanks." He accepted it from me and glanced up. "Your new bed is under the drip."

"I thought I—oh, in Loxa's name!" Annoyed, I went over to pick through my bedding. Aside from a fair share of water, a heavy amount of ice had frozen into my blankets' woolen fibers. Although I could've sworn I'd careful about the cot's placement, the aetherium had been shifting in the wind. The cot had slid beneath the drip yet again. This was the third time!

"I should really just bolt it to the floor." I sighed. "Can I sleep with you?"

"Sure." Leofa thumbed through the newspaper casually.

I sat down at the desk and peered out our small window into the darkness. We didn't have shutters, but at least the glass was quite thick. I rifled through my own papers aimlessly, knowing I couldn't get any work done, and I turned my chair so that I faced Leofa. I hadn't planned on saying anything in particular. I'd wished simply to look at him.

"You ever think about leaving?" he asked.

"I can leave whenever I want," I said, dryly, "as long as I'm interested in going to Newland as a farmhand."

"Yeah, I've got my reasons for staying too," he said, but didn't list them. "But you know, if you could go. No consequences. No worrying about anyone else. Everyone's going to be fine if you go. Where'd you go then?"

"I've not…thought about that." I supposed my dreams had been vague. More on the lines of winning back my family's fortune and reputation, either through hard work or sudden academic discovery. Then finishing my doctorate, and going on where I'd left off, though older than in my original plan. But I knew how unrealistic those dreams were—how childish they seemed in retrospect—and this saddened me.

I decided to shift our conversation away from this fruitless inquiry, and I nodded at the stars, which stood crisp and clean in the deepness of the sky. "Look, the Huntress is up."

"The Huntress?" Leofa seemed comfortable with my changing the subject. "*Binhwasl*. Means the same thing in Hei."

"I meant it," I said. "About wanting to learn Hei from you."

"Sure," he said. "But not right now. Get yourself some sleep. You got that big party to attend tomorrow."

"You're right." I pinched out our tallow candle.

I started to undress in the darkness, but then paused uncertainly. I could feel him watching me. His regard made me feel flushed and nervous, but pleasantly so, and I could only hope that my body would not betray me too obviously.

I reached out to the bed, trying to find it in the dark, and encountered his stomach, flat and hard. Leofa laughed, that low noise that filled me with such warmth, and I apologized. I found the edge of the cot and seated myself.

I forced myself remain sitting there longer than necessary, as if the chill in the air could cool my misplaced ardor. I needed to stop thinking like this, as if I were some sort of predator and he my prey. I had to act the gentleman.

I had to stop imagining how it would feel to slide the length of my body across his, to brush my fingers over the coarse hair of his stomach, to feel the pulse of him just there—

This wasn't appropriate.

Leofa leaned up against me companionably, and I felt a real ass for mistaking the desire for human reassurance in this nerve-racking situation for something sexual. I had to control my perversity.

"Come to bed," Leofa murmured.

I lay down with him. I savored how our bodies pressed together, how they lined up so comfortably, that it simply felt natural and right to be lying with him.

I turned away and curled up tightly, as if by making myself smaller and inconspicuous I could hide my desires from myself—and more importantly, from him.

The pipes clanked in the wall beside us as the turbines released a hot spurt of gasses. Snow caressed the roof above us and glistened in starlit whorls outside our window.

Leofa turned onto his stomach, taking up the lion's share of the cot, propped a leg up under my buttocks, and wrapped an arm around me. He splayed his hand out across my stomach…and this certainly led to some intriguing sensations. His fingers curled but an inch or two from my groin and my cock twitched disobediently, as if trying to leap out to meet him.

I shifted around to make myself slightly less comfortable. I could feel his warm breath on my neck, the rise and fall of his chest, as he gripped me more tightly. I listened to the wind whispering outside and resigned myself to a long night filled with many wicked thoughts.

The day of the Nobbsnipes' Herrow-on-Fire party started as well as any other. Leofa left early, giving me time to ease my physical yearning in private before I shaved and went to breakfast. By midmorning I had the boys reviewing the history surrounding the holiday. Herrow-on-Fire commemorated a historic fire which had occurred almost two hundred years ago, reducing much of Herrow to ash.

"But it spared the palace and the royal family," I explained. "And that was when the palace was on the ground."

Roger burst through the door like Demos on a rampage. He said, "In the yard! Everyone line up and strip."

"Again?" If I hadn't seen him routinely harassing young Peggy I would have wondered at Roger's constant demand for young male nudity. Could he think of no other disciplinary measure than that? If not, his idea of punishment probably illustrated more about his secret fears than even he knew.

In the yard, Roger strutted back and forth in front of the boys, his boots crunching over the frost blooming up from between the cobbles. Mentally I counted the watchmen. Roger had assembled the lot. The boys turned blue from the cold.

"An entire cake is gone. An entire cake," Roger snarled.

In the distance, I could hear the musicians practicing for tonight's dance. I stepped forward, down from the steps. "Roger, isn't this an overreaction?"

"An. Entire. Cake. Is. Gone!" Roger ignored me. He thumped each boy with each word as he passed by. He'd already left his mark on them, in the form of dark welts that seemed to swell as I watched. He gritted out, "I. Won't. Give. Up. Until. Someone. Confesses!"

"You've no right to discipline my pupils," I said, my voice tight with fury.

"I won't let disgusting little thieves live under my roof!"

"It isn't your roof," I said. "All of this belongs to my uncle."

Leofa ran into the yard. He skidded to a halt, almost slipping on the ice, and flushed from running. Leofa stared at the tableau—me, Roger, the boys, the watchmen—and he turned pale despite his flushed cheeks. Before he'd arrived, I'd thought Roger's intensity ludicrous, but now I began to have an inkling of his earnestness.

When one of the boys burped, Roger spun around and stalked forward like a dog sniffing out his prey. He stopped in front of them and grinned. He said, "You know who you are, little thief. If you don't step forward now, I'll punish you all."

Hooker, with his big mouth and puppyish enthusiasm, edged forward. I wanted to curse at him, to shake him for this childish show of bravery. Hooker said, "I did it, sir! It was me. I sneaked down last night. It was delicious."

Roger grabbed him by the hair, wrenching him around and pushed him down so that the boy's head pressed near his knees. He glanced at me. Roger said, "You know, I do believe he did it. Come on. Let's get this over with, boy."

"Wait—" I seized Roger's shoulder. "You can't—"

He said, "Get your hand off me. Now."

I released him, feeling cold with fear for Hooker and deeply humiliated.

"Roger, wait." Leofa seemed relaxed as he stepped forward, even casual. "I was in charge of Hooker."

Roger strode up to Leofa, the ivory-headed cane clenched in one fist, Hooker dangling from the other. Roger paused, flexing his fingers around the cane. For an instant, I thought he would strike Leofa.

"Let me punish him instead," Leofa said quietly.

I felt all of my muscles clench, hearing that, as though my body rebelled at the thought of even witnessing such a thing. It seemed like the antithesis of everything I knew to be true.

"I don't think so." Roger shook his head. "Stealing is against the Good Writ, you know. And 'suffering in this life lessens suffering in the next.'"

Roger dragged Hooker away. Jerome and the watchmen fell in behind him. The other boys scooted over to their clothes, fumbling and dressing. I followed after Roger, determined to stop this, but Leofa caught my shoulder. He leaned in and commented tensely in my ear, "Don't do it. Don't."

"I wasn't—" I turned around to face him.

"Roger won't hurt Hooker badly. The child is too valuable to the school. I promise. Please don't do anything stupid. Roger'd like the excuse to go after you."

"It would not be so easy as that!" I said hotly.

"You wouldn't be the first he's killed," Leofa said, his voice flat. His eyes were calm, his hand clenching around my shoulder. I searched his face, hoping he joked, because if Roger had truly killed anyone, surely he would have gone to jail? Surely this could not be true?

But if it were true, I could not allow him to simply carry Hooker away. I shoved Leofa's hand aside and followed Roger.

"For fuck's sake," Leofa muttered. He fell in behind me as I dogged

Roger and his prey through the busy kitchen, the engine room, and down into the bilge.

The water in the bilge tank stank and glistened darkly with machine oil. By now, it had already been run through the turbines as coolant and remained as ballast.

Leofa stopped beside me. From behind I could hear the other boys gathering. I could hear their shuffles and fearful mutters. But no one dared stop Roger when he had the watchmen on his side.

Roger shoved Hooker's head beneath the filthy water.

I watched numbly, my horror and outrage overwhelmed by my new knowledge. Roger, a murderer. It did not fit the world as I understood it. I had dined with him. The sound of Roger's grunts, the boy gagging, the stink of the bilge, the hum of the turbines above us, it nauseated me with its realness.

Roger went on longer than I thought possible, until the boy vomited up water and cake through his nose into the bilge tank.

My heart stuttered in my chest. Inadvertently, I pushed toward the scene. But Leofa clenched a hand over my shoulder, silently telling me to wait.

What if Leofa was wrong? What if Roger meant to kill this boy right before us?

Roger hauled Hooker up. Hooker hung limp as a drowned cat.

"See the wages of sin!" Roger gloated.

Hooker whirled and slammed his foot into Roger's groin. Roger dropped him. Hooker paused over Roger's hunched form. He shouted out, "You can—you can go—go eat a dick!"

Hooker bolted away. No one laughed. No one moved. Inside, I felt like cheering. But I did not. Roger gradually straightened up and glared at us. Still, no one even coughed. His eyes fixed on me, bright with hatred, and but then he looked at Jerome. Roger said, "What're you standing there for? Go get your watchmen and get that little motherfucker!"

With that, everyone scrambled away. If Jerome caught Hooker first, Hooker would get the beating of a lifetime.

The other boys scattered in front of the watchmen, blocking their paths and obscuring Hooker's escape.

Leofa hurled a pursuing watchman to the ground, swearing.

I charged past Leofa, sprinting up the stairs after Hooker. I had to ascertain whether Hooker had been injured and to protect him from Jerome.

Hooker scampered up the spiral staircases with the agility of a monkey.

I ran after him, following him upstairs, through the dining room, and out into the courtyard. He fled across the cobbled expanse into the starboard hall's staff room.

I pushed through the open door after him. Not one watchman guarded the starboard hall—Roger had brought them all when dunking Hooker and apparently none had regained their posts. I saw a flash of motion. Hooker scuttled up the staircase and shot through the door, leaving it ajar in his wake.

At the top of the stairs I paused before the door. An open blood-lock dangled as if it were a spider waiting for its prey. The metal glistened as if malevolent. One touch of the metal spines and I could be dead.

I heard voices behind me. Jerome searched the courtyard, bellowing out threats.

I slid through the gap into the forbidden.

I halted almost immediately, stricken with shock, incredulity, and awe.

The vaulted workshop was ringed around with an upper gallery where glass showcases flaunted a wealth of grimoires. Dozens, perhaps even hundreds of leather-bound spines glittered with gemstones and gilt. These showcase windows, glass embedded with nets of en-spelled wires, glimmered blue with the light of protective spells.

A brass ladder led to the upper gallery. The lower floor had large polished tables on it, many scarred and blackened. The sturdy chairs had charred sacking thrown over their backs.

In one protected stone-lined corner was a small forge with a hood. Its pipes went into the wall, no doubt so that the smoke could escape via one of the school's exhaust pipes.

The opposite corner had what looked like a small chemist's lab, with labeled beakers of chemicals locked into glass cabinets. There was an array of burners, retorts, and tubes set out on a broad square workspace. Shimmering agents traced neon paths throughout tubes, sparkling as they percolated along, their multi-hued lights hinting at some sort of intricate chemical magic at work.

Other cabinets, cupboards, and chests lined the walls, no doubt containing more tools of the trade. A heavy metal vault stood beside them.

What unspeakable wealth! I had never seen so many grimoires in my life, not even in Elmstead's graduate labs, and looking upon bound spine after bound spine imbued even me with superstitious nervousness.

Hooker had swung up the brass ladder to the upper gallery. He startled a tracker into flight. Other trackers, dozens of them, crawled along the gallery's polished rails, their dragonfly bodies flashing copper, their oiled leather wings iridescent with live aether. Perhaps they presented an evacuation route for the grimoires if anything threatened the aetherium.

Stanley sat at a table close to broad multi-paned windows. Pained, Stanley had tightly clenched his eyes shut. His blue iolite goggles pushed up his hair. He leaned forward, his elbows braced to either side of the most girlish grimoire I'd ever seen. And he held his swollen hands out at an odd angle.

"What in Iskar's name is going on here?" I asked.

"Mr. Franklin!" Stanley opened his eyes and gazed at me in an expression of what seemed like unadulterated horror. Varnish-scented smoke drifted up from the singed tabletop around Stanley's grimoire. He said, "You're not allowed to be in here! How did you even get in here? Nobbsnipe never leaves the door open! You have to leave immediately."

"Where did you get all of these grimoires?" I demanded.

Hooker peered down from an upper gallery, with black machine grease from his bilge-water dunking streaking his face. He hopped up on the rail, his arms out, and sent the flock of trackers swooping through the air.

"We're cracking them!" he announced.

The trackers flashed brightly around me. The metallic whirr of them vibrated the air.

"I'm the best there is. Except for Leofa. I did almost ten of them by myself," Hooker bragged. "But Stanley can't even crack open that girly thing!"

"Don't you know how illegal this is?" I said. Hadn't anyone ever explained to him that these had been stolen from the queen? "You could hang!"

Stanley turned a dark red and hunkered down behind his swollen hands. He looked ashamed, almost to the point of agony.

"Like the queen's men are ever going to catch me, when not even Roger can," Hooker scoffed. "Hey! Did you see how I got him? It was good, huh!"

I regarded him. My heart sank in my chest, weighed by an emotion that wavered on the cusp between pity and fear for these boys.

Leofa rushed into the room. He stopped when he saw me, as still as a man trapped in the stocks. "Neil. We have to get you out of here."

Below I heard the sound of raised voices. The watchmen had returned to their staffroom, still searching for Hooker. Jerome shouted something. Footsteps thudded on the stairs.

Hooker grinned. He jumped down from the railing, landed on a table, ran to the window, and hied himself out. He pushed the window shut behind him before clambering away.

Leofa opened a closet, pushed aside some rolled-up maps, and held out his hand to me. He said, "Come on."

Although the need for self-preservation tangled with my anger at Leofa, the will to live won out. I crammed myself into the closet with Leofa. I would not have considered it large enough to be a proper broom closet.

It would've been a tight fit for one, but with the both of us, the only way I could avoid our knees knocking involved straddling one of his legs. We were pressed hip-to-hip, my face against his shoulder. He hunched down around me, his face against my neck.

"Where'd he go?"

Jerome's voice filtered through the closet door. Floorboards creaked as he stepped into the room.

"Who?" Stanley asked.

"Hooker, the little sod."

"Isn't he out in the yard with Roger?" Stanley asked.

"What're you still doing here?" Jerome demanded.

"Because Nobbsnipe told me to finish this, or else," Stanley said grimly. "You know Nobbsnipe doesn't like it when you're up here."

"Then he shouldn't have left the door open," Jerome said. "You think you're going to tell him about that little lapse?"

Silence. Jerome's footsteps ranged around the room, heavy and predatory. He came toward us. Something about this situation seemed unreal, like a game of hide-and-seek gone awry.

I pressed my face into Leofa's chest as if that could muffle the sound of my breathing. I could feel the thudding of his heart, the heat of him with my lips.

Jerome's footsteps paused. Floorboards creaked again. He stood directly in front of the closet where we hid.

"There's a hidden lock on that." Stanley's voice sounded bored. He said, "Open it at your own risk."

Jerome snorted, as though he didn't believe Stanley, but he didn't search the closet. He turned and walked away. "You should report to Nobbsnipe about your pretty book. He'll want to know how badly you fucked it up."

I heard the sound of retreating footsteps as Stanley wordlessly followed Jerome out of the room. The door shut with a click and left us in ringing silence.

We remained in the closet, as if we could not believe, could not be sure, that we were alone in this room. I pressed too close to Leofa, so close that he could surely feel how I shook.

Although out of immediate danger, Leofa did not release me. He straightened, smoothing his hands down my back.

"It's all right," he whispered. "You're fine now."

Warring emotions paralyzed me. I wanted him. Yet I feared him— and I held Leofa in contempt for what he allowed to happen to the boys. And at the same time I had the urge to do things that I knew were totally unacceptable, that were not permissible under any circumstances, especially these. I wanted more from him than I should.

I pushed free of the cupboard. I panted as though I'd run a hard race, and I turned to face him. It felt so disorienting to be standing surrounded by broken grimoires, as though I should've been someone else entirely. I wished that I were.

"Neil, you don't understand..." Leofa ran his hands through his silky dark hair.

I watched him uncertainly. I said, "No, I don't think I do."

"You have no idea. You're so…" Leofa stepped much too close to me now and a delicious unease kept me there. He reached out, slowly, to give me time to step away, but I did not. Yet the instant our skin made contact, his hand stroking my cheek, shock prompted me to pull back.

Leofa withdrew as soon as I did. He didn't apologize. Leofa didn't say a word. But I knew I'd done so much wrong in those few seconds I couldn't contemplate it all. I felt awful. I sank back against the cupboard. I trembled with self-loathing and desire.

"We have to find Hooker," I said.

Leofa turned away from me with a frustrated sigh. "Yeah, I know. He'll probably be back in the dormitory by now. We have to leave. You can't be found up here. Nobbsnipe'll be back here in a minute to take a look at Stanley's latest failure."

I glanced inadvertently at the outlandishly feminine lavender grimoire, studded with pearls and encircled with char. I asked, "What kind of grimoire is that?"

"A grimoire for ladies' spells. One color coordinates your cat with your evening wear. Another fixes lapdog breath. There's one called 'Never Tipsy' that keeps you from wobbling on your heels no matter how drunk you get." Leofa's mouth twisted wryly. "We can't go out through the staff room."

In the end, we dropped down from the windows onto the deck below. The slippery ice made our landing difficult, and I wrenched my knee, but did myself no real damage. No windows but those of the empty workshop above overlooked us where we stood between the stone edifice and the drop three feet away, giving us the illusion of an odd privacy. A rising wind spat ice and snow across our skins.

"I want to explain," Leofa said.

"Well, how can you possibly countenance exploiting children like this, using them to perpetrate criminal activities? Boys younger than this have been hung for stealing purses—and they're working on grimoires stolen from the queen! How can you let this go on?"

"Is that what you think I'm doing here?" He recoiled as if my words stung.

I crossed my arms, nodding up at the workshop above. "How else can you describe what happens there?"

"I'm protecting these boys," Leofa growled. "Without me, they'd be thrown away. Greater villains are at work here."

"Oh yes?" I asked.

"Yes. I keep them safe—"

"Not all of them."

Leofa's jaw clenched with anger. "That was uncalled for."

"And the rest of them are kept as slaves."

Leofa seized my arm. "You don't know what you're talking about."

"Don't I finally?" I shook free. "If you please, I have the Nobbsnipes' odious party to attend. We will discuss this later."

10

The Nobbsnipes' Herrow-on-Fire soiree had been—by their standards—a smashing success. I'd represented myself plainly, the new schoolteacher engaged in charity work, a lord, a coup for a party filled with middle-class tradesmen. I'd entertained them by playing the piano duet I'd been working on with Louisa, stunned them with my manners, and had given them something to laugh at with my threadbare suit.

Outside the Nobbsnipes' residence, the temporarily hired servants had decorated the courtyard with artfully trimmed potted evergreens, a colorful stone garden, and carved ice sculptures. All of which brutally mimicked the more sophisticated gardens above.

Beneath the small red-striped pavilion and beside the glowing braziers, I'd eaten spiced nuts and fortified my sense of humor with more than a few rum toddies. After the fireworks from the city below and the aetheria above had petered out sometime past midnight, I'd made my excuses and returned to the garret.

Leofa awaited me there, seated on the cot and illuminated by our solitary candle. I wondered if he'd seen the fireworks at all. He ran his hands through his dark hair, apparently nervous, and glanced up at me.

"So." I shut the hatch to the garret quietly. Perhaps the rum toddies made me ask so directly: "How to you plan to make this right?"

"What?" he asked.

Leofa clearly expected to have a different conversation.

"You must know that you cannot continue to endanger these boys and still call yourself a good man," I said, employing the idea that drunkenness made personal criticism reasonable. "How do you plan to rectify this situation?"

"Come on, Neil." Leofa sounded impatient. "Can't you see that there's nothing we can do?"

"Nonsense." I waved his defeatism aside. I said, "What I can't do anything about is my debt. I'm going to have to live with that for the rest of my life. This could be solved with a single letter to the authorities."

I liked the idea of an anonymous tip off—as though we lived a penny dreadful—but maybe I'd given the rum toddies too much say in this discussion.

Leofa said, "You really are naïve. Do you really think the authorities are going to believe that Nobbsnipe is the mastermind? I'd be the first to hang."

I considered this and could find no good answer. I realized I needed to know everything.

"How do you come by the grimoires?" I asked.

"Jerome gets them from some lord," Leofa said. "At first I thought it was your uncle, this being his property and all, but now I'm not so sure."

"Why is that?"

"Well, because you're not in on it." Leofa smiled ruefully. "Which is strange, with you being family."

"I'm not related to Uncle Gerard by blood," I said. "But I can see your point."

"Nobbsnipe tracks down people he knows to be bastards, or suspects that they are, and convinces their guardians that Highfell is a golden opportunity for advancement. Once they're here, Nobbsnipe tests them."

"To see which grimoires the boy's blood will open, I presume," I finished.

"Yeah. It's handy enough, when a boy's blood opens a tome no trouble, but after that, they only keep on the boys who're good enough to crack the other grimoires as well."

I asked, "Wouldn't it be easier to simply keep the boys with useful blood?"

"You don't have to keep a boy to keep his blood," Leofa said. "We've vials and vials of blood to work with, and it only takes a drop to open up a tome."

I thought about the boys, illegitimate all, and how bright they were. How clever with their hands they all were. How easily they learned what I'd seen my own classmates spend months struggling with, and I was awed.

Her Royal Majesty's government confiscated criminals' grimoires and claimed any grimoire without a bloodline. I'd hoped, in school, that I would end up in the cracking laboratories, trying to decipher recently unbound pages that no one had yet dared to read. If I thought about it, Leofa lived my own dream in a debased way.

"How many tomes do you have in the workshop?" I asked.

"More than fifty. At least. Probably closer to seventy, if you count all the pieces."

"Is my family's grimoire here as well?"

"Well, what does it look like?" Leofa said.

I could visualize it clearly. My mother, her lovely face candlelit and serene as she had lifted it from its locked display case, unchained it from the wall, and cradled it in her hands. How I had loved that grimoire while growing up.

"It's bound in emerald green leather that's tooled with vines. The flowers and buds are semi-precious gems. I always wished I could inherit it," I said wistfully, "but since it's matrilineal—"

"Wait, it's matrilineal?" Leofa said. He looked like he wanted to smack his own forehead with his hand, but instead he just shook his head. "No wonder I haven't been able to crack it! I've been working the lock in the wrong order! Wyrd, I feel like an idiot! That should've occurred to me weeks ago. Matrilineal, but eh, they're *rare*."

I stared at him. He seemed to realize it, and then he laughed.

"Sorry, professional pride," Leofa said. "I can usually crack a grimoire maybe two months at tops, but this little lady has been really tough. It's driving me crazy! And it's been getting me pretty good, as you can see. That bloodlock burns."

I contemplated him. He had to be very good at his work. I knew some grimoires that had been in Her Majesty's libraries when the laboratories had been founded, and they still hadn't been cracked fifty years later. I'd heard that the average time for cracking a grimoire stood in the range of five years, not months.

I related what I knew of the queen's laboratories to Leofa, who compared them to what he actually did. Contrasting the methodology proved fascinating for both of us.

As we spoke, I sobered up and weariness from the long day weighed upon me. I longed for sleep to descend and cleanse away today's complications. I wanted to forget that dire scene in the court-yard, the discovery of the workshop, the fight I'd had with Leofa, and the noxious party. I didn't want to think about the discussion that had allowed me to work out exactly how deeply in trouble we were. Even as I desired this ignorant bliss, I knew I would never trade away any knowledge.

"Come here." Leofa stood, moved the desk chair, and then shifted the cheap little desk aside with ease. He pushed open the window. He repeated, "Come here. I want to show you something."

I considered refusing out of sheer tiredness. Leofa watched me closely. But the expression of expectation on his face prompted me to smile.

"Well then. Lead on, Lord Blackwater." I tried to sound more irritable than I was. Leofa smiled. His eyes lit up. His obvious happiness made me suddenly breathless and created an echo of unwanted warmth within me.

Leofa squeezed his shoulders through the narrow window and then grabbed at a dangling rope. Before I could blink, he scooted out the window and climbed up, feet braced against the side of the building.

"Follow me," he called.

I peered out the window. Below, the cobbled promenade glimmered with ice. Heights did not terrify me—nor did they to anyone who'd lived in aetheria as long as I had—but it seemed positively dangerous to climb the rope in such ice and cold. Yet I didn't want Leofa to think me a coward.

I leaned out and tugged on the rope. It seemed secure enough. Suddenly a thought occurred to me. What I'd learned about Leofa gave me the power to injure him—as well as the boys. He had managed to convince me not to write that letter to the authorities, but what if he felt he could not take a chance on me? Leofa did have the boys to think of.

If Leofa had planned to kill me to conceal his crimes, this would be his opportunity. But I did not want to believe him capable of murder. Now one question hung within me. Did I trust him?

Wyrd knew I had little reason to, given his criminality. And yet I could not believe that he would harm me. If he planned to do that, he would have given me up to Jerome in the workshop.

I closed my eyes, offering up a prayer to the gods I did not believe in, particularly Loxa, the goddess who loved fools, and then I started out the window.

Terror becomes irrelevant when one must focus on the task at hand. To do anything else would be insane.

I concentrated on bracing my feet against the building and moving hand over hand up the rope, stepping up along the side of the building. The bitterly cold wind whistled around me, tugged at my coat, and made the tense rope buzz in my hands. I sensed the distance below me to the ground much as I would a monster's gaping mouth. Was my heart pounding like mad? Or had it stopped altogether? In either case, it couldn't be healthy.

I encountered the eaves. I managed to both step and hunch over it. I clambered onto the slate-tiled roof.

In the ambient light radiating from Herrow below and the aetheria above, I could see that Leofa sat cross-legged near the apex of the roof. I picked my way up the gentle slope and sat down by his side. He had a plate on his knee and proffered a wine bottle.

When I took it, I found the glass oddly warm to the touch.

"It's only tea," he explained.

I took a swig. It had been sweetened with treacle, rather than honey. I handed it back and looked down at the plate. "Is that—"

"The cake Hooker stole?" Leofa laughed. "Yeah, he saved us some."

"How wonderfully pilfered," I said appreciatively. The two cake slices were beautiful with candied ginger, rose petals, and gold leaf artfully decorating it. I'd refused to partake of any of the sweets at the party because Roger's actions had sickened me so. But now I found myself eager to eat.

Leofa shared it out and we ate the rich almond-orange cake with our hands in silence. To one side, I saw the water-intake valves that led down to the rain tank; the slate tiles there looked razor-sharp. On our other side, the exhaust pipes also spewed hot vapor.

A few late fireworks blossomed, shuddering the air with their thunder. Startled birds that roosted on the aetheria took flight, swirling in confusion. Gunpowder, smoke, and the metallic scent of the aetheric turbines' exhaust gusted around us. Small snowflakes spiraled through the air.

I finished up my cake. "Please don't crack my grimoire. The process will destroy it."

"Neil, now that I know it's yours…" Leofa passed me the tea. "Look, I'll tell the boys we're stalling on it."

"It's been stolen, clearly," I mused aloud. "I need to inform my uncle. I'm sure that, once I explain the situation, we'll be able to recover the grimoire without any problems."

The more I thought about it, the better this idea seemed.

"Uncle Gerard owns Highfell. Naturally, he will behave with discretion regarding the stolen grimoires. He can have the Nobbsnipes and their lackeys removed from the school quietly, without involving the law. With such measures, you and the boys would be safe from any charges of treason."

"You're sure he's not in on it?" Leofa asked.

"No." I shook my head. "Certainly not. The fact that our grimoire is here as much as proves that. He has my sister as his ward. He could ask her to open the grimoire at any time, and I'm sure she would oblige him."

The logic behind this pleased me. I disliked Uncle Gerard, especially after he'd struck me. But I couldn't imagine a man of his wealth and standing risking all to become embroiled in a crime of this enormity.

I thrummed still with euphoria from my climb. Perhaps this—or a lingering influence from the rum toddies—caused me to act so unusually bold. Golden fireworks boomed out above, belatedly, and illuminated us brightly. I reached up and touched Leofa's dark hair. So black and fine, like jet made into silk by some alchemy. His lips parted slightly.

I leaned up and kissed him as though nothing could be easier. He tasted like treacle, oranges, and almonds. Leofa groaned against my mouth, pushed me back down on the roof, and pinned me with his weight. The kiss overwhelmed me—and I had no doubt that he shared my interest. His need pressed against my thigh, hot even through the layers of clothing between us.

I'd known that I'd wanted him, but I would have never been able to stay away so long had I known how good this could be.

His obvious arousal removed my last shreds of compunction and I gripped Leofa tightly across his shoulders, twining a foot around his.

I savored the play of his muscles under his clothes, the very shape of him.

His lips were soft and his skin was rough with stubble, a contrast in textures that invigorated me. He teased my mouth open gently with his teeth. When our tongues touched, it felt electric. I gasped, and Leofa laughed softly, that deep sound that I loved so, and then he kissed my neck, nipping my ear. I wanted to beg him for more, but I did not even know what to beg for.

All at once, we suddenly began to slide down the tiled roof. He grabbed the roof's ridge and held us in place.

Now I laughed softly, somewhere between relieved and disappointed that we'd been interrupted, because I'd had no idea what to do after this.

Leofa flipped over onto his back. He sighed, a contented noise.

The air seared me with its cold and I missed his closeness already. If I had even imagined this earlier, I would have suspected myself of feeling repentance, guilt, and shame after such a kiss. But instead I could only think that it had been perfect. I wanted to feel his skin on mine. I wanted to touch every inch of Leofa.

What was I thinking? Not an hour before I had despised him. When I'd climbed up to join him here, I had considered the possibility that he could murder me to preserve his secrets.

"I'm sorry," I said. "I didn't mean to impose."

Leofa huffed a sigh. His tone, when he spoke, carried with it both impatience and resignation. "You weren't."

"Oh." I quieted, trying to discern exactly what he'd meant by that.

"Look. You got to figure this out." He pushed himself up and leaned back on his hands. "I'll be around. I do live with you, right? Now, let's go inside before that rope ices over."

"I hope my bed isn't under the drip again," I muttered. If I had to lie beside him, I didn't know what I'd end up doing.

"Sadly," Leofa said, laughing, "it's not."

⌒

The next morning, I determined to relate all to my uncle—well, not those portions pertaining to Leofa and I—but on all other counts I intended to come clean. To do that, though, I would have to begin with a lie.

Nobbsnipe said, "Your uncle sent for you, you say?"

"Yes, the message arrived this morning by tracker," I said politely. "He will reimburse you for my passage."

Nobbsnipe seemed perturbed by this but said nothing.

I ventured to keep the conversation going. "How are Frank Smalley and Yorick Upping settling in? I assume I'll see them, when I go to visit my uncle. It took me quite aback, you see, that you'd reassigned my students without my knowledge."

"Pardon?" Nobbsnipe said. "Oh, yes, I'm sure they're doing well. They've been posted…to a country estate, I believe, so I doubt you will see them unless you're flown out to Thornshire."

"The aerophaeton should arrive soon," Miss Louisa said. She had gone up to the signaling tower to summon one at my request, slightly to her parents' disgruntlement.

"Oh, do you think so?" I said. Disappointment spread through me. I wouldn't have the time to filch anything from the Nobbsnipes' table, much less to distribute my takings. Increasingly, I only appeared for breakfast in order to secrete away tidbits for the boys. I truly enjoyed stealing from these people.

"Hmmph," Nobbsnipe grumbled. "You know what this about? Seems sudden."

I would have liked to excuse myself, perhaps to search for Leofa. Last night had been a restless night, sleeping apart in our separate cots, and he'd left sometime before dawn. But, before I could make my excuses to pursue him, Peggy came in to announce that the aerophaeton had arrived and awaited me on the landing deck. I bowed and then left via the front door.

Outside, in the courtyard, the temporary staff that the Nobbsnipes had hired for their Herrow-on-Fire bash packed the ornamental silk plants into crates. The former paradise stood half disassembled and in disarray. Out past the windbreak on the landing deck, the aerophaeton had already been turned around for takeoff.

I'd never ridden in an aerophaeton before—a massive six-seater with double wings—and this vehicle-for-hire had clearly seen better days. The silk wings had faded from a deep violet to lavender on the upper sides. The body had been repainted black to hide a crest, but the edges of the ancient gilt glimmered through the paint. This hinted that it had once been a family vehicle, but had been sold and retasked. The turbine at the vehicle's nose looked large and unwieldy.

On the journey out, I stared down at the winding streets in the city below and thought of Leofa. He'd been gone this morning when I woke. Now I wondered what it had been like for him. How young had he been when Nobbsnipe lured him away? What dreams had Leofa cherished before life in Highfell Hall? Somehow I couldn't imagine him wanting to join Vernon in pig farming.

At the airfield, I paid for a hansom to take me to the western end of Knave's Court. The Tremont Reform Club was a modest four-storey brick townhouse with only a brass plate on the door bearing its name. When I knocked, a doorman with a soldierly build answered.

I handed him my card with a brief smile. "Please inform my uncle, Lord Gerard Franklin, that I am here."

After studying my card, the doorman gave me a dubious look. "You don't meet the dress requirement, sir."

I looked down at my garments, concerned, and realized I wore no cravat. The last of my cravats had been damaged in the ice storm when that girls' school had gone down.

The doorman had to lend me one of the clubs' cravats, which had shockingly ugly with red, brown, and orange checkers. Once I had knotted on my badge of humiliation, my awareness of my clothes, last year's fashion and shabby to boot, prickled at me.

Showing me into a modest reception room done in cherry wood, the doorman offered me refreshments and tobacco to occupy me during my wait. I declined both. Ten minutes later, the doorman showed me into the dining room.

Uncle Gerard breakfasted. The fare on his table was sumptuous by my standards, though once I perhaps would not have considered it so: rolls, jellies and anchovy paste, sculpted butter crusted with sugar, liver, pickled salmon, salted tongue, pork pie, muffins, bread, boiled eggs, goat cheese, sausage, baked haddock, and oranges. And thank Wyrd, coffee.

Spreading anchovy paste across his breadroll, Uncle Gerard asked, "Did you invite yourself here for any reason in particular?"

He did not ask me to sit, which didn't surprise me, considering how we'd last parted company. I gazed with longing at the porcelain coffee pot.

"I wanted to apologize," I said, my love of coffee lending sudden inspiration. "I'm afraid I may've…drunk a little too much at my sister's birthday and spoiled it for everyone. I truly am sorry for my behavior at your townhouse—as well as for the behavior of the man I brought along. I'm afraid I borrowed him from the Nobbsnipes. I'd no idea he'd such a temper. I do hope that ruckus didn't cause too much trouble in the end?"

"Not at all. Not at all," said my uncle gruffly as he poured himself some coffee. "I should've been a more attentive host on Nora's birthday. You young people worked yourselves up and I wish I'd been able to get in there and defuse the situation earlier. But now you've learned, haven't you, never to bring a creature like that into a world for which he is not suited?"

I didn't bristle—externally, at least—at my uncle calling Leofa "a creature." I had to get through this conversation without offending him. Instead, I accepted his words with a quiet nod and a murmured, "Indeed."

"You ought to endeavor to avoid drink, I believe. Particularly in light of your father's weaknesses."

"Quite." Rage burned within me, but I forced it down, focusing on my task.

"Is that all?" Uncle Gerard asked.

"It's all that I came for," I said. "But while I'm here I wondered if you could spare a few minutes to talk about Highfell Hall."

At this Uncle Gerard glanced up sharply. "Have a seat then. We can discuss the school after breakfast."

I seated myself across from him, served myself from his broad selection, and ate heartily in spite of my recent breakfast with the Nobbsnipes. I drank some coffee while he chatted about recent events. I related the drama of the girls' school going down, which impressed and entertained him. I did not hurry my uncle or speak at all of Nora.

After he'd concluded his meal, he took me upstairs to his small suite. In addition to a brass plate reading G. Franklin, he had a bloodlock on his door.

The bloodlock was in an older style, a sterling silver box the size of the palm of my hand. It was inscribed artfully with knotwork and prickling with needles. With a casual gesture, my uncle pressed a finger onto one of the needles, a drop of blood ran down its length, and sparked when it hit the bloodlock. His door popped open.

"You can't have too much security," he said. "It's a premium service, you know."

"I would think so," I agreed.

I revised my intentions to tell him about the grimoires. The bloodlock on his door brought him into question. Could Uncle Gerard—and not Nobbsnipe—control Highfell? I wished I knew for certain. With Nora in his care, I knew I had to err on the side of caution. I had to test him, to determine exactly where he stood without letting slip what I knew.

Uncle Gerard showed me into his suite, which consisted of a small but luxuriously appointed sitting room, study, and bedroom. The walls were all paneled with mahogany. Although the windows in his sitting room stretched broadly across the wall, he'd smothered them in green curtains and his suite gave the overall impression of a dimly lit trap.

He offered me champagne or a sherry, but I declined. I feared it would go to my head. I wanted all my wits about me.

My uncle said, "Before we get to Highfell, tell me, what did you think of Lord Slackleigh? I believe, before everyone got ruffled, that you two had quite the chat about archaeology."

"Is that so? I can hardly remember." I sat and absently examined the small daguerreotype standing on the table beside me. It was a yellowing image of a beautiful young woman, who by the look of her old-fashioned gown and jewels, must have been quite wealthy.

I found something about the set of her lips, the easy serenity in her shoulders, oddly familiar. I wondered, vaguely, who she was and why my uncle had this woman's image here. Then I set picture aside.

"Lord Slackleigh was in high spirits," I said finally. "I am… I do not suppose we have much in common by way of temperament, but he has donated much to the museum."

"You should see his private collection some time," my uncle said. "I think you'd enjoy it very much. He has some astonishing pieces there. He had a whole gate from a fallen city shipped and set up as a garden folly. I'm sure I could arrange a time for you two to visit, if you'd like to take a look at it."

"I would be interested in knowing what he has," I said, conservatively.

"It would be no trouble at all to arrange a visit. I'll speak to him about it."

"Are Frank Smalley and Yorick Upping working with you well?"

"Who?" Uncle Gerard eyed me blankly.

"Frank Smalley and Yorick Upping," I said. "Weren't they sent out at your behest to work as watchmen? I hope they're doing well in their new posts. Though in the future, I would like to receive some sort of notification if you've found a place for one of my students."

My uncle seemed to remember. "Ah, yes. I can see what you mean. I'll send you a letter the next time. You can hardly keep discipline if you don't know where they are!"

I found myself fairly sure, despite my uncle's words, that he had no idea whatsoever who these boys were or where they'd gone.

"Speaking of Highfell," he said, "I've been looking into a few things since you sent me that note, and I'm afraid we might have a real problem on our hands. I never thought, sending you to Highfell, that it would be like this."

"My note?" I asked. At first confusion dominated, but then I understood. "Oh, you mean my request for school supplies? I must thank you, sir. They were a great boon to me and the boys."

"Yes, yes, quite so," he said. "But the problem is, the boys should've had those things already. I charged the Nobbsnipes with buying them before your arrival, and it seems they hadn't."

"Ah. I think I understand." I tried to assemble these puzzle pieces. Uncle Gerard was hardly a perfect savior or philanthropist, accepting money for hiding away the peers' bastards as he did. But he also did seem to want to give these boys a good education and a good start in life.

But the Nobbsnipes had taken advantage of my uncle's goodwill and fortunes; stealing all from the boys so that they might have more, even selling shit for pennies. They were embezzlers and close-minded bigots, sadists of the worst kind.

Perhaps the bloodlock on his door was nothing more than a coincidence.

"Unfortunately, I cannot simply dismiss Barnabas Nobbsnipe for embezzling at this point," my uncle said.

"Whyever not?" Disappointment did not begin to describe my feelings on this matter. "Uncle, you say they are criminals. Let the police find the evidence. You're a lord in good standing. Upon your accusation, these embezzlers would be arrested and investigated. The Nobbsnipes are doing the boys harm. At the very least, the Nobbsnipes would be no longer able to inflict any injury upon my charges."

"Neil, I cannot," he said, sadly. "If I had the Nobbsnipes removed without first acquiring the funds to hire new staff at the school, there would be no school. I would have to ground it. If you were under-staffed and a storm took the aetherium by surprise, well, that does not bear thinking! With the school closed, you would no longer have a place as their teacher and they would have nowhere to live. Would you see them on the street?"

As most of them had living kin, "on the street," seemed an exaggeration. But I did not argue that point.

"Certainly it cannot be so hard to find replacements. I can easily see to the running of the school myself," I countered instead. "I'm certain I can find new staff. One of the students, young Stanley, is already qualified enough to teach the young children. I would forego my wages—"

"Absolutely not, Neil. Think of the scandal. My reputation would be irrevocably damaged by any such action. Alerting the police... It would like using a hammer to do a needle's work. You must swear to me now that you will not involve them."

I leaned back. I thought about confronting Uncle Gerard on this. My thoughts reversed again. Fear of the authorities was plain in his eyes. Much as I did not want to believe it, I had to see that he'd involved himself not only with hiding away illegitimate sons but also the gri-moire-cracking operation.

"And what would become of you," he said, "to be associated with embezzlers? Surely it would finish your academic career and dirty your already tarnished reputation."

Suddenly, I felt as though I walked on the edge of a precipice. Was my uncle threatening me? Or just trying to frighten me? A single word, a misplaced phrase, I realized, and it could be my doom—and the doom of others.

I thought about my sister, in his house and under his control. The boys, kidnapped and isolated, were his prisoners. Leofa, his longtime employee, if abandoned to the law and charged with treason, would be hung.

This decided me. I could not let my uncle know that I was not the high-minded popinjay he thought I was.

"Sir," I said, "I think I understand your meaning. I swear to you that I will do my best to sort this out—subtly, of course—for we would not want to tip our hand to the Nobbsnipes. I stand, as ever, with my family."

"Good." He granted me a thin smile. "You're a good lad, Cornelius."

I stood to shake his hand, when he offered. Then he affectionately brushed my shoulders with the palm of his hand, tugging on jacket seam. The cloth here had been rubbed thin and shiny. I flushed with embarrassment.

Uncle Gerard smiled, patted me much as you would a dog, and said, "You're looking ragged about the edges. If you wish, before you head back up, I can have the hansom take you to my tailor so you can have a new suit. An early Darkest Night present, if you wish."

"Oh, thank you, sir," I said. "If it is all the same to you, coal and a brazier would not go amiss. You know how chill aetheria can get in the winter and it is cold in my room."

Actually, that vastly understated the situation. Sometimes I thought that more ice coated my room than the building outside.

"Done," he said, cheerily. "Let me write you a letter."

As he wrote the check, with his back turned toward me, I palmed a handful of candies from my uncle's table for the boys. When he turned back to look at me, I smiled at him hopefully.

"If it's possible," I asked, "I would like to see my sister while I'm down here."

"I'm afraid that's rather short notice for a lady of your sister's standing. I do believe she's out today, at the museum with her maid-servant. She does love it so." Uncle Gerard handed me the letter for credit at his tailor's. "Here you are."

I accepted this with a smile and retraced my steps, pausing only to deposit the ugly club cravat at the door. I thought of the letter in my pocket. However I might need a new suit, my uncle could not buy my complicity with one. I wouldn't accept his bribe.

But then that would show me to be duplicitous, wouldn't it?

I went to the tailor and, for the first time, took no pleasure in the process. The small neat man assured me that my suit would be ready well before Darkest Night and that I would look wonderful in it. I barely heard the tailor.

When I returned to the aetherium with my pocket full of candies and a new coal brazier, I felt as though I came bearing the treasures of Iskar. In the courtyard, the boys rushed out to greet me, like so many puppies when their master had come home, slipping across the ice, their arms wheeling out, crowing and pushing at each other.

I could not help laughing at them. I used the candy to bribe them to haul the coal downstairs to the boiler room, where it could be kept outside of the Nobbsnipes' own stores.

The boys raced along the stairs, both eager and slightly reluctant in their help, because of the number of stairs and the amount of candy involved. I helped with unloading the aerophaeton so it could leave in a timely fashion. After that, I took my new brazier upstairs to my room.

Leofa sprawled across the cot, his arms hanging down to either side like a dead man's. He'd closed his eyes. Leofa breathed evenly. The sunset light poured in redly through our small window. I put the heavy brazier down and sat down on the cot beside him.

His hands swelled with blisters and burns. I'd never seen anyone's—except maybe Stanley's—hands look so terrible. Leofa had blisters along the side of his neck, a few along his singed eyebrows, and the heat of some blast had curled his dark eyelashes.

"You're back," he said, opening his eyes.

"I'll get you some ice," I said.

"I can't bend my fingers," he said. "Had to use my elbows to get up that fucking ladder."

I cracked some ice off the windowsill and filled our chipped basin. Leofa pressed both palms into the ice chips. I said, "After the swelling goes down, I'll put some of the last of the balm on the burns."

I sat beside him, reluctant to tell him what had transpired with my uncle, though I knew he waited for the news.

He looked down at his hands and flexed his fingers slowly. "So I guess your meeting didn't go as planned?"

"I think my uncle might be in on it." As I related my conversation with to him, Leofa nodded as though he had expected as much. But now I understood my own foolishness.

"Well," Leofa said finally, "I suppose we're on our own then."

I felt lost. I hadn't known much I'd been invested in Uncle Gerard's help until my expectations had been dashed. My most overt leverage as a peer had been through my still-wealthy uncle. Without him and his connections, what, other than my useless title, would separate me from, well, anyone else?

"What will we do?" I asked.

He sighed. "I really don't know."

Perhaps, without even knowing it, I'd imagined a future. And now this crashed down around me, crushing me. When I'd gone to my uncle, I'd honestly thought I could save everyone. I'd thought I could be forgiven everything—including my debt. I'd dreamed of working alongside Leofa on these treasured grimoires, his skill acknowledged, my theoretical expertise lauded, both of us safely in the queen's laboratories.

"Would you ever work for the queen's laboratories?" I asked out of curiosity.

"They'd never take me. What could I say? Hey, I've been cracking grimoires that rightfully belong to the queen, now please give me a job please?" He snorted. "I don't have a degree from Elmstead, and I've hardly got lords lining up to give me letters of recommendation."

"I'd give you one," I said.

He looked at me fondly. "What would you tell them?"

I sighed. His burnt hands had melted the ice chips into slush. I said, "I have to go soon. I'm to teach Miss Louisa the piano after supper."

Leofa grimaced. "You know, when I was younger, they kept on trying to match me up with her. Setting us up like we were two childhood playmates who'd just happen to fall in love."

I wondered why the Nobbsnipes would even try to set their daughter up with Leofa. I could certainly see why he was desirable as a partner: only an idiot could overlook how attractive, how intelligent and capable, how hardworking and loyal and perceptive and kind Leofa was. But the Nobbsnipes wouldn't care about that. The Nobbsnipes were class climbers.

Leofa continued, "Sure figured out otherwise when they caught me with another one of the boys. Louisa was embarrassed, I can tell you that."

"Who was the other boy?" I asked abruptly.

"His name was William Larson. He's dead now."

I felt like a complete fool because of the sudden surge of jealousy that had prompted the question. I said, "You mean—Roger?"

"Nah, Roger was just a mean little snake then, slapping Louisa when he thought he could get away with it." Leofa sighed. "The Nobbsnipes hadn't worked out yet how to track likely boys down and all. Some of us weren't even related to peers, just kids they'd picked up. They told my ma that they'd educate me to be a gentleman and she paid them to take me. But anyway, none of us had a clue how to crack a bloodlock then. It was all just guesswork. Will died trying."

I tried to imagine it, the accident that had caused his death. I'd seen burns on his hands often enough in this place to know that, however grotesque they looked today, the swelling would eventually go down. Then the blisters would darken into scabs, and in the end, a few pinkish flecks would join the silvery scars on his hands.

"When I came back from Herrow," he added, "they'd brought new boys in. Had me teach them what I knew, and what could I do? Most of them they kept on as watchmen later, because they knew what was going on in the workshop, but they couldn't crack like me. Addison, Odwin, Kendall, Danebury, Edmunds, and Harkon, I taught 'em. Uckfield and that lot, Jerome brought them in and the only place they'll retire to is overboard."

"Joining Yorick Upping and Frank Smalley," I said in a small voice. "When did it happen?"

"Probably during the storm."

"I thought—I thought they—they'd been sleeping over with the watchmen—they—"

"They were idiots," Leofa said. "Dead idiots now. They believed what Jerome told them, rather than me, because that's what they wanted to believe."

"Roger's handiwork?" I asked.

"Most likely," he said. "But it could've been Jerome or any of them."

I stood up and paced to the window. I felt about to vomit. This sickened me—that I could have been ignorant to such ignominy. I shook with fury. I wanted to go kill Nobbsnipe right now for arranging all this.

I'd never actually wanted to kill someone before. I didn't mean in the sense of how people said it, playfully, when angry or frustrated. I did want to do it. I actually wanted to kill him. I owned a pistol. I had excellent aim.

It seemed so simple. All I had to do was walk up and shoot him. I would not feel remorse. I knew exactly what I would feel, and it would be the beatific calm, the sense of majesty, that I got after hitting a target dead on. I wanted this so badly, so awfully that my eyes stung with tears, that I didn't know how I'd ever be able to be in the same room with him—

"Don't think about it too much," Leofa said.

I turned back and faced him. "I could kill Nobbsnipe tonight."

"All right," he said, "but first tell me what you think you'd be accomplishing with this murder of yours."

"He'd be dead," I said.

Leofa shook his head. "And then you'd be dead."

"We could take a glider—"

"And leave the boys behind here?" he said, and when I didn't answer, he continued, "You see? It's not that simple."

"We can call the police," I said. "We can explain it all."

"They don't give a shit about people like us."

This truth saddened me. I said, "I'm a lord, even if I've been disgraced. If I can find proof…"

"Me and the boys would still go to the gallows for cracking," Leofa said soberly. "And the Nobbsnipes would slither away, fat as snakes with bellies full of gold. Dunno what would happen to you and your sister."

I frowned but didn't argue the point.

Leofa sighed. "You can't do anything now but go downstairs and act like you haven't the faintest idea of what's going on in starboard hall. Entertain the Nobbsnipes over supper, bow your head to Roger, and teach Louisa the piano."

He was right. So I did exactly that.

Over the Nobbsnipes' sumptuous supper, as the boys dined on flour soup in the next room, I related to them an edited version of the breakfast I'd shared with my uncle. I said that my uncle wanted me to meet with a lord whom he believed could be a good prospective match for Nora.

In retrospect, I realized I'd spoken the truth—Uncle Gerard had wanted to talk about my sister's marriage prospects with me.

I entertained them by singing a beggar's ballad that I heard on the streets about the Siovanese king's new mistress. I taught Louisa the piano. Whenever she tried to place her head on my shoulder, I found a way to evade her. After all, her mother did sit but a short distance away. Louisa tried all but to climb on my lap, attempting to get me to show her the fingerings via an embrace method.

I played my role meticulously, as if nothing at all had happened, as if I didn't know anything untoward. I was, truly, still a gentleman.

11

When I headed upstairs, past the schoolrooms and through the boys' dormitory, I heard a soft murmur and saw a shadowy figure hunched over a boy's bed. Alarm filled me.

"Who's there?" I asked.

A female voice said, "Oh, sir, Lord Franklin, sir, it's me!"

"Molly?" I asked.

"Mommy!" young Thaddeus said.

The long and uncomfortable silence in the darkness broke when Thaddeus started talking about squirrels. He'd seen one, drawn in the margins of a grammar, and now he now fixated on squirrels eating up our building. Thaddeus seemed to class them, size-wise, alongside elephants.

"Hush, hush, I didn't mean to wake you." Molly stroked Thaddeus' hair. She said, "Be quiet now, my sweet. I'm going to go, but I'll be back soon. You stay there and sleep tight. Don't let the bed bugs bite."

"Okay," young Thaddeus said.

Desperation edged Molly's voice as she faced me. "Sir, I can explain everything, if you'll give me the chance."

I replied, "Let's speak in the schoolroom."

"Sir, if it's all the same to you, I'd rather not," she said. "Watchmen patrol the schoolrooms on occasion, sir."

"The garret then?" I offered my elbow and escorted her between the boys' beds to the ladder. Seams of light shone down from the trapdoor below. Realizing they illuminated her ascent up the ladder, I rapidly whipped around to preserve her modesty.

Golden light poured down as she opened the hatch. I could hear the scuffling as she climbed up into our room, then the perplexed greeting that Leofa gave her. I followed her up.

Leofa struck a match and lit a second tallow candle.

I offered Molly our chair and something to drink. When she refused, I filled our single cup with water from the rain tanks, gulped it down, refilled it for Leofa, and handed it over.

I took a seat on my cot, and then noticed that the bedding at the foot had a puddle of ice forming on it. I had located it a good distance from the drip this morning, and now this! I'd have to ask Leofa if I could share with him again tonight, after Molly had left.

Molly stared downward, fidgeting, and then said, "Well, it's like this, hold your peace and try not to think too badly of me until I finish speaking, right? I was sixteen when I got a real good place at a lord's house in the city, a fine house. The work pleased me. The lord of that house, he saw me tending the gardens. I'm passing well at the household garden."

"You can say that again," Leofa said. "I can't believe you can make those cabbages grow up here."

Molly flushed and smiled, but her nervousness showed. "He said he wanted to work with me, help me put together a folio on city gardening. It'd be real popular, he said. I wasn't stupid. I knew what he wanted from me and I'd go only so far without a wedding. So he married me."

I could see where this was going, but I didn't interrupt.

"He wanted to keep it secret, you know," she continued, "for political reasons. Something going on Parliament. I said yes. I mean, I was seventeen then, and it seemed so fun, like something out of a story, to sneak around with my own husband."

"Shit," Leofa said.

"Yes, well, that all changed once I had a baby," she said. "It didn't seem so fun then. I wanted him to stand by me—by his son—and I wanted the boy raised right and recognized as a proper heir. I wanted him to have a governess, not to be tossed in the kennel to play with the hounds like some sort of stable boy in the making. I wanted my boy to have what he deserved."

As I listened to her, I realized she had been but Nora's age when this had happened. My heart ached with sympathy—and with helpless compassion for the younger Molly's plight.

"I told him, my lord husband," she continued, "that he'd recognize the boy all right, or I'd bring the child straight to Parliament with me. I'd stand up in front of those other lords, and I'd demand recognition right there and then. Politics be hanged! And I would have done it."

Molly buried her face in her hands. She didn't cry. When she looked up, her composure held. "The next morning, he had me brought in front of him, accused me of stealing, and had me put out on the street. I went to find the marriage contract. It was gone, along with my boy. He was six weeks old."

I couldn't imagine it. I couldn't imagine her fury and her terror. Being so young, her child taken from her, and her husband acting like a stranger. I had no idea what to say.

"It took me three years to find my boy." Molly clenched her hands in her skirt. "But I did it. I'm going to find a way to take him back. And then I'm going to track down that marriage certificate, and I will stand before Parliament and I will get my son the recognition he deserves."

I believed Molly would do it. I believed it completely.

I also understood why it wouldn't work. Even if she gained access to that chamber, her husband could merely declare her a forger or insane. He'd have her locked away. In the end, I'd stumbled upon another hopeless situation in the massive disaster of Highfell Hall.

Molly stood and smoothed her skirt. "Thank you for hearing me out. I got to go downstairs. If Cookie sees me gone much longer, she's bound to think the worst. Peggy can only cover for me so long. You two are good ones, you know. You take care of my boy."

"Good night, my lady." I bowed and opened the hatch above our ladder for her.

"Yes," Molly said with a glint in her eye. "I *am* a lady."

When I closed the hatch behind her, I could hear her slight murmur of reassurance as she bid goodnight to Thaddeus. Her life was hard—the Nobbsnipes were not easy masters to serve.

"Well, shit," Leofa said, lying back.

"You know, it's a fine irony that his lordship, in order to get the divorce he would need to legally remarry, would have to bring his marriage before Parliament," I said. "Whatever she said, he could always denounce her as a trollop out for revenge."

"If he'd ship his own son up here," said Leofa as he tucked his hands beside his head, watching as I prepared for bed, "then he'd sure use more than words to keep her quiet, with a scandal like that. Snuff the candle and come over here."

I did so nervously. I didn't know how our sleeping together would change, now that I'd kissed him, and I sat beside him in the dark. Both nerve-racked and thrilled, I imagined the possibilities. I could feel my cock stirring.

Suddenly, I wished I'd read more pornography or folios or anything that would give me an idea of what, exactly, to expect. I had deliberately kept myself away from such things, because I had hoped that by ignoring this spark in me it would go away. I did not want it to go away now that I had Leofa.

"Relax," he said. "I'm not going to grab you. I'm covered in blisters."

"Oh. Right." I sounded so disappointed that he laughed. But I lay down beside him. It felt wonderful to be so close to Leofa, even knowing that nothing would happen, and I loved how his body fit to mine. I craved him. I felt as though I could never have enough and yet being close to him made me so very satisfied. I pondered this paradox before deciding to just enjoy it.

"I didn't know it could be like this, between two men," I said, into the darkness.

"It's not always," he said. "I've never...I was with blokes, down in the city, not as a betty or mandrake or anything like that. But I got tired of it, groping in alleys, and then he goes rushing back to the missus. It's not that great to fuck people who are ashamed of what they're doing. They aren't that kind, either to themselves or to me. I got pretty tired of it, once the novelty wore off. You know."

I didn't know. His words filled me with a concoction of inadequacy and envy. I couldn't see myself as just going with a stranger in the alley. I wouldn't know where to start. How had he even known which men to go with?

"You can get arrested for doing things like that in an alley," I remarked.

"Yeah..." Leofa sounded amused.

Swallowing hard, I said, "I've never..."

"But I thought—you went to a boys' school and all—"

"No," I said softly. "Otherwise, I wouldn't have kept going to that school."

In silence, I contemplated these separate experiences, how they shaped us, and how they brought us together. It reminded of melody and countermelody, but played as equals. So at first it sounded like nothing but chaos, nothing but competing noise, and then, they came together, suddenly, in perfect balance, and the entire song made sense.

The music became then like a spun thread—because each half twisted in the opposite direction, they held together as one and they became the stronger for it.

Leofa knew me. Around him my innate qualities fell into place and expressing myself with genuineness came to me with unexpected ease. I could be myself.

How ironic, that I had found this freedom in a prison of a school. In the world outside, I had feared most being revealed, shamed for the nature I'd kept secret. But that paled in comparison to the possibility of being killed. The precariousness of our position here heightened the fleeting beauty of being together—and gave me the chance to treasure him, if only for now.

⌒

Over the next week, a snow cloud caught the aetherium. Downy snowflakes broke through the soft fog outside our window. Moisture froze across the aetherium's walls, so that a bright and icy shell encased the school.

As the fog prevented the boys from chipping ice off and no one here would ever consider buying salt, Nobbsnipe ordered our rain tank drained. The school released ballast, showering Southside below with filthy water, to compensate for the weight of the ice.

Long winter nights provided time to work on my aetheric studies. I corresponded with Professor Pike about my transducer, explaining my new theory on how spell language controlled how the ink medium interfaced with the wire matrix in the paper, which then shaped the nature of the magical output.

The outputs, I theorized, were what was incompatible.

The language and the wording of the spell was irrelevant—any academic knew this. But analyzing the basic wire matrices in the paper—as well as the language's spelling and grammar—could allow me to predict fluctuations in the aetheric output. Knowing that, as long as one held off speaking the spell-key, which would convert the aetheric output into non-aetheric physical energies, one could then make any given spell work with any other using my transducer.

Or at least so I theorized.

"What's that?" Leofa asked, leaning over my shoulder to look at the schematic I'd sketched.

"I'm trying out another idea for the transducer," I said. "But I still have too much data to fit on a single spell page, much less inscribe around a wire."

"Huh." Leofa looked at it thoughtfully. "You know, I've noticed working on grimoires, when I'm wearing my goggles, that some of the language, uh—"

"Output fluctuations?" I suggested the technical term.

"Yeah," he agreed. "Some of them look pretty similar even for different languages. They're more like types."

"Hm." I had to think about this. I relaxed back against him.

He rested his hands on my shoulders, stroking his fingertips across my tense muscles.

The swelling in his fingers had gone down completely, and the blisters had turned into hard, pinkish bumps. By next week, Leofa would have more scars speckling him whitely, like so many snowflakes burned into his dark skin. He would probably go back to the workshop on the morrow.

"Do you read them out often?" I asked.

"Mostly we don't. We got reams of pages in there, and what do they do, we don't know, so no one's going to sell them until we can figure out that," he said. "Does the spell make a firefly light? Does it throw down Hem Cho's Great Wall? Does it make the person reading it explode?"

I snorted. "Suicide spells are a myth."

"Yeah, that's just because no one's read one yet and lived to talk about it," Leofa said. "Shit, there was this one…Stanley figured it out after I cracked the grimoire, because he can do Accadian, but what a nasty piece of work we handed over, maybe, late spring, early summer this year. An ill-wishing spell that brought down the ague. Sometimes I think I should've just burned it."

I flinched. Although the suggestion of burning a spell would've normally upset me enough, the spell that he described sounded altogether like what had killed my parents. But it couldn't be the same spell, I told myself. I saw patterns, even desired logic, where none could be found. I was glad Leofa stood behind me and could not see my expression.

"You can't stop progress," I said, trying to push the conversation away from this sensitive topic. I did not want to accuse Leofa of releasing the spell into the world that could have killed my parents. I didn't want to blame him for it.

"Sure, I'm not saying that," he said. "It's more that I wish I knew what I handed over. That I had more of a choice. You think of a spell like that, and you know you can't trust someone not to use it. Even war doesn't excuse some crimes."

I had always focused so much on getting into the queen's labs that I had never contemplated this aspect of the work.

"You wonder if you hid it or destroyed it," he continued, "if that'd save someone's life or someone's town. Or if wouldn't matter, because whoever'd use a spell like that, they'd have to be either real desperate or real heartless. And someone like that would find a way to get what they wanted whatever the cost."

I could see that the guilt weighed on him. I did not envy his position and wondered, had I ended up in the queen's labs, if I would have soon felt the same. Queen Isolde was a fine ruler, but there had been unwise rulers in the past, and tyrants. Seeing such a store of spells in the hand of someone cruel, insane, or both, would give anyone pause.

"Is that why you've been trying to teach yourself Accadian?" I asked.

"Seemed like the thing to do," Leofa said.

"Some of the boys will be able to read the grimoires soon." I folded my schematic into an envelope and then sealed it. "Ashby is good at languages. He's progressing well. Northwall and Carlsworth are both doing fairly. Stanley probably already can, considering his education."

"Stanley is hopeless at grimoires," he said. "If I wasn't covering for him—but you're right, the other boys have been piecing together some of the pages, translating here and there."

I nodded, because that fit with my idea of their skill level.

"But the problem is," Leofa continued, "we don't know if they're getting it right. I seen the work they do. You've half marked it in red. We can't afford for them to make some dumb mistake."

I wondered if Leofa wanted me to volunteer my services, but then I decided he didn't. If he had wanted to bring me in, he would have done that already.

Leofa leaned down over me, kissing me from above. I closed my eyes and kissed him back, savoring the softness of his lips, and the roughness of his unshaven face against mine. Sensations thrilled through me, making my cock stir with need, my body prickle with want.

He smoothed a hand down my chest to my groin, brushing his hand across where my cock pressed against my trousers. Arousal rippled from there throughout my entire body. I had to break our kiss, gasping with surprise and desire.

"Your hands—" I began.

"—are fine," Leofa said, roughly, and kissed me again.

The hatch to the garret slammed open, and Hooker bounded into the room. Leofa lifted his face and then, very nonchalantly, moved his hands to my shoulders. I had to turn around in my chair to see Hooker properly, where he gaped at us. I hadn't ever seen someone's mouth drop open from surprise before, but his had, like a fish out of water.

"What brings you up here without knocking," Leofa said.

"What? Oh. Um. Stanley's, he's got, he needs some help," Hooker said. "You-know-what in the you-know-where. And Miss Louisa wants to talk to you, sir. Hey, are you two stepping out or something?"

I was mortified. I expected Leofa to answer, but he didn't. I could feel his hands on my shoulders tense. He awaited my response. I knew that Hooker would accept my word, whatever he'd seen and whatever I said. I knew also that he would repeat it.

"Yes," I said slowly. "I think we do have an understanding."

"Oh," Hooker said, and made a face of disgust.

"You got a problem with that?" Leofa said.

"No, it's more like…" Hooker screwed up his face as he thought. He said, "It's like seeing your mama and papa go at it or something. It's really, you know, horrible. But also kind of good, knowing they're getting along?"

"Oh, merciful Loxa," I said, burying my face in my hands. "Tell me I'm not the mama."

"'Course not. Leofa's the one who makes us dinner." He jumped down to the boys' dorms below with a thump that even Cookie could've heard belowdecks. I could hear him shout, "Come on! I meant it about Stanley being in trouble!"

I glanced at Leofa. "I guess that makes me the papa."

"I'm fine with that," he said, and then leaned in to give me a quick kiss. "So long as we're officially stepping out together."

⁓

Before I headed to speak with Louisa, I tidied my attire and put on my holster and pistol. I'd striven to make a habit of it since learning of Smalley's and Upping's deaths.

Louisa waited on the piano bench in the drawing room. She wore white muslin, entirely inappropriate for the season. When I rifled through the sheet music, Louisa abruptly mentioned she had forgotten to bring down a letter meant for me.

She invited me up to the signaling tower so she could get the letter from the dovecote. I suspected she had an ulterior motive, nonetheless I followed.

After all, I did have a letter to send. Because I still had to make Nobbsnipe believe I reported to my uncle. As my uncle expected me to attempt to discover the Nobbsnipes' embezzlement, I'd written Uncle Gerard stating that I'd been unable to find Nobbsnipe's account books. In addition, I'd assured my uncle that he could count on my loyalty as I searched for the proof he needed.

Upstairs in the dovecote, a few of Mrs. Nobbsnipe's letters lay on the writing desk. Though the cote stood open, the dank and almost fungal smell of the birds permeated the enclosed space. The pigeons remained on their perches, feathers fluffed so that that they looked as round as snowballs. Miss Louisa handed over a letter from my sister.

I cracked the seal, and Louisa stood on tiptoe, digging her pointy chin into my shoulder as she tried to read my mail. How strange, that when Leofa had done this, I'd found it comfortable and endearing, but when Louisa did this, I wanted to shove her off the edge of the aetherium. I shrugged my shoulder out from under her chin and sidestepped away.

The text was brief, saying mostly that she'd had a fever but had become well, thanks to my uncle sparing no expense on physicians and tonics. But below the words, I saw an intricate fleuron.

"Your sister has pretty handwriting," Louisa said, edging around me to look over at the letter. "Very feminine. She didn't seem very interested in the more delicate pursuits when I met her. Mathematics is a little mannish, don't you think?"

"Excuse me?" I glanced at the letter. Just in time. I dodged Louisa, who sneaked up on me again, and I tucked the letter into my pocket. I edged away.

The girl rubbed her arms artfully, shivering.

"It's so cold up here," she said. "Why don't you lend me your jacket?"

I stared at her. Removing my jacket would invariably reveal my pistol and I didn't know how I'd explain that. Instead I said, with a smile, "Well, why don't we return downstairs? You can play me that new hymn you've been practicing."

"Oh, I don't want to play boring old hymns for you," Louisa said. "Besides, I have to feed the birds, don't I? What should we talk about, now that we're alone up here?"

Downstairs, I could hear some shouting. Leofa's voice cut through the noise, raised in a thunderous roar, and then Roger's snigger drifted up. It sounded like something had gone very, very wrong. I glanced at Louisa, but she did not seem at all upset.

"I should go and see what's happening," I said.

"Oh, it's probably nothing," she said. "It sounds like Leo's done something wrong, and Roger's going to punish him. One must keep the lower echelons in order, you know. But it will keep my family busy for quite some time, and we will be up here…alone…"

I could not believe she had said this. I'd thought Louisa a girl sheltered by immoral and overly religious parents. A girl who had a cruel and overbearing brother, whose perspective had been shaped of forced ignorance rather than enlightenment. I'd wanted to believe her good.

But now I could see her for what she was—as selfish as her brother, though not as cruel, and Louisa schemed as much as her parents, though not yet as well. She saw her brother Roger's cruelty toward Leofa only as an opportunity to thrust her dubious charms upon me without interruption.

"No matter how much time we have alone, I assure you, there could be nothing between us," I told her quietly. "If you persist in these repellant advances, I will have no choice but to treat you unkindly."

Louisa flushed and then blanched rapidly. She raised her hand and slapped me on the cheek. Hard.

I turned my back on her, face smarting. And I left her standing there, shocked and furious. I loped downstairs. The back door had been left open, slamming against the wall in the wind, and I sprinted out to the yard.

Roger had tied Leofa to one of the poles with laundry lines strung from it. Leofa was shirtless. His bare back had a few thicker scars striping it. Several boys waited in silence. Stanley struggled where two watchmen held him. Five more watchmen flanked Roger. Peggy waited anxiously beside Molly.

Leofa glanced up at me. His expression wasn't relaxed, precisely, so much as in control. He made something designed for humiliation into an act of defiance and pride without saying a word or even resisting. Something in the look on his face, or perhaps in the way he held himself, made it so.

I paused, indecisive, and distinctly aware of the pistol beneath my coat.

Roger, in a way that he no doubt thought dapper, used his foot to kick his cane off the icy ground into his hand. He toyed with it, tossing it between his hands, and then leaned over and spoke with Leofa, who answered calmly. I couldn't hear what they said, but Roger sneered, raised the cane, and cracked it so hard enough across Leofa's back that I instantly feared broken ribs. A broken rib puncturing a lung could kill him.

My hand went beneath my jacket, then stilled. Every one of the watchmen carried a gun. I would be dead before I could fire two shots.

Roger's cane fell on Leofa's back a second time. He lifted it for the third blow, and I charged forward. I flung my hand out and I twisted the cane out of Roger's grip and flung it away. It clattered to the ground a good deal away, skittered along the ice to the aetherium's edge, then plunged off the side.

The watchmen smirked at me, moving in a protective phalanx toward Roger.

"How dare you?" I said quietly. "How dare you treat him like this?"

"You think you're so fucking superior, don't you, my lord?" Roger's face twisted with anger. He seized me by the shoulder and pulled me so close I could smell the tobacco on his breath. He said in a low voice, "We ran this school before you came around. We'll run it after you're gone. Your uncle wanted you out of the way, so he put you where he puts people that he wants out of the way. Do you think he'd care if you vanished?"

"Perhaps my uncle had me brought here for another reason." I glanced at the watchmen as I spoke, smiling, with a confidence that I did not truly possess. "Perhaps he expects me to report back to him on who should stay...and who should go."

I made a deliberate survey of the watchmen, meeting their eyes as if making an accounting. Several of the men shifted nervously, hands dropping away from their guns, their palms out as they stepped back, as if washing their hands of Roger's mess. The men holding Stanley released him.

"You are all employed by my uncle," I said. "All of you. Don't forget it."

I began to untie Leofa, who shook his head as if he couldn't believe in my idiocy. I took him by the arm and marched him back between the cabbage beds to the door. My calmness pervaded me so deeply that anything could have happened and I would have taken it in stride.

In the doorway, I paused and looked back. "Keep up, Stanley."

Stanley left the stunned watchmen behind and hurried after me. I did not watch to see if he caught up. The boys assembled in the dining hall watched in silence as I helped Leofa toward the stairs. Stanley bolted in after us, sagging down on at a table beside Quincey. Immediately, Hooker leaned forward to question him.

Back in the garret, I barred the hatch leading down to our ladder.

Leofa sagged down on his cot, drawing the blanket over his bare shoulders, but I knew that two bruises already darkened along his back and ribs. His expression communicated quiet stoicism.

"What happened back there?" I asked. I wasn't angry, so much as burning with concern.

"I'd covered for Stanley at the workshop," Leofa said. "He can't crack a tome to save his life. Literally. His life depended on it, and he couldn't do it. What was I supposed to do?"

"I meant, with Roger." I had begun to shake with the aftermath.

"He caught me," Leofa said, wearily.

I sat down on the bed, rubbing my temples, and then I laced my fingers together, perched my elbows on my knees, and leaned forward to look at Leofa. I felt ill but also very alert. I didn't know what to say, really, about that. Clearly this had happened before. Yet he was not some cowed indentured servant. He remained his quietly insolent self.

Earlier in his life, he had escaped. Knowing Leofa now, I did not believe for a second that he had returned to take Nobbsnipe's money.

"Why did you really come back here?" I asked him.

Leofa moved over to the floorboards, under which he hid his personal things. He pried them up with the ease of long practice. Kneeling down, he searched through his treasures. He brought me a sheaf of letters all bound with a string.

"It's my mother," Leofa said, handing the letters over and sitting down beside me. "You know, she sent me here to become a gentleman, but she knows about what's really going on here. You know how folk are in Hetta. Under the flag, sure, but wanting to stick it to the Crown. She's all for me cracking them grimoires, stealing from Queen Isolde. Anyhow, my mother's real sick. Has been bedridden for years. I'm her sole provider, you know. I send all my money to her, almost."

"Why don't you just go to her in person?" I asked.

"Can't," he said. "Don't know where she is. She's being taken good care of, but I think the Nobbsnipes have paid off her doctors or something, because they won't say a word about where Mum is."

"Did you try to find her?" I frowned.

"Yeah, when I ran off," he explained. "I earned enough money in Herrow so I could afford to go out to Hetta. I tried to track her down. Found where I used to live, but none of the neighbors knew anything. I had to come back to ask the Nobbsnipes, and by then she was real sick, and I owed those doctors a good amount."

"May I?" I opened a letter that looked as soft as fine leather, it had been opened so many times, and I read it.

The words were laudatory. His mother thanked her son for his hard work here. She commended his rebelling in this small way against the oppressors. Asking for his patience, she expressed the hope that they would see each other again someday, if he obeyed the Nobbsnipes who saw her cared for so well. And so forth. The letters expressed sweet, poetic, yet motherly sentiment.

I could not help but notice that the handwriting bore a strong resemblance to Mrs. Nobbsnipe's.

Moreover I couldn't credit any theory that involved the Nobbsnipes sending away money on Leofa's behalf. Somewhere, deep inside, Leofa had to know that these letters weren't authentic.

"Mum's as good as a star." He gazed at the letter with such fondness it broke my heart. "She always tells me that, whatever the Nobbsnipes might do, I've got to stay here and look after these boys. She's right, you know. They don't have anyone else."

I wanted to rip up the letters and burn the scraps. I folded them gently and handed them back. The consolation that he'd found in these letters, written by one of his tormentors, had shaped the person he was today. It had kept Leofa from bitterness, urged him to focus on a work that he excelled at, reaffirmed his loyalty and virtue toward the boys, and probably so much more.

Unfortunately, I'd to have to tell him who'd written this.

"Have you ever been to the dovecote?" I asked.

He shook his head. "You know Barnabas doesn't allow anyone up there."

"Well, I need to go up there and send some letters before Barnabas or Mrs. Nobbsnipe learn what I've done," I said. "I have people who need to know they won't be able to reach me by pigeon anymore. I can hardly expect the Nobbsnipes to pass on my mail after this."

"We can do that," Leofa said. "I think Roger's going to take Louisa below to shop for Darkest Night masks tomorrow. I can ask the boys to keep Barnabas busy in the workshop, and then we'll only have to look out for Eudora. If we time it right, she'll be bossing around Cookie in the kitchen, talking about menus and such."

"I can't believe it's almost Darkest Night. But, yes, that does sound like a plan," I said.

I knew I ought to tell him now. I knew I should've said, *You've been fooled*. But I could not make myself say such a heartbreaking and terrible thing. Those words caught in my mouth and I looked down at my feet.

"You're not—" Leofa began, and then cleared his throat. "You can probably still go back and tell them you're sorry. You're the golden boy, right? They'd have to accept it, seeing as you're Lord Franklin's nephew."

I shook my head. "Fuck them. I'm not sitting down for another meal with those bloody monsters. I'm not apologizing for doing right."

When I glanced over at Leofa, a smile tugged at his mouth. He said, "Say that again."

"What? Oh. That." I shrugged. "I meant it."

"Say it again." His dark eyes lit up. He tilted his head at an angle somewhere between inquisitive and amused. His long smooth hair fell across his face. He truly needed to get his hair trimmed, though I couldn't imagine Leofa sporting the short cut gentlemen favored. I touched his sleek hair, moving it aside, and brushed my fingers over the rough stubble along his jaw.

"Fuck them," I said, softly.

He laughed, that low rumble that came from deep in his chest, and he framed my face with his scarred and work-roughened hands. Leofa kissed me, hard. I pushed him down into the bed, and we almost tipped over the cot, and he laughed again.

I'd had no idea that kissing could be a wondrous eternity. I'd had no idea I could love his body so much, his muscles flexing under my hands. I could feel his restrained desire, while his expression was one of wary hope.

I stroked his length through his clothes, watching his face transform with need. The heat of him, his arousal, filled me with nervous excitement.

"I don't know what to do," I admitted. "I mean, I've never…"

"You'll do fine. For starters, though, you're always wearing too many clothes," he said, as he tried to unbutton my jacket.

"I like how little you wear," I said, "though it's not decent at all."

"Me, I'm known for my decency." Leofa pulled upon the buttons of my trousers and reached into my smallclothes to grasp my cock's length. I gasped. He worked me, artfully, into a frenzy, thrusting against him into sudden release. And even as bliss engulfed me, so did shame—not so much in what I'd done, but for my inadequacy about being able to return the favor.

Leofa watched me, looking relaxed and lazy and flushed, and I fumbled at him. His breathing quickened when I began to touch him. I felt grateful for his patience as I toyed with him, hot in my hand, slick with his fluids, trying to figure out what pleased Leofa.

"Ah, yes," he said. "Like that."

Although I was sated, I loved watching him. Finally, Leofa groaned, climaxing, and in that moment he seemed so wantonly innocent, so perfectly mine, that I had to kiss him. We lay spent in each other's arms, our skin warm as we pressed together. I wished it would never end. But then we had to clean up. I went to search for a cloth among our things.

"Thanks, Your Majesty," he said, "for taking responsibility for my beating into your own hands."

I glanced back at him, surprised and confused. I saw his dark eyes gleaming wickedly as Leofa stretched along the cot, arms over his head and feet sticking off the cot's end, his ribs and abdominal muscles visible. When I understood his pun, I threw a rag at his head. He caught it, grinning at me, and I decided I wanted to do this as often as possible with him.

12

While I taught the next day, Leofa popped his head in through the door. I held up a slate, with the embarrassed and proud Vernon beside me. Vernon tried not to squirm as I illustrated how he'd done his algebra correctly.

"Mr. Franklin," Leofa interjected, "can I borrow you?"

"Of course," I said. "Vernon, please help out the boys who didn't get the right answer for these sums. I want them to be able to explain to me what they did wrong by the time I get back. As for the rest of you, it's time to work on your translation projects. I want to see ten sentences done."

As I left, I could hear chaos and chatter burst out behind me. Vernon looked hopeless, clutching his slate against his chest, still standing at the front of the schoolroom. I glanced back just in time to see him, his eyes darting, let out a silencing whistle and start talking. I continued walking alongside Leofa.

"Carlsworth's keeping Barnabas busy in the workshop," he said.

I nodded. I'd seen Louisa and Roger leave early this morning from the schoolroom window. I hadn't breakfasted with them, of course. In fact, I'd skipped it altogether, and now I felt peckish.

"Good. Eudora is ill this morning," he said. "Molly told me so. When she gets one of her headaches, she usually takes smoke of the poppy, so she should be asleep right now."

I frowned. "I had no idea she indulged."

"Well, her family likes to keep it quiet." Leofa opened the door from the storage room to the dining room. The two of us slipped upstairs. Every creak of the beautifully polished floorboards rose up around us, seeming to me as loud as an alarm. The scent of the beeswax polish was thick in my nostrils, almost as cloying as the smoke that drifted around Mrs. Nobbsnipe's boudoir door.

My heart pounded. I wished I had my pistol. But at least no watchmen were posted up in the dovecote. They focused their guard around the workshop and the boilers, with the occasional random patrol through the port hall, kitchen, or bilge.

At the top of the staircase, I paused and touched Leofa lightly on the shoulder. He glanced up at me, and I knew I should have said this to him before now. I could feel my stomach clench with anxious sadness.

But I braced myself. I told myself that I had to do this, and I said, "I brought one of your mother's letters with me. I thought—I thought the handwriting reminded me of something, that it was very similar to—to Mrs. Nobbsnipe's—"

He looked down. His eyes narrowed only slightly, thoughtfully, and then he said abruptly, "Give me the letter."

I pulled it from my breast pocket and handed it over. Leofa held it in his hands, caressing the envelope with his thumbs, and then he turned away from me. I didn't confront him, but tried the dovecote's door handle instead. It moved loosely, but the door was locked.

"Let me try that." Leofa removed his lock picks from his trouser pocket. Meant for cracking bloodlocks, he'd fashioned the picks from silver, bronze, and iron. He fiddled with the lock. It clicked. He pushed the door open and smirked at me, though his heart was clearly not in it. "Harder to crack than a bloodlock, that is."

The dovecote itself was freezing cold, as the cote was open and the flag raised. Icy wind and snow gusted through the air. The pigeons fluttered in their cote. I'd always found the noise of pigeons' wings eerie.

I nodded over at the writing desk meaningfully, and Leofa began to search its drawers. The papers were all tucked away out of the elements.

I found the harnesses, stowed carelessly in a box, and I pulled out an alert-looking bird from the cote. Quickly, I fitted a loop over the pigeon's head, pulled up its wings, and snapped together the bird's harness behind its wings, moving aside any feathers.

The pigeon bobbed its head around curiously, passive in my hands and accustomed to handling. I fitted the backband, ensuring its snugness, and then slipped the letter into the pocket in the breastband pouch that descended down along the bird's keel. I'd double-folded the envelope so that it was no more than two fingers wide without damaging the seal.

Carefully, I traced my finger along the band on the bird's leg, murmuring the seek incantation and my finger rubbed the notches in the metal band. This handy spell let me set anywhere as the bird's "home," including places that the bird had never been. The bird's other leg band was plain leather, with the bird's name, owner, and home cote on it. Using the spell, I set the bird's home to Elmstead's cote.

When I opened my hands, the bird flapped out the window.

The bird would be delivering a message meant for Professor Pike. In order to circumvent the Nobbsnipes, I'd told him to use only trackers for my mail; they could bring mail directly to me as long as I was located in an aetheric current. I had enclosed a drop of my blood in the envelope for the professor so that he could use it to set the tracker's homing spell.

In the end, the process took around five minutes. By that time, Leofa had found letters written by Mrs. Nobbsnipe. He examined them closely, comparing them to his mother's handwriting. Even from here, I could see their similarity. But, with tears in his eyes, he kept on searching for differences.

Mrs. Nobbsnipe had been falsifying those letters from Leofa's mother. Obviously. But Leofa's own heartbreak made it impossible for him to see it clearly. My chest and my throat tightened with my unspoken sympathy for him.

I sent out Nora's letter next, inquiring after her health. I sent a separate bird to my uncle, and finally, one last bird to my former fiancé.

In addition to my new contact information, I had written Madeline an apology. I had told her, that even should I win my fortunes back, I doubted I would take the government post as had been expected. I enjoyed teaching too much for that.

If only to myself, I had to admit I'd used a euphemism. I couldn't see myself giving up Leofa.

When finished, I walked up behind him. He bent up over the desk, curled in on himself, and it made me feel sick to see him so shattered. I touched him lightly on the shoulder, to indicate we ought to leave. Leofa lifted his head, wiping his face on his sleeve, and then he left with me as though nothing had happened.

I expected him to go back to the workshop, but he didn't. He headed upstairs, to our garret, and I meant to follow him. But first I had to check on the boys. I made sure they occupied themselves with their translations, though they hadn't gotten done as much as they would have had I been there, and then I went to go upstairs. Molly stopped me in the passage.

"Lord Franklin, sir," she said, sounding concerned, "I've been looking for you all over. The boys said you were out talking to Leofa. Mrs. Nobbsnipe wants you to know that you're not to come to dinner or such any longer, and that I'm not to help you out with any of your washing. Nor is Peggy."

I shrugged wearily. I had expected as much. I wondered if my exile had been the result of insulting their daughter or embarrassing their son. Perhaps I could attribute it to a combination of both? I couldn't bring myself to feel cut. I despised them. I said, "Well, thank you for telling me."

Molly bobbed a little curtsy.

Upstairs, I found Leofa burning his treasured letters. He didn't look at me when I came in, and I watched him from the bed without commenting. Black smoke spiraled up around him, and gobs of melting wax spattered down across the desk, a greasy lavender color, flecked with gold. Ashes as large as rose petals fluttered around.

"You must think I'm a real idiot," Leofa said. "How long did you know about this?"

"I first suspected it yesterday." I hung my head. "I should've—I should've warned you. I should have told you right away. I just—I just didn't know what to say."

"Aw, fuck." He pressed his face into his hands, exhaling shakily. "She's probably dead. My mum's probably been dead for years, or at least she's so far gone I'll never find her. The Nobbsnipes will have made sure of that."

He turned, stalking over to the other side of the room, and slammed his hand into the wall with the rain tank. The tank gave out the massive boom of a drum and dust showered down from the ceiling. He hit it again, rested his forehead against the icy wall, and then turned back to face me. I didn't know what to do or say, knowing nothing could make this better.

"You wanted to kill the Nobbsnipes," he said. "Now I want to kill them. You know what I put up with, for my mother's sake? You know what…I let that fucking bastard Roger beat me, and for what? For what! You don't know…"

Leofa slammed his hands against the wall again, and the hollow boom that rang out had to be audible throughout all of the port hall. He actually growled, or near enough.

"Ten years! Ten fucking years of my life."

I didn't say anything. I could tell him later how those years hadn't been thrown away—he'd helped at least some of the boys. He'd learned how to crack grimoires with unrivalled skill. And he'd become an expert in aetheric dynamics in a way university-educated specialists were not, and Leofa could give any one of them a run for their money.

I knew this for a fact. But I told myself I'd say these things later, when his anger had waned.

"Those sly motherfuckers owe me more than thirteen hundred guineas," he said.

I nodded. Leofa earned well, then, better than he could've ever expected as a laborer. He'd been theoretically paid ten times the amount I earned in a year as a schoolteacher here. No wonder he'd stayed on. But, since that money had been supposedly going to his mother, they'd really fleeced him instead.

"I should demand all that money back."

"Then they'll know you know," I said.

"What the fuck does it matter anymore?" Leofa sat down next to me. When he placed his hand on my knee, I entwined my fingers over his. Oddly, our hands were almost the same size, though he was significantly taller than I. I'd always had large hands, ideal for stretching across a ninth on a piano.

I liked the contrast—my golden skin, splotched with ink, with his bronze skin, speckled with pale scars. I couldn't say I understood what, exactly, developed between us or what it meant, but I found myself relieved that this hadn't broken it.

"We have to find evidence against them," I said. "It's an offense against the Crown to crack grimoires. If we can find enough evidence to persuade the police would search the aetherium, they'd be locked up for those crimes at the very least."

"I work for them, you know," he said. "We've already talked about this."

"I've been thinking… You'd probably have to give some testimony about being unaware that the laboratory was unsanctioned," I said. "As a hireling, it will be expected that you're unaware of these circumstances. I hate to say this, but in terms of setting them up, it's rather a good idea for you to have burned those letters, as they did incriminate you."

Leofa nodded, thoughtfully. He still looked furious, but at least he was rational now.

"I have to find—shit, she must have all the letters I wrote her," Leofa said. "She must have them. Before we can turn them in, I need those letters back. I know—I knew—in those letters, it's dead obvious I know what's going on here. I don't want to hang as an accomplice. I got to get them back."

"They weren't in the writing desk, then, in the cote?"

"No, I would've taken them if they were," Leofa said.

I felt cold with trepidation—as if I'd already informed on him accidentally—and I tightened my hand around his.

I had to figure out how to find them. If only my mother were here to speak her seeking spell. She'd been able to find almost anything with that spell, as long as she had a physical connection to the lost object.

After my own father had drunk himself to death, and before she'd married my stepfather, she'd earned a modest living through selling the spell's services. My mother had sought everything from lost children and dogs to manuscripts, necklaces, thieves, and even corpses.

"In my sister's grimoire," I said slowly, "there's a seeking spell."

"Yeah? How does it work?" Leofa asked.

"I only saw my mother perform it a couple of times," I said, for she had only brought me on business when she could find no one to watch me.

I could still remember the emerald green grimoire drooping open over her palm. Her delicate face fierce with concentration, she'd traced the spell with one finger, with the connecting item placed over her heart.

"You need a connecting item for the spell to work," I said, "something with a physical or emotional association to the items you are seeking. If you're looking for a corpse, the murder weapon is best. For your letters, your writing hand would work."

"As long as it remains connected to my body," he said, with a spark of his usual humor.

"You'd just have to place it over my heart." I could remember what my mother had looked like as the spell had taken effect, her pupils blazing gold with aether. "From what I understand, the person who has read the spell then sees a sort of... 'invisible thread' between the connecting item and the item sought. Then the caster is drawn to the item sought. I think I could perform the spell."

"Your grimoire's in the workshop," Leofa said. "It's possible for us to get at that spell. But you know I'd have to crack it, right?"

I nodded. It would have to be done, and I could always return the leafs to my sister. I thought that Nora would understand, given the stakes, and she would rather the spells be in my hands than another's.

"If I did it real delicate, we cut out the spell, only the right leaf, yeah, then they wouldn't even have to know I'd cracked it," Leofa said.

"That might work," I said.

"I'd need to get you inside the workshop," Leofa continued. "So you could point out the right one. The way I figure it the Nobbsnipes would have to report if something seemed amiss with that tome, seeing as what your uncle's done to get it, so it's best to leave light tracks."

"It seems quite difficult, logistically," I said. "When working the spell, I would have to be sure I would encounter no one else. It's not precisely subtle. One's pupils glow."

He smiled. "We can work around that."

⌒

When I entered the schoolroom, Hooker had somehow managed to get onto the ceiling. He clung to the central beam like a spider. I knew Ashby had something to do with this, since he presented the image of virtuous industry beneath my gaze.

I hauled Hooker down and punished him by telling him to clean up Thaddeus and Ingram's mess. The two of them had decided to illustrate a beasel's adventure on the wall using ink from my inkwell. I looked over the boys' translations, what little they had gotten done, and corrected where necessary. Soon the bell rang for dinner.

The boys bounced with ecstatic glee when I announced that henceforth I would be dining with them—until Stanley pointed out that I would no longer be sneaking them treats from the Nobbsnipes' table. Then the boys' spirits drooped. But they perked up again when they stood in the serving line, pushing each other, shouting.

Peggy served me cabbage soup. The grayish broth contained only a few sad strings of cabbage, lurking at the bottom of my wood bowl.

I sat down across Leofa at the unfinished table, moving carefully so that I didn't snag my jacket sleeve. The tables had been thoroughly desecrated by the boys—obscenities mingled with erect penises, proudly carved names, and short messages. EAT A DICK! arced over BOOBIES, HOOKER IS A LADYS MAN, and FUCK OFF.

"Any of these your work?" I asked Leofa.

He grinned. "Some."

After I finished my soup, I still hungered. A briny taste lingered in my mouth. I found focusing on the afternoon lecture difficult with my mood so soured. Dinner involved hard bread, a slice of dry cheese, and a beef broth whose brownish color resembled that of marsh water.

"Beef missing, presumed absent," I muttered into my soup.

Leofa laughed at me. He was not exactly sympathetic. After supper, I played several tunes for boys in the dormitory and retold some ancient myths. The boys found them unexpectedly entertaining, but then they concerned massive feats of strength, tricking bull men, and getting seduced by well-endowed goddesses.

Peggy darted into the dorm just as I started a story about a hero's quest into Iskar's underworld.

"Storm rising!" she called. "Barometers are falling fast. Batten down!"

Only a second after she'd left, the bell began to ring wildly, warning everyone. I bolted to my feet, panicked by a thought of a repeat to the last storm's disaster and ready to leap into action. Leofa stood more calmly and placed a reassuring hand on my shoulder. He said, "We're following regular procedures only, Neil."

"Maybe you are the mama after all," Hooker quipped.

I glowered at Leofa, which made him laugh unrepentantly. But I did settle down enough to put my urgency to good use. I loped upstairs to our garret, secured our window and our belongings, and Leofa headed out to close the rain intakes. I sent the boys downstairs to double-check the schoolroom windows.

I'd developed the habit of closing everything down in case of storm before leaving the schoolroom, but in this case, better safer than sorry. Then I told the boys to secure themselves. I headed downstairs to help Peggy and Molly flip and tie down the trestle tables in the dining hall. As I worked, my hands knotting ropes quickly, I lamented the fact that the tables hadn't been bolted down.

In the midst of this, the storm hit.

A trestle bench tumbled, slamming onto Peggy, and the aetherium careened sideways. I kept my legs, barely, and Molly gripped my arm hard to steady herself.

Fear clenched my heart as I watched the door for Leofa. If he hadn't finished his duties outside before the storm had hit, he could have been thrown overboard. I couldn't bear to think of that.

The walls shuddered, the metal struts of the aetherium groaning, as we leveled out.

Molly and I helped Peggy to her feet. She dusted herself off, looking as though she might cry.

"You'll be fair black with bruises come the morrow, but you'll be fine," Molly told her. "I'll be checking downstairs on Cookie to see if she needs help with the fire. You go into the house to help the mistresses."

"Yes, miss." Peggy trotted away.

I could hear a strange absence of sound. Although the aetherium quivered with the force of the winds, there was a sense of something missing. Something that I'd become so accustomed to that its absence unnerved me.

Then I knew.

"I can't hear the intake fans," I said.

The boilers, or one of them at least, had to be out. I turned to the stairs. Did no part of this blasted aetherium function correctly?

I could wait no longer for Leofa. I thudded down the stairwell in a controlled panic. I'd be no use to anyone with a broken neck. In the back of my mind I could hear myself silently chanting *let him be fine, let him be fine, let him be fine.*

As I entered the boiler room, steam gusted over me, bearing the bloodlike reek of aether. Glass pipes filled with copper trapping wires radiated with golden light as aether coursed through them.

Carlsworth labored at the working boilers frantically. Quincey and Northwall strained at the anchor chain's mechanisms, trying to wheel the links up. At the far side of the room Derby dodged into the aetheric turbine tunnels, which sparked blue with magic.

The aetheric turbines yet worked, the spellcraft all intact, or we would have been plummeting out of the sky. But without the power of the boilers, we wouldn't be aloft for long.

The boilers ran the fans that drew in the aether, and powered the pumps that forced cooling water around the turbines. If we didn't get the boilers running at full tilt soon, then we would fall right out of the sky like that poor girls' school had not so long ago.

"Where's Leofa at?" Carlsworth shouted at me, as he shoveled coal into the functioning boiler's firebox while I rushed to the cold one.

"He's still on the topdeck!" I got tinder and matches lit. A tiny spark flickered up. I seized the bellows, working it until my arms hurt, trying to get the faint sparks to ignite the coal.

"How did this happen?" I demanded.

"Derby fell asleep," Carlsworth said.

Such rage at Derby's incompetence flared within me that it could have been used to power a hundred boilers. But I forced it back down. He was only a boy after all. Nobbsnipe's refusal to hire real stokers—or any other true crew—was not his fault. But surely the watchmen should have been here. If not to work, at the least they could have ensured that the boys did their jobs. All of our lives depended on these machines.

I pumped the bellows. Now a strong flame burned and the coals began to glow, but not enough to move the steam.

I looked at the glass tubes above us. The aetheric glow flickered as the metal began to overheat. A long crack splintered down one glass tube, dripping boiling water on to the floor.

The aetheric turbines stuttered, and for a second we hovered in midair. The boiler chugged back into life with a clatter and a hiss of steam. The coolant water gurgled as it gushed through the glass pipes, as it bathed the copper wires. The turbines hummed now.

The school steadied, and I could feel the press of gravity in the soles of my feet as we regained lift. I could barely breathe for gratitude that we would live, and then Carlsworth yelled, "I need more coal, sir!"

The next five minutes seemed an eternity. As I hauled bucket after bucket of coal, time was somehow suspended and slowed by urgency.

Once Carlsworth had enough, I went to help Quincey and Northwall crank the anchor chain, adjusting it for tension. My arms, back, and thighs ached with unaccustomed agony as I leaned into the mechanism. I pushed it forward on the count of three, releasing a slow breath, and then I did it again. Hydraulics hissed. Chain links, large as a man, slowly unspooled.

Quincey banged on the chain with a hammer and listened to it sing. I could barely hear that beneath the noise of boilers and turbines. He beckoned us to move again. Northwall and I unspooled another link. Quincey tested it again, and then held up his hand to signal that we'd finished.

It was then that Quincey seemed to notice who I was.

"Fancy meeting you here, sir," he said.

I glanced around. Strange. I would have thought that some of the watchmen would have come into help, considering our danger.

"Where are the watchmen? Why aren't they working alongside you boys?" I asked.

"Sometimes they do, sir," Quincey said. "Not today, though. We can handle it from here, sir."

I smiled warmly out of relief. But Leofa, had he tumbled from the edge when the storm had hit? What else could have prevented him from running down to the boiler room when the machines had so obviously failed?

"Call me if you need me. I have to go above." I bolted from the engine room, cold with dread, taking the stairs two at a time.

Then I charged up through the kitchen. Molly was helping Cookie finish netting down her hanging pots and pans. She turned to watch me go past, her eyes huge and dark. I ran up through the storage room, into the dining hall, and nearly collided with Leofa.

The world seemed to go still around us as I took him in—wind-blown but alive. He embraced me forcefully, near driving the air from my chest. We clung to each other, warm and alive in the chill of the empty dining hall. I could feel the trembling of his freezing body, but the solidity of him reassured me on a primal level.

I kissed him fiercely, so hard that he gasped. Leofa broke away, his face smeared with soot from mine, and his eyes sparkled with mischief.

"Never thought I'd see you ruin a suit," he said.

I smiled in wry acknowledgment. "Where were you going?"

"To find Stanley. We need a good pilot for this storm."

"Isn't he already in steerage?" I asked.

"No, Barnabas is at the wheel, but he's half drunk already," Leofa said. "I thought Stanley must've been down in the boiler room."

I shook my head.

Simultaneously, the two of us turned and looked upstairs. We rushed for the dormitory, hoping to find Stanley there. But my quick glance did not reveal his lanky figure.

"Where's Stanley?" Leofa said.

Vernon straightened up and confessed quietly, "Roger brought some watchmen. He came and got him."

My heart sank. Leofa shook his head grimly.

"I think Roger put him out to freeze," Ashby said.

Thaddeus began to wail.

"Where?" Leofa demanded.

"He's hanging on the laundry line." Hooker gazed at his feet, his usual blitheness dampened. He said, "Roger said he'd kill us if we helped him."

Not a boy met my eye.

"We have to get him," I said, but Leofa had already turned. We pounded down the stairs to the dining room and threw open the back door. The wind tore it from my hands, slamming it open.

I ventured out into the roaring winds, hunching down, and placing one foot after another on the ice. I was bracing my feet against the raised cabbage beds, and then I saw him—

Lashed to a pole with laundry line, Stanley slumped unmoving. He didn't seem conscious or aware of us. His skin had become tinged blue with cold.

Leofa rushed out before I could stop him, slid along the ice, and then caught himself. Withdrawing a knife from his pocket, he sawed through the line. The wind roared around us. I reached Stanley just as he finished. Stanley sagged toward the cobbles, but I caught him and heaved him up. Together we dragged him back in and bolted the door behind us.

Leofa touched Stanley's neck. He said, "He's alive."

We carried him to the dormitory and put him in his bed. As if ashamed for their inaction, the boys crowded around him, warming Stanley with their own bodies like a pack of apologetic puppies.

At last he regained consciousness enough to drink and speak. Only then did Leofa and I go upstairs and collapse on our shared cot.

Leofa's fingers brushed my numbed palm and we grasped hands. It felt as though our lives depended on this grip, the refusal to let each other go. We held onto each other like that, in silence, as the aetherium rode out the winter storm.

In the morning, soft snow drifted as innocently around us as though the blizzard had never raged. Although snow and ice coated the aetherium's hull, the boys weren't sent out to chip ice. The pulleys for the abseiling raft had frozen solid and the landing deck had to be cleared before ice could be collected and sold to the frostmongers.

Under Roger's watchful eye, we scraped ice from the landing deck that morning. As was his habit, Leofa kept his distance from me by daylight. So Vernon taught me how to use the ice scraper.

The work was backbreaking, especially after the exhausting events of last night. The sound of blades screeching and thudding across the decks made my teeth ache. Halfway through the morning, Stanley joined us, haggard, but still doing his part.

Roger strutted back and forth, thuggish. He'd bought a new gold-headed cane, garish with inlaid jade and mother-of-pearl. He didn't say a word about Stanley's presence.

I feared that Roger would just take Stanley out back and shoot him, put him down like a dog. But, I supposed, even the Nobbsnipes would have questions to answer if a boy with a bullet hole in his head came plummeting down from their aetherium.

Stanley worked slowly but surely. I'd been worried he'd gotten frostbite out there, but he'd come through unscathed. He was only exhausted, with dark crescents under his eyes, and deeply shaken. I heard Leofa tell him not to go to the workshop again.

When we came in for dinner, Peggy informed us softly that she'd been forbidden to serve Stanley. The portions of boiled suet pudding were pathetically small, but nonetheless everyone donated a spoonful into Stanley's bowl under Leofa's watchful eye. I led by example, though I was so hungry that stitches from a wound would've come easier, it seemed.

We returned to the decks to chip ice. In other circumstances, perhaps food would have rejuvenated me. But I had eaten so little, with no meat at all, and so my hunger gnawed at me as I worked. My muscles tormented me. I felt I could barely breathe between the cold air and my own exhaustion.

I'd been so spoiled—even here, when I'd thought I'd been deprived, with no fire in my room, no servants, no coffee in the morning or claret at dinner, no beeswax candles, a shabby and increasingly filthy wardrobe. Even then I had been so spoiled when compared to my charges.

The hard work took its toll. I ached with hunger and from physical exertion so much that I complained silently to myself. I imagined no few revenge scenarios wherein I charged into the Nobbsnipes' home, knocked Roger out with a single blow, and took everything I could carry from their laden table.

Roast beef. Capon in lemon sauce. Even mutton, that greasy middle-class staple, would be welcome now! Fish. Bread, fresh baked, with melting butter. Gods living and dead, I would have even eaten turnips or cattle feed. I sighed, watched my breath freeze in the air before me, and bent my head. I continued scraping ice. By supper, we'd cleaned the landing deck.

The watery broth, meagerly enriched with flour, tasted like wallpaper paste. The faintest hint that the broth could have, possibly, once, been introduced to a chicken was the only thing that made it at all edible.

Still Stanley went unfed and again we all shared.

That night, I sprawled down on the cot. I couldn't believe that Leofa had the energy to scramble onto the roof and check his traps. I would eat any bird he brought back, whether it was Silver-Edged Thurgeon or even a Wald's Black Peacock Dove. I would eat a pet cockatoo that could say the alphabet backwards, I was that hungry. He came back empty-handed and sat down beside me.

"I could take advantage of you," he said, "but you're too pathetic."

"It's miserable here for you and the boys." I stated the obvious, because until now I had never truly understood it.

"Sure is," Leofa agreed.

I knew that I should be plotting with him, trying to figure out the best way to recover his letters, so that we could persuade the police to lock up the Nobbsnipes. But all of my mental faculties felt benumbed. I couldn't figure my way out of a paper hatbox.

This, I reflected, must be how poverty kept people low.

Very gently he began to rub my shoulders.

"Senna bless you," I moaned, and mustered the energy to strip off my shirt.

Leofa laughed again. "If I knew you liked massages that much, I would've started giving them to you months ago. You were a hard man to get naked."

"Decency," I said. "You tried to get me in bed then?"

"Well, why do you think your cot was under the leak?" he said, philosophically.

"I knew it!" I flipped over to look at him, smiling triumphantly. "I *knew* I hadn't left it there on accident! I knew it. Ha! I'm not that careless with my things."

He leaned forward and kissed me. Leofa plucked at my hair, stretching out a tight curl and watching it spring back, and then he tangled his fingers through my hair. It had grown out longer than I liked it. I felt vaguely embarrassed that I'd forgotten my pride. He said, "I like your hair."

"You do? But it's so…lower class," I finished.

"Everyone has curly hair in Hetta," he said. "Except me. But my mother came originally from the south, you know, and moved there before I was even a babe in the womb."

"My mother passed curly hair along to my sister and me," I said. "It always made me look the cuckoo, though. And everyone knew that my stepfather had adopted me. But I wasn't his heir. His blood. Nora was. Is. But I could have stood to have it be less apparent that I didn't belong."

"Did you know your father?" he said. "You never talk about him."

I shrugged. "He died when I was young. Seven. They had a runaway marriage, you know, my mother going with a childhood sweetheart of hers, and it didn't go well."

"Ah," Leofa murmured.

"He was a brawler and a drunk," I said, "a man embittered by the fact that marrying a woman of a higher class only lessened them both in the eyes of the world. What about you?"

"Mine died when I was a babe. He farmed, my mother said," Leofa answered. "She sold his lease after, then moved for a fresh start."

"Do you miss the Barrens—Hetta, I mean?" I said.

Leofa shrugged. "Flip over so I can rub your back."

I turned back onto my stomach and he continued, "I don't know if I miss them as such. Used to, you know, when I first got here. But I think what I missed most was being anywhere but here. The culture, I guess, it differed. I miss the food, and the mountains."

His hands were strong and capable on my shoulders, his touch warm and relaxing as he rubbed the sore muscles along my back.

"For me," I said, "it's the aetheria. They aren't like this one, you know, my old schools." I sighed, dreaming of Elmstead's vast hall at suppertime. "I suppose I never interested myself in managing the estate out in Midshire. I focused on academia. Except when I wanted to be a pirate."

Leofa laughed. "You?"

"That, or an explorer," I said. "Thus the early fascination with firearms. I liked hunting with my stepfather, as well. We saw eye-to-eye there, had something to talk about when we couldn't talk about much else."

Leofa made an understanding noise.

"It pleased my mother, I think," I added, "to see us head out together. He could understand the prestige attached to higher learning in theory, I think, but he appreciated my role in the marksmanship society more."

"You'd go back there?" he asked.

"In a heartbeat," I said.

"Not if I'm on top of you, you can't." He hunkered down on top me, pinning me against the cot, and then it turned out that I wasn't so tired as I'd thought.

⌒

In the weeks coming up to Darkest Night, Leofa attempted method after method to crack my mother's grimoire. I adapted to my new place as an outcast.

On Mondays, Tuesdays, and Wednesdays, I got up two hours earlier and went down with the boys to the laundry rooms. Considering how we rationed the fuel my uncle had given us, the laundry became the only warm place we passed any time. This almost, but not quite, made up for the back-breaking labor.

I found that I took additional care of my clothes, knowing that I'd be the one to remove the ink stains. The one time I chanced a complaint to Molly she met me with days of gentle, yet accurate, mockery.

In the schoolroom, the older boys progressed slowly but steadily in their study of the ancient languages. The younger boys became more solid in their reading and reckoning. Wallace had almost mastered the alphabet and the numbers up to one hundred. I started Thaddeus on learning them as well, though he had already picked up the basics from his older friend.

While I did my teaching, I knew peripherally that Leofa labored in the workshop, trying to crack the grimoire now, but in such a way that Nobbsnipe couldn't observe his progress.

It was a tricky procedure all around. Nobbsnipe was not the laissez-faire employer I'd encountered in my schoolroom, but rather a hawk-eyed and strict commander in the workshop.

Nobbsnipe had the only key to the workshop. He unlocked it to let the boys in mornings and locked it again at night—apparently having watchmen sleeping in front of the only door did not content him. And even if he so much as needed to go out for a piss during the workday, he'd almost always lock the boys in.

Inside, he had a keen eye and a good feel for how far a boy had gotten on cracking a tome. He searched every boy before they left, lest they conceal a spell leaf on their body.

No one, in Leofa's memory, had ever tried this.

So, in addition to concealing his work on my sister's grimoire, Leofa plotted to smuggle me into the workshop so that I could tell him which leafs to cut. Getting those out again would be another matter.

At mealtimes, Stanley still received no ration, surviving off our assembled donations. I'd always had a slim build, and now, sharing the boys' diet, I dwindled alongside him. My clothes draped from me like so much sacking. It looked like I'd bought them secondhand while blind drunk.

Stanley showed occasional sparks of life, but they never lasted long. Mired deep in misery, he seemed to console himself with an imaginary world. One where he could construct the perfect flying machine, powered by miniature boilers that drove steam-powered propellers.

Sometimes, the Nobbsnipes left their windows open when they knew the boys and I were outside laboring. We could hear them laughing, smell the roast beef and fresh baked bread and all the glory of other hot foods perfuming the air. They meant to torment us. They succeeded.

Once, Roger left supper early to watch me as I slurped gruel in the boys' dining hall. He swaggered around, tossing that ludicrous faux-Cho cane from hand to hand, telling us to be grateful for his father's generosity.

Several more storms rocked the aetherium in varying severity. Sometimes we lost half a day, sometimes two days, to scraping off the ice. As I worked, I thought often of my sister. I found it hard not being able to write to Nora, not being able to know if she did well.

I imagined drafting letters to her in lieu of the real thing, which, going unsent, would simply depress me. I tried to think of her preparing for her presentation on Darkest Night. Nora would be corresponding with her school friends, finding out who would be coming into town for this grand event, and arranging to meet them. All the chaos and the excitement, as the possibilities of her life began to unfold.

I hoped that she was happy. But I could not risk contacting her because I did not want to get her in trouble with Uncle Gerard.

I did send letters to Professor Pike via tracker almost daily. He had taken to sending extra trackers to me, in spite of the expense, so that I could send him small updates as I worked them out. I often returned in the evening to see the aethero-mechanical devices glommed onto the garret window, like so many moths attracted to the light.

At night, Leofa took to strolling around the aetherium under the guise that he had difficulty sleeping. He searched, quietly, for the letters.

When he went out, I worked on my transducer.

Although hunger made me feel vague and distracted, sometimes it gave me a sharpness—a strange alertness—that worked to my advantage. I'd spent years thinking about the transducer and years working on it. Now it suddenly seemed as though my disparate theories, thoughts, all those little pieces, combined so beautifully.

It reminded me of playing an unfamiliar piece on the piano. It could seem initially out of order, even confusing. And then suddenly one could hear it, the intention of the song, the poetry and rhythm of it, so that it became more than disparate notes. Suddenly it transformed into tightly woven melody.

I would have been worried that that my ease led me falsely, or that my hunger had sent me into a euphoric delirium. But Professor Pike seemed to think that I pursued the right course.

When I encountered a stumbling block with my work on the transducer, when I needed to divert myself and step back, Leofa was always there for me. He taught me Hei. With his permission, I wrote out what I learned and passed it along to Professor Pike so that he might give it, in turn, to his language specialist friend, Professor Vassily.

Leofa taught me how to trap birds and I taught him courtly manners. He humored me, somewhat, out of affection. But I still treasured a secret hope that someday, if our circumstances had altered, perhaps he would be able to put his skills to work in the queen's laboratories.

"Shrugging is ill-bred in mixed company," I said. "You'll need to know that when you work for the queen."

"You do it." Leofa tapped his hands on the knee of his grayish trousers. He wore his singed navy blue sweater to combat our room's abidingly low temperature.

"Not even I am perfect," I said with mock hauteur. "But truly, do not use your index finger to point. Rather, gesture with the whole hand, or nod. If you encounter a countess, you'll want to tip your hat."

"I have to do this for every lady I pass?" he said. "If I walked through the Royal Shadow Gardens, it'd take me an hour to get fifteen feet. How do you manage to get anywhere?"

"You calculate how long it will take and then add an extra hour for courtesies," I said dryly. "Really, you do get accustomed, and if you must get anywhere in a hurry, it's wise to take a closed conveyance."

During one such discussion, a tracker arrived. The tracker smacked against our window. It was heavier, cheaper, and more primitive than the ones employed by Elmstead, shaped more like a dragonfly rather than a moth—and I opened up the window to retrieve it. Curious, I brought it inside.

I grasped the tracker's coppery spine, popping loose its suction-cup feet from the window glass, and then turned it over. I opened the hatch on its abdomen and fished out the letter inside. I recognized Nora's handwriting immediately, though the envelope had no seal and the paper possessed a much shoddier quality than what she'd normally use.

Dear Brother,

~~*I'm sorry I haven't been able to get away. The maidservant spies on me. I eluded her at the museum to send this*~~. *Wish I could say more. Stay safe and well. I remain,*

Ever Your Loving Sister

Her secret code followed, the dots unembellished.

"It's from my sister. It's in code." Worry surged through me. What did she need to communicate so urgently that it could not go through other channels? Why had Nora sent me a letter clandestinely—and in her secret code? Was she in danger from my uncle?

I handed the letter to Leofa and released the tracker from the window. The dragonfly-like device plummeted. Then as the aether rushed in through its fans, its mini-turbines whirred into life. I saw its dark shape zip away, returning to the private postal service from which it had come. When I turned back to Leofa, he'd raised his eyebrows. He smoothed the letter down on the desk.

"I have those trackers from my professor," I said. "If I reprogram one, I could send her a message. Reassure her, at the very least."

"That's a bad idea," Leofa said. "If she escaped her maidservant tonight, and a tracker comes for her tomorrow, they'll connect the two and know that she's communicating with someone. What with cracking grimoires being treason against the Crown, the stakes are too high to let that slide."

"Then may Loxa the lucky watch over her." I rubbed my temples, pained.

Nora was my little sister. Of course I wanted to swoop down there, like some rash fool, and take her away. But I had to trust in her, not make her living circumstances worse.

But still…still, she was my baby sister.

Leofa rested his hand on my shoulder, giving me a gentle squeeze to show that he knew what I thought. I could hear him shift beside me. Together we sat down to decode her message.

UNCLE KILLED MAMA AND PAPA AGUE TO GET GRIMOIRE

Leofa inhaled sharply. I stared at the decoded note, stunned.

I'd wanted to believe, so badly, in that fairytale that Uncle Gerard had told about himself. I'd wanted to believe the story about the second son making it in the big city through good investments in stocks.

He'd reached out to my family as if he'd wanted to share his good fortune with us. He'd gone out of his way to invite my parents to visit him in Herrow so that they could look into that business opportunity—

—gone out of his way to invite them to Herrow, paying for their stay at a fine hotel—

—a fine hotel, that had been located where the ague had broken out, where they'd been among the first stricken—

"Oh, Wyrd, father of all wisdom." I sat there, stunned, between tears and fury, as I contemplated a possibility I hoped impossible. It wasn't true. It couldn't be. That my own kin, even by marriage, could do such a thing, defied comprehension.

"What is it?" Leofa knelt beside me, his hands on my knees, looking up at me. Had he been speaking before? Had he tried to get my attention? Had I not heard him? I did not know. Dazed, I took a shaky breath.

"It's true. What she wrote. The ill-wishing spell, the spell you handed over," I said, "it caused the ague, yes?"

Leofa nodded. "Within a radius of where you'd set the spell, yeah."

"I think he may have set the center of that radius on the hotel where my parents stayed." I stated this quietly but surely, going to a calm and clinical place inside of me. I felt as though I stood before a committee of professors, taking an oral exam, and logic banished all else. I could not react any way but this.

I continued, "He would have known which hotel to focus the spell on, considering that he put them up there. He must have—he knew about the debt. Either he engineered it, or he knew they'd incurred one; and he took into account debtors seizing everything, everything but the family grimoire, which could not be seized save by the Crown and only then if the family bloodline had died out."

I took another breath before my conclusion. I finished, "He came in like a savior, and in our gratitude, we gave him exactly what he was after all along: the grimoire."

My throat ached with pent-up emotion, small tremors dancing through me.

"Neil, I am so sorry." Leofa's voice cracked. "It's my fault."

I was still too stunned to even begin thinking of something as crass as blame.

"It's done," I said quietly, because nothing could bring them back. I stood up. Leofa looked at me with torment in his eyes. But then I leaned up against him. He embraced me tightly. I needed him there as strong as an anchor, his warmth real. He needed this too, because I knew that Leofa feared I would hate him. I did not find him at fault.

Only...

Suddenly I felt as though my parents had died yesterday rather than months ago, the knowledge driven home with torturous exactitude, like iron splinters under fingernails. How could they have suspected such infamy?

I could imagine them, all too easily: in the city with their rusticated fashions. My stepfather—a hale country gentleman—greeting his brother with a friendly handshake. And my mother greeting her brother-in-law with an embrace and a kiss on the cheek.

I knew my parents had been generous people, paying out more scrumpy to their seasonal workers than most. If my uncle had simply asked to have access to the family grimoire, surely they would have worked out some deal more than fair to all. But no, clearly that would not have worked for him. His greed had overwhelmed his good sense.

I rubbed my temples as I thought. Downstairs, the boys had gotten rather rambunctious.

"What makes this grimoire so valuable?" Leofa asked.

"I told you, it's the pyxis spell," I said. "It must be that. It's a spell that can capture and hold infinite amounts of aether, so that aether can be used even when you aren't in a current. Modern spells can only use ambient flowing aether."

Leofa made a gesture that indicated I should get to the point.

"If the pyxis could be made to work with modern channeling

spells," I continued, "such as those that draw the aether from the school's fans through the turbines and the spells that keep us aloft, then it would change everything. Warfare. Travel. Communication. Everything."

"That's why you're working on a transducer," Leofa said. "Do you think he has a key to making the pyxis work?"

"Maybe. Maybe not." I sighed. "He might simply give up and sell it. I know my family had offers to sell."

"Did you think of selling it yourself?" Leofa asked. "You know, when your estate was sold?"

"The grimoire is not mine. It's my sister's," I said. "I don't know if Nora thought about selling the spell or not. We never discussed it. I think we were too stunned by circumstances, and then my uncle came."

"If none of this had happened..." Leofa began.

I brushed my fingers along his jaw. I still found it remarkable that, when we were alone, he let me touch him however I wanted. I hoped my wonder in this would never die away, in having the freedom to press my skin against his.

His cheekbones beneath my fingertips, the roughness of his stubble along his jaw and chin—I savored all these sensations as I bent to kiss him where he knelt. I could feel him smiling throughout this soft kiss, the barest brush of the lips.

"You know," I said seriously, "I can't bring myself to regret coming here, even given these misfortunes."

Leofa smiled and glanced away as though shy, and again I wondered what would become of us.

Discovering the extent of my uncle's infamy did make my own loyalties clear. But this knowledge, though strengthening my resolve to bring him to justice, got me nowhere.

For I could not let justice come at the expense of Leofa and all the boys who I'd come to hold dear. So I needed proof not only of the iniquities but I also needed to extirpate whatever evidence that could inculpate Leofa and the boys. In practical terms: I needed to find Mrs. Nobbsnipe's fraudulent letters to Leofa. And I needed to destroy them.

But right now we had to discover a way to infiltrate the workshop without tipping off the watchmen.

Downstairs, a blast of whooping followed by a crash and several panicked thuds broke my thoughts. I couldn't focus with the boys creating such a racket downstairs.

Affectionately, I brushed a hand across Leofa's shoulder, then lifted up the hatch, and leaned down to see what had happened. The action, as per usual, seemed to center around Hooker, who'd opened a window that I had not even known could open and already had a leg slung out of it.

"Hooker!" I bellowed. "Don't climb out of the windows! And the rest of you, keep it down. Demos, it's the middle of the night!"

The boys stared at me, astonished, as though they'd forgotten our room stood directly above theirs. Hooker froze and then slowly eased himself back indoors. He closed the window with a false nonchalance and grinned at me. I shook my head, shut the hatch, and looked up at Leofa from where I knelt.

"All we need to do," I said, trying to resume my chain of thought, "is get into the workshop."

"The door is always guarded," Leofa said.

"But are the windows?" I asked, my pulse racing. "Do they have windows that open?"

"If I unlock them when I'm working they will," Leofa said. "But I know what you're thinking. It's too dangerous."

I started to smile as a thought occurred to me. "That is not at all what I'm thinking. I suggest we recruit Molly."

13

As a landed lord, I'd never had eye for the girls—obviously, though I could have described each of the stable hands in detail. I hadn't noticed the maids-of-all-work anymore than I would notice the furniture. Was it well kept? Did it serve its purpose? And so forth. But since coming to Highfell I had been enlightened as to Molly's integral role in running the household.

She laid the fires and swept the ashes. Molly dressed the ladies, she made repairs to their wardrobes, she served the food, and whatever was needed, she presented herself with her head bent, ready to do it.

Most importantly, Molly was allowed in any room.

"Your main task," I told her, "would be to take Nobbsnipe's keys. We'd need them to lock the watchmen into the port hall and also to gain access to rooms during our search."

"Well, can't say I'd like getting caught doing that, my lord." Molly was seated at the desk. Beside her our brazier blazed. In spite of the toasty heat wafting from the coals, frost limned the rain tank wall. She said, "And I don't see why I should really help you, considering I could lose my place, and we all know I got my reasons for keeping it."

"You won't help?" I asked. I had never considered this an option— that she would refuse.

Night had darkened the sky—Molly was too busy during daytime for her to meet us then. The tallow candle's wick had grown long, drooping down against its side and melting a dent. I moved over to the desk, clipped the wick, and seated myself back on the cot Leofa and I shared.

Molly looked at him and then down at her hands, clenched on her lap. "Not for nothing, I won't."

"What do you want?" Leofa said, sounding curious.

She glanced back up, her head slightly cocked. "My marriage certificate, that's all. I need it. But I can't—I can't read. So the chances of me finding it in all those papers his lordship kept around... Well, it's unlikely, you see? The seeking spell, do you think you could use it to find my marriage certificate?"

"Only if we were within a thousand feet of it already," I said, apologetically.

"No matter. That's what I want," Molly said.

I glanced at Leofa. He met my gaze and nodded.

"I say it's a deal," he said.

Molly regarded us thoughtfully. I could see snow falling outside, flecking against the window. The lit brazier, coals glowing red and throwing up a sulfurous stench, barely mitigated the chill. The brazier's fumes escaped through our window, which was cracked open. Molly shivered slightly in the draft.

"You two will need a dark lantern." Molly sounded practical as she lifted her hands to warm them above the brazier. She said, "I can get that for you."

I knew that we couldn't guarantee that we'd find the marriage certificate, due to the spell's own range and limitations.

I looked askance at Leofa. He'd made progress on my sister's grimoire, but I could not say whether he could currently crack it.

He gave a casual shrug. "How about tomorrow night? 'Course, depends on whether I'll be able to fix the window. Should be able to get the rope in, at least, seeing as we aren't searched on the way in."

"If that isn't too soon..." I said, glancing at Molly.

"I can get the keys and the lantern tomorrow," she said. "Have no worry on that account. But you're going to have to swear it to me, in blood, that you'll find my marriage certificate."

I agreed reluctantly. I knew my chances of my finding it were slim, but we needed Molly's assistance.

We pricked our fingers on her sewing needle and then swore it in blood. Before Molly left, we went over the plan with her once more and she said she'd bring us the dark lantern in the morning, before starting on her daily work.

Directly after Molly left, I noticed a tapping at the window.

As I opened the window to let one of Professor Pike's moth-like trackers in, Leofa busied himself with fixing his pigeon traps. He wasn't catching much. The other aetheria's cotes had been mostly shut up in this weather, and the pigeons in the city below didn't venture into the winter storms. But he'd been faithfully trying nonetheless.

The tracker wiggled in my hands, light in spite it size. Insect-like legs scrabbled against my wrist as I reached under its head and flicked the off switch. The tracker locked into stillness, and then I turned it back over again to open its fat grub-like body.

Professor Pike had enclosed a note. There Pike said, among other things, that he had a copper-and-gold mesh ready to be inscribed with the pyxis spell in his lab. And that he could inscribe any number of other wires for me, even at short notice, if it would mean my being able to test my work personally.

I glanced up at Leofa, where he muttered as he mended a net. He sometimes talked to his knots as if they lived, striving to spite him, and it looked as though Leofa currently discussed the best way to subdue a knot rebellion.

"Professor Pike says he'll do whatever he can to help me test out my theory on the transducer. He'll even set me up with a working pyxis, though right now I can't give him the spell to inscribe on the mesh because I don't have it," I told him. "He also thinks we should submit my work on the transducer to the Royal Society of Aetheric Studies."

"Huh?" Leofa stopped his work. "Say that again?"

"Well, the professor says I need to finish a few of these equations here and there, but other than that, I'll soon have a working model. He said he'd inscribe wires for me so that I could test it here."

"What's he get out of this?" Leofa asked.

"Well," I said, "he is essentially funding this work and he has advised me on the equations, so I think that asking to be a co-author on my work is hardly unexpected."

"It's your idea," Leofa groused. "Don't see why his name should be on it all."

"I don't have my doctorate," I said. "No one would take it seriously if I submitted. But he has quite a history, and my name would be on it, so at least I'd get a publishing credit. He says he'll ensure that I receive credit when he fills out the submission forms."

"You trust Pike not to steal it?" Leofa asked.

"If he meant to, he would have done it already," I said. "This could be a way out for me."

"Then Loxa look upon your endeavors," Leofa said, too politely, and returned to crushing the knot rebellion in his net. He conscripted repentant twine into his new army of more obedient knots.

After drafting a cautious response, and sending it out in the tracker to the professor, I turned to Leofa and asked him if I could snuff the candle. When he assented, I pinched the hot wick out with my fingers. It made my hands smell like singed mutton.

At times like these, I felt uncertain. Somehow, I never knew what I ought to do, or where I ought to go. Was this thing between us a series of moments, or had the precedent built into habit, and then something more? Could I make presumptions, simply because of what had gone before?

I couldn't tell what made me more nervous: the possibility that this could lead to something that had always seemed impossible to me, or the possibility that this could end. But I knew what I wanted. I would go to Leofa as long as I could, savor the sound of his heartbeat, his pulse against my lips, the taste of his skin.

"What are you waiting for?" he said, laughing. "Come to bed, Your Majesty."

⌒

In the earliest hours of morning, I climbed down the ladder from the garret and waited for Leofa to follow. The boys all slept in their beds with such quiet that it almost seemed suspicious; no one snored, no late-night troublemakers whispered to each other, and Vernon, who sometimes talked in his sleep, made not a sound.

Leofa descended the ladder. He'd brought with him a cloth sack containing his gauntlets, goggles, and bloodlock picks. He touched me on the shoulder, indicating that we should go.

Downstairs, Molly waited for us in the boys' dining room. We were far enough from the sleeping boys, the kitchen, and the Nobbsnipes that we did not have to fear being overheard here. But still, we kept our voices down when we spoke.

"The last watchmen just came in." Molly handed Leofa the dark lantern, and pressed a box of matches into my hand. She said, "You might need these. I'll want them back, though. I'll meet you out front in an hour. Loxa love you."

Venturing outdoors into the bitter wind, we crossed the icy courtyard. The caution light on our aetherium's prow and the illumination beaming down from the higher aetheria gave us more than adequate ambient light.

I found it odd to think that we now acted rather than merely talking about it. I had thought I would feel like a boarding boy breaking curfew. But this was very different. If caught I would not face a disapproving schoolmaster, but a man who would happily beat me to death. No thrill emboldened me. Rather, terror invited prudence.

Passing the front door, we went around the starboard side. The wind hissed past us here, driving old snow against our faces and into the fabric of our coats. The air's chill stung my nose.

"That's the one," Leofa said, gesturing at the middle window.

I squinted up at it, my eyes watering because of the wind. The window seemed very far from me. Prior to this, Leofa had smuggled a rope and secretly fixed its grapple onto the sill. Most of the rope coiled on the windowsill. Only the tail end hung down—still far out of reach.

"You'll have to get on my shoulders," Leofa said.

I wanted to give him a skeptical look. It hardly seemed safe, considering the ice underfoot, but truly, we had no choice.

Leofa crouched down beside me, grunting as I climbed up to stand on his shoulders. I braced against the wall as he straightened his legs and stood. I wished for something more solid, like a ladder, as I wobbled with my feet on my lover's shoulders. The rope's end hung mere inches from my fingertips now.

I stretched up. My hand slipped off the ice-coated rope end—and then I snagged it. The rope unfurled downward in a tangle. I dismounted from my clownish acrobatics display.

Leofa tugged the rope to make sure it had remained and gave me a mock salute. Then he walked up the ice-slick wall, climbing until he reached the window. He pushed open the shutters. The wind snatched them from his hand and slammed them against the wall—once, twice, before he grabbed the shutters again.

I flinched at the noise, my eyes darting around the courtyard. I hoped the sound would rouse no conscientious watchmen.

Leofa, legs tight around the rope, held the shutter back with one hand. He pushed the window inward with the other. Then he slid in with relative ease. Once inside, he leaned out and gave me the all clear. He tied the lantern to the rope and pulled that up before dropping the rope back down for me.

I climbed up after him with considerably less ease. I was glad he has gone first, for I would have been incapable of the maneuver he'd just pulled. Once inside, I reeled the rope back up, then closed the shutter and window.

The dark workshop now seemed cavernous. The ladders leading up to the second-story gallery looked incomplete without trackers crawling across the rails. The showcases filled with grimoires, cracked and uncracked, glimmered with the eerie blue light of protective spells.

On the ground story, the bulky shapes of the tables, the strange curls of alchemical glassware, the small smithy, all seemed strange, and therefore, foreboding, in the dark.

Leofa slipped his gauntlets on, put his iolite goggles up on his forehead, and tucked his bundle of lock picks under his arm.

I lit the lantern and flipped its hatch closed, and then used a small knob to slide the cover off a round opening. A crescent of light escaped, and so I caught a glimpse of Leofa beckoning me. He headed over to a brass ladder that led to the upper gallery. I handed the lantern up to Leofa and joined him.

The nearest showcase contained, to my surprise, empty grimoires. The intact covers had been shut but there were no pages inside. I gestured at them, curiously, and Leofa leaned in to whisper, "We've kept the completely cracked ones for practice."

He brought me past several more cases containing empty grimoires and then past several full ones. Finally, he paused, aiming the crescent of light at a particular spine. I knew it from its emerald green leather, decorated with citrine flower buds and opal moths. I nodded. It was definitely my mother's grimoire.

Seeing it overwhelmed me with nostalgia and a certain possessiveness. And it also made me quite pensive regarding our endeavor. I whispered a silent apology to my mother's memory.

Leofa handed me the lantern. He flipped his goggles down over his eyes and knelt to examine the case's lock. I held the lantern up for him, angling the light so that his own shadow would not block his view.

I could tell from how he turned his head that he analyzed the aether's currents. Leofa selected an iron pick, peered at the lock, and got to work. A few seconds later, the lock clicked and the metal netting in the showcase's glass flashed blue. He opened the showcase and retrieved the grimoire.

Once we'd finished that part, we returned to a table downstairs and he got to work on cracking the grimoire. He selected each lock pick with care, retracting the blood collection needles delicately, using an iron pick, pressing them down, then switching to bronze.

I stayed at a safe distance. How he disabled the enspelled mechanism fascinated me.

His face was relaxed and serious, his eyes almost closed, as though Leofa listened more to the lock than looking at it. His current expression reminded me of the one he wore when leaning in for a kiss. But the tension around his dark brows differed. His eyelashes flicked as he manipulated an iron pick.

Once, he made a mistake and a spray of blazing white sparks fountained up. He flinched back reflexively, instantly whipping the cloth sacking off a nearby chair and smothering the grimoire with it. Leofa rubbed out the embers smoldering on his gauntlets.

It'd hadn't been exactly inconspicuous, that. I wondered if the watchmen had noticed the light beaming out from the workshop door, but I could hear no commotion downstairs. I could feel time ticking away. Surely we had to meet Molly soon? I forced myself to remain myself patient and still.

"Wish your blood'd work to open this," he muttered. His leather gauntlets still smoking, he returned to his work.

Twenty minutes later, the bloodlock quietly popped open, with the straps that bound the grimoire's covers slithering away of their own accord. He flipped open the book and smiled up at me.

"Cracked her," he said quietly, satisfaction evident in his voice. "See what you can find. I'm going to get a cutter."

As Leofa went back to open one of the supply cupboards, I stepped up to the grimoire. The paper was soft and thin beneath my fingertips, fine as a flake of ash for all that each page was embedded with metal strands.

I paged through the grimoire slowly. For each spell leaf, two larger and thicker woody pages served as a buffer. This was to prevent inadvertent contact between the spells, which could have catastrophically explosive results. When I turned the pages, I touched only the clean margins.

The grimoire had been made before indexes and tables of contents had been invented. Even though the alphabet was Accadian, no one could read the spells any longer. So at one point some enterprising ancestor of mine had written small descriptions of some of the spells (not many) in an inert ink in the upper corners of the pages. By the time Leofa returned with his cutter, I had found the seeking spell.

He held the cutter, which appeared to be a small scalpel with a wooden handle and sporting a blade of volcanic glass. Both were substances that did not react to aether.

Giving way to his expertise, I stepped back with my hands up, indicating that he ought to do the honors. Carefully, he sliced the leaf out of the grimoire without damaging the page below. He set it aside, and I went back to the search. The seeking spell was important, but to me the pyxis spell would be my real prize.

Then I found it. Leofa removed that as well. Expertly, he packed up the spell leafs in protective layers of blank paper and then slid them into my emptied shaving box. I slipped the shaving box with its precious contents under my clothes, keeping it close to my body.

Leofa packed away all of his tools, replaced the cutter in the cabinet, relocked it, and then returned the grimoire to the showcase in the upper gallery. When he shut it into the cupboard again, the enspelled wire in the glass flashed blue as the alarm spell reactivated. Leofa hurried back over to me. I extinguished the lantern.

After that, we slid down the rope. The wind buffeted me, sending me spinning. I slid the last few feet, hit the ground, slipped, and regained my footing. Leofa lowered down the lantern and his tools first. He then unhooked the rope and dropped it into my waiting hands. I lifted the rope and started coiling it over my shoulder.

Leofa, being more at ease with scaling icy building than I, now had the tricky part ahead of him. I could feel my jaw clench as he stepped out onto the icy windowsill. He shut the window behind him, reached out for the open shutter, almost slipped, and then caught himself and latched the window shut.

Slowly, very carefully, Leofa crouched down on the windowsill, and then swung himself down. He dropped to the ground with a thud. He slid on the ice and landed ungracefully on his side. I reached over, helping him up, and he dusted off some snow with a smile.

Molly awaited us out front, shivering on the stoop. I returned the lantern and matches. She departed without a word.

We slipped inside the boys' dining room. Leofa gave me a confident smile. I smiled back at him, feeling something in my chest warm in response, and then paused. I'd heard something. Leofa gave me a look that told me he'd heard it too. I shut the door to the outside carefully and then we both listened. Voices.

At first I thought watchmen came for us. But then I heard something that sounded suspiciously like giggling, and the door to the storeroom opened. Peggy came out, an apple in her hand. She stopped when she saw us, her mouth dropping open with surprise.

Hooker bounded out after her, holding dry sausages and grinning. He gawked at us. Ashby and Quincey collided with them. I heard some thuds coming from upstairs. Stanley came down.

"Don't you think we should get some of the—" he began, excitedly and none too softly, and then he saw us. Stanley flushed and said, "Uh. Good evening, sir."

Leofa closed his eyes and shook his head.

"Here I thought it'd gone well," I said.

While we'd been quietly sneaking through the workshop, the boys and Peggy had picked the locks on the storage bins. They'd gulped down several links of sausage. And then they'd started moving the rest of the delicacies for the Nobbsnipes' Darkest Night feast into the unused schoolroom upstairs.

The damage could not be undone. Peggy and the boys, now fidgety and acting defiantly proud of themselves, watched keenly as Leofa and I drew aside to confer privately.

"I cannot believe they did this to us," I muttered, feeling a surge of anger toward my students for selfishly, unknowingly, jeopardizing our plan. But I took a deep breath, putting that aside. What was done was done.

"We'll have to do the seeking spell tonight, because the Nobbsnipes are sure to increase security after this," I said, pitching my voice low so that only Leofa could hear it. "Molly's already unlocked the watchmen's staffroom."

"We got to make it look like raiders did the stealing," Leofa said.

At first I didn't understand the conclusion he'd leapt to, but then I saw that he was correct. The Nobbsnipes, if they discovered the missing supplies and the children's full-scale insurrection, would punish the boys more severely than ever before.

The spell would have to wait until the boys were safe—or safer, at least.

"Are those rumors of raiders even true?" I asked.

Leofa nodded. "They'll be true enough tonight. Get the boys out of here."

I turned around to face the miscreants and saw terror on their faces. I said, "You boys aren't in trouble, not with us, and not right now. If we're going to steal, we're going to do it right."

I had their attention now. I glanced over at the line of boys, mentally counting them and assembling an idea of who was present, and then I said, "Falcons, Wolves, you're with Leofa. Beasels, Skunks—"

"We're the Rhinos now!" Hooker said.

"Fine, Beasels and Rhinos, you're with me," I said.

Leofa smiled and shook his head. "Falcons, go upstairs and get the ice skates and the ice scrapers. Meet us outside on the landing deck. Wolves, you pick up those bags of flour and follow me. Let's leave a trail that not even Roger can miss."

I followed the Beasels upstairs to their stash and ordered them to stash it under the classroom floorboards, which we could pry up easily. We handed up food, shifting it faster than a fire brigade shifted buckets.

"A patrol's coming," Hooker said.

"Run outside and warn Leofa," I told him.

In my urgency to preserve the boys, I'd left our bag in the dining room downstairs. Leofa's grimoire-cracking tools would be exposed.

Panicked, I dashed downstairs. I searched for the bag by feel, not able to find it in the dark. When I heard the floorboards creaking, I reflexively pressed under a trestle table. I expected to see Hooker.

But it wasn't Hooker. Instead Addison and Yardley, two of the watchmen, strolled in together. Holding up their lanterns, they made a cursory examination of the dining room. I could barely breathe. I remained still as a hunted deer. Now I could see, but a few feet away from me, the bag. What if they saw it?

Just then, Ashby and Hooker galumphed down the stairs with all the subtlety of elephants. The boys saw the watchmen and paused. Ashby tucked something into his pockets quickly and casually. Hooker squeaked when he cleared his throat, he was so nervous.

"What are you boys doing?" Addison demanded.

Hooker almost answered. My eyes followed his gaze as he caught sight of something. The storeroom door stood open a crack. Peggy stood there, looking as timid as a rabbit. Ashby knocked Hooker on the shoulder so hard that Hooker actually stumbled down a step. Ashby replied, "Going to take a piss, sir."

"Both of you?" Addison sounded skeptical.

Peggy sank back into the shadows, away from the door.

"Yes, sir," Ashby said, coming down a step to stand beside Hooker. "He's afraid of the dark."

Hooker opened his mouth, no doubt to protest.

"We'll escort you," Addison said.

Yardley smirked. "What were you going to do, Hooker, piss the bed?"

"Fuck off!" Hooker shouted, and the watchmen seemed to find this hilarious.

The two watchmen escorted the boys out. As soon as they'd gone, I snatched up the bag against my chest and bolted outside. I sprinted across the courtyard to the landing deck, pressing myself up against the windbreak. I could not see anyone.

The deck was well torn up. The winch lead had been unwound and snaked across the deck. Several split bags of flour had been discarded to the side of this. If anyone ought to get in trouble over this caper, the watchmen would. I would not weep to see any of them beaten or dismissed.

Surveying the area, I realized that Leofa had to be hiding beneath the gliders. I skidded over to the hangar, my entire body thrumming with nervousness, and slipped under one of the wings beside Leofa.

"It safe?" Leofa asked in a low voice.

I shook my head. "Maybe. Maybe not. I don't know where the watchmen are. And the boys?"

"I sent them back with Quincey." Leofa had a dusting of snow on his pitch-dark hair and his hands, which were flat against the frozen ground where he crouched.

I handed the bag to him and removed the seeking spell from the shaving case. My hands trembled as I held the spell. I'd never cast it before.

The page felt light in my hands in spite of the hair-thin wires embedded in it. In the ambient light, the metallic inks glistened. I read over instructions on how to cast the spell, located in the lower margin in inert ink (penned, it hurt to see, in my mother's own hand).

"You're going to have to guide me. I won't be able to see normally," I told him. "You will have to place your writing hand over my heart when I'm pronouncing the spell. Please try to keep in mind what we're looking for. That should help."

I edged out from under the glider and stood up. Leofa pressed his hand to my chest. Necessary though it was for the spell, it made me feel as though a greater affinity connected us. Warmed by this, I smiled at him. He nodded, signaling that I start.

I held the page in one hand, and then with my index finger, traced the letters and whispered out the spell. Leofa twitched as I spoke and watched me as though startled. I kept in mind, always, what we searched for.

As I enunciated the last words of the spell, as my finger brushed the last letter, a strange tingle flashed through me. It hurt, much like the intensity of pins-and-needles in a benumbed limb. My bearings and sense of balance felt subtly altered.

"Shit, that's eerie," Leofa muttered.

I blinked, my eyes watering. The world around me looked smeary, like I viewed it through grease-streaked glass, and my eyes could not quite make sense of the proportions of the building. The skewed architecture made my head throb.

My aching eyes gravitated toward the one point in the world that seemed supernaturally, keenly, in focus. The thin line hung as if etched in the air. I grabbed for it reflexively, almost losing my balance, and Leofa steadied me.

I stared at the thread. It seemed to pour out from Leofa's hand, where he'd placed warmly over my heart, and then forward toward the aetherium. I swiveled toward it and started following it. The thread passed directly through the windbreak.

"Watchmen," Leofa said in a low warning tone. "Close your eyes."

I shut them, trying to smother out the glow that I knew burned in my pupils.

"No luck," he said. "They're glowing through your eyelids."

I pressed my free hand over my eyes. Without sight, my sense of distorted reality and instability increased. I thought, Please, don't let them notice the food's theft yet.

"They've gone into the staff room," Leofa said. "We should have a few minutes before the next patrol starts. Let's move!"

Although I unreasonably wanted to follow the invisible thread through the windbreak, Leofa forced me to go around. The thread led me directly across the courtyard and angled upward into the Nobbsnipes' residence. I reached along the thread, with a yearning, grasping gesture.

Leofa lifted his hand away from my heart and the spell snapped. I shook off its remnants, dazed and achy. Leofa gazed up at the windows and said, "They're in Mrs. Nobbsnipe's boudoir."

⤙

When we'd once more reached the safety of the dining room, Molly waited beside the table. She pressed the box she'd been carrying into my arms. It gleamed metallically, like some sort of cash box. She said, "The Nobbsnipes' lockbox. If raiders were here, they would've taken it."

"If we're caught with this—" Leofa sounded on the verge of anger.

"That's why I'm giving it to you," she said shortly and turned away.

We kept the currency and tossed the lockbox over the side to land in the icy river far below.

Upstairs, we had a lecture to deliver. I did not want anyone's imagination running away with him: should someone claim to have heard anything, should one boy begin to embroider upon it, the lie would unravel. The most eloquent lie would be silence. The firmest opinions that individuals developed were conclusions that they thought were independently gained.

Leofa's lecture was, admittedly, more concise.

"One word about what happened tonight," Leofa said, "and Roger will hang you all out to dry come the next storm. Got it?"

Then he stormed upstairs. I found him sitting on his cot.

The instant I got upstairs I sent off the pyxis spell to Professor Pike so that he could inscribe it on the wire mesh he'd already prepared. In my note I also said that, should anything happen, I trusted him to hold the spell for my sister. I knew him to be honorable. I had full confidence that he would respect my wishes in this. At least the pyxis spell would be safe.

"We need to get some sleep if we can," Leofa said.

In his words lurked the tacit knowledge that the morrow might be a disaster. Would the Nobbsnipes believe that they'd been robbed by flying pirates or would they suspect us?

14

The bell ringing furiously at half past five did not signal a rising storm or the start of the workday, but rather the fact that the "raid" had been discovered. Leofa and I dressed hurriedly in the dark. Someone thumped on the garret's hatch, summoning us to the dormitory.

Downstairs, Roger held his jade and mother-of-pearl cane, clearly threatening the boys. He gave me a sneering look. Gilford, Kendall, and Edmunds paced around the assembled boys, holding up oil lamps that cast a wavering light across the boys' frightened faces.

"What are you doing, rousing us at this hour?" I rubbed at my eyes, which felt gritty and sore from my lack of sleep.

"Did someone shit in the wrong hole again?" Leofa asked, his words distorted by his yawn. He leaned back against the ladder, blinking sleepily, and I wanted nothing so much as to ease my body against his warmth and close my eyes. Leofa glanced at the boys, looking amused. "I thought I taught you apes better."

"Apes," Hooker said. "We could call ourselves the Apes!"

Roger granted us all a sour look.

"Did anyone hear anything last night?" he asked.

"Nothing abnormal," I said. "Leofa snored like a guinea hen being strangled, but other than that…"

"I don't snore," Leofa said.

"And you boys?" Roger turned to them.

Ashby and Quincey, the most accomplished liars of the lot, told him no, they had not heard anything. The boys looked as sullen, grumpy, and whiny as anyone who'd been woken up an hour earlier than normal. Hooker sat back down on the edge of one of the boxbeds and rubbed his face as if trying to scrub away a veil of dreams.

"Can we go back to bed now?" Northwall complained.

Roger frowned at Leofa. "It seems like raiders may've hit us last night."

"Really?" Hooker asked excitedly, apparently having forgotten our ruse.

Roger shot him a look of annoyance. "Yes."

"Search the premises," Roger said, and Gilford, Kendall, and Edmunds moved to obey. Since Kendall had once been a student here, one of the first bastards who'd worked at cracking tomes, he knew the boys' usual hiding places. He opened up nooks and crannies I hadn't even known existed, digging up Vernon's "erotic" drawings and other boys' secret treasures.

I wondered, with a sinking heart, if Kendall would think to search under the classroom's floors. Surely, no boy would confess. None of them, I told myself, would be stupid enough to believe Kendall's or Jerome's promises.

"Why're you searching here if you think it's raiders?" Leofa asked.

Roger ignored him. The search took long enough that no one got back to bed, but rather, we had to head downstairs to start in on our laundry. Inside the windowless lower decks, lamps cast a dim light that illuminated machinery, laundry vats, drying racks, and mangles.

Peggy heated water for us and the boys chattered, loudly energetic, so happy to be warm for once that they almost did not mind doing the laundry. As my laundry sloshed, hot steam scented with lavender plumed up into my face.

I found myself glad we'd had the foresight to throw so much overboard.

When Roger came into the laundry, everything snapped into sudden motion. I felt dread and anticipation, as if I faced a test. I was eager to get started and see how well I'd do.

Roger had two watchmen at his side, Gilford and Harkon. Roger also wore my own pistol openly. Anger flashed through me. He must've taken it after searching my room, probably while I'd been slaving away in here. But then it occurred to me—had he found the grimoire pages too?

I feigned surprise when he curtly gestured for Leofa and I to follow him.

Nobbsnipe and Jerome waited in steerage. Roger lurked behind his father, shoulders slouched. Nobbsnipe retracted the brass periscope and laid one hand across the curve of his belly in a casual, habitual gesture. As his gesture indicated relaxation, my own tension immediately dropped a notch.

I went over to the mercury-filled stabilizer, and as per boarding boys' tradition, touched the brass-bound glass globe for luck.

"I wondered if you knew anything about the identity of last night's raiders," Nobbsnipe said.

I let my own puzzlement show. "How would I know that?"

Nobbsnipe gave me a long look. His jowly face screwed up shrewdly. He nodded at his son. Roger came forward, passing around me, tossing that cursed cane of his from hand to hand, and then he strode around behind me and lingered there. It was most disconcerting.

He leaned in and spoke quietly into my ear.

"A learned man like yourself might have some insight," Roger said.

"I can look at the…scene of the crime, if you wish, and I could see what I could find," I said, my stomach churning. "But, honestly, I think you would certainly be better off contacting the police. It's your duty to step forward, sir. If the police can discover a pattern to the attacks, then perhaps they can discover the raiders' base of operations. Such outlaws must have one."

Leofa addressed Nobbsnipe directly. "What's this about, Barnabas?"

"It's not like you to be caught unaware, Leo," Nobbsnipe said.

"What?" Leofa laughed, startled. "You think I worked with the raiders?"

"I know it," Nobbsnipe said. "So what did they offer you? How much?"

Leofa shook his head, bemused. "That's absurd."

Roger unholstered my pistol and pressed it into the small of my back. The muzzle nudged me through my coat, and cold fear melted through me. I could not tell whether he threatened me genuinely. I doubted whether Roger even knew himself. Roger, I knew, liked violence and would be all too glad to engage in it.

"Roger, be civil." Nobbsnipe looked annoyed but not dismayed at his son's behavior.

Roger grinned at Leofa and asked, "You want to change your story now?"

Leofa went still. His dark eyes fixed on me, the gun, and the man holding it. He said, "You've gone too far. Lord Franklin has nothing to do with this. And neither do I. You're unlucky. That's all. Raiding always increases around Darkest Night."

"When my uncle hears that your son has drawn a weapon on me—" I began.

Nobbsnipe cut me off. He said, "We are all aware that this is where the families store their unwanted baggage. I can only conclude, Lord Franklin, that your uncle must consider you as such. If you had value to him, no doubt you would be serving him in one of his other business ventures below."

"I told you to leave him alone, Barnabas." Leofa's commanding physicality intensified as he strode toward Nobbsnipe.

Nobbsnipe smirked and directed his attention to Roger, saying, "I do believe you're right, my lad. Lord Franklin is Leo's new toy after all."

"You're wrong. Leofa is *my* new toy." I could only see one way out of this. But I had to sound perfectly confident and self-assured for it to work.

Ignoring the muzzle of my own pistol pressed up against me, I stepped forward, gazing at Nobbsnipe, and then smiled as though amused. I let the tone of a spoiled brat creep into my voice. "How can you still think I'm not in my uncle's complete confidence?"

Leofa smiled as if glorying in a fact he knew to be true.

Roger's attention swung between me and his father. He clearly wanted so badly the opportunity to use his power, to beat me, but would not dare attempt it without his father's permission. Roger was truly no better than a dog.

"Oh, you are?" Nobbsnipe looked at us, his own confidence wavering. He smiled. "We shall see."

Roger made a noise of disgusted frustration but I felt him withdraw the pistol.

I exited the room with Leofa. Once on the stairwell and away from their eyes, I felt shaky. I'd never been threatened with a pistol before. Demos the Guardian, how I wished that Roger had never taken that pistol from me, and how I wanted its reassuring presence.

"Give me that cursed pistol." I heard Nobbsnipe say through the door behind us. "What were you thinking, drawing on him?"

As pleasurable as it would have been to hear Nobbsnipe scold his son, getting caught at it probably would have been less so. I started up the stairwell, Leofa beside me.

He shot me a worried look, but said only, "We'd better get back to the laundry."

I understood his terseness. No doubt, if we could hear Nobbsnipe so clearly, Nobbsnipe and Roger would be as able to hear us. Any discussion concerning what had just passed needed to happen elsewhere, in a location more private.

At the top of the stairwell in the house's entry Louisa awaited us. Her face expressed bitter triumph. Leofa ignored her completely, continuing on with the ease of long practice, but she caught me by the arm as I attempted to move past.

"I should've known you were an *invert*," she hissed in a low voice, and I could only assume that she had been eavesdropping.

"Please, Louisa. Don't say it like that." I removed her hand. "You have found me out. I suppose I could have only hidden it from you for so long."

"You don't have to be with Leofa simply because he is..." She paused, licked her lips. "Convenient."

I realized that with Louisa again on my side I could have easier access to the Nobbsnipe residence and to Mrs. Nobbsnipe's boudoir. I smiled at her apologetically. "I am sorry that we fought, Louisa. I did not mean to be so harsh with you. It was really quite ungentlemanly of me. Do you think I could make it up to you somehow?"

Louisa smiled. But I could see in her eyes that her wariness had not yet vanished. She said, "Well, I'm trying to learn the *Sonata of Flowers*, but there are some difficult passages near the end where I need help sorting out the best fingering. It would so please Mama if I could play it for company."

"Consider it done," I said. "I have missed our duets."

"Don't worry," she said. "I'm sure Mama will let us practice more together, now that we know how you're harmless."

"Yes. Harmless," I agreed.

⌒

I was so jittery that I could not bear the thought of either laundry or teaching. Rather, I returned to my room. I took the steps at a run, climbed up the ladder, and all but flung myself into the garret. Here, I stalked in circles and imagined throttling Nobbsnipe, his son, the watchmen.

Ire invigorated me, being far more comfortable than fear. I'd never been so angry as I had been at this place, or had so many things to be angry about, I supposed.

"I thought I'd find you here." Leofa pulled himself up into the garret. "What delayed you?"

"I spoke with Louisa," I replied.

"Louisa? Why?"

"Nothing important." I did not feel inclined to share my plan of using Louisa to gain access to the Nobbsnipe residence, fearing he'd think me a cad.

He came to me, stroking one hand down my back, touching my face. "My heart fair stopped when Roger drew on you."

I flushed, embarrassed and yet pleased by his concern, and I leaned into his touch. His touch sparked an arousal that mingled with my fear and anger. I had to keep a clear head, I reminded myself, and truly think about where we could find evidence against the Nobbsnipes. And also how we could deliver that up to the police in a manner in which we would be believed.

I murmured, "Schemes upon schemes."

"What's that from?" Leofa asked.

"Well, the Prince of Mirrors—you know, it's from *Bright Lake* by Stanshaw." I registered that he hadn't heard of it. I said, "The famous playwright? He also wrote *King's Funeral* and *The Forgotten Glorious* and *Bygones By*? I'll have to take you to the theater sometime."

"Take me to the theater—that's—I think I'd like that," he said.

"Certainly," I agreed, "once we're independently wealthy men."

I knew I sounded more than a little sarcastic and laughed bitterly. Such a future seemed impossible, and I hated being in this position. Turning the Nobbsnipes in would most likely result in my unpayable debt being called in and my being transported to Newland, away from what I held dear. Going to the theater with Leofa—it seemed ludicrous to even discuss it.

"We'll work it out," he said, and kissed me so hard that I leaned back and pressed my palms against the cot's canvas surface to keep my balance. He ran his hands down me, gripping my hips.

Breathless with want, I gasped as he fumbled with my clothes, cursed, unbuckled my bracers, then pulled my trousers down. He pumped my cock in his hand, slicking it with saliva, and knelt in front of me, taking my cock in his mouth. It felt unbelievably good.

I groaned. Then I tangled my hands in his sleek hair. He glanced up at me. Leofa looked so very wicked, his lips stretched and reddened around my cock. He gulped me down until I could think of nothing but him until I came.

A white blaze of pleasure left me feeling drained, shaken, yet sated.

When I looked back down at Leofa, he finished himself off, his eyes slitted with bliss. Watching him come, I'd never had the pleasure of witnessing a more exquisite sight.

I drew him up and kissed him thankfully, tasting myself on his mouth and tongue. He leaned his forehead against mine, one hand braced on the desk, and he said, "I love you."

"You... love me?" I stared at him.

His eyes flicked open. Leofa pulled himself back. He looked messy and oh so beautiful. It made my heart ache, to see him looking at me like that. But it still felt as though my heart had stopped, my breathlessness now a product of anxiety and confusion.

"You love me," I said again.

Hurt flashed across his face. His smile faded. He gazed at me searchingly and whatever he saw evoked a hard and brittle smile. Leofa said, "Don't worry your curly little head about it, Your Majesty. It's not like I love you that much."

15

On the morning of Darkest Night, a tracker waited for me at the garret window. Professor Pike had sent along the wire mesh box inscribed with the pyxis spell. In metal alone, much less the cost of having an inscription done on the wires in secret, it was worth a fortune. He urgently requested the final inscriptions for my proposed transducer spell so that he could have the wires etched in his laboratory.

I had nothing for him. I tried to focus on it, bending all of my mental strength to the task. I sighed and leaned back. I pushed around my papers.

I saw the syllabary I'd been making for the Hei language. I could remember working on it with Leofa, listening to him tell me stories in his native tongue, his voice settling into a deeper tone, taking on an unfamiliar cadence. It had made me want him, simply to hear him talk.

Thinking this didn't help me. I pushed forward the diagrams of the pyxis spell and sighed. I removed the pyxis box from its hidden location and looked at the written text. It was lettered in Accadian, but did not express the Accadian language. The Accadian alphabet had to represent another tongue, much as Pythian once had…

I sighed and began to mutter it aloud, careful not to let any of my skin make contact. I did not want to inadvertently activate the spell, after all, but I did want to feel it out.

Suddenly, something about the cadence struck me. I frowned. I read it aloud again. The truth struck me. I read aloud phonetic Hei written in Accadian letters.

Since very few matrilineal tomes still existed, and as no one among the scholarly community learned Hei itself due to its political ramifications, no scholar had ever the chance to work this out. Until me.

I jotted down a quick note to Professor Pike. I sent trackers as my work neared completion.

He sent me back the inscribed wires I needed. I wove my transducer wire around the lip of the mesh pyxis box, the delicate and flexing metals requiring a deft touch. I only needed a trapping spell to connect into it and a spell to wire it to—and I had it!

A working pyxis! It would make my fortune as well as my sister's. I tried to rein my elation in. Most importantly, I told myself that I'd made a lasting contribution to knowledge and it would change the very course of history.

Leofa climbed up into the garret, moving with a leaden slowness, and I reached down to grab his hands and haul him up.

"I've done it!" I greeted him, fit to burst.

"Done what?"

"Finished it! The transducer." I grinned at him like a fool. I said, "With the fortune this will bring me, I'll be able to pay off my debt to my uncle, collect my sister's grimoire, and get off Highfell once and for all! I'll be free."

"Oh. I see." Leofa smiled, but it seemed forced. I paused, quizzically regarding him. He tried to meet my eyes. "You'll be—leaving then? After you sell, uh, the rights to it?"

"Leo, move out of the way!" Molly called from below. "I've got a letter for Neil."

Leofa moved aside. He reached for me briefly, and let his hand fall.

When she'd come upstairs, Molly slammed the hatch down over the ladder and handed me my letter, clearly irritated. She said, "You need to get me that marriage certificate *now*."

"I need something of yours to make the seeking spell work," I said absently, turning the letter over in my hands. "A lock of your hair, perhaps?"

I'd received a letter from my sister. I snapped the wax seal and unfolded the letter. Seeing her handwriting and the recent date in the corner relieved me, because I'd been so worried for Nora. After our brief communication via code, we hadn't had any exchanges. She could have been dead or ill, and unless my uncle had deigned to write me, I would have had no way of knowing.

Leofa handed Molly my shaving razor, which she used to cut a curl from her hair. Molly's voice trembled as she informed Leofa she could not risk losing her place here without first obtaining the marriage certificate. She could not—she would not—put her son's future at risk because of our schemes.

I could not believe what my sister had written me. "Lord Slackleigh," I said, almost under my breath, incredulously. "*Lord Slackleigh?*"

"What did you say?" Molly turned dead white, her face draining of her angry flush.

"She's getting married…" I muttered, pressing the letter to my forehead.

"What *did* you say?" Molly said again. "I can't read it."

"Sit down. Now!" Leofa belted out in the tone he used on the boys, which brought them to silence.

To my surprise, I sank back down into my chair. I felt an instinctive and sullen anger at my ready obedience.

When I looked over at Molly, she'd seated herself on my cot. She looked as subdued as a girl sent to the headmistresses.

"Molly," Leofa said in an even tone. "How about you go first?"

"That name…you said your sister would marry…" Molly paused uncertainly.

Leofa nodded at me. "You want to clarify all that?"

"My sister is engaged to Lord Slackleigh," I said. "She says Slackleigh will pay off our debt. I'll be free of it."

"But—but he can't marry her." Molly sounded puzzled and stunned. "He's married to me."

Leofa, startled, glanced up at her and asked, "You mean he's that asshole?"

"They are to announce the engagement tomorrow." I refolded my sister's letter, placed it on the desk, and stalked around.

I glanced at Molly, who'd gone from infuriated to calm and speculative. Yes, this news had changed my plans significantly. I tilted my head and spoke as though I asked her the time.

"Would you mind terribly if I pummeled your husband?" I asked.

Leofa snorted, trying to repress his laughter.

"No, not at all," Molly said.

"Great, great," I muttered. I sized up Leofa and then glanced at Molly, now hopeful. "Do you think you can nick me one of Roger's spare suits? Preferably one that's not too out of fashion?"

"I'll keep watch," she said in a tart tone, "but don't think I'll do the stealing myself."

"What are you planning?" Leofa said, eyeing me with suspicion.

"You're of a size with Roger," I said. "Let's go below and find Slackleigh. If we're both well dressed, between the two of us we should be able to brazen our way into his house and force him to tell us where the marriage certificate is."

"That's your plan?" he said, giving me a long look.

I looked at him pleadingly. He shuffled his feet. Leofa growled. He stared up at me, shook his head, and muttered to himself.

Finally, he turned to Molly. "Are you sure you want to be married to this man? Aren't you worried he'll have you locked up? He's already sent Thaddeus away. So that means he can't hold you all that dear. Wouldn't it be safer if we could just help you take your son and get away from Highfell?" Leofa asked.

"I know all that. I did my thinking." Molly sounded firm and unyielding. "But I want my due. If Slackleigh wants a quiet divorce, I'll give it to him. For a price. I won't let Thaddeus grown up in want."

This to me seemed risky. But in the end, how she conducted her life was her affair.

"You mind if we can have a word here?" Leofa asked Molly.

"We'll need the clothes as soon as possible," I said. I picked up Molly's curl, snapped a loose thread from my worn suit, and knotted the hair off. I tucked the little brown curl into my breast pocket. Beside it I placed the seeking spell—just in case we happened to need it.

"I'll go scout Roger. Soon as I know if his room's clear, I'll be up to fetch you two," she said, and moved to leave. "You and I aren't square, Neil."

"I know." I nodded in acknowledgment.

As soon as Molly had left, Leofa stalked across the room to where I sat on the desk chair.

I still urged Leofa to help me with my plan to keep Lord Slackleigh from gaining control of my sister, a plan that mostly centered upon my desire to punch Lord Slackleigh in the face.

Leofa stood directly in front of me, leaned down, and combed his fingers through my hair. I'd stopped putting pomade in it, because he liked the curls, and now he took a lock in his fingers, stretching it out, then letting it spring free.

I looked at Leofa hopefully. I knew I'd hurt him the previous day, when I had not immediately returned his declaration of love. But how could I have, when I had not known what to say? And would he help me now?

Leofa shook his head, framing my face with his hands, then teased my lower lip with his thumb. He said, "If you weren't so fucking beautiful, my life would be a lot easier."

Downstairs, I could hear the chaos of the boys returning back from dinner. Leofa paused, listening thoughtfully. I had become so attuned to the boys' background noise that I could hear it too, a tone that wasn't quite right.

Leofa dropped down into the dorms and shouted for me to come down as Stanley and Vernon had gotten into a fight. Young Thaddeus had somehow got walloped during their exchange and now he wailed his head off, more apparently out of surprise than any real injury. Associated with this, general chaos resulted from maniacal hungry adolescent boys seeing a scuffle.

Holding Stanley back didn't require strenuous action. He mostly lunged at Vernon as if to strangle him. When I tried to ask him why, Stanley transferred his glare to me and muttered sullenly, "Nothing. It's nothing!"

"I see." I gave him a hard stare. "You know better than to be fighting."

I released Stanley and Leofa let go of Vernon. The fight did not resume, although the boys exchanged no few black looks.

The boys would need some time to settle down. Shortly after this, Molly returned upstairs.

"You boys keep out of trouble while I'm gone," Leofa said. "Don't think I won't beat you if I hear you done something stupid. Stanley, you're in charge."

Stanley nodded, adopting an expression of sober respectability slightly undercut by the mark on his face where Vernon had hit him. Vernon and his friends glared at Stanley but didn't kick up a fuss.

A fight between boys would normally not have worried me, but this altercation showed that the boys wearied of supporting Stanley and would soon reject him as their *de facto* leader. What would happen to Stanley after such a rejection? Would Leofa and I be able to keep him from starvation?

My actions had allowed the situation to worsen. Was this how Leofa had felt all these years, blackmailed into staying, observing the waste of life after young life?

Did he feel shame, as I now did? In his face, I could only read sadness.

We followed Molly downstairs.

"Mistress Nobbsnipe is in her boudoir, indulging," she said. "Roger's in steerage with Master Nobbsnipe, talking. If you want those clothes, now's the time."

I could only imagine what Nobbsnipe and Roger discussed. Surely, they had enough to occupy them for a good while. Now I had an unprecedented opportunity—not just to nick Roger's clothes, but to seize the letters that incriminated Leofa.

Molly led us to Roger's bedroom. Leofa went inside.

I didn't follow. When I started instead for Mrs. Nobbsnipe's boudoir, Molly grabbed my arm. "What do you think you're doing, my lord?"

I leaned in close and whispered, "Mrs. Nobbsnipe has a packet of letters that she keeps hidden. Where are they?"

"I don't know what you're talking about," Molly whispered.

But now that I understood more of servants and what they actually did, I highly doubted the truth of that. Molly had cleaned every inch of this house. Nothing would be secret from her. I said, "They're from Leofa addressed to his mother."

Guilt flashed across Molly's face. "That's not what you're here for. It's too dangerous."

"Tell me." Through Roger's open door I could see Leofa carefully removing a clean white shirt from the large wardrobe. A scarlet cravat already hung over his arm. Molly followed my line of sight to Leofa. Then I turned back to her and saw compassion there, tinged with fear.

I whispered, "Tell me. Or I'll tell him you knew about it."

Molly closed her eyes, clearly ashamed and angry at having her hand forced like this. "Fine. But you're not doing him any favors. Under the middle cushion of her chaise. The one she's sleeping on right now."

When I entered the boudoir, a smothering scent of lilac powder and cloying poppy smoke rolled out over us. Odd shapes swelled out from a chaos of strange shadows as I moved forward.

A delicate gilded dressing table was covered with pots and bottles of cosmetics. A small daybed, a lounging chair, a writing desk, and a hip bath formed oddly angled hummocks before a fireplace. Falls of damask, lace, and crocheted doilies cluttered all surfaces along with dried flowers and porcelain trinkets.

I knelt in front of a chaise lounge. Mrs. Nobbsnipe slept on it, sweating, her loose hair plastered on her face. I slid my hand beneath the cushions, groping for the letters and attempting to ignore the woman's dishabille. But I could not help but pay scrupulous attention as I feared her waking up.

She shifted around again, her weight crushing my palm. I gripped the packet of letters and drew them out…very, very slowly. Mrs. Nobbsnipe did not seem to notice. Close beside me stood a metal bowl, lamp, and pipe, blackened with residue and stinking.

I eased myself to my feet as gently as a dancer and crept out of the room, letters in hand.

Ostensibly, Molly tidied a small table on the hall that held a dried bouquet in a vase, but in reality, she kept watch for us. She told me to make it quick as I entered Roger's room. It was decorated in a conspicuously masculine manner. Heavy dark wooden furniture and deep green brocade dominated, along with slightly pornographic nudes and taxidermied trophy animals.

As I knew from previous conversations with Roger that he had never been hunting or deer stalking, I found the display ludicrous.

Disgustingly, this room not only stank of tobacco but smelled like Roger.

Leofa gestured at the open wardrobe. "You pick."

I handed the letters to Leofa. He glanced up at me sharply when he realized what they were. But I ignored that, focusing instead on the contents of the wardrobe. Quickly and expertly, I fingered the suits, identifying cool linen, soft worsted, and whispering silk.

"The letters, they're all here," Leofa said.

I found a suit very high in quality, but so far out-of-date that it would be useless. Set in the rear of the wardrobe hung an evening suit in the utmost fashion. I pulled it out and held the suit up to Leofa.

"Perfect," I said. "Don't you—"

I heard a knock at the door. Molly. Warning us.

Leofa frowned and pressed his finger against my lips to quiet me. I met his eyes. I could feel the heat and the roughness of his callused fingertip resting on my lower lip. I wanted to kiss him teasingly. But then I heard sounds.

Footsteps moved lightly across the creaking floorboards. Louisa. It had to be. Surely, secreted away in Roger's room, we would not have to worry about discovery. As long as we remained quiet, we would be safe. Her footsteps retreated.

Leofa brushed his finger across my lower lip once, an expression of wry sadness touching his own lips. He was here because he did love me, and I—what did I even feel for him?

He spoke in a low voice, "Let's get out of here."

As soon as we stepped out of Roger's room, Leofa paused. I stopped, startled, and saw Louisa peering out from her bedroom door at us. She must have only come up here in passing, perhaps to get something, because she stepped now out of her bedroom. Louisa bit her lip. She held her thin body ramrod straight as she approached us.

"What do you think you are doing here?" she demanded. "And what are you doing with—are those my brother's clothes? Are you stealing his clothes?"

I smiled at her in what I hoped what a disarming manner. If we could get out of here without Louisa setting off the alarm, we would have to convince Louisa to be, at least temporarily, on our side. I'd have to deceive her—much as I had worked to deceive the other aristocrats around me for nearly all of my life.

"Leo, take the clothes and wait for me downstairs," I said, imperiously and draped the suit I held over Leofa's arm. I softened as I turned toward Louisa. "Please, Louisa, I'm afraid we have to talk."

"We do?" She paused, uncertain now.

I smiled at her. "Yes. Leo, do give us a moment."

Leofa gave me a long look, but said, "Sure. Fine."

I drew Louisa aside to the drawing room, where I seated myself on the piano bench and faced out toward the room. I wanted to remind her of the times, at least unconsciously, that I had spent carefully teaching her. I needed her to respect me, to believe me, to be flattered by my confessions.

"May I tell you something in confidence?" I asked.

Louisa sat down on the chaise lounge rather stiffly. "If you must, I suppose."

"Oh, thank you," I said, as if relieved. "I feel like I can truly talk to you. After all, we've so much in common. We're both intelligent, capable, musically gifted, and we're kept out from what makes Highfell work, though I know you're capable of handling it."

"They don't let me do anything," she said in a small voice.

"You could run this school," I agreed. "You're certainly capable enough. Look, Louisa, I wouldn't normally say anything, because of the reputations at stake...but I think you'd understand. My sister is about to be taken advantage of by a very unscrupulous man, and I must save her."

Louisa watched me, troubled. "What do you intend to do?"

"Only warn him off," I said. "But I need to get down to Herrow below before I can do that. And we need the clothes, or we'll never be admitted into his presence. What I'm wearing is just too ragtag, isn't it?"

Louisa laughed uncertainly at my weak joke. She said, "But I don't know what you expect me to do, Neil. If I helped you and my father found out..."

"He need never find out you helped," I said. "You can always blame us two troublemakers, after all."

Still, she hesitated. I needed to persuade her.

I changed tactics. I sighed and leaned forward, resting my face in my hands and rubbing at it. Not as though I wept, not quite, but as if emotion overcame me. My voice muffled by my palms, I said, "If I can't get the glider, then I don't know what I'll do. She'll be at this man's mercy. Can you imagine that?"

As I spoke I realized that, despite my blatant manipulation, my words were sincere. "Please, Louisa. It'll only be for a few hours that I need the glider. It's not like I'd steal it. I'm as bound to this aetherium as you are."

"Oh, Neil..." Louisa sounded reluctant and nervous. "Will it only be for a day?"

"Of course," I said.

"She's really lucky to have you," Louisa said wistfully. "I'll get you the keys from my father's room, and I won't say anything. Only return as quickly as possible. Do you promise?"

I promised, though I knew I could do no such thing. As Louisa left to fetch the keys, I remained behind. I did not know how I felt about using her, even though I knew she had been a passive accomplice in many of her father's and her brother's misdeeds.

When Louisa returned with the keys, I embraced her effusively and left before she could change her mind.

Leofa awaited me in the foyer. As I held up the keys, the skeptical expression on his face changed to chagrin. He shook his head and said, "Sweet-talked her, did you? Should've guessed you'd do that."

I tossed him the keys with a triumphant smile.

16

Below in Herrow, the afternoon light shone brightly across the cobbles. The polluted black snow had left dark sooty streaks along all the storefronts, heaping in drifts that the carts slowly mashed down into the streets.

Street children threw vile snowballs and the air smelled like blood as the wind spread the aetheric turbines' exhaust across the city. Clerks rushed to work, eager to be done with their half-day so they could spend Darkest Night with their families. The street vendors sold glittery masks. Balladeers sang holiday hymns while shaking tambourines and ringing bells.

Leofa looked better in Roger's clothes than Roger ever had. He filled out the shoulders of the greatcoat, and the lean lines of his torso made it look as though it had been tailored for him. The pale cuffs peeking out from under the black wool sleeves framed his large scarred hands.

The coat had been left open to reveal a single-button jacket, a cream-colored vest, and a dark ruby silk cravat. The trousers, slightly tighter on Leofa's more muscular frame, displayed his form to admirable advantage. He wore a top hat with his iolite goggles on the brim, and held Roger's ridiculous jade and mother-of-pearl cane in one hand.

With his new haircut and clean-shaven jaw, his manicured fingernails, and the orange water scent he'd borrowed, he seemed every inch the perfect lord. His unstudied grace and command made him look born to wealth and opulence. With his natural physicality, he radiated an animalistic sensuality as he strode down Markbury Street.

Normally I wouldn't contemplate the idea of lovemaking in an alley. I'd even been flummoxed when Leofa had mentioned doing those sorts of things himself, so incapable was I of even imagining myself doing something so racy, so illegal. But now, watching him made me want him so much that I felt I would almost give a finger for the chance to drag him somewhere only slightly more private.

At the courier storefront, he paused in front of the window to gaze at himself in its reflection before strolling in.

Acting as the obedient manservant, I bought some paper. I wrote out a note requesting the honor of calling upon Lord Slackleigh, quietly accepted Leofa's card—well, it came from Roger's pocket and had Roger's name on it. Then I folded the card into the note, sealing the note shut. I wrote Lord Slackleigh's name on the outside and handed it over to the balding man behind the counter.

"It really is quite urgent," I said. "If you could deliver it immediately, my lord master would be most pleased. You do know the location of his lordship's house?"

"I've a canny lad," the courier said. "He knows every lord's house in Herrow and their mistresses' too. He's fast, my lord. He knows if he don't run, it'll be back to the workhouse for him and I'll get a boy who's faster."

"Ah, excellent," I said, as though nothing could please me more, yet in reality I wished to throttle the man for his easy disregard of this boy's life. "Your charge for this service?"

"That'll be triple the going rates then, my lord," the courier said, nodding at Leofa.

Leofa looked bored. I had to admit that, at least, he expressed a gentleman's mannerisms accurately. He toyed with Roger's cane absently.

I paid without question, even giving the man extra to be certain that it would be done. He didn't overtly count the money, having expected the extra payment, but bellowed, "Oliver! Expedited letter to Lord Slackleigh for immediate delivery!"

I glanced at the twelve-year-old boy who took the letter—his unusually pale hair made him distinctive enough to follow easily. I thanked the balding man on behalf of my lord and bid him a good day. Then we left his establishment.

"Let's follow the poor blighter," Leofa said, his accent so at odds with his clothing that a passing lady shot him a startled look.

We pursued the messenger past the beautifully broad windows of storefronts. Soon that gave way to residential neighborhoods, where townhouses had small brick walls enclosing barren rose gardens.

By the time the boy reached the out-of-town suburb, we flagged. The shops here clustered around "country-style" pubs and the houses stood at ease behind tall snow-covered walls.

I would have known Lord Slackleigh's house, even had I not seen the messenger deliver the letter. The wrought-iron gate stood framed with two stone simurghs, half-dog half-bird creatures excavated from Zisth. Behind the gate, the sprawling brick mansion had the simple grace of a newly renovated building, with arched windows and dozens of white-washed chimneys.

"You need to call upon Lord Slackleigh," I said, hoping that bluster would get us through this.

Leofa stopped suddenly, and he shot a panicked look down at me. He said, "Neil, I can't do it after all."

"You look fantastic," I blurted out, so frank was my admiration.

He flushed and shook his head. "Neil, don't."

I would have liked to touch him, but I stood before dressed as a manservant. In my own worn-out clothes. "It will be easy. Ignore everyone. I'll do the talking. Remember, I'm your man."

After gatekeeper granted us entrance, Leofa remarked, "We're in Molly's garden."

The ornamental beds arced around smooth lawns, concealed by snow, and cascades of evergreens had been sprayed down with water so that falls of ice draped them. Nature glorified the garden's centerpiece, the gate of the fallen Ashkanavra, jewel of the ancient south, that Lord Slackleigh had excavated and imported to make his garden folly. The red and blue geometric mosaic shone shockingly bright in the snow.

"Beautiful," I said.

I rapped on the door and the butler answered.

Lord Slackleigh, he informed us, was out and would not return until after Her Majesty's Darkest Night Ball.

He offered to take a card and Leofa handed over Roger's. Outside, Leofa strode away with me at his heels. Once we had distanced ourselves from Slackleigh's house, I said, "Well, I suppose we've learned of one place where he'll be."

"That's insane, Neil. How will we even get in?"

I clasped my fingers around his palm. He stilled. Two passing girls, chaperoned by a governess, sent shocked glances our way.

But I did not care.

"I could go to the ball to see my sister debut," I said. "I could even bring you in as my guest. Your clothes are almost fine enough."

"Yours aren't."

I flushed. But he was correct. I pushed down my embarrassment, thinking, and then it occurred to me: "When I went to visit Uncle Gerard, this was before I knew he conspired with the Nobbsnipes, he commissioned a suit for me. The tailor said it would be fine enough for Darkest Night."

"Well," Leofa said, "we have to get there before he closes shop if you want to carry out this plan of yours."

Leofa and I headed back into town, cutting through a poorer district. The buildings around us seemed to contract in size, from the airy houses of the rich to the densely packed tenements of the poor.

The lights, set out on stoops and window sills festively to dispel the smoggy darkness, possessed orangey halos. Playbills, political posters, and advertisements, caked the wooden walls. A man, already drunk, shouted up at the closed windows of a bawdyhouse.

Urine sheeted from the tin slop guards above us, and inexplicably, a clock fell from the sky. It thudded into the thick sewage in the street's central gutter, so cushioned by the muck that its crystalline face did not even break.

"Huh," Leofa said.

Celebrating men and women wore their finest, hiding their faces in cheap brightly painted paper masks. Some, from the country tradition, had crowned themselves with raven feathers. Enterprising vendors sold mulled wine, hot rum punch, cakes, puddings, oranges, and roast chestnuts. The stink of the muck underfoot and the earthy scent of unwashed bodies wafted around us.

Two harlots groped me. I turned down their advances politely, much to their ribald amusement. When I felt little fingers prying at my belt, I slapped the offending hand lightly and sent the girl on her way.

As we passed back into a wealthier district, the tenor of the parties changed. Although still rowdy, men and women here sported leather and wooden masks above their silken finery.

Public teahouses had been packed with private parties. Buskers playing frantic reels collected donations. Mongers selling schnapps in tiny bottles catered to a spirit of drunken exoticism. Men presented hothouse flowers to masked ladies it seemed like they'd never been introduced to.

At the tailor, I picked up my suit. With the cream silk shirt, the warm gray and brown herringbone wool possessed quiet elegance. Fine golden feathers had been embroidered onto the russet vest. I also bought a cravat of coffee brown silk. Over the tailor's protests, I dressed in the store.

So long as no one looked too closely at our shoes, we were sufficiently outfitted for the ball.

After that we found ourselves a mask maker who still had some of his finer pieces in stock. All rejects, claimed the clerk, from lords who'd changed their minds at the last minute. If we did not mind that, then he would sell them to us cheaply.

The masks were all made of wood carved thin. They were all half masks, descending to just above the cheekbones, so that one could partake of conversation, food, and beverage without difficulty.

Leofa and I brought him down by nearly half of his asking price, though they still did come dear. The mask that Leofa settled on was fine work, the wood so thin it felt as light as paper on my fingertips.

The raven's visage was elegant yet harsh, with a strong beak and angry brows in glistening black, red glass over the eyeholes, each feather edged with gold. The red, I thought, would match his cravat wonderfully. I chose an owl mask, the white feathers limned in russet brown and bloody red, with large gilded irises and the eye slits almost lost in the larger mock-pupils.

"Guess you're never going to take me to the theater." Leofa seemed strained. He added, "Or recite that poem."

"What do you mean?" I asked.

"We stole from the Nobbsnipes and we're going to assault a lord. We're not going to get away with this. We're finished."

"Don't be so pessimistic." I wanted to divert the conversation, but somehow I knew he wouldn't let me get away with my usual tactics. "We're bringing the glider back. At most we'll be punished by Roger."

"You know that's not true," he said. "We can't go back. Roger really will hurt you this time. Maybe even kill you."

"He wouldn't dare to kill me," I scoffed.

Leofa shook his head stubbornly. "We've got to take the letters to the police and tell them about Nobbsnipe. I'll throw myself on the mercy of the judge and beg for leniency for the boys."

I recoiled. "You cannot mean to give up now."

He contemplated the mask, glowering at it.

"I promise you that everything will work out," I said in a soft and persuasive tone. "Professor Pike and his friend Professor Hammerton would step in for us if it ever became an issue for the courts. Hammerton'll see us through, I'm sure. We must go on."

"Fine. Let's do it." Leofa held the mask up to his face. "I really hope you're right about this."

17

Even from a distance, the Darkest Night Ball's extravagant decorations dazzled the eye. The celebrations would begin the Royal Shadow Gardens, beneath the lofty Mile Palace.

Ice sculptures the size of townhouses hung suspended from the palace hull. Carved into tangles of vines and moonflowers, the queen's own flower, and preserved by magic, the ice was colored with the light of aetheric wires. The moat around the gardens below had been stacked with frozen blocks, forming a wall. Pale aetheric lights, reflecting through mirrors cleverly imbedded into the ice, made it all shine.

At the gate, the queen's guard stood in rows wearing immaculately pressed uniforms. Bustling heralds greeted guests. As the queen's heralds were notorious for their memories, no invitations were required at the gate. They knew each peer by sight. I stood behind a young girl who would debut—I could tell by her white dress—and I waited to be recognized, my mask in my hand.

"Can't do this," Leofa muttered, clutching his raven mask and nervously fingering the gold leaf that edged the carved feathers. "Shit, Neil, I just don't like to pretend to be someone I'm not."

"You can do this," I said. "And how do you know you're not a lord? You're at Highfell, after all."

Ignoring those around us, I turned to him and smoothed down his lapel. I leaned in close to him. I had to reassure him somehow. I had never known how to comfort people, so I was awkward at it.

"Tell me what I can do to help you get through this," I said in a low voice.

Leofa searched my face and then shook his head. When he replied, his voice murmured almost inaudibly beneath the hubbub of the peers around us. "I'll tell you what you can do. You can let me fuck you tonight, after all this is done. That's what I want from you. That, and nothing less."

"Yes. I will." I looked down and away from him, ashamed.

"Fine." Leofa straightened his shoulders, took a deep breath, and stepped forward. I remained beside him.

"Ah, Lord Franklin," the herald said, hurrying up to me. "We did not think that you would be attending this year. I'm afraid your response to Her Majesty's invitation with the name of your guest may have been lost in the mail."

I gave him a slight smile for this transparent courtesy. I said, "I do apologize for this. I'm afraid that my change in circumstance may have made my responses less than reliable."

"Please," the herald said, "allow me to give my condolences regarding your parents. The Herrow ague was indeed without mercy, taking the best among us."

"Thank you. It was ruthless." I felt the numb ache of grief reawaken. Ruthless. I wondered if I had been referring to my uncle.

Several lords and ladies, who had already entered, had drawn themselves aside to put on their masks. The ladies' masks seemed to take some tinkering. I didn't see Nora among them.

"Your name?" the herald asked Leofa.

"Roger Nobbsnipe." Leofa handed over the stolen name card.

"Thank you, Mr. Nobbsnipe." The herald wrote this out, placed the card in a basket, and then showed us through. I asked the herald whether my sister had yet arrived. He checked the lists, and informed me that Nora had not. I dared not ask after Lord Slackleigh.

Above us, the palace above blotted out the stars. The massive anchor chains had been decorated with more of the new aetheric lights. The glowing globes were imbedded in brass petals like the centers of flowers. Hundreds more of these lights were strung above the paths, suspended in glittering wire nets.

Coal braziers on the paths provided intermittent sources of heat, around which the ladies fluttered, and more warmth radiated up from the paths at our feet.

"Let me help you with your mask," I said to Leofa. He held the cane in his hands patiently. I helped him fix the mask upon his face, knotting its satin laces behind his head.

Although it beautifully complimented Leofa's coloring, I did not find the Raven to be a guise that suited Leofa. The Raven, who'd tricked Demos into making him a Mortal Constellation, didn't match

Leofa's openly commanding posture and frank nature.

After that, I held up my owl mask to my face so that Leofa could assist me. I felt comfortable in its concealment, because ultimately, I realized, I wore a mask at all times without seeming to wear one at all. I liked the ease that hiding my intentions gave me. I rarely had to battle for what I wanted.

So often the protection of courtesy and attractiveness allowed me to approach my goals indirectly. Leofa and I were fundamentally dissimilar in that way.

As I stepped out into the path with Leofa, acquaintances from boarding school who had seen my approach accosted me. Some had gone onto Elmstead while others had chosen to attend the rival aetherium, Alton. I'd never kept up with these classmates as they had clearly only been studying to go into politics.

I didn't introduce Leofa, by false name or real, and after an exchange of remember-this, remember-that, we parted ways with them. I took Leofa down a separate trail, between some night-blooming phosphorescent balsam that had clearly been brought to bud despite the season.

"Your friends are louts," Leofa muttered.

"Future politicians," I said.

"You don't have to be mean now," he said, and I laughed.

He stiffened slightly. I gazed at him, suddenly aware again of the unanswered question between us. Did I return his sentiment?

I found it difficult to remember to keep myself at a distance from him. Leofa clearly felt the same about me. All too easily we slid back into intimacy. But intimacy wasn't love.

As soon as we were alone on the trail, he caught me by the hand and drew me back into the ferns and underbrush. He touched me lightly on the lips. I thought he might kiss me, but sadly Leofa meant it as a gesture for silence.

Together we sneaked back around to watch the influx of guests filtering through the front gates. I could hear gaiety in the distance, the now-unfamiliar trill of women laughing, the coil of violin music. Away from the heated paths, the air tasted dull, cold, and wet, and it smelled of greenery and earth.

We waited for Lord Cyril Slackleigh to pass before us.

Instead Nora stepped through the front gates. Her white silk dress ranked among the more fashionable. Her décolletage was modest, due to an ancient Imrian-style necklace that fell in a cascade of sapphires and tiny golden leaves across her chest. And I felt warmed to see that she wore the chatelaine I'd given her for her birthday.

Nora had bound back her dark hair, elegantly straightened, in a mignon. She looked healthy, though not exactly happy, as my uncle assisted her with her white crane mask.

With a cry of delight, she saw a friend from school who, from her white dress, was also clearly set to make her debut that night. The two of them greeted each other with excited embraces, clasping each other's hands, admiring each other's masks and white dresses. When a third friend arrived, the girls all linked arms and walked down along the path.

Lord Cyril Slackleigh arrived just then and my uncle assisted Lord Slackleigh in tying on his mask. It was a golden hawk stylized like an iconography from the Ollundi tombs. When the two of them moved to leave, I nudged Leofa, so he knew that the time had come to go. I sidled out of the bushes as quietly as I could and moved onto a smaller path parallel to the main thoroughfare.

Leofa touched my shoulder lightly, then removed a leaf from my hair, and we moved on. He strolled beside me. I could hear the rise and fall of my uncle's voice, but not make out his words in the surrounding noise.

When we passed an older couple walking arm-in-arm, Leofa tucked aside his cane and bowed. He didn't quite get the angle right, considering that the lady was a countess, and the gentleman shot us an odd look.

Leofa slouched and said, "Failed at that."

"It wasn't that bad," I said and then drew him back into more shrubbery. I drew him close, touching the soft hair at the nape of his neck, and kissed him. He relaxed slightly as his lips parted and pulled me against him hard, taking control of the kiss. I shivered with excitement and broke away.

"You're lord enough for me." My lips brushed his as I spoke.

Where the paths intersected in a small glade, young ladies and lords mingled under aetheric lights like so many butterflies in the midst of flowers. Caterers circulated between them with trays of drinks and delicacies. A violinist played songs upon request. A poet-for-hire also declaimed borderline bawdy lines, making the younger girls in their songbird masks flutter.

But for the lush hostas and ferns, this could have been a scene from a drawing room.

At the edge of the glade, my uncle drew my sister aside and "introduced" her to Slackleigh. Nora turned her face away as he bowed over her hand. Her smile, not covered by the mask, was bright and pained.

"She hates his guts," Leofa commented.

"Most certainly," I agreed. Nora had never been able to hide herself or her opinions from others. It had been both a boon to her and an onus. Clearly, my skills at misdirection, fitting in, and politeness weren't so much family traits as learned ones.

Nora spoke with Lord Cyril Slackleigh longer, gesturing at some nearby phosphorescent greenery. Then, courtesies done, she curtsied, he bowed, and they separated. I could see my uncle smile as he watched my sister depart. After finishing his conversation with my uncle, Slackleigh also took his leave.

Leofa and I kept our distance. We lost Slackleigh when I encountered one of Professor Vassily's disciples, who expressed his excitement about the work on Hei that I'd done.

I gave Leofa a slight nod. He made his apologies and followed Slackleigh away.

Included in my Hei syllabary and grammar, I'd written out a folio containing the stories that Leofa had told me about the Mortal Constellations and their alternative names. As the young man spoke about how my work had evoked a desire in him to collect Heton folklore before it died out, my attention wandered. I wondered what it would be like to visit the wild mountains and forests of Leofa's childhood. How would it change him to return to Hetta? What could he show me that no one else could?

After the student thanked me effusively, I continued on.

Society was smaller than one might think. Between attending Evermore and Elmstead, between my parents' friends and associates, I knew one in five people that I passed. I proceeded through the pleasantries smoothly. I accepted their condolences and disregarded their controlled unease.

I knew they felt that I shouldn't be here, that I should have had the courtesy to hide myself away from society, to be properly ashamed of my destitution.

I adapted to their pity.

I conducted myself well.

But anxiety gnawed at me. I'd lost sight of Leofa. With every conversational gambit, I felt more and more exposed to discovery. I wasn't meant to be here. I felt as though I raced against ticking time. I had only until one of those friendly faces encountered my uncle and said, "Your nephew is looking well."

Deadly, those innocuous words.

From behind, someone tapped me on the shoulder. I turned, my heart thudding with anxiety, expecting to see my uncle or my sister, but Leofa's raven mask poked out of the bushes. He said, "Found him. He's excused himself for a piss."

I disappeared into the bushes after him with a rustle of leaves, a crackle of branches. He held me by the wrist, using the cane to push aside the thick bracken, and once we had to pause to brush glowing golden pollen off our clothes, before we continued on again. His grip tightened on my wrist, warning me to be both silent and still, because we'd gotten ourselves right up against a path.

Multitudes of ladies walked past, all rustling skirts, high-pitched chatter, and clouds of lilac perfume. With their flitting fans, their coy murmurings, they seemed so foreign to me. I'd become accustomed to the likes of Ashby and Hooker. When I thought that the trouble those two would raise in a gathering like this, I restrained my smile.

When the trail cleared, we darted across and continued our journey through the bracken. Leofa eventually stopped. We'd arrived near the men's loos. The rank smell of sewage thickened the air. The small booths, barely visible in the dark, had lights hanging above their doors.

"There's a clearing back there," Leofa said very quietly and handed me the cane. "We can bring him over to it."

Lord Slackleigh came along, no doubt intending to relieve himself. Leofa darted out, grabbed him by the collar, and hauled him behind the shrubs. His lordship yelped like a lapdog and his voice went silent. Leofa had him in a choke hold, or so it appeared in the dim light.

Leofa dragged him back to a natural clearing beneath a massive rhododendron, the thick leathery leaves crunching under our feet. He forced Slackleigh to his knees. Slackleigh emitted a grunt and clawed at Leofa's arm reflexively, his fingers scrabbling on the silk.

"You will not marry Honoria Franklin," I said. I felt numb and cold and slightly ill as I held Roger's cane in my hands. "You will recognize your true wife."

Leofa relaxed his grip on Lord Slackleigh, enough for his lordship to sputter out, "Who are you?"

"No one important, my lord." Leofa kneed him in the back.

"You will recognize Molly Paxton as your bride, true wife, and mother of your legitimate son," I said.

He started to shout for help and I discovered how depressingly easy it was to kick a man who was already down. It didn't feel very honorable, to be sure, but I did so nonetheless.

"I don't think you understand," Leofa said. "We know that Molly Slackleigh is your wife and Thaddeus Slackleigh is your son and heir."

"Who are you really? Her brother?" Slackleigh demanded. "How much do you want?"

"We want their due—what you promised them," Leofa said.

"I will recognize them," he croaked.

"What excellent news," I said. "I'll expect to see your marriage announcement reprinted in the city papers tomorrow. Or perhaps the next day. It is a holiday, after all. Now we will escort you to your house and you will give the marriage certificate into our safekeeping."

"I can't!" he said. "I can't do it. I don't have it."

"You're lying," Leofa said.

Slackleigh said, "I'm not. Someone has it. For safekeeping."

"And who might that be?" I already knew who it had to be—but I wanted it confirmed. I wanted to hear it.

He said, "Gerard Franklin. Your employer, most likely."

Leofa didn't relax his grip. "Where does Franklin keep them?"

"How would I know?" Slackleigh said.

He wasn't lying, I realized. But I knew where Uncle Gerard kept his papers—at Tremont Reform Club behind a bloodlock.

"Well, you must find a way to retrieve that paper then, the sooner the better," I said. "You have two days, Lord Slackleigh, before my associate and I come for you. Deal with your affairs before then." Then I addressed Leofa, "Come."

Leofa slammed Slackleigh onto the ground, and we made a run for it. As soon as we hit an unoccupied pathway, we stepped out onto it.

Continuing in an unhurried walk, through unspoken agreement, we acted as though we'd been wandering here all along. I couldn't speak, I was so worked up. I could hardly listen to Leofa as he explained his opinion regarding an article he had read recently in the *Herrow Inquirer*.

I noticed my former fiancé being escorted by another man. I acknowledged them with a genteel nod and pretended to be occupied with whatever Leofa said. I tried to focus on him like nothing mattered more.

"You left the cane." Leofa kept his tone conversational.

I must have dropped it without meaning to when I'd bolted. I felt all the urgency drain from me, leaving me shaking. I said, "Shit."

He said, "Well, it's too late now."

Accepting two tumblers of whisky from a servant, Leofa smiled at me as he took a sip. He guided us methodically toward the gate and against the flow of foot traffic—people had to be congregating for the first dance.

During a solitary lull, he splashed the whisky across himself. The fumes made my eyes water. I stared at him, nonplussed, and Leofa draped an arm over my shoulder, suddenly limp and staggering.

"Let's get out of here," he said, his breath hot against the side of my neck. "You still owe me."

Passing an acquaintance at the gate, I explained that I needed to take my drunk friend home before he embarrassed me further. The heralds expressed no surprise and called us a hansom cab, instructing the driver to take us to my uncle's house. I did not correct them.

Once we'd gotten a few blocks away, I rapped on the roof and told the driver my companion was about to be sick. The driver reined his horse to an immediate stop and leaped down, about to harangue us for fouling his cab. I tipped him extortionately to desist and let us be on our way.

Leofa spat into the gutter, leaning down as if drunkenly contemplating the effluvium, and there he tilted up against me until the hansom pulled away. The hansom would no doubt be returning to the stand right outside the ball, so I had to keep up the show for now. Once the cab had gone, I loosened my cravat and we moved away.

Leofa slung his arm across my shoulder, guiding me across the bridge to Southside.

Red bawdyhouse lamps lit the street around us. The wooden shanties were darkened by the foul black rain and the windows were unshuttered gaping holes, protected only with slop guards.

Pimps and pullers in red cardinal masks pretended to play games of chance, watching us with snake-like eyes as we passed. The smell of gin saturated the air. Other drunken revelers strolled through in defensive clots.

Leofa and I looked like we were slumming it, out to get our cocks wet and probably our purses cut. Under normal circumstances I would have tried to maintain appearances—to rise above that impression. Tonight I hardly cared.

I sank down onto an unoccupied stoop, removed my mask, and pressed my head against my hands. "I never want to do that again."

Leofa removed his raven mask. He said, "Being a pirate wouldn't have worked for you then."

I glared at him, only to earn myself his wry smile.

"You'd do it again if you have to," he amended.

I sighed and relaxed minutely. I didn't know what I would have done without him by my side. I couldn't let my sister marry that man.

"I wish that it always came to reason rather than force," I said. "I suppose it comes down to wishing that the world were fair, and that's… that's childish."

"No, not childish," he replied. "Justice and fairness are sure signs of civilization. Children are savage." Leofa had his elbows on his knees, his hands clasped together. He gazed out at the slum.

A couple of boys played in the black snow. The cowhide leather sack they kicked around looked to be filled with river sand, and by any objective standards, one would think their life was misery, but they still laughed.

Leofa continued, "You see some of the boys above, they rage at not getting what they want, and that's something else. Sometimes, accepting what is unfair is part of growing up. But there's the things that are worth getting angry over."

Leofa withdrew the letters he'd written to his mother from his pocket. He'd been carrying those letters all night long and now he smacked the bundle of them up against his thigh. He stood up and walked away from me, heading toward a nearby fire where vagrants gathered. Leofa dropped the letters into the flames as if they'd meant nothing to him. As he turned back to face me, the burning letters flared with light.

"It's time for us to be moving on." He gave me a hand up.

High above us, the aetheria blotted out the stars. The black snow drifted around us darkly, melting on our clothes. Our finery, meant for the ball, couldn't repel the weather.

Because we had little money and no letter of introduction, no legitimate inn would let us overnight. But we did manage to find a small hostel near the airfield. Although the hostel looked like a dilapidated townhouse outside, its bright interior displayed a high level of care.

"Down on your luck, my lords?" said the widow running the hostel. She wore a dress in mourning black fifteen years out of style. Her iron gray hair was tightly pinned back.

"We were robbed on the way back from the ball." I applied a rueful expression to my face and held my mask in my hands.

Leofa said nothing, keeping his eyes lidded, playing the drunk again.

"Oh, what's the world coming to?" fretted the widow, showing us up a narrow staircase. "It's hard to believe that two nice gentlemen like yourselves couldn't go about unmolested. What times we live in! Are you sure you wouldn't like to have separate rooms?"

"I'm afraid we're lucky to have a sum enough to pay you as it is," I said as if embarrassed.

"How thoughtless of me. Of course." The widow had a true chatelaine with multiple keys and she splayed them, looking for the correct key to the door in front of us. "I run a nice establishment, my lords, though it's poor compared to what you must be accustomed to, and I have several permanent boarders with me."

I nodded attentively.

"In fact," the widow added, "my late husband's brother has a room right down from the hall from you. He's a watchman, so if you hear any commotion down on the street, be sure to wake him right away."

"I think I grasp your meaning, madam, and we shall be sure to do that," I said.

"Sleep well, my lords," the widow said, handing me the key.

I stepped into a small but clean room with white and blue striped wallpaper. I put the lamp on the table alongside the blue-flowered porcelain washstand. I would have once considered the brass bed narrow, but it seemed broad and roomy compared to the cots in the garret. The straw mattress seemed vermin-free and fresh.

Leofa locked the door. His act, done in silence and with predatory grace, had such meaning to it that I flushed to think of what would come next.

Doubts overwhelmed me. Would it hurt, to have him inside me? How could I possibly compare, inexperienced and nervous, to what he'd had before? Would my body please his?

I calmed my breathing. I would not quail. Looking at his expectation I knew I could not retreat. I could not disappoint him or, if I had to be honest, myself.

I had to know.

I set down my mask and slipped off my jacket. Leofa watched me. His raw desire fueled my bravery. I turned my back to him and stripped away my filthy clothes. The black snow had left my suit stained and my hair dirty. I rinsed off my face and hair in the basin.

Leofa stepped up beside me, so close that his presence made me shiver with expectation. But he leaned forward, dunking his head in the basin, rinsing out his dark locks. He drew his hands through his wet hair and smiled at me. His eyes met mine in silent acknowledgement of how this bedtime routine seemed overshadowed and intensified with our mutual knowledge of what we intended to do next.

When I wetted the washcloth, Leofa took it from me. He washed my back slowly and thoroughly. I turned around. Standing before his inspection, I felt like a recently won trophy. With his scrupulous care, he took stock of my every inch at his leisure. He prepared to own me tonight, I knew.

At this thought, I shivered and my cock rose with anticipation. I blurted out, nervously, "I wish I'd thought to bring a razor. To shave with tomorrow, I mean."

Leofa laughed, low and soft, and reached to tease one finger across my cock. "I'm sure we'll survive."

"You look rugged with stubble," I complained out of nervousness.

"I look like I have mange. You know, the boys are probably wondering where we are right now. I did think we would be celebrating Darkest Night with them."

"Hush now," he said and kissed me. He tasted of smoky whisky.

The sensation of his clothed body against mine so overwhelmed me I had to break away from the kiss and moan. The rough damp wool rubbing against my bare skin contrasted with the texture of his lips, softer than the finest silk. He drew back from me and looked me up and down. My body ached with need.

"Some kiss, huh?" Leofa flashed me a confident smile that left me breathless and dazzled.

"Oh. Um. Yes." I realized how incoherent I sounded and, embarrassed, I shut up.

But now he disrobed. He stretched out on that bed in that way he did, one arm folded under his head as he looked up at the ceiling, one leg slightly bent. His lean muscular frame dominated the space with a beautiful ease. "I never thought I'd see anything like that ball. The Royal Shadow Gardens were heated even though it's outdoors. Demos, how much do you think a ball like that costs?"

"Hundreds of thousands," I said. When I'd attended such balls in the past, I had never given a thought to cost. Contemplating money was crass. But what staggering sums were spent on mere entertainment! It made me ashamed.

Leofa had successfully distracted me in an attempt to ease my fretting. I scowled at him for this gambit. He laughed at me, and then his smile faded.

"You looked so natural there." He sounded wistful. "It's where you belong."

I realized he waited for me to come to him. He did not mean to bend me over and brutally take me. I had to want this, and I did.

"Well," I said, "I have been trained to mingle since childhood. Of course I do it perfectly. But it's so dull."

I sat down beside Leofa, aware of myself and my proximity to him with such keenness, the brush of the naked skin of our hips. With the arousal lengthening my cock, concentrating on conversation seemed too challenging.

"I can see why it matters to you, though." He stoked down the outside of my thigh in a most distracting manner. "You knew almost everyone there."

I shook my head. With only so many peers in the nation attending the same schools, the same parties, familiarizing yourself with those reappearing faces came easily. My family had been hardly the elite among the elite: we were lords, not dukes, and an immeasurable distance separated my station from the highest of the high.

And everyone Leofa had seen greet me had known of my father's low station, and how my blood was that of a common wastrel. It was only because of the charity of my stepfather that I had a title at all. I could never be good enough for some of them.

"You know," I said, "it is Darkest Night. I meant to recite that Imrian poem for you."

"Yeah, the one from the museum." He smiled and caressed me lightly, watching my reactions as his fingertips grazed my ears, my neck, my chest, my navel, and then the fine line of hair leading downward. Leofa stopped there, a teasing inch away from what I wanted most, and murmured, "Anthar, the god of the growing grasses, and Hemnan, the god of the spring rains."

I stretched out beside him. The straw mattress crackled beneath my weight. His arousal matched mine. His thick strong cock looked perfect to me. I interlaced my fingers with his and drew his hand down.

He wrapped his fingers around my cock's length but didn't stroke me. Leofa leaned up on his elbow, bracing his head on his hand, in order to look at me. I reached for him and he shook his head warningly.

"I don't think so," he said. I saw wicked amusement glinting in his dark eyes. "You think you can recite that poem for me?"

I realized what game he played and I glared. "You prick."

His hand tightened ever so slightly around my length and I gasped. His smile broadened. "For some reason, I doubt it starts like that."

As I began to recite the poem, he stroked me. My breath catching in my throat, I murmured how it ended for the two gods, the rising of the grasses and the rain that fell, how spring came, rippling across the lands and bringing with it all good things. Leofa worked me into forgetting what happened next, into missing beats and rhymes.

When I lost track of what I said—it certainly wasn't poetry—he bent his head and took me into his mouth. As he flicked his tongue, he breached me gently with his saliva-wetted fingers. The sensation discomfited me with its unfamiliarity, but I didn't dislike it.

As he engulfed me in the wet heat of his mouth, I pushed back against his fingers. I needed to prove to myself that I did not fear this, did not fear being unmanned—not from his acts.

Much to my surprise, this eased the ache. Between his mouth and his hands, skillfully keeping me on the edge but never driving me over, I felt lost on the brink of endless bliss.

He released me from his mouth and withdrew his fingers. Leofa disengaged and brushed his body up the length of mine, so that our cocks nudged each other, a sensation that made me gasp. He kissed me ruthlessly. I writhed against him, begging for more.

"What would you do for me, my lord?" he asked, slicking his length with spit. He drew my knees up so that his cock nudged against my ass.

"Anything," I moaned, because I wanted him so.

"I wish," Leofa murmured, and impaled me on his length. I gasped at the not unpleasant pain, pushing up against him, forcing him deeper, loving how he filled me, made me feel like I'd been missing something all of my life: him. He groaned, shutting his eyes tightly, almost as though pained, and he kissed me hard.

"You don't know how fucking good you feel," Leofa said roughly. "Tonight, Neil, I own you. You're mine tonight. That's got to be enough. Say it."

"I'm yours," I wished aloud, shaking with need. I would have said anything for him. "You own me. Tonight I'm all yours."

He moaned and guided my hand so that I could grip myself. Too far gone for embarrassment or shame, I stroked myself in time to his thrusts. He moved ever harder and faster, his eyes focused on my face, his expression both fierce and hungry, like he wanted to take all he could and could never take enough.

"I want—I want—" I pleaded, hardly able to comprehend my own words. "Please, Leofa. Please."

"I know what you want," he said, his voice grown more rough with affection and sadness. He wrapped his hand around mine, now slick with my fluids, and I groaned with shocked pleasure. He ordered me, "Come for me."

"I'm yours. Yours," I gasped out. Convulsions of ecstasy shook my body and I could feel my muscles tightening around him. I could feel his own spasms, felt him shudder as he leaned down into me, then drove himself into me that final time. My seed spilled across our two intertwined hands. I saw the beauty of his face locked into that moment of eternity.

Afterwards, when satiation relaxed us and he withdrew from me, he curled up behind me. I ached from our unfamiliar exertions, but pleasantly so. Leofa clutched at me as if he feared I'd fade away like a dream. His grip reassured me and sent such ripples of soft contentment through me.

As I faded into sleep's oblivion, he pressed his face against my neck. My pulse thudded against his lips. I felt the soft brush of his lips, like a kiss, as he murmured something in Hei.

I will love you always.

18

In the morning, quiet hung over the streets. Discarded paper masks lay on the cobblestones, the damp turning them into colorful pulp. The neighborhood where we'd stayed had a depressed look, like once its residents had been striving to better themselves, but now they'd simply given up.

The terraced brick houses around us had rippled glass windows the greenish color of fishing floats. Occasionally, as an early riser carried a candle to the kitchen, the glass flashed and shimmered with warped light. The front gardens slumbered beneath snow-twisted weeds.

But as Leofa and I walked side by side, little could dim my mood for long. He let his shoulder brush mine and I glanced at him in surprise. Leofa smiled—a private smile, to be sure, but I could see the radiance beneath. I flushed, pleased with myself.

Last night had been wonderful. He'd been skillful, more than skillful, and he'd taken so much pleasure in my body that I now found it hard to be embarrassed. If I had been a religious man, I would have said that I now felt blessed. Only such an exalting word could describe my deep and abiding, yet tranquil, joy.

Everyone spent Charity Morn with their families or their households. Presents would have been distributed late last night and this morning; after everyone slept in, the servants would get first pick of used and worn goods.

Later in the day, anyone who had anything to give away would take to the streets. Even countesses would be holding up old handkerchiefs and warped pots and stained tablecloths, shouting out what they had to give like they were fishwives.

Somehow it seemed appropriate for us to be together now.

"You know what I'm thinking?" Leofa said.

"Hm?" I asked.

"Bet you anything Eudora's not about to give Molly her cast-offs. What do you say we give her an even better present?" Leofa grinned at me.

I felt my heart skip a beat and couldn't help but return his smile. I said lightly, "Why not? My uncle should be at his townhouse this morning. It *is* Charity Morn after all!"

"No one will be at the club," Leofa added.

I patted my pocket. "I even have the seeking spell with me."

When we arrived at my uncle's club, we hardly looked like the sort that anyone would let into an establishment of quality. But we strode up the steps to the modest brick townhouse wearing yesterday's filthy finery as though we could not think to belong anywhere but here.

I rapped on the door. The heavyset doorman on duty had let me in previously and recognized me on sight, and though our clothing did not meet with house standards, he raised his eyebrows when I proclaimed my mission's urgency.

"What a Darkest Night!" I leaned my arm over Leofa's shoulders. "You wouldn't believe it! But really, we do have to gain access to my uncle's rooms."

"Sorry." Leofa squinted at him. "Hung over."

The doorman gave me the long-suffering glance of a man who thought he'd seen every trouble a lord could get into, but he did permit us entrance.

I showed Leofa through the cherry wood reception room and into a broad and square stairwell, made claustrophobic despite its generous size by its ebony paneling. Aetheric lamps emitted sleepy light from the sconces studding the burgundy wallpaper.

Leofa strode up the stairs beside me and I directed him toward the door.

"And there it is." I gestured at the door with the brass nameplate.

He knelt to look at the bloodlock. Leofa said, "Oh, you beauty, let me have at you. What a lovely little beast you are."

As I watched him, he flipped his iolite goggles down from his hat and buckled them on. He wore a look of concentration that endeared him to me, his brows drawn together and his lips in a slight frown. Yet a fierce serenity deepened his expression.

"I see these bloodlocks most often on grimoires with Middle Sio-vanese text," Leofa said quietly. "Particularly the grimoires from the Chanclaria. You can tell they were bound by monks sworn to Senna, because those grimoires often had woven straw covers. And the knot-work on the metal, here, if you look at it closely, it's the unquenchable ivy pattern. Very unique. Definitely Senna, yeah? And let me see... no maker's mark. Maybe that's why no one repurposed it? You might want to stand back. I'm going to feed it and see what happens."

I stepped back a good five feet, wondering how the lock would react when he tried to crack it. With my sister's tome, the lock had sprayed out sparks, but I did not know what might happen with this bloodlock. Would it spray fire? More sparks? Acid? Or something even more formidable? What if he failed, and we had to smuggle him out of here, our quest aborted, and his hands ruined?

Leofa regarded the sterling silver box, delicately and beautiful-ly inscribed and bristling with sharp little needles, and then flipped through his picks. He took out a long iron pick that'd been burnished so often it gleamed rust free and shiny as a file.

Leofa pricked himself on the finger with it and rolled the iron pick through his blood until a large sticky drop hung from it. Then, standing as far from the bloodlock as possible, he extended an arm, touched the blood to a needle, the blood ran down the needle to lock, it sparked, and—

The bloodlock popped open the door. Simple as that.

He gaped. I stared at the bloodlock and the open door.

"How did you do that?" I asked, astonished. I had seen no reaction on the part of the bloodlock at all. I had known he was good, but I found it unbelievable that Leofa could disarm it so easily.

"I don't know," he said, mystified. "I really don't... I don't know."

I blinked and gathered myself. "Let's go in."

Inside, darkness swathed the sitting room. The curtains had been drawn closed across the broad window so the room seemed caught in a smothering twilight. The fireplace had been banked, but a few coals still smoldered. A selection of candies, fruits, and jellies was heaped on a small table between the dark upholstered chairs.

"I'll keep watch." Leofa turned to stand beside the door. But then he paused, frowned, and seemed transfixed by a small portrait on one of the side tables. He picked it up, stared at it, and then glanced up at me. "Why does he have a picture of my *mother*?"

"I don't—Leofa, we have to focus on tracking down the marriage certificate and the files," I said.

He scowled at the portrait, tracing his fingers over the glass, and then deftly slipped the picture out and returned the empty frame to the side table. Leofa replied, "Sure, sure. I'll keep you from walking into any doors or anything."

I adjusted Molly's brown curl in my breast pocket. I patted it to make sure the curl rested firmly over my heart, and unwrapped the spell from its protective paper. It had remained intact and in good order in spite of the night's adventures.

With the index finger of my writing hand, I began tracing out the letters and murmuring the spell. As my finger finished caressing the last letter, a painful tinge sparked through me and my eyes teared up. Even though I had been expecting it, seeing the world again through this strange blur nauseated me almost instantly.

I braced myself against the skewed proportions looming around me and focused on the invisible thread, the one point in my world that sharpened. Slowly, I followed it.

Practice did make this slightly easier.

"Wait—shit, let me get the door!" Leofa lunged past me. He must have been pushing open a door. "You're in his study now. The desk is—oh."

The invisible thread had led me directly to a smooth wooden paneled wall. I could only discern its nature from the slickness of the finish and the striations of the grain beneath my fingertips. I brushed my fingers over it, searching for a way through the wall.

"Let me see," Leofa said from beside me. "I think there's a catch."

I felt a slight pop as a wood panel depressed beneath my fingertips, and when I let up, the spring-loaded door sprang open. I felt forward, my fingers combing over thick wooden slats, the edges of paper, and then I touched the object of my search.

The spell switched off. The world closed around me with disorienting suddenness, flashing back into proportion and sharpness, and my eyes throbbed painfully. My muscles ached.

I stood in my uncle's study, beside his large desk and before a secret cabinet that had been built into the wall. It had been concealed with the same dark paneling that encased the rest of my uncle's suite. Wooden slots separated the neatly labeled files.

I pulled out a drawer and found the file labeled SLACKLEIGH. I saw the marriage certificate, the son's birth certificate, a record of payments made, and a marriage contract drawn up concerning my sister. But there was more. Apparently Lord Slackleigh sold my uncle the grimoires he found on his travels for extravagant sums. I tucked those papers down my shirt. Near SLACKLEIGH was STANLEY.

In there, I found papers concerning Baron David Stanley—and his son's abduction. When Slackleigh had given my uncle a prized grimoire recovered from a beggar believed to be a distant relative of the Stanleys, my uncle had ordered the younger Stanley abducted for the purpose of opening the volume's bloodlock.

The papers even contained references of how the kidnappers had evaded the father's desperate search for his vanished son.

I stashed those papers away as well and searched through for evidence of grimoires and more ill-doing. In these files I saw clear proof that my uncle had been blackmailing other peers.

Reams of evidence lay before me, more than I could hope to carry out without notice. But likely any one of these files could bring the queen's law smashing through the doors of my uncle's club to snap a noose around my uncle's neck.

The idea of that I could kill a man, even a man as cruel as my uncle, with just a few sheets of paper sobered me. Little in my life had prepared me to hold another man's entire fate in my hands.

Then my eyes fell upon another file. This one marked BLACKWATER. Leofa's surname. I pulled the file out, my stomach tight with a sudden anxiety. The first document inside was a marriage certificate. Eileen Blackwater had married my step-uncle Gerard Franklin twenty-six years ago.

The pages after that comprised several battered reports from a variety of agents commissioned by my uncle to discover the whereabouts of his runaway bride. None of them ever found her or the child she'd been carrying when she'd fled from my uncle. One of his agents had discovered Eileen's grave and had sent my uncle a copy of the woman's death certificate, supposing her son had passed away along with her.

I glanced over to Leofa.

He appeared deep in his own contemplation of another panel in my uncle's study. With a quick motion of his hand, he flicked a tiny nail and the entire panel swung open.

Inside a shelf of wooden slats not only organized but also kept unbound spell pages separate and buffered. The slots were labeled with the family name, the grimoire page number, and the spell title if known. Some of those family names belonged to quite prominent peers who definitely still lived.

Leofa grinned with delight.

"Well, aren't these a familiar sight? I think I cracked a good half of these. And here's Stanley's 'Never Tipsy' spell." He glanced at me, his delight dying as he caught sight of my expression.

"What is it?" he asked.

Nothing I could say could ease the burden of this knowledge. I could not mitigate it. Nor could I spare him pain by keeping it from him. Too many people had done him that disservice already.

So I handed it over. I said, "You ought to see this."

"Blackwater? He's even got a file on me, has he?" Leofa opened it. His face expressionless, he stared at the page as though he could not make sense of it. The emotions dawning on his features—fury, disbelief, grief—dug into me.

"This can't be right… How could he, of all people, be my father? Whose perverse joke is this?" he asked.

I didn't argue. We both knew the truth. The bloodlock had verified it when it had opened to Leofa.

As he read more, Leofa sank slowly down with his back against the mahogany cabinets. He dropped the file onto the ground and leaned his head back, his eyes closed, his hair falling away to reveal the pain etched onto his face. Leofa pressed his fists against the floor.

"I don't think he knew who you were," I said because I couldn't let this silence continue between us.

Leofa took a shuddering breath. He tilted his head, drew his fingers across his eyes, and then tangled them in his hair. "No. I don't think so either."

His hands clenched over the file. He said, "But how much would you bet that those petty shits, the Nobbsnipes, knew?"

Leofa hurled the file away from him, scattering the pages across the floor of my uncle's office.

"I'm sorry," I told him.

Leofa shook his head.

"You've got nothing to be sorry for." He straightened, glowering at the scattered papers, before he set to retrieving them. Leofa picked up one page and glanced back to me.

He said, "I always had a sense the Nobbsnipes were smirking at me whenever they mentioned your uncle but I could never see why. They knew. They had to have found out from my mother."

I grimaced, but didn't comment.

"That must have given them endless hours of amusement," he continued, voice bitter. "All that time knowing they had Lord Franklin's son right under their fucking thumbs, working like a dog for the lout."

I'd seen too much of their petty amusements and tortures to doubt Leofa's interpretation. Yet I suspected that Nobbsnipe may have acted out of more than spite. Surely Nobbsnipe had considered the advantage that exploiting Leofa gave him. After all, with a few drops of Leofa's blood, he could have accessed Uncle Gerard's most private files and bank safes without ever even tipping Gerard off.

As a hostage, Gerard's long-lost son would've offered leverage if ever Nobbsnipe discovered himself at an impasse with Uncle Gerard. Little wonder the Nobbsnipe family had gone to such wretched lengths to keep Leofa.

"I'm going to see them rot in jail," Leofa snarled. He caught up several of the loose spells and handed another two to me.

"Evidence," Leofa stated.

Heartened by his resolve, I snatched the files detailing my uncle's dealings with Lord Slackleigh and his misdeeds against Baron Stanley. Molly at least would be overjoyed when I read the papers to her.

"First, we have to get these papers to Molly," I told him. "Tomorrow we'll take this to Hammerton. He's well known in law circles and Pike's good friend. He'll advise us best on how to see the Nobbsnipes in jail and the boys liberated."

"We can't let them know what we're planning," Leofa said. "Or they'll run. We got to spring this one on them, Neil."

"What about Roger?" I asked. Leofa had been so concerned about how Roger would punish me yesterday. Now I needed to know if Leofa had a plan for this.

"I don't know," Leofa said. I could see his desire to protect me warring with his need to see the Nobbsnipes imprisoned.

"Let's return the glider," I said, so he wouldn't have to make this choice. I could handle Roger. "I'll act the penitent. With Louisa on my side, Roger won't dare harm me. You'll have to keep Molly from taking off with Thaddeus after she gets that marriage certificate. You're right. We can't let them know that anything's amiss."

After carefully restoring my uncle's office to its pristine state, barring certain documents, we departed the club, determined but silent. Then we made our way to the airfield.

19

Wet snow swirled around us, chaotic and catching the light, as Leofa and I circled Highfell Hall in our two-seater. We'd been quiet the entire flight up, both preoccupied with our own troubled thoughts. But now Leofa glanced from the controls to smile at me.

"If the court does right by Molly, we're going to have to get used to addressing her as 'my lady.'"

I grinned. I almost commented that he might have to accustom himself to being addressed as Lord Franklin. But better to let that lie. I said, "At least we didn't discover that Hooker's a legitimate noble as well. He'd never let us live that down."

"Loxa forbid." Leofa grinned.

He brought our craft down carefully despite the miserable weather. I forced my fingers, stiff with cold, to unlock my harness buckles and then slithered out onto the icy cobblestones. Leofa secured the glider and then glanced back towards the house.

"Speaking of Hooker…" He nodded and I turned from gathering up the files we'd taken from my uncle's club to see Hooker bolting towards us. Hooker grimaced as heavy flakes of snow spattered his face and then skidded to a halt in front of Leofa. His eyes shone bright with excitement despite the cold.

"What's going on?" Leofa inquired.

"Early this morning a *girl* showed up here with the dung collectors and she asked for Mr. Franklin." Hooker spoke with both wonder and bewilderment.

I thought immediately of Nora—and from Leofa's expression I guess he'd drawn the same conclusion. Nora wouldn't have come here—of all places—unless she was utterly desperate.

"Stanley recognized her. He took her up to your rooms even though she's a girl," Hooker added.

"Must be your sister." Leofa took the files from my clenched hands. He said, "Something's gone wrong."

"She's your *sister*?" Hooker gaped. "But she's beautiful!"

Without exchanging a word, both Leofa and I bolted from the windbreak and started for the dormitory. Hooker raced along with us, continuing his report of the morning's excitement.

"Your sister said she gave the dung collectors her necklace to get here, but they wanted her fake key too. When she wouldn't give it, Stanley punched one of them in the nose." Hooker grinned through his chattering teeth, obviously proud of Stanley's solution.

Once we reached the shelter of the hall, Leofa paused. He turned to Hooker.

"You and the other boys keep an eye out for anyone else coming around. You come up and warn us, all right?" he said.

Hooker nodded.

Then Leofa and I raced up to the garret. Stanley hunched in the dormitory beside the ladder, looking troubled and holding a rapidly melting chip of ice against the badly bruised knuckles of his right hand.

"Thank Demos!" he cried out at the sight of us. Then he quickly lowered his voice. "Your sister—"

"Hooker just told us," I cut him off in my agitation. "Let me past to see her."

Stanley moved aside and I clambered past him. Behind me I heard Leofa and Stanley exchange a few words. But it was the sight of Nora that seized my attention.

She stood in the middle of our squalid room, holding my pyxis trap in her shaking hands. Nora stared past it, her face haunted. She still wore the white dress in which she'd been presented to the queen, but now grime stained the cloth and the hem appeared torn. Her hair had lost all semblance of order and hung around her pallid face in tangled curls.

Nora looked up at me. Dark smears of the little makeup she'd worn to the ball circled her eyes.

I'd never seen her in such a state; not even on the day we'd learned of our parent's deaths had she appeared so stunned.

"Neil!" She rushed forward and I embraced her. Nora felt cold as ice in my arms and she trembled.

"What happened?" I asked.

"I—I thought—" Her words seemed to catch in her throat. "I'd—I had spoken with Lord Slackleigh, but he avoided me after I was presented, and I thought I'd gotten it wrong. But then when we went home, I couldn't sleep because I'd been drinking, and I saw his carriage come and I heard him arguing with Uncle Gerard…"

Suddenly guilty, I feared that her anguish somehow stemmed from the romantic loss of Slackleigh. But I couldn't believe that Nora had been infatuated with a disrespectful reprobate like Slackleigh. A broken engagement wouldn't upset her so.

Leofa and Stanley came in behind me and shut the hatch. Nora didn't seem to even see them.

"They argued…" Nora whispered. The pupils of her eyes were wide with shock.

"What did they argue about?" I asked.

"Oh, Neil, Neil, please don't make me go back there," she begged, her eyes welling with tears and her voice now cracking. "Uncle Gerard—he—it didn't stop and I couldn't look away—"

"Calmly now." I used my best older brother voice and very gently took the pyxis from her shaking hands. I reflexively slipped it into my coat pocket.

Leofa snatched up our cleanest blanket and draped it over Nora's shoulders. Only then did she seem to take in her surroundings. She absently thanked Leofa. As her eyes fell on Stanley, she pushed a lock of her dark hair back from her face.

"Tell me what happened," I coaxed.

"Yes. I'm sorry. I'm not feeling quite myself." Nora nodded and her voice steadied, though I could still see the fear in her wide eyes. "I saw Slackleigh's cabriolet from my window and I'd wondered why he would visit at such an hour. Considering how he did not speak to me after my presentation, I felt rather curious."

I nodded encouragingly for her to continue.

"He'd gone to Uncle Gerard's smoking room." Nora bit her lip. "So I—I stopped outside to listen. I pushed the door open just a crack and I could see the two of them as they argued…"

Nora's voice shook and Leofa looked at me, alarmed. I could see what he wondered. Had we set off this chain of events? But a moment later Nora regained her composure and went on.

"At first I couldn't understand but then I realized that Slackleigh was demanding his papers back. Something about a marriage, a previous marriage, I think. Then they both became quite agitated and Slackleigh made accusations about Roger and Highfell Hall."

Leofa grimaced. I felt guilty. Stanley watched her, the expression on his face intense and yet kind.

"Then he claimed that if it came down to it he'd go to the police," Nora said, her voice rising in pitch, "because he wouldn't hang and he wouldn't be bullied. He waved this garish Cho cane at Uncle Gerard and…"

"And?" I asked with an uneasy feeling.

"And…" Nora swallowed hard. "All at once Uncle Gerard snatched the cane from Slackleigh's hand and struck him across the face with it. Slackleigh fell, but Uncle Gerard kept beating him until his head wasn't…" Nora shuddered. "He killed him."

"You're sure." I felt sick, even nauseated with guilt. I'd wished Slackleigh hurt and out of the way—but not dead. Now I could only feel horror. I hoped that somehow she had been mistaken.

"Quite sure." Nora nodded firmly. "No one survives having his head turned to pulp, Neil."

"Shit," Leofa muttered. Belatedly, he added, "Excuse my language, my lady."

Nora shrugged. Obviously she had greater concerns than an overheard obscenity.

She gripped my hand and said, "I was terrified that Uncle Gerard would realize that I'd seen what he'd done, so I fled. I didn't know where to go in the middle of the night like that. But then I remembered that Slackleigh had mentioned Highfell. I thought maybe—maybe you might be in danger."

After hearing Nora's story, I thought we might all be in danger. Who knew what Uncle Gerard might do if he discovered that we'd taken his files? We'd closed everything back up.

But then I remembered the daguerreotype of Eileen Blackwater that Leofa had slipped out of its frame and secreted in his pocket. Uncle Gerard would notice its absence—and the doorman at the club would readily inform him of my visit.

A hard rap sounded at the garret hatch. Leofa jerked the hatch open and Hooker popped his head in. He announced, "Lord Franklin's just arrived in an aerophaeton and he's furious!"

Nora blanched. Stanley lunged to her side as if to catch her, but she didn't swoon. He hovered beside her nervously.

"We must leave here. We must leave at once!" Nora said.

"Oh, he's not looking for you, my lady." Hooker beamed at my sister. He said, "It's Roger he's after. I think he's going to cane him with Roger's own cane! He wanted to know where Roger was. And I told him that Roger was in steerage—"

"We have to stop him," I told Leofa. Uncle Gerard blamed Roger because we'd inadvertently framed him. We couldn't be responsible for another death—not even Roger's.

Leofa nodded in grim agreement.

"No, you mustn't!" Nora said.

"We have to try." As gently as I could I pried her hand off.

"We don't have the time to argue." Leofa glanced to the bed where he'd set aside the files. "And someone has to fly down and go to the police."

Leofa scooped up the files and proffered them to Nora. But I did notice that he didn't offer her the grimoire pages, which remained in his pocket, presumably because he judged them too dangerous. I agreed with that determination.

"Lady Franklin," Leofa said, "the police are more likely to hear out a woman from a good background. Will you go, tell them everything you told us just now, and give them these files? They were taken from your uncle's room at his club."

I almost expected Nora to refuse. She'd already been through so much. But, with a very dignified nod, she accepted the files. Her eyes narrowed as she noticed Slackleigh's name. Nora glanced up at me sharply and I could see her wondering what kind of trouble I'd gotten myself into. But she said nothing.

"Stanley—" Leofa began, only to be cut off.

"I'll fly Lady Franklin," Stanley volunteered. "And escort her directly to the police."

"Good man." Leofa nodded and then gazed at Hooker, who appeared more excited than frightened by all of this talk of police, pilfered files, and Roger taking a caning. Leofa said, "You and the rest of the boys see what you can do to distract the watchmen until Stanley and Lady Franklin fly out of here."

"Done." Hooker launched himself back down the ladder. I heard his voice ringing through the dormitory below as he called out for the other boys.

Before I left, I gave my sister a quick embrace and followed Leofa out. We had to get to steerage before blood spilled.

We burst past Mrs. Nobbsnipe. She appeared so distracted by contents of the teacup in her hands that she hardly registered our passage.

"How inappropriate, Mr. Franklin…" Her voice drifted off into a faint, jumbled murmur.

Leofa bounded down the spiral staircase leading into steerage and I took the metal stairs just as fast. Our steps reverberated through the narrow stairwell.

Then Leofa hurled the door open and we both charged into the cheery room with its perpetual scent of wood polish and tobacco.

In an odd tableau, Uncle Gerard stood to the left near the stabilizer, glaring imperiously across the aetherium's massive steering wheel at Roger. Opposite him, Roger leaned against the periscope, a sour smirk on his lips and a lit cigarillo tucked behind his ear.

Uncle Gerard clenched Roger's cane in his hand, but Roger appeared largely unimpressed by the threat. I realized why as my eyes fell upon the pistol—my pistol—clenched in his right hand.

Both Gerard and Roger glanced angrily at Leofa and I when we burst in upon them, but neither man shifted from their standoff.

"You dare to betray me, to steal from me!" Uncle Gerard snarled. "I will thrash the life out of you, you little shit!"

"Please, Uncle Gerard, Roger, calm down," I said. Such words sounded absurd, even to me, but I did need to explain to Uncle Gerard that we'd all but framed Roger. I didn't want another death on my hands. I could hardly take my eyes from the gleaming muzzle of the pistol in Roger's hand.

"I'm sure we can work this out without anyone getting hurt," I added.

A very soft disbelieving sound escaped Leofa's throat, but he said nothing. He edged towards Roger.

"None of that from you, Leo!" Roger swung the pistol towards Leofa, who froze. Roger smirked. A sadistic pleasure lit his eyes.

"Roger," I called, hoping to divert his attention. "Don't do anything stupid. The poli—"

"Stupid?" Roger cut me off with a sneer. "You mean like stealing my cane and setting me up for a fall with your old uncle? Or—" Roger's grin turned truly nasty as he looked at Gerard. "—maybe you mean stupid, like losing track of your own son so long that you don't even recognize him when he's standing right beside you."

Uncle Gerard stilled like a crane above water. He swiveled his head to take in Leofa. The family resemblance, if looked for, became clear. Leofa nodded, his acknowledgment tight with restrained anger.

"No. That can't be…" Gerard whispered.

Roger's laugh rang out. He waved the pistol lazily at Leofa. "I wonder if there's any point in keeping you around now that the secret's out, Leo."

I felt inside my coat pocket for something to hurl against Roger's head, but my fingers only brushed over the insubstantial wire mesh of my pyxis trap. I might as well lob a butterfly for all the damage the pyxis trap would do. My heart pounded so hard it felt like it might kick free of my chest.

"I have sent for the police," I said quietly, trying not to betray my desperation.

That seemed to sober Roger. He narrowed his eyes at me.

"It's over," I said. "They're going to seize Highfell Hall and if you and your family are still here when they do, you'll all hang."

I hoped to distract Roger with my little speech more than to convince him to relent. I did not want him pointing that pistol at Leofa again. I'd have recited dirty verses if I thought it would keep Leofa alive.

I continued, "I won't take the blame for what goes on here. Neither will my uncle. And Leofa won't either. You know we won't. We have titles behind us and the boys will back us up. Who do you think the police will believe, your tawdry little family—or lords?"

Roger's face twisted with fury, and I knew he'd all but forgotten about Leofa. Only at that point did it occur to me that if I kept baiting Roger, I might end up shot myself.

"I'm giving you fair warning, Roger. You still have time to save your skin." I shrugged, feigning nonchalance. "Or you can stand around here, wagging an obviously stolen pistol at peers, and see how the police interpret that."

Roger said nothing. From the way his jaw clenched I guessed that he wanted to swear but couldn't think of words obscene enough to suit the situation. Ash flaked off the cigarette tucked behind his ear, exposing the smoldering cherry.

In the quiet, the mechanical murmurs of the tiny gears moving behind the wall of brassy barometers, thermometers, altimeters, and flight gauges filled the air like insect songs. The stabilizer glinted faintly as it automatically made some minute adjustment in response to the winter winds buffeting the aetherium.

"Move away from the door," Roger commanded at last. Leofa and I both stepped back to allow him past. Roger sidled nearer. The smell of his cigarette carried with it the distinct odor of singed hair.

Roger's left hand touched the doorknob. But then he lifted it away, turning back to smirk at Leofa. Roger said, "You've been some good insurance all these years. I'd hate to give it up. After all, we're going to need money to resettle."

"Not a chance," Leofa snapped.

He jerked back as Roger reached for him.

Suddenly Gerard swung the cane in his hand, bringing it down hard against Roger's right arm. Roger yelped and pulled the trigger. The loud booms of gunfire echoed through the room. I grabbed Leofa, pulling him down and out of the way.

Uncle Gerard crumpled to the floor a few feet away, blood welling from his gut. Roger looked shocked. He bolted out of the room. Amid the thunder of his footsteps up the stairs I heard him howl, like a frightened child, for his papa.

"No," Leofa whispered as he caught sight of Uncle Gerard.

He stood, starting for Uncle Gerard, but then lurched left, nearly tumbling into the base of the steering wheel as the entire aetherium tipped to the portside. Overhead I heard alarmed shouts and furniture crashing to the floor.

Both Gerard and I slid several feet left. A calligraphic swash of blood traced Gerard's motion as he slumped into the far wall. I clawed at the floorboards, just managing to keep from skidding into the shattered glass of a barometer that had dropped from the wall.

"One of the bullets hit the stabilizer." Leofa remained on his feet, gripping the base of the steering wheel.

Behind him, one tiny alarm bell after another rang out signaling that the boiler tanks had faltered. I feared that because the boiler tanks down below had pitched sideways, they threatened to overturn. Not only would upended tanks flood the boiler room—likely killing anyone down there in a sea of searing water—but if we lost more than two tanks, our turbines would stop and the entire aetherium would drop from the sky.

The starboard side of the aetherium continued to tilt upwards, setting off even more alarm bells. A wrenching metallic noise echoed from somewhere above us.

If the aetherium rolled any more, it would all be over.

Then, having tilted some thirty degrees, the aetherium stopped moving.

Against the wall, Gerard groaned and cupped his hand over his bloody abdomen. Leofa hunched down and in a crouch edged to Gerard's side. Leofa seemed to struggle with his own concern, but then he pulled off his cravat and pressed it over Gerard's wound. Gerard's eyes looked like dark pits in his pale gaunt face. He gazed at Leofa, his brown eyes intent, and then patted Leofa's bloody hand weakly.

"I can see her face in yours," Gerard whispered. "My Eileen..."

Stark sorrow flashed across Leofa's face. But then he caught himself and hardened his countenance.

"You hold this cloth down good and tight, Lord Franklin," Leofa ordered gruffly. "I won't have you die before I can give you a good piece of my mind."

To my surprise a hint of a smile lifted Gerard's whitened lips. He took the cravat, his own blood turning it from scarlet to nearly black.

Leofa fought up to his feet then. He used the instruments on the wall to pull himself back to the steering wheel. I managed to slip and crawl to it myself. Bracing myself, I stood and surveyed the damage Roger's bullet had dealt us.

A furrow of twisted brass gaped from the left side of the orb of the stabilizer. Streams of mercury dribbled down its face to form shining balls that cascaded slowly down the slope of the floor. Several more beads of mercury spilled out.

The aetherium listed just a little more to the left. Although it was standard practice to keep multiple stabilizers aboard all aetheria, I didn't hold out much hope that Highfell would have one. Still I looked at Leofa.

"We wouldn't keep a backup on board, would we?" I asked.

"No," Leofa replied grimly.

I nodded. It would've been too much to expect.

The room had gone quiet. Glancing to the instruments on the wall I saw why. Most of the alarm bells now hung from their yokes at such a steep angle that their clappers lay against the bell walls, shuddering faintly.

"We do have you." Leofa gave me a wry smile. "You don't happen have an idea for keeping us from rolling?"

I scowled at the stabilizer and suppressed the urge just to grab the damn thing and turn it upright. Even the slightest shift in the orb would translate to a magnitude of degrees for the entire aetherium. Exactly how many I couldn't say, because I hadn't calibrated the stabilizer.

I thought Roger's bullet might have violently re-calibrated it in any case. Better to let it be, than to let my fear overwhelm my good sense.

We still tipped. But the rate had slowed. It would stop at some point, but there was no way of knowing if that would come before or after the boilers overturned.

"We could attempt an emergency landing on the river," I said at last. "But the lower we go, the less aether we'll have to keep us aloft. The aetherium might hold together if we can glide..."

Leofa grimaced and said, "Highfell Hall will glide like a sack of bricks."

Suddenly the sound of Ashby and Hooker's hoots filled the room. The boys themselves tumbled down the stairwell in a series of lurching falls. They caught themselves on the door. Both boys quieted as they took in the blood-streaked floor and Gerard's supine body.

Hooker's eyes popped wide. "I've never seen a dead person before!"

"You still haven't," Gerard hissed weakly. He fixed Hooker with his dark gaze. Hooker almost lost his grip on the door. He gulped, but the shock only seemed to inspire a burst of words from the boy.

"I thought you should know, Leofa, the Nobbsnipes tried to flee in the four-seater and pitched over the side and they're tangled up in the arresting wire and dangling!" Hooker's hand mimicked the glider's skid and plunge off the aetherium's landing deck.

The Nobbsnipes being caught in the ruin they had landed us in should have consoled me. But all I could think about was the pendulous weight of them disrupting the stabilizer even further.

"Jerome and two watchmen went over," Hooker added. "So did a bunch of laundry, but Vernon caught Peggy and hauled her back inside."

"The two-seaters are gone," Ashby stated quietly.

A terrible thought gripped me.

"What about Nora and Stanley?" I asked.

"Oh, they were well away before we went all sideways," Hooker assured me. "Why have we gone all sideways, anyhow?"

"Roger shot the stabilizer," Leofa informed him. "Do you know if anybody's down with the boilers?"

Ashby shook his head. But I wasn't certain if he meant that he didn't know or that the boiler room had already been evacuated.

"Everybody scarpered and the alarms went off. We're all holed up the pantry." Hooker stole a glance at Uncle Gerard but then flicked his attention back to Leofa and me. He said, "Peggy said that we might as well have a feast, since we're all going to die anyway."

"We're not going to die, are we, Leofa?" Ashby asked quietly.

"No." Leofa flashed the boys a smile. Although I saw the effort behind it, Hooker and Ashby grinned in response. Leofa said, "Mr. Franklin's going to fix everything. We'll glide down and float right along River Wyrd light as a turd."

Ashby smiled and Hooker laughed.

"Both of you get to the pantry and tell everyone to hold tight," I instructed. "It's going to be fine."

The boys turned and climbed up the stairs as nimbly as monkeys. I waited until they were well beyond earshot to say anything.

"We could try to flag another aetherium. Maybe get a stabilizer from them?" I suggested. "Most schools do have spare stabilizers."

Leofa shook his head, resigned.

He knew as well as I did that if gliders had pitching off the aetherium, then a man out on the icy deck didn't stand a chance of flagging out a message before he slid over. Other aetheria near us would notice our listing to the port.

In fact, our very instability would prevent anyone from delivering the device we needed to fix it.

The aetherium shuddered and tilted another degree to the left.

"Let's get her to the river then." Leofa peered at the wall of lopsided thermometers and gauges. He added, "Someone is going to have to steer us just using the periscope."

I nodded. Leofa reached down and gripped the dull steel lever to the right of the steering wheel—the release for the emergency sails.

Leofa ground his jaw and grunted at the effort of pulling the lever back. I scrambled over and gripped the lever, planting my hands below Leofa's. On the count of three we threw our combined weight against the lever. A low noise growled up from the hull of the aetherium. The whole structure bucked as the supports of the sails tore away from the hull and spread the canvas wide to catch the air.

Dust from crumbling plaster sifted down across us as cracks spiderwebbed the ceiling. A larger chunk thunked down, revealing naked and splintering boards.

Inches from my head the steering wheel suddenly began to spin. I reached up and caught it, feeling the resistance of the emergency sails.

Leofa gripped the periscope and drew it down. He peered through the eyepiece.

"I can see snow and fuck-all," Leofa announced.

To my surprise, that elicited a raspy laugh from Gerard. I, like Hooker earlier, had mistaken his stillness for death.

Without warning, the aetherium lurched again. We dropped. My stomach rocked into my throat. I whipped the wheel hard starboard, hoping the emergency sails might catch the wind and provide a greater lift.

Our decent slowed.

But now the aetherium listed at a vertigo-inspiring forty degrees. The port walls had all but become floors.

"Gliding isn't enough," Leofa said softly. "We need a stabilizer or we'll lose the boilers."

His words brought out a spark of guilty anger in me. Here I was, the man who'd mastered the pyxis trap, but when it mattered, when lives stood at stake, I couldn't even repair a cursed stabilizer.

"I'm sorry," I snapped. "But I just don't have anything to work with! Unless you happen to have a stabilization spell up in the workshop, or better yet tucked into your pocket—"

"My pocket…" Leofa murmured as though the word were a revelation. His face lit up with a wild delight. "How could I have forgotten it? Stanley's 'Never Tipsy' spell!"

He dug into the pockets of his coat like a man possessed, tossed aside two grimoire pages as if they were trash, and then held up a third. Leofa grinned like a maniac and nearly lost his balance. I grasped his arm to keep him from tumbling into the far wall.

Leofa hooked one hand on the base of the steering wheel and thrust the grimoire page at me.

"It's the spell from that lady's grimoire," he announced. "No matter how intoxicated or discombobulated, it will keep the speaker balanced and upright."

"A stabilizing spell!" I felt fit to burst with unlikely happiness. "Take the wheel. I'll speak it."

Leofa caught the steering wheel in his strong grip. I took the grimoire page in my hands and read it over to figure out if it would act as we needed it to.

At turns elation and disappointment swept through me as I took in the exact specifications of the spell. A strong winter gust struck the aetherium. Leofa wrestled with the steering wheel even as he kept stealing glances at me.

"Well?" Leofa asked.

"It's not just a stabilizing spell." I didn't look up from the page. My thoughts worked at just how to implement a tiny spell designed to effect offset the mass of a single person rather than an entire aetherium. "It keeps the person invoking it from falling down as well as tipping over."

"That's even better, isn't it?"

I frowned at the fine wires running through the silky paper. Then I nodded.

"What's wrong with that?" Leofa asked.

"I will require a huge amount of aether to stabilize something as large as an aetherium. If I cast it directly on the stabilizer, it'll likely drain all the aether from the turbines before the spell builds up enough to take effect."

"So we go to a more direct source of aether," Leofa responded. "I'll take it up to the roof. The higher the more aether—"

"Ambient aether isn't going to be enough." I steadied myself as another powerful gust struck the aetherium's emergency sails.

Leofa turned our prow into the wind so that the aetherium could catch a slight lift.

"My pyxis trap might just do the trick," I said. "But I'm the one who's going to have to wire it into the 'Never Tipsy' spell. I'm going to have to climb up onto the roof."

Unwillingly, I remembered Hooker's report of Jerome and the other watchmen who'd pitched off the side of the aetherium. Then the visceral memory of that day when Leofa and I had clung to the abseiling raft shook me. The icy fury had nearly taken our lives. How much worse would it be up on the roof?

"No." Leofa said it softly. "Neil, I've been up and down Highfell the better part of my life. Even all off-kilter I'll be better at navigating my way up. And I'm stronger—I just am. I should be the one to carry the spell up. Look, you can wire it down here—"

"I haven't tested the pyxis trap, so I won't know how to wire it, or re-wire it, until I get it out into the aether and see how it meshes with this other spell. You can't do that. I have to go."

"We'll both go then. I'll keep hold of you—"

"Who's going to man the wheel if we're both climbing up to the roof?" I spoke harshly. I had to get him to agree with me. We'd wasted too much time and our argument served no purpose. I had to bring the pyxis and the stabilization spell up to the greatest concentration of aether.

I even had the pyxis trap in my pocket. If I were to believe in fate, I'd see this as meant to be.

"I'll take the wheel."

Both Leofa and I started at Uncle Gerard's voice. He pushed one bloody hand against the wall and levered himself to his feet. His other hand clenched Leofa's blood-soaked cravat against his belly.

"I was something of a pilot in my school days." Uncle Gerard's eyes lingered on Leofa. With a grunt of pain, he lunged for the base of the steering wheel. I caught his arm with my free hand and pulled him to us. The tang of blood rolled off of him and his skin looked as dead as tallow. Still, he gripped the wheel with certainty.

"Go on," he spoke to Leofa. "I'm not going to die until you've given me a piece of your mind, remember."

Leofa met his father's gaze and held it. Then he released the wheel into Gerard's pale hands.

"Hurry," Gerard told us both. With that we threw ourselves up the incline of the floor and climbed hand over hand up the winding stairs. Leofa led the way out of steerage and through the Nobbsnipe residence, moving fast and making the best footing of overturned shelves, wall hangings, and plaster moldings. Walls became floors and doors swung overhead like battering rams.

My body thrummed with tension as I and Leofa cleared one floor and then another. Cold wind whirled up from the cracks in the hull below. The aetherium's turbines sputtered. We dropped, a lurching sensation that left me feeling without a stomach, and then the aetherium turbines coughed back to life and our descent slowed.

But it never stopped. We fell even as Leofa and I climbed. What had been staircases now presented us with only hand and foot braces in a hard vertical climb up.

As we passed into the dovecote I glimpsed the fluttering forms of the agitated pigeons. A few lay still, their feathered bodies draped over the cote bars.

My muscles ached. Despite the bitter cold, sweat beaded my brow. Leaning awkwardly in the tight space around the school's flagpole, I managed to jump up after Leofa through the small porthole that led out onto the roof. I hung from the edge and then squeezed myself up through the opening. Snow and shards of ice pelted my face.

Already outside and braced in the crotch of a steaming chimney, Leofa reached out and caught my hand. He gripped my wrist with bruising intensity as I scrambled across the ice-glazed roof tiles to share in his meager protection. Overhead icicles jutted from the brick lip of the chimney like fangs.

I drew the "Never Tipsy" spell from one coat pocket and handed it to Leofa. Then I withdrew my pyxis trap. The innocuous mesh of copper and gold turned deathly cold in the winter wind. My bare fingers ached just gripping it.

Leofa braced me as I twisted the tracking wire onto the transducer and hooked that up to the pyxis. To my relief the trapping wire took on a glow, emitting an almost living heat as it captured more and more of the aether flowing over us in the grip of the cutting wind.

"Is it working?" Leofa shouted over the wind.

I nodded. Snow poured down on us. Flakes turned to steam when they touched the pyxis trap. The back of my hand beaded with droplets of water. I tried not to think about the likelihood that I might electrocute myself.

But why fear that when I was so spoiled for choices?

"Give me 'Never Tipsy' now," I called to Leofa over the storm's gusts. He handed the page to me carefully. Only the strength of the wires underlying the paper kept it from being torn to shreds in the onslaught of wind and snow.

With half-numb fingers, I worked the unbound wire ends of the grimoire page into an aetheric transfer wire feeding out of the pyxis trap. As I twisted the last wires tight, a low hum began to vibrate through my body.

Leofa gripped me as I traced the spell over with a finger, activating it. All the while the hum grew stronger and deeper, seeming to drop below hearing into a bone-shaking resonance. Even in the face of the wind, I could feel my hair standing up on end as the resonance expanded out from me in building waves.

An oath escaped Leofa as the resonance reached him. Strands of his dark hair rose around his face. The whirling snowflakes began decelerating, their tumbling slowed, leaving them suspended. The delicate twists of ice floated perfectly still as if stopped in time.

But the aetherium still dropped.

I kept reading, tracing the lines of the pyxis spell. The power pouring through the spells seemed to rush through me in hot waves. Snow seared away before even brushing against my skin. Halos of water droplets hung all around me like dew suspended in a spider's web.

In my hand the pyxis trap blazed the palest blue, the grimoire page sang with light, its purpose flooding out from it in resonant wave after wave.

The aetherium swayed, rocking to the starboard side.

We were thrown up against the roof. My feet slid from beneath me. Leofa caught me and held on so hard I could barely draw a breath. I gripped the pyxis trap desperately as I saw city spires and rooftops rear out from the banks of snow—directly below Highfell Hall.

I gazed up at Leofa where he gripped the edge of the chimney and stared down at me fiercely. His dark hair whipped around his forehead, his coat whitened with snow, and nothing could have seemed more beautiful than he was, suspended in that wild and yet still moment.

Our descent slowed so fast and so completely that I felt almost left behind. Dazed did not even begin to describe my state of mind.

Only a half dozen feet below, the river roiled past.

The aetherium hovered, impossibly, outside of the aetheric current. We hung in the air but a few feet above the River Wyrd between two of Herrow's greatest bridges. The tiny box in my hand with its feverishly bright glow kept us from death.

Above us, I could hear the sound of sirens. Police gliders began to converge upon Highfell Hall.

20

Of course Leofa was arrested on the spot, along with the remaining watchmen, the Nobbsnipe men, and all of the boys. Except for Thaddeus Paxton, who was deemed too young to take to prison.

But with the help of Elmstead's formidable law school, Professor Hammerton, true to his word, made what would be his foremost historical argument before the queen. He secured the release of all servants deemed to be the victims of slavery and coercion. And he did this in less than one week.

I expected to see Leofa after his release, but he didn't come to me. Hooker and Ashby did, looking for a place to stay while they waited for their parents to collect them. And Vernon asked to borrow coach fare back home, which I gladly loaned him, on condition that he write to me once he arrived.

The tweeny Peggy also darkened my doorstep, looking for work. With Nora's permission, I took her in.

The rest had done well for themselves. Now acknowledged as the deceased Lord Slackleigh's wife and mother to his legitimate heir, Molly busied herself learning how to manage his estates.

Stanley, who had thought his father had sold him to the Nobbsnipes, was shocked when his father paid his bail. Upon learning of his father's desperate search after the Nobbsnipes had abducted him, Stanley reunited with his overjoyed father and was named his father's legitimate heir. Most of the other boys had been returned to their closest kin.

Uncle Gerard died from his wounds before he could be prosecuted. To Nora he bequeathed his house. He left Leofa his fortune, Highfell Hall, and my debt. I sent tracker after tracker to Highfell with letters of increasing urgency, but Leofa replied to none of them.

Thirteen days after his arrest I saw Leofa for the first time.

The secular temple of Iskar was a square room lit by torches and filled with backless stone benches. In silence, Nora and I took our place beside Leofa. He didn't look at me. Leofa fixed his gaze on the hanging mask of bronze and the dark altar where my uncle's corpse lay supine.

After the funeral, I tried to track Leofa down. I wanted to ask him to stay with me and I knew he'd say yes. But he evaded me like one avoids a guilty pleasure.

As he slipped away from me, my sister cornered him. I hovered at a distance and afterwards tried to approach him. But Nora intercepted me, her face bright with happiness. She announced proudly, "We've arranged that my accountant will meet with his lawyer to pay off your debt! You will be free of it."

She hugged me tightly. As I returned her embrace, I could see Leofa leaving.

Two days later, as I lunched with Nora in the house that used to belong to Uncle Gerard, I received three letters—none of which turned out to be from Leofa. The first indicated that the Royal Society of Aetheric Studies awarded me the Laureate of Scientific Achievement, in conjunction with Professor Pike. I didn't think that anyone so young had ever achieved this.

With the laureate came a handsome prize and a knighthood. However my parents' debt might have shattered my family's reputation, a knighthood from the queen went far to restoring my honor.

Nora's plans to sublease the rights to the pyxis spell would do even more to regain our family's reputation. As my transducer had made the pyxis a functioning alembic, the military's researchers had made an offer on the rights, which would make Nora a very wealthy woman indeed.

If not for Leofa, I would have achieved none of what I now had. I missed him.

He kept now to Highfell. If I could only see him, I thought, I knew we could work some situation out.

Before my smile faded, I ripped open my second letter, which was from Professor Pike. He'd written to inform me that in light of the prize and the paper we submitted, the university had decided to grant me an honorary doctorate and invite me back as a research fellow.

If I'd ever thought this possible, I would have dreamed this for my future.

The final envelope was from my former fiancé.

Madeline Havensea's letter stated simply that, with my honor and fortune restored, her family would be delighted if I would again consider choosing to take their daughter in marriage. She stated that, while other offers had been made for her hand, due to our long understanding, she would give me special consideration.

If I wished to discuss this in person, she would await me at the Green Rose Tea Shop from noon until two.

My parents would have wanted this life for me: the academic accolades, the rich and beautiful wife who'd give me a family to provide for, and the social acceptance. And I knew I could easily fall into the rhythm of providing for my family, coming home to a perfect house and kissing my wife on the cheek. I would be expected to do my conjugal duty by my wife. I'd have progeny.

I could slip into respectable complacency as easily as I'd become a criminal accomplice at Highfell Hall. And this, I knew, was what Leofa expected of me. He had called me his for only that one night because he believed that I would, like water, take the course of least resistance. Perhaps he even believed I should take that path. Leofa did not want to stand in my way because he did truly love me.

And because of that, Leofa avoided me. Perhaps he also feared his own response to me. Leofa feared how far he would go, what he would do, what it would make him, if I did ask him to be with me.

"What's wrong?" Nora asked.

"Oh? Pardon?" I glanced up at her. She sat in one of Gerard's oversized red velvet chairs, eating neatly from a table too uncomfortably tall for her. Uncle Gerard's thick smothering green curtains had been thrown aside so that light poured into the room and cleanly illuminated the freshly polished ebony wall panels. Peggy entered the room with a tea tray to refill Nora's teacup with freshly brewed Dayshon.

"I asked if anything were wrong," Nora said, cutting through a slice of carrots in aspic. "You haven't been yourself."

"Peggy, what time is it?" I asked, for she'd taken to wearing a watch like a chatelaine.

"Quarter to one, my lord," she said.

"Have the driver bring the carriage around," I said. "I need to be taken to the Green Rose immediately. When I return I'll want my belongings packed."

"What in particular, sir?" Peggy asked.

"Everything."

"My goodness, Neil, what's gotten into you?" my sister asked.

"I'll explain later."

Nora said, "I shall be away by the time you get back from your tea. I must catch the coach quite soon. I have given you a few instructions concerning the household I want you to pass along to Peggy this evening." She reached over to tuck a scrap of paper into my breast pocket. "Please read them out later tonight, if it's not too much trouble."

"Of course not," I said. "Have a delightful romp in the countryside."

I hared off to the cabriolet.

The driver did his best to get us through the press of the Herrow streets. He circumvented a group of pigs, who seemed to be attempting to root up the cobblestones, and then followed behind two lords who the police chased for horse-racing in the streets. The young lords' breakneck antics and the police alike had left the way clear for us.

The tea shop had dark-green painted columns and broad windows. Lady Madeline Havensea sat at a small table inside. She remained as pretty as a doll, reading a folio and eating cakes as she waited.

When I seated myself before her, Madeline lifted her face and smiled politely. Her raven dark hair swirled smoothly around her face into an elaborate hairstyle visible beneath her bonnet of stiffened rose silk. Her dress was done in a dusky rose and white herringbone wool.

"Lord Franklin, it is a pleasure to see you," she said, and poured my tea with her own hand.

"Please, call me Neil," I said.

Her shoulders straightened slightly, as if she went on guard, but she smiled. "But then you must call me Madeline again."

"How have you been?" I asked. I surprised myself in how much I wanted for her to have done well. I knew it could be hard on a girl to have an engagement broken. I hoped she hadn't suffered too much from gossip.

Madeline regarded me thoughtfully, and she said, "Honestly, I've been doing quite well. I think my father became resigned to the fact that he's never going to get a son-in-law who will take over the business. He let me invest in a portion of the cargo with one of our ships in the summer, and…we received an excellent return. He's given me partial supervision over three of our Hem Cho routes now. I hope to be supervising them fully in another year or two."

"In your letter, you said you had other marriage offers," I said.

"Not ones that I plan on accepting," Madeline said. "But the understanding between our families was made some time ago, and I would honor it."

"I'm glad to hear you phrase it like that," I said. I understood now. She would marry me because of that, and because she could be certain that, with my academic pursuits at the forefront of my mind, I wouldn't interfere with her family business. But she'd much rather keep her property to herself, thank you very much, rather than give it away in marriage.

"Madeline, I formally release you and your family from any considerations of our former understanding," I said. "If you'd like me to draft that up in writing, I will."

Madeline looked at me. Suddenly, she smiled sunnily. "You've changed, Neil. It suits you. I'm glad that I could discuss this so frankly with you."

"And I you. If I ever have any shipping concerns, I know who to bring them to." I stood up and held out my hand, as if she were a businessman, and Madeline took it, with a glint in her eye.

She shook my hand firmly. "It was really nice seeing you again. Good luck."

"I hope I don't need it," I joked.

As I hailed a cab for the ride home, it occurred to me that my sister could have verbally instructed Peggy before she left, rather than giving me a note to read out to the girl. Inside the jouncing cab, I pulled out the scrap of paper, unfolded it, and read the note addressed to me.

In small and delicate handwriting, Nora wrote that she intended to elope with Stanley, because they were in love. She joked that she had to snatch him up before a lady adventurer saw his worth and whisked him away.

Nora apologized for not trusting me enough to tell me in person, but she had feared I would try to stop her because of their youth. And she hoped I would not be angry once they returned from their honeymoon.

I considered pursuing them, begging them to wait until they'd grown older, but as soon as the thought had occurred, I discarded it. As an adult, Nora could make her own decisions regarding her life's course. Stanley was a good man.

And now I had my own flight to take, and my own plunge.

↬

The aerophaeton's airman helped me unload my baggage—trunks of clothing my sister bought me, even some furniture and other necessaries. When I saw it all heaped on Highfell Hall's landing deck, I noticed how I'd acquired so much in a remarkably short time.

As I turned from tipping the airman, I saw that Leofa stood on the front steps of the Nobbsnipes' townhouse. His feet were bare, though I reckoned the temperature to be well below freezing. He wore his worn trousers, a knit sweater, and a thin wool jacket. His hair had grown out into shaggy layers that the wind tossed back.

When I finished, I stepped forward to the foot of the stair. He looked at me consideringly. To the waiting airman he said, "Don't go anywhere," and gestured me into the house.

I remembered the house's stuffy clutter well, but when I now entered it, the air in here remained cool and scentless, like the icy wind outside. The luxuries had been stripped away. If it weren't for the dark walnut floors and wainscoting, the green wallpaper, and the layout, it could have been any old townhouse for sale in Herrow below.

Leofa dragged his hand through his silky dark hair impatiently. "I don't want to be rude, but why are you here?"

"It doesn't look like their house at all," I said, sliding my hand along the banister as I moved upstairs. I didn't know how to approach this directly, how to explain my reasoning or how my last few weeks had been without him.

"Neil... Please, don't." He came up after me and caught me on the arm, but not before I saw into the drawing room.

I turned to face him, delighted. "You kept the piano!"

Leofa released me as if scalded. I moved into the drawing room and stood before the battered piano, letting my hands drift across the keys in a scale. The racket appalled me; the townhouse had not been kept warm, obviously, and the temperature change had made the piano go horribly out of tune. When I looked up at Leofa, he tried to hide his wince.

"I have your pistol for you," he said. "You know, they thought it belonged to Gerard."

"Oh. Oh, thank you," I said.

"It's upstairs," he said. "The Crown confiscated almost everything 'associated with criminal operations' here and I sold most everything not in the workshop. Gerard didn't actually leave me much aside from this aetherium, and it's going to take most of my funds to repair the neglect to the turbines and the boilers."

"You shouldn't stay up here alone," I said. "It's dangerous. If a storm rises…you can't be in the boiler room and in steerage both. You need to hire a crew to help you."

"Yeah…Yeah, I know. It's just…" Leofa shrugged and led me into a room that I'd never before visited. A walnut bedstead sat in the middle of the room, draped with a plain gray woolen blanket. The portrait of his mother stood lonely on the wall, and a single wash basin dwelt on the floor with a straight-edge razor beside it.

Leofa could obviously read my expression, because he laughed. "It's not their bed."

"Oh, thank Loxa," I said, relieved. "I'd have thought it cursed."

He found my pistol, which had apparently been living in a paper box under the bed, and handed it over. His face turned troubled as he regarded me. "Really, Neil, why are you and your furniture here?"

I set the pistol back down in the paper box. "You know, I received a fellowship from Elmstead—"

"With which you can take your proper station in life," he said.

"I don't want to take my proper station in life."

"I think I need to get some air." Leofa led me down the stairs and out out back so we wouldn't be in view of the still-waiting airman. We passed the outhouses and the abandoned cabbage boxes. Leofa stopped a foot from the edge. Unlike other aetheria, no guardrail ringed the promenade. I stood beside him, aware of the ice-coated cobblestones beneath my feet and the wind whipping tiny ice flakes around my face.

"You want to crack grimoires. I want to study them, and the more esoteric the better." I hesitated, and then I said it. "I have a plan."

His lips quirked into an involuntary smile. But then he shook his head and gazed out at the city. "You have a plan. I wonder when I've heard that before?"

"I'd need your help," I said.

"You always do," he said, and looked away. "Well, tell me your plan, then."

"I aim to negotiate with the committee and Elmstead's dean of research to be an at-distance researcher. I think they'll agree, provided that I give six lectures per term, as well as take on and put up two students."

"Congratulations," he said, in a tone that indicated that he really wanted me to get to the point sooner rather than later.

"Professor Pike says he knows someone in the queen's labs," I said. "There's a grimoire bound in red reptile leather. The last time someone tried to crack it, the grimoire ate his hand. The lab wants it off their shelves. And, you know, we have as set of shelves here."

"You know I'd want a try at a beauty like that." His breath hitched. "Look, Neil, I don't want to be your student or go into business with you. You know what I want."

"I do," I said quietly. I looked down at the city. At the geometric shapes of the tarred-over roofs in Southside, the half-frozen river glistening blue and black, and the slate roofs of townhouses jutting up. Snow, some clean white and some filthy, made the city look piebald. I thought I could see the packed stir of foot traffic on the bridges.

"I wondered..." I said uncertainly. I could feel his eyes on me. "I'd wondered if you'd like to see *New World Outlaw* with me. It's one of Stanshaw's latest plays. Very good reviews in the *Herrow Inquirer*."

"I know. I read them." He smiled. His dark eyes lit up. I wanted nothing more than to lean forward, to touch the rough day-old stubble on his jaw, to press my lips against his, to feel the warmth of his hard muscles beneath my hands. He said, "You came up here, in person, with all of your luggage and furniture, in order to ask me to go to a play with you?"

"Well, I hoped to stay the night," I said.

"One night?" He was amused now.

"Well, I didn't bring a bed." I knew I babbled now but somehow couldn't stop. I tucked my hands into the pockets of my greatcoat. "I got box seats. You did say you wanted to go to the theater."

"I said I wanted you to take me," he clarified. "You'll see people you know there. I won't pretend you're not mine."

I stepped forward to stand directly in front of him, so close that we almost touched and I gazed up at him. He smelled slightly like oil soap. Everything about Leofa, from his broad shoulders, his scarred and clever hands, his rumbling laugh, his direct and no-nonsense care, to his clear-sighted intelligence, was what I wanted.

I brushed my hand across his stubble and said, "All the better. They'll get used to it."

I kissed him. I couldn't rationalize how something so invigorating could also be so relaxing, but it was. When I touched Leofa, the world clicked into joint, as though everything had been off-kilter without my noticing and now it was all as it was meant to be. I broke the kiss and told him, "I love you. I want to stay with you. I want to buy you decent shoes. You need socks."

He laughed, his dark eyes glinting. "Say that again."

"You need socks?" I repeated.

"Not that."

The look on his face gave me a breathless happiness. A warm elation that defied the cold snow glimmering around us opened within me. With quiet fervor, I said it again, "I love you."

He grinned at me. "I love you too, Your Majesty."

About the Author

Langley Hyde first fell in love with steampunk while studying at Oxford University. There she divided her time between reading about alchemy and heresy in Duke Humfrey's Library, and visiting London to gawk at Babbage's Difference Engine.

A graduate of both Sarah Lawrence University and the Clarion Writer's Workshop, Ms. Hyde's stories have appeared in *Cicada* and *Polluto* as well as anthologies such as *Magic in the Mirrorstone*. Her hobbies include making wire sculptures, talking to cats, and wearing tiny hats.